SONG OF THE HOLLOW

EMMA T. SHANNON

ISBN: 979-8-9898487-0-6

eBook ISBN: 979-8-9898487-1-3

Description: First edition. | United States, 2024. | Series: Song of the Hollow; Book 1

Cover designed by Emma. T. Shannon

Map by Emma T. Shannon

Published by Emma T. Shannon

Formatted by Emily B Rose

Dedicated to the third-grade version of myself who discovered Greek mythology for the first time.

Your insatiable hunger for myths was never quenched, and may it never be.

THE NORTHERN ISLES
FOLOI FOREST
LYSAEN
LAVOISIN
WALLAEKVA
LAVOISIN FOREST
KELTOS
CAIRA
WELINAS
BERTANA
ORINOS
XAETHES
SVADAEVA
N
W
S
THE SOUTHERN ISLES
IA

PROLOGUE

As the world outside ended, Amelia Jäger sang. She sang the way her mother sang when she had nightmares as a child, with a voice soft and gentle and full of love despite her body being full of fear. Clutched to her chest was her trembling eight-year-old son, who had no idea what was happening. Who wouldn't know what was happening, because Amelia Jäger would distract him with her voice until the end.

> *Drift upon the waves*
> *And the stars will align.*
> *Until we reach the end*
> *Just know that you are mine.*

"Mama?" Her son asked, voice wet with tears. Amelia Jäger had been holding back tears of her own. She wouldn't cry. She was going to be strong, for her boy if not for anyone else.

"My angel," she whispered. "Just focus on me. Just look at Mama."

Her son looked up at her. He'd inherited his mother's stormy blue eyes; eyes that shone brighter now that they were wet with tears. Amelia Jäger kissed each fat tear from her son's rosy cheeks. Outside, the smell of smoke had grown thick.

The screams from the people of Wallaekva had become nothing more than background noise. Black shadows passed in front of the shuttered windows, just visible enough to cause Amelia Jäger's heart to flutter each time. She pressed her son's head against her breast, forcing him to close his eyes.

A heavy weight slammed against the door, nearly splintering the wood. Amelia hugged her boy tighter and tighter still. Another slam and the door gave way.

Amelia Jäger looked up. She hadn't meant to, but instinct sometimes outweighed survival. Beneath the heavy hood of the Hollow, whose face was shrouded in darkness, were two glowing eyes the color of rubies.

And Amelia Jäger, upon looking at those eyes, felt her soul leave her body.

Her son screamed as his mother's body fell back, but not once did the boy look up. Not once did he pull his tear-stained face from her chest.

"Just don't look in their eye," she had told him earlier. She'd heard of Hollows attacking other cities outside of Wallaekva, and she knew the vampiric demons

fed off souls they stole by making eye contact. Amelia Jäger had explained to her son that he was not allowed to leave the house until *human* authorities came. And even then, he was not allowed to make eye contact with anyone.

He didn't hear the Hollow leave. But he did hear the screams outside and his own sobs as he clutched his dead mother's still-warm body.

"Are there any survivors here?" An unfamiliar voice called. The boy didn't know how long he'd been there, and he was almost tempted to look up to see who had come to his rescue. But he remembered his mother's warning, so he covered his eyes with an arm and stood.

"M-my mama..." he said in a voice so weak, he himself could barely hear it. He pointed to the corpse.

"Your mother is dead," another voice said. "We're going to take you to some people that can help you. You didn't look them in the eye, right? You didn't give them your name?"

The boy sniffled and shook his head, not trusting his voice to speak. Something warm was wrapped around his shoulders—a blanket, he realized—and his arm was gently lowered. When he opened his eyes, a piece of fabric had been tied over them.

"What *is* your name, kid?" The first voice asked. "I'm August Hawthorne. My friend is Cora Bellamy. We aren't Hollows. Hollows can't speak like us."

The boy took the smaller hand as he felt around blindly. *Cora Bellamy's,* he assumed. The Hollow that devoured his mother's soul hadn't spoken like that. And he figured Hollows didn't have names, since they didn't have mothers to give them one.

"I'm Cassiel Jäger," the boy said. And, when death didn't come for him, he knew he could trust these people. He knew they were human, and that they would keep him safe.

PART ONE

SEVENTEEN YEARS LATER

CHAPTER ONE
DIORA

The shock and realization that they were, in fact, dead tended to stay plastered on my victim's faces long after they took their final gasping breath. Even after witnessing it several – no, dozens – of times, I still could never help the wicked grin that formed when it happened. Every single person I set out to kill was a piece of filth – *scum* – and I never once felt guilty, even as they choked and panicked, gurgling out their final breaths as their faces were forever encased in betrayal.

I bent down and picked up the pouch of coins on the wooden nightstand, not bothered in the slightest when the ends of my braids touched the still-warm body of the disgusting human man who had just consumed lethal amounts of arsenic. The pouch was heavy in my hand. Grinning, I stuffed it into the deep pocket amidst my heavy skirt and petticoats.

"Well, you had gods-awful information and you were a cheating scumbag, but, hey. At least you had money." I winked and grabbed the man's fur-lined coat from a hook on the wall. I didn't need it. The harsh night temperatures of late-fall Lysaen, the capital of the Unseelie Kingdom, had trained me to face worse, but nobody would think twice if they saw someone wearing the same coat that the man wore into the inn *leaving* it. Though I was slimmer than him by a mile and a half, I had that lanky height human men seemed to have. I pulled the hood over my braids, hiding my ears.

Sure, it would have been easier to just create another glamour, but my magic had always been weak, and I was too exhausted to cast one over myself. I still had to open a portal home.

The room I was in was on the fourth floor. I could jump from it if I really tried. I didn't want to risk broken legs, though, so I opted for heading out the front door. At this late hour, the poor concierge at the front desk was practically asleep. I breezed past him without him even looking up.

Welinas was such a drab kingdom. Even at night, when revelry clogged the streets and men and women alike poured out of brothels and pubs and other shady establishments, I couldn't get over how...grey everything was. The sky, the cobblestone road, the stretching buildings... All of it was sickeningly *boring*. Even the dullest of cities in Lysaen had more life than Welinas.

Oh, well. It wasn't my problem. Not anymore.

Humming, I slipped through the shadows, making my way to a secluded alley so dank and rancid with the stench of human waste and vomit that my eyes watered. The smell was just what I'd been looking for. The smell masked the scent of magic.

Magic had a smell no mortals could detect, but one Hollows could. It left behind an oily shimmer that an untrained eye wouldn't be able to pick up, but in enemy territory, the last thing I wanted to risk was having a Hollow *smell* my portal and follow me home.

I pulled one hand from my pocket and began tracing a simple pattern in the air near the brick wall. I shot a quick glance over my shoulder to triple check that no revelers were watching, then waved my hand in the air. Blue and green light erupted as the space between me, and the wall became a doorway to Lysaen. As soon as I crossed the threshold, I was greeted by the familiar Lysaeni chill that I loved. I pulled my hood down, allowing my pointed ears to poke free.

"No information," I said once I reached the office space owned by the agency that owned me. I dropped the pouch of coins, still warm from being tucked into my pocket, onto the mahogany table. The woman behind, who was both my owner and employer, looked bored, her yellow eyes betraying no emotion.

"No coins, then." She snatched the pouch and stuffed it into one of her desk drawers. The grin on my face faded at once.

"What?!" I exclaimed, slamming my hands on the desk. "That's not fair! It's not *my* fault he knew nothing! I *need* those coins!"

"What you need, Diora, is information," the woman said tightly. "We hired you to find information on the Hollows. We did not hire you to sleep around on our dime. I want you to return to Welinas in three days' time. There will be a man wearing a black scarf and red boots waiting for you on the corner of Main and Sixth. He will have the details of your next mission."

I opened my mouth to argue, but the woman had already started to ignore me. I cursed her in my head as I ripped off my stolen jacket and threw it to the ground in one final *fuck you* protest. I dragged my boots through the mud, not caring that my torn skirts only got more destroyed. The sooner I got home, the sooner I could rip this damn thing off and free the wings that were stuffed under the boning of my stays.

Four and a half blocks from the office building, nestled between two taller buildings that reached high into the inky night sky, was the two-story flat my adoptive brother and I somehow managed to afford. I shoved open the front door, frowning when it was unlocked, and stepped inside. I kicked off my muddy boots and followed the delicious scent filling the air to the kitchen.

Tristan Edelweiss was not my brother by blood, if that wasn't obvious from our complete opposite appearances, but he was my brother, nonetheless. Like me, he'd been orphaned as a child. He'd clung to me, for whatever reason, and years later, we were stuck together.

I tiptoed over and peered into the iron pot over the stove.

"Soup?" I asked, grabbing a spoon, and dipping it into the pale broth. Crisp vegetables and slippery noodles swam in the pot. I nearly moaned as I put it in my mouth.

Tristan whacked my hand with his wooden spoon. "Get that mud off you before you touch my soup. It'll be done soon." When he turned his back to me, the pearlescent multi-toned wings against his spine were visible. I'd always been jealous of the whorls and splatters of blues and greens and golds that marked the massive things. Tristan had always been self-conscious, because most fae had *single*-colored wings. It was a rare sight to see them out. I reached out and tugged on one.

He flinched and whacked me with the spoon again.

"Brat."

"Jerk."

I stuck my tongue out at him before hurrying to my upstairs bedroom to shed the muddied slip of a dress I'd been in all evening. As much as I adored dresses, the skirts were just too heavy from all the mud and rainwater, and human clothing didn't boast the necessary holes for my wings. I changed into a pair of wool trousers and a loose linen shirt. There was no need for propriety and decorum when it was just me and my brother.

Tristan was setting the bowls on the table when I hurried back down. I pulled out a chair and sat down, reaching for a piece of bread with one hand and my spoon with the other.

"Did you get paid?" he asked. I tore off a chunk of bread and dunked it into the vegetable broth, soaking it up before stuffing it into my mouth. Fae, despite the elongated canines we all had, were unable to digest meat.

"No," I said between bites. I stuffed another spoonful of crunchy root vegetables into my mouth before Tristan could ask me to elaborate.

He brought his spoon to his mouth but stopped. A crease formed between his pale brows. "Why?"

"Because Aea can't seem to wrap her head around the fact that not all of my marks are loaded." Aea, my boss, seemed to care more about money than anything else, and since I was beneath her in every way, I got the leftovers of whatever I brought to her.

Tristan set his spoon down. "Dio, we need money. We have bills we need to pay. I don't bring home as much money as you, and unless you want to dip into our savings..."

I slammed my hands on the table. Between Aea and now...now *this*... I'd had enough. I was *tired*. I snapped, "I'll get the money. *Fuck.* I don't need *you* treating me like some incompetent child, you know. I'm doing this for *you.* "

His wings twitched. His throat bobbed as he swallowed.

Of all the banned topics in our house, my employment was at the top of the list. I'd lied about my age years ago and signed my soul over to the assassin's guild so I could build up a record satisfactory enough to adopt Tristan, instead of letting him rot in the orphanage alone. It had been ages and I still couldn't shake Aea off my back.

"You don't need to be a bitch about it," he said defensively. "I was just –"

"You were just being a condescending ass," I said. "It's not *my* fault I couldn't bring home money today."

"Then pick better marks!" he shouted.

I stood, my chair falling over with a clatter that caused him to flinch again.

"Fuck you too, then," I growled.

He started to protest, but I gave him the middle finger and turned on my heel, stomping up to my room and slamming the door behind me.

Three days came and went in the blink of an eye. Tristan had left two days before, going out on his own mission. His lasted longer than mine, since he was there to spy, and I was there to kill. Returning to Welinas wasn't ever my definition of *fun*, especially since I had to spend an hour glamouring myself to hide my ears and teeth and wings – *gods*, it exhausted me. It didn't help that I didn't know *when* to meet my mark, only *where*. So, as I opened the portal and stepped onto the rain-slick cobblestone in an alley in Welinas, frowning as I was instantly soaked with rain, I could only hope that my informant was still there.

Black scarf, red boots, Main and Sixth, I silently repeated as I ducked my head and hurried down the streets, pausing every now and then to seek shelter under various awnings.

There. Black scarf and red boots, approaching the intersection between Main and Sixth, standing there as if he was lost. I grabbed my skirts and skipped over puddles to catch up with the man.

The man looked down at me, one dark eyebrow raised as though he was irritated to see me standing there. His hair was long enough I almost mistook him for a woman, his eyes the color of spilled ink.

He was taller than me, that human bastard. There was a shimmer to the air around him.

"You know why I'm here," I said.

When the man spoke, lips curled into a tiny smirk, his voice was low and accented, unlike the accent of the Welinas peoples. "Do I now?"

And before I could open my mouth to respond, or even will my legs to run, something solid hit the side of my head and the whole world went black.

CHAPTER TWO

SHASI

The chalice in my hand was dry, drained of every last drop of maireya, which I had guzzled down moments before as a means of both avoiding the heat and avoiding the conversation with the man seated across from me.

Man was such a generous term – he was more of a *boy* than anything, with a rounded face and a stature that barely rose over mine. He wasn't even a prince, but a second son from a somewhat wealthy family who thought his *genius* and *innovative* ideas to put an end to the Hollows was enough to get into my dress.

It was not.

"...we blindfold every citizen, we'll be able to cut through them like butter," the second son whose name I couldn't remember, drawled on. Khalid? Ali? It was something incredibly plain and common. I eyed my goblet, silently praying that it got refilled before I had to listen to another second of this man's speech.

"What weapons will we use?" I set my chalice on the low table between us. The second son looked up, his grey eyes wide and childish. I curled a strand of inky hair around my tattooed finger. "Tulwars? We've already tried. They *break.*

At this point, fighting the Hollows themselves is useless. We have to go right to the source. To the fae. And have you found a way to enter Lysaen? To kill the fae and their leaders? Didn't think so."

Gods, I needed another drink. Even in the late fall, Svadaeva was *sweltering*. Beads of sweat dribbled down my back. I met the eyes of a servant standing near the doorway and silently begged her to refill my glass. She, thankfully, walked over and poured more sweet wine into my goblet. I guzzled it down greedily.

"Shasi –" the man began. I slammed my empty chalice down. There were three things I never tolerated: liars, cheaters, and disrespectful assholes. The only people who could call me by my name – in *public,* no less, where Hollows could be roaming and listening – were my mother, my father, the members of my mother's harem, and my best friend.

"Princess," I corrected. "I am the future queen of this realm. You are to address me with my full title if you are going to try to convince me to fund your...battle strategy."

It was probably a mix of the sweetened juice I'd been nursing and the lack of sleep from the night before that made me so irritated, but I couldn't help the satisfactory chills that raced up my spine when I saw how taken aback the man was.

He cleared his throat. "Princess Shasi Dārayavahush, going after the fae is impossible. Nobody knows how to get into Lysaen or Caira, and those who *have* stumbled into the fae realm die before they can give us a map. Fighting the Hollows is our only option."

Lysaen and Caira – the two fae queendoms – weren't some hidden realms. They just had magical wards to keep those with ill intentions from entering.

The gods were likely just as irritated as I, as the gossamer curtains leading to the balcony where the second son and I sat parted, and an older woman stepped into the scalding sunlight. The second son, knowing who the woman was—likely judging by the number of heavy jewels dripping from her deep ebony skin—dropped to his knees to bow.

"Amma!" I exclaimed, hurrying over to the older woman and enveloping her in a crushing hug.

Amma was not my birth mother, but I loved her as such. As one of the six in my mother's harem, she was treated like royalty herself, and as one of the members that had been there longer than two decades, she helped raise me.

"Shasi," Amma said, smoothing out my mess of curls that had sprung free from the thick plait down my back. "Your mother wishes to have a word with you."

Typically, when my mother the queen wished to have a *word* with me, it was never for a good reason and usually because I've stirred up some sort of trouble. Again.

I resisted the urge to role my eyes, opting instead to just huff. Keeping my spine pin straight, I waved the second son off and followed Amma into the palace.

The throne Mother sat on was solid gold, a gilded beauty next to the ivory one my father, the king consort, rested upon. Women inherited the throne here, and Father was little more than her eye candy used to give her an heir.

I dropped to my knees and pressed my forehead against the smooth marble floor. When three seconds passed, I raised my head and stood, as fluid as water.

When Mother spoke, her voice was clear and resonate, filling the entire room even though she only directed her words towards me. "Hollow activity has died down here. Your birthday is approaching, isn't it, Shasi? I think it's finally safe to have a proper birthday celebration, don't you think?"

The last time I had a *proper birthday celebration* had been three years ago when I turned eighteen. Men and women of varying noble status from varying kingdoms came in hopes of winning my hand and heart. All I'd cared for was drinking ungodsly amounts of wine and getting into a sword fight with my personal guard.

I'd won said sword fight, despite being drunk enough that that I'd slipped from my native tongue into Wallaekvan, which I hadn't even studied since I was a child.

However, if there was one thing I loved more than swords and wine, it was parties. Especially parties where I didn't have to dance and could simply host.

Lips curled into the whisper of a smile, I nodded. "I think that would strengthen morale in the kingdom. I'll get to planning it."

CHAPTER THREE

KORE

D id you sleep with him." The question that came from Mother's mouth wasn't much of a question, but more of a seething statement laced with venom and ice that struck deep enough in my belly that primal fear took over every sense of reason.

I had not slept with him; the *him* being a human stable hand who tried to woo me with white chrysanthemums that he'd picked from the rickety fence around the graveyard. Nobody in their right mind would sleep with someone who gifted them funeral flowers meant to bring bad luck. Mother didn't seem to see the reason. She'd just seen the boy handing me the flowers and jumped to the conclusion that I had made passionate love with him in the barn. Just the thought of it made my skin crawl.

"Mother—" I started, but she wasn't having any of it. She removed her soft white leather glove and struck my cheek with it hard enough to leave an angry red mark in its wake. I barely flinched. This was the third time she'd slapped me today. Her other glove lay discarded on the marble floor.

"Do *not* even *think* of lying to me, young lady," she hissed. "Tell me, Kore. Did. You. Sleep. With. Him."

"No!" I finally shouted, my ice-thin patience shattering. Tears burned my eyes, no matter how hard I tried to blink them back. "I didn't! I'd never! He gave me flowers and I turned him down! I even threw the flowers out!"

If there was one thing that pissed Mother off more than random human stable hands who offered me funeral flowers it was me talking back to her. When she slapped me again, it was with the strength and fury of a demoness. I tasted blood, only realizing I'd bitten my tongue when the blood dribbled over my bottom lip. My cheek stung, raw where skin split from the metal of her rings biting into my flesh. I squeezed my eyes shut, ignoring the sting of my salty tears seeping into the cut on my cheekbone.

Mother didn't even seem fazed by the injury she'd caused me. It wasn't the worst she'd given me.

My entire life itself was the worst thing she'd given me.

I quickly reached up and wiped my mouth with the back of my sleeve before any blood could hit the floor. Mother had found the marble in a cave nearby and hauled it out herself. She hired a lapidary from the city to cut and polish the raw chunks and make it into the flooring.

I sometimes wondered if she loved that damn floor more than she loved me.

Mother reached out and yanked on my hair, adjusting the crimson locks until they covered my ears. My *pointed* ears.

"Go to your room, Kore. I cannot stand to look at you right now." She jabbed a finger in the direction of the stairs, giving me no choice but to grab the hem of my tattered skirts and scurry up to my bedroom. The door locked, but it locked on the outside, so in order to have even a second of privacy, I had to shove the chair from my vanity under the doorknob.

Using the natural light pouring in from my window to illuminate the room, I walked over to my vanity and stared at my reflection. The cut on my cheek had already begun to bruise and heal. My tongue was already back to normal, leaving a metallic aftertaste in my mouth and speckles of blood on my lips.

Being half-fae, I was able to heal just as fast as they did. Which is why Mother got away with hitting me as hard and as frequently as she did.

I forced myself to look away from the mirror before I made myself sick. With no freedom, nowhere to go, and nothing better to do, I grabbed one of the seven books off my shelf and flopped onto my bed. Every year on my birthday, Mother would buy me a book. She'd done so since I turned fifteen and needed to be locked away. Since she was a botanist who bred plants to sell in the city, all she got me were books on plants.

I opened the cover of the book I grabbed and began reading over the passages I'd long-since memorized.

As a half-fae, I had access to *some* magic.

As I skimmed the words, I willed tiny vines speckled with little white flowers to grow from between my fingers. They wound around like rings and bracelets, climbing up my arm and over my shoulders. The vines and flowers brought me a strange sense of comfort, and before I knew it, the pain in my cheek was forgotten.

Mother usually came knocking when the sun set to offer me a half-assed apology that I had no choice but to accept and dinner that was still warm. The sun had vanished beyond the horizon hours ago, and Mother hadn't once so much as pass by my door.

We'd had worse fights, but I still couldn't shake the feeling of unease that gnawed at my insides. I shoved my stack of books aside and slid out of bed. As I stepped close to the door, I stopped.

You could run, I thought. *You could slip out the window and run and have a night of freedom. If she hasn't come looking for you yet, I doubt she will.*

I lowered my hand, having had outstretched it to move the chair. Instead, I turned and hurried to my wardrobe, an old wooden thing that I'd decorated with painted flowers over the years. Opening the creaky doors as quietly as I could, I reached in and grabbed a pair of sturdy leather boots that I still hadn't broken in and a wool overcoat with a hood that I stuffed my hair into.

Then, silently as a mouse, I pried open the window and slipped into the dark night.

CHAPTER FOUR

DIORA

The first thing I noticed when I opened my eyes wasn't the cloth stuffed between my teeth or the shackles binding my wrists above my head or the cold stone ground I sat on. The first thing I noticed was the lack of magic running through my veins. I yanked on the manacles, trying to break free, but they held fast. It wasn't until I felt the burn against my skin that I realized they were iron.

The knowledge that iron was a magic inhibitor wasn't uncommon, but the metal wasn't used at all in Lysaen. Which meant I was still in Welinas. Humans had captured me. Unless...

No, I told myself. *If they were Hollows, you'd already be dead. Only humans take live captives.*

As if on cue, a creaky door opened, and heavy footsteps approached my cell. I looked up, glaring at a greasy human bobby. His belt barely held his gut in.

"Well, well, well," he drawled, his accent thick and Welinese. "Look what we have here. A fae bitch. We could catch a pretty penny for one like you." The man was *lucky* I was gagged, otherwise I'd insult him in every language I knew. The man chuckled.

I'd killed men without my magic. In fact, I rarely used my magic to get my marks. But without it, I felt empty, like I'd lost one of my organs.

He said, "I'm going to take that gag out, and you're gonna tell me what a bitch like you was doing here." He reached to his belt, removing a large ring of keys. They jingled and clanked together as he made a show of *slowly* figuring out which one went to my cell door. I couldn't tell if he was being stupid on purpose, but most human men were stupid regardless, so I didn't waste my breath thinking about it. When he finally figured it out and unlocked the door, I glared daggers at him and scooted as far away as possible. I didn't want his filthy hands anywhere near my mouth.

"Damn brat," he hissed. He shot out a hand and grabbed my jaw hard, holding it in place while his other hand yanked the ratty gag out.

The second he did, I spat on his face.

I heard the slap before I felt the sting across my cheek; before I even realized what he was doing. Fury bubbled in my core. I yanked on my shackles, trying to get free.

Deep breaths, Dio, I silently told myself. *You're an assassin. He's just another mark.*

The man leaned in close. I slammed my head against his. White hot pain erupted behind my eyes, but it was nothing compared to the satisfying crunch and gushing of blood that followed when my skull collided with his nose. He cried out in pain, dropping his ring of keys as he reached up to cradle the wound. *Bingo.* With the man distracted, I reached for the ring of keys, hooking the toe of my boot through the metal hoop.

"You godsdamned bitch!" The man shrieked before I could even grab the keys and begin to figure out which one unlocked my shackles. If he was going to lunge at me to get the keys...

Without thinking twice, I kicked, letting the ring of keys soar through the air and crash into a brick wall opposite of where I was. The man looked between me and the keys and decided to chance it. With blood still waterfalling from his nostrils and dripping down his set of chins, he turned and ran for the keys.

As awkwardly as possible, I reached for my chest. Breaking the boning of my corset was easy but slipping that snapped bone out of the fabric and using it to pick the locks of my shackles would take longer than it would for the man to fetch the keys and return. Wishing I had my magic or a knife or *something*, I snapped the boning on my side with a *snap* that echoed.

With a *snap* that caused the man to look over.

I barely managed to pull the bone free before he stood and began walking, his bloodied face contorted into a vicious look that told me I'd fucked up.

The slicing of metal through air caused even my bound wings to bristle as my entire body went rigid.

The man slowly fell right into a thick puddle of his own blood, a knife sticking out of his throat.

"I guarantee that little piece of bone there is going to be too thick," said the assailant. His accent was thick and harsh – Wallaekvan for sure. He bent down and ripped the knife free, sending a spray of blood that didn't let his grin falter. His teeth shone straight and white like pearls. "Here. Catch." He tossed something through the air; I barely managed to drop my broken boning as I caught the keys. Quickly, I figured out the smallest one would unlock my shackles, and once they were off, I quickly stood, standing with some distance between the man and myself. Like a sweet dose of opium, my magic seeped back into my bloodstream.

I narrowed my eyes as I studied the man. He stood as tall as me, if not an inch taller. Impressive for a human. His short, rounded ears and small canines gave that away, if not for his lack of wings. Dark hair hung to his shoulders, though half of it was gathered into a messy bun at the back of his skull. He wore black clothing that looked too nice to belong to a street urchin but too ragged to belong to someone of the upper class. Scars on his face cut through the stubble that kissed his razor-sharp jaw; one through his lips, one across his straight nose, one curving under his eye...

"Relax, sweetheart." He held his hands up. Fingerless leather gloves hugged the warm bronze skin tightly. "I'm not a threat. If I wanted you dead, you'd already be in whatever afterlife awaits us. I want your help."

In the distance, sirens began to wail. The damn *bobbies*. The dead one must have called for backup before coming here.

The strange man grabbed my wrist before I could protest and began pulling me along with him as he started running. I stumbled, tripping over the mess of petticoats and overskirts that had tangled around my legs.

Once we made it out of the cell room and into a thin, dank corridor that smelled uncomfortably like sewage, I yanked my wrist away.

"Who the *hell* are you?!" I snapped. The damp ground made me realize this likely *was* an entrance to the sewer. It was a small blessing that I didn't have a lantern with me.

"Ah ah ah," the strange man *tsked*. "You think I'm going to just hand over my name to you? You fae must be dumber than I thought."

I crossed my arms over my chest and gave him a pointed look. "Your eyes are visible. If you were worried I was a Hollow, you wouldn't be showing me your eyes. *You* must be dumber than I thought."

Muffled footsteps and yelling pulled our attention towards the entrance we'd come from. The man began running and I was left with no choice but to hike up my skirts and run after him.

"Sclera lenses," he explained as he rounded a corner. He glanced around, blindly feeling the walls until he found a ladder that he quickly began to descend.

Once he was halfway down, I went after him. "What lenses?" I asked, grimacing when my boots hit a shallow puddle that I *prayed* was nothing more than water. The smell said otherwise.

"Sclera lenses," he repeated. "They cover my eyes so the Hollows can't see them. I've seen Hollows, sweetheart. You look *nothing* like them. Come on. I don't really want to stick around in the sewers all day. Or you can just stay down here. Doesn't really matter to me."

Begrudgingly, I stepped closer to him.

"Clearly, neither of us are Hollows," I said. "So, I'll ask again. Who are you? Why did you bother freeing me? You *killed* that man, you know."

"I am well aware. Fine, then, sweetheart. Since you're *clearly* not a Hollow, I'm Jäger. Cas Jäger."

I narrowed my eyes, but the man – *Cas* – didn't seem to be lying. I rolled my eyes. "Dio Hyoscyamus."

"Isn't Hyoscyamus a poison?"

"It's my preferred method of killing. Are you going to tell me where we're going and what you want with me?"

Cas ignored me. I opened my mouth to ask the question again, but never got the chance to. Instead, he led me through a circular opening and into another corridor with a deeper pool of water. I cursed loudly as my boots and skirts were soaked almost instantly. Still, the squelching footsteps and shouts of angry men in the distance forced me to trudge on.

Just when I thought we'd never escape the sewer, Cas shoved on a metal grate and we both tumbled onto a cobblestone street.

The city surrounded us from where we'd emerged in a tight alleyway. Rats scurried out of our way. Cas stood and brushed himself off, as if that would somehow instantly remove the smell of septic fluid and sewage from his clothes.

"Will you *please* explain what the *fuck* is going on?" I demanded. My eyes slowly adjusted to the light from the gas-fueled lamps lining the street and the warm glow emanating from the windows of nearby buildings.

Cas didn't stop walking as he spoke. "I need to go to Svadaeva. The royals there have information on the Hollows that I *need*. And you, dear fae *sweetheart*, will be my bargaining chip."

CHAPTER FIVE

AURI

Blood, thick and hot, dripped between my fingers and splattered against the cobblestone pavement. It wasn't my blood. I wished it was. It would make this whole situation more ideal.

The body at my feet was not human.

I dropped the slim dagger I'd been holding. *Technically* I couldn't get into legal trouble for killing a Hollow. Hell, I'd probably be praised for it. But the knife I'd used was stolen and I hadn't intended to kill the Hollow.

I thought it had been human. A bobby, or some other authority set to catch me because they saw me steal a leather purse of jewels from a market vendor fifteen minutes prior. I'd meant to slice their side as a warning to not follow me, but that had taken a turn for the worse and now there was a dead Hollow on the ground, its blood seeping into the soles of my boots.

If it had been human, I would've been a thousand times calmer. I could kick the body into the greedy river that cut through the city. I could flee and let the bobbies assume it was some drunken squabble in which the poor bastard had left the fight with one more hole in their body and a lot less blood in their veins.

But it was a Hollow. Which meant people would know. People would track me down. The fae would find me and track me down. The damned *Hollows...* There were already more Hollows than humans in Welinas, and if they found out I'd killed one of their own...

I took a tentative step back, my eyes unable to leave the corpse on the ground. Curiosity itched inside me, whispering in my ears to remove the cloak that shielded the Hollow's body. Telling me to see what they really looked like. But how was I supposed to know if their creepy eyes stopped working when they stopped breathing?

Instead, I turned and *ran.* It was midday, and the market was still bustling with life, despite the Hollows stalking the streets of Welinas. Nobody seemed to notice the blood on my hands, or the hood pulled over my head despite the clear skies. I squeezed through the tight crowds, shoving my way through the maze of people as I tried desperately to get as far from the body as possible.

When I emerged on the other side of the market, I didn't realize my hood had fallen. Not until a pair of burly bobbies stopped right in front of me.

"Well, well, well," the first—a stocky, muscular man with biceps the size of my thighs—drawled. His accent was so thick I could barely understand a thing he said. "Lookie what we 'ave here."

The second, taller man grinned. One of his teeth was gold. I longed to rip it out and claim it as my own. "White hair. Thought it'd be shorter, eh?" He reached out and twirled a strand of my silver hair around his finger.

The people of Orinos – a city just outside the capital of Welinas -- knew me as Luther, the thief. I typically wore my hood or a cap to hide the tresses of white hair that fell to my mid-back, but clearly that had failed. I paled, trying to hide my hands while taking a step back to avoid the pair of goons.

"If it ain't the thief of Orinos. Luther," Goon One said. He didn't reach for the baton at his hip. Instead, he reached his grubby hands out towards *me.*

And *that* was my cue to flee.

There was only one direction to go, back towards the Hollow corpse, so that was where I ran. Fleeing was second nature to me by now and shoving through the crowd was nothing. I'd rather get yelled at by a few grumpy pedestrians than face life in the jail or risk my neck at the gallows.

Every decision I made was risky. Killing the Hollow had been risky. Going back to its body was risky. But still, that was the direction I ran. The stench of death, sticky and thick, soon caught up to me. I nearly tripped over the body of the Hollow as I leapt into the alleyway. Goon One and Goon Two were nowhere to be seen. Which would have been comforting had there not been a hooded figure in the alley with me.

At first, they looked like a Hollow, with a dark hood pulled over their face. I instantly reached up to shield my eyes when the person turned and met my gaze. The eyes that locked with mine were not a Hollow's eyes. They were not human, either. They were yellow, almost feline. I could only assume they were *fae.*

Great. You killed a Hollow and now the fae are after you.

Footsteps rapidly approached behind me. I hadn't thought about the Pair of Goons seeing me with the Hollow corpse.

Then, a song cut through the air. Soft and melodic, the voice too beautiful to be human. But...I knew what they were, deep down inside.

Drift upon the waves
And the stars will align...

"There he is!" Goon Two yelled. I glanced over my shoulder.

And, taking a gamble, I ran in the direction of the song.

CHAPTER SIX

KORE

The stories I'd heard as a child were not, in the slightest bit, accurate, because the silvery light of the moon did *nothing* to aide me as I traipsed through the woods, tripping over my own feet and upturned roots left and right. My arm caught itself on a prickly bramble vine, which only irritated me further.

The deeper I got into the Lavoisin Forest, the more overwhelming my magic seemed to become, and the more *lost* I got. Around me, tiny six-petaled flowers bloomed, creeping up trees like vines and curling around roots and logs. They choked the life out of the forest, as they trailed after me like obedient dogs. It was like the grip I had on my magic had become loosened the closer I got to the border of Faerie.

In the distance, a branch snapped, and I stilled. While I knew it probably belonged to a deer or a fox, part of me couldn't help but wonder that it was Mother, come to find me and drag me home. Or a faerie. Or a—

"Who do we have here?" The wind whispered in my ear. I stiffened, spine going pin straight as I went still. A warmth wrapped around my torso, squeezing

like a serpent. Warm tendrils of *nothingness* crept up my throat, holding it like a hand-shaped collar.

"Who are you?" I demanded, trying to make my meek voice sound stronger and braver. It still came out as a terrified squeak.

"I cannot be seen, though I am there," the voice crooned. It was light and airy but deep and silky at the same time. I couldn't tell if it was masculine or feminine, both or neither. *"I can fill a room, much like air. I cannot be touched; you cannot come near. I am mostly harmless, there is nothing to fear."*

I forced back the lump in my throat.

At once, the warmth grew cold as something—no, someone—materialized behind me. The hand at my throat prevented me from looking back, so I just closed my eyes.

"I do believe I asked for your name first," a husky voice cooed from behind me. Flesh colder than ice brushed against my jaw as the stranger leaned in close to breathe his words into my ear. It was so deep my stomach churned and my heart nearly stopped.

For a town so close to the border of Faerie, Lavoisin had less than three Hollows a year. Still, everyone *knew* the two rules when it came to the creatures; don't look them in the eye and don't give them your name.

"Etoile," I breathed. It was the fake name I always went with since it was *similar* to my surname.

"Liar." I could *hear* the grin in the male's voice.

"Am not."

The male chuckled, and my knees nearly gave out. I wet my lips with the tip of my tongue. The grip he had on my throat tightened ever so slightly, pressure applied to the sides just beside my jugulars. It didn't hurt. If anything, it almost felt...pleasant.

"What are you doing out here alone so late at night, *Etoile?*" The male asked. He hooked a finger around a strand of my hair, curling it gently as though the red lock was made of real fire.

"I could ask *you* the same thing," I shot back. The further his hand strayed from my throat, the more confident I became. Tiny blossoms of white flowers tangled themselves around the male's ankles. He didn't seem the slightest bit bothered. He chuckled again. I nearly gave him my name.

"That still doesn't answer my question."

"Nor does it answer mine."

Tendrils of darkness, inky and thick, reached out to wrap around my limbs. Vines shot out of the earth and pried them off in an attempt to keep me safe.

"I was going on a nightly walk," I said. It wasn't *technically* a lie. "Now answer my questions. Who are you? Why are you out here? What do you want with me?"

"You wouldn't want to know," he finally answered. "I was, too, going on a nightly walk. I just want to converse with you. Satisfied, Little Star?"

I was not satisfied in the slightest. I finally pried myself away from the male and began to turn to face him.

Tendrils of shadow shot out and spun me around, so my back was to him. That one tiny gesture was enough for me to realize who he was. *What* he was.

"Are you human?" I asked, already knowing the answer. It was nothing short of a miracle that I wasn't dead. Yet. "Or are you fae?"

His voice distorted once more, become neither male nor female, both nor neither. The cold presence of his corporeal form behind me was gone. "I believe you know the answer to that, Little Star. Your mother is not going to be happy to find your bed empty in the morning."

I blanched, my stomach twisting and knotting as it threatened to heave. I wanted to ask what he knew of my mother. *How* he knew I'd been running from her wrath. But the eerie stillness that had smothered the Lavoisin Forest moments before had faded away, and I knew I was left alone once again.

That man. No, I couldn't even call him that. He was neither human nor fae. Which only left one thing.

He was a Hollow.

CHAPTER SEVEN

SHASI

I quickly learned that I hated planning balls just as much as I hated attending them. While I'd never minded the loose, heavy fabric that made up gowns or the gilded slippers designed for dancing, I much preferred soft trousers and a sword at my hip. I doubted Amma would be fine with me dressing in such for the celebration. She was more...*particular* than Mother.

I also doubted that I'd stick around the party long enough to *care*.

I'd decided I'd drink plenty of wine and excuse myself at the ball's climax. It was *my* birthday, after all.

I tapped the end of my pen against my chin. The paper before me was more incomprehensible chicken scratch than legible notes. Huffing out a sigh, I reached over and tugged on the cord to turn the light off. Darkness befell the room, casting my notes in a swath of shadows.

Out of sight, out of mind.

The palace and its inhabitants were asleep, and I realized just how long I'd been working when I stepped into the hallway to see darkness filling the walls.

A princess was supposed to be a morning person; I was anything but. With a whisper of a grin, I pivoted to the balls of my feet and silently dashed down the gilded carpet that stretched down the hallway like a plated tongue.

The arched doors leading to the grove where I spent most of my time were unlocked. I opened them with ease and stepped into the cool night air. The days were sweltering hot, but the nights dropped to freezing temperatures that rivaled the cold weather of the Northern Isles. The smell of citrus blossoms and lily flowers mixed with the rich aroma of jasmine. I breathed deeply, letting the sweet fragrance fill my lungs. I tiptoed over the stone pathway to the fountain in the center.

Three figures all reached up to hold a gilded bowl encrusted with emeralds and sapphires. Water filled the dish and overflowed over the dipped sides to created waterfalls that sluiced over their bare breasts and cascaded into the tiled pool at the base. The statues themselves were plated with gold and precious gems, making the fountain worth more than a wealthy merchant's house.

The three figures were fae once, but their gilded wings had been cut off, leaving jagged scars of raw stone along their otherwise perfect backs.

A branch snapped. I whirled around; my hands already balled into fists. I didn't have a shamshir or anything else sharp that could be used for stabbing, so I'd have to rely on the weapons my mother birthed me with.

"Relax!" The figure hissed. As he stepped into the moonlight, I lowered my hands. He pushed the scarf covering his short mess of curls back, his blue eyes catching in the light. My closest friend and personal guard Mirza grinned lazily. I damn near punched him for that alone.

"Medea's *asshole!*" I exclaimed. I grabbed Mirza's arm and yanked him close, pinching his pierced ear tightly and tugging on it, careful of the emerald there.

"It's just me, Shas! No need to curse!" Mirza wriggled himself free and brushed his dark clothes off. "I saw you from the window and wanted to join you. How did your meeting with what's-his-face go? Mister Potential Match?"

When Mirza and I were children, we vowed to marry each other if we never found a match. Mirza pretended to hate every one of my potential courtiers while I pretended I hadn't caught him kissing one of the kitchen staff when he was sixteen.

"I can't even remember his face." I sat on the edge of the fountain. Cool water sprayed my curved back, sending shivers down my spine. I pressed my elbows into my thighs and cradled my chin with my hands. Mirza sat adjacent to me and began plucking stray willow blossoms from the thick braid draped over my shoulder.

"It could be worse," he quipped. "Your mother could be forcing you to wed a faerie ambassador to strengthen forces, or whatever. Or, worse, a Hollow."

I rolled my eyes and shoved his shoulder. He scooped up a palmful of cold fountain water and splashed me with it. I cursed again, my spine suddenly rigid.

"Bastard!" I seethed. I opened my mouth to call him another string of profanities, but Mirza clapped his hand over it. The sudden lethal glint in his eyes told me he was done playing.

It wasn't Mirza Issawi, my closest friend sitting next to me anymore. It was Mirza Issawi, Personal Guard of the Crown Princess

He stood, pulling his curved scimitar from the sheath at his hip.

"Cover your eyes, Shas," he instructed. His playful tone had left, replaced by the steely stern voice he reserved for shouting orders. With his free hand, he pulled his scarf over his head again, covering his ocean eyes. "There's a Hollow here."

CHAPTER EIGHT

CASSIEL

The last thing I planned on was teaming up with a fae. But, I realized as I pulled the fae woman – *Dio* – through the streets and tight back alleys, what better way to get information from the fae on the Hollows than to siphon knowledge *from* one? In a fated chance of me being in the right place at the right time, I'd witnessed Dio get arrested and thrown in jail. If I freed her from her inevitable death sentence, it would be *child's play* getting her to trust me enough to share her secrets.

That *was* the plan. Until Dio kneed me in the groin with the strength of a full-grown man and snapped, "Why the *fuck* do *we* need to go to Svadaeva, and why the *fuck* am I being used as a *bargaining chip* like this is nothing but a giant game of *Crimson Crowns?*"

I sank to my knees, my face devoid of color and twisted up in pain. *There goes my chance of continuing my bloodline...*

Yeah, right. As if there was one in the first place.

"Crimson Crowns doesn't use chips," I said through clenched teeth. The pain slowly diminished, allowing me to stand. She raised her foot again, and I instantly shielded my groin.

"I'm surprised a *human man* even knows what Crimson Crowns is," snapped Dio. She crossed her arms over her chest. "But the version *I* know *does* use chips. And that's besides the point! You haven't answered either of my questions!"

"You only asked one question!"

"I asked two within one sentence!"

I dragged my hand down my face. This woman was going to be the death of me. It wouldn't be a Hollow or my own stupidity that led me to my untimely fate, but this damn *fae girl.*

Maybe she wasn't the right person to team up with.

"I heard a rumor—" I started.

Dio cut me off, "Wait, wait, wait. You *kidnapped me* and are *using me against my will* over a silly little *rumor?* What are you, Cas, a *schoolboy?*"

Oh, this *bitch.*

I sucked in a harsh breath before continuing. "I heard a factually-based *rumor* that the princess of Svadaeva is working to create a weapon capable of eradicating the Hollows from Welinas – from the whole continent. But I heard she's not fond of meeting with people, *so,* I need to bring something to her that will make it so she can't refuse a meeting with *me.*"

Dio stared.

And I knew I had said the wrong thing.

Because *Dio,* that damn fae *bitch,* started *laughing* at me.

"I'm not in chains," Dio laughed. Tears like tiny diamonds glistened at the corner of her almond eyes. I could deal with Hollows. I could deal with the monstrous beasts that slithered across the border and congested the Lavoisin Forest. But I simply could not handle Dio.

"I could walk away *right now*," she continued, "and you'd lose your little game Crimson Crowns! I'm not going to Svadaeva. It's hot. It's full of humans. I have a home to get to."

"Crimson Crowns doesn't use bargaining chips!" I blurted, exasperated.

Dio stopped laughing, her eerily vibrant eyes locking with mine the way a predatory cat would stare down its prey.

Then, she lifted one of her elegant shoulders.

"Fine," she finally answered. "I'll venture to Svadaeva with you. Under three conditions." She held up three slender fingers. As she began walking, forcing me to follow, she listed her reasons. "The first: you can't reveal that I'm fae. Not to the princess, not to anyone. The second: we use my method of travel, since I am *not* walking from here to there, especially with the Svadaevan heat. The third: you're going to show me what the fuck kind of Crimson Crowns you humans play, because it most definitely *does* use bargaining chips."

She looked over her shoulder, tossing her braids against her spine, and grinned.

"Find me a deck of cards," I said, having no other choice than to agree, "And I'll show you that we can play it just fine without. What in the hells would you even need chips for?"

"For placing bets, duh," she responded, like it was the most known fact in the world.

It bothered me, I came to realize, how uncannily human Dio could appear. Her height posed an issue, but she assured me it would be fine, and proceeded to slouch, taking her height down at least a head. She pulled her hood over her long braids, covering her ears and hair.

It also bothered me how incapable of shutting up she was. As we walked, she rambled on and on about *anything* and *everything* and the nothing in between.

Every hour or so, I'd ask when she planned on using her fancy travel method, only for her to ignore me and continue on, talking about something her brother had done three and a half years ago that she still held a grudge against.

"Dio." I put a hand on her shoulder. She spun around, pulling a dagger from gods know where and pressing the blade against my throat.

"Touch me again, and I'll kill you," she hissed. I raised my hands in surrender, and only then did she slowly lower the knife.

"We're not getting anywhere fast like this. We're just wasting time and energy."

"Maybe *you're* wasting energy, human, but I'm not."

"Can you at least tell me where we're going? It feels like we've just been walking in circles for hours now." *Maybe,* I realized, *this is her ultimate goal.*

Suddenly, a carriage zipped past, sending a muddy spray of puddle water at our legs. Dio flipped her dagger around, ready to throw it at the driver's head. I grabbed her wrist and yanked her into the closest alley before the knife could leave her hand.

"Tell me where we're going," I hissed. Dio glared, and for a second, I worried she'd plunge the knife into my gut. Then, she sighed, and sheathed the dagger.

"I can't open a portal to a place I haven't seen before," she said matter-of-fact-ly, arms crossed over her chest. "So, I need to find a library or a museum or *something* that would have anything useful. Dumb*ass.*"

I blinked, dumbfounded.

I was more shocked by the fact that she *didn't* knife me than anything.

"We aren't going to find either of those by walking loops around the same two streets over and over again, dumb*ass,*" I retorted. "There's a library not too far from here. We can take the tram to get there faster."

Dio stared at me like I'd just spoken a different language. Of course. The fae wouldn't have trams when they just had magic to get them from place to place.

I jabbed a thumb at the mouth of the alley. Nestled between the stones making up the road were parallel iron rails a few inches thick each. Larger cities in the west had begun using trams after people began complaining about how carriages clogged up the streets and made it impossible to walk through. I avoided trams for the most part, since they got crowded enough to make *me* anxious, but the idea of wandering around the city with Dio, aimlessly looking for something, made the tram seem bearable.

"Humans don't have magic," Dio retorted, staring at the tracks like they might come alive and eat her.

"No," I said, and walked out of the alley. Dio, more silent than the stealthiest of mice, followed after. She continued to eye the tracks, wary.

"But we do have this." Just then, a boxy car came rolling down the tracks. A few people were seated inside, and a few held onto the rails lining the outside. I grabbed Dio's wrist and pulled her onto the tram. Two empty seats greeted us; Dio sank into one, her eyes wider than saucers. Nobody seemed to notice the fae sitting among them, and the tram continued.

A few people passed by us to hop off the tram as it neared a popular café. The strong aroma of lemon and fresh bread wafted through the air, nearly enough to make my mouth water. Killing Hollows didn't usually result in a good pay, so pastries were a rarity.

"So," I said, tamping down the hunger gnawing at my belly. The tram moved away from the bakery without stopping. "What's the plan once we get to the library? You just need to find a book with, like, a map of Svadaeva so we can..." I gestured vaguely with my hands, hoping to mimic what Dio would interpret as magic.

By the blank look on her face, her brows perfectly arched, she did not interpret it as such.

"I never cared to learn your human geography," she harrumphed. "I know this city and a few others, and that is all I need. I need to know what Svadaeva looks like so we can—" she exaggerated my hand gestures "—do whatever the hells you were trying to do here."

Before I had the chance to reply, the familiar brick building crested with needle-sharp spires came into view. I grabbed Dio's wrist—much to her evident dismay—and jumped off the tram. The library was one of the tallest, and oldest, buildings in the entire city. The windows had long since been boarded up, after the Hollows attacked and destroyed the delicately painted stained glass. There had been a rose window, with scenes of the gods and goddesses of old painted intricately in bright hues that caught the sunlight, but that was gone, the pieces smashed beyond recognition so much so that the museum couldn't even salvage them. The tarnished brick and soot-stained oak doors made the hairs on the back of my neck stand on end. I just had to get to Svadaeva. I had to get whatever weapons I could to kill the Hollows, because those bastards deserved it.

"Come on," I said to Dio, leading her up the stone steps to the oak doors. They were arched, with old runes inscribed on the frame. Bits of moss clung to the cracks, and a spider too big for comfort made its web in the upper corner. I shoved one door open; it groaned like an ancient ghost as the hinges worked. Then, with Dio close behind, I stepped into the library.

CHAPTER NINE

AURI

Orinos was a city people easily got lost in. Usually, I was not one such person. I knew the city better than the back of my hand; I had to, otherwise I wouldn't have survived this long. I would've died in the mazing streets that cut through the city like sinister veins. I could get from one end of Orinos to the other in fifteen minutes. At night. With my eyes closed.

Yet, somehow, for the first time in my life, I found myself completely and utterly *lost.*

The alley I stood in was brick wall on three of the four sides, the fourth opening to a city somehow shrouded in a thick, smothering blanket of fog that hadn't been there a moment ago. Dense ivy clung to the wall opposite of the foggy mouth, suffocating the brick in a deep green tapestry. Vines wove in and out, almost like a blanket. The other walls were eerily naked, save for bits of dirt and grime that stuck to the worn bricks.

That's what you get for following some creepy song, I scolded myself. *Now you're lost.*

I couldn't hear the bobbies anymore, though, so all things considered, maybe fate was on my side for once.

What had that song been? It wasn't a human voice, that's for sure, and nobody else seemed to have heard it. Could it have been a fae, come to lure me to my death in reprimand for killing that Hollow? Had the Hollows themselves come?

No, Ri, that's impossible. Hollows don't even have mouths. How would they sing a song?

Not wanting to risk stepping into the fog to find myself face-to-face with the pair of goons responsible for chasing me here, I took a tentative step closer to the ivy. It wasn't the sturdiest thing in the world, but it should support me enough to climb over the wall. As I took hold of the waxy leaves, a cold burst of air kissed my knuckles.

I recoiled quickly, staring at the ivy like it had just bitten me.

"First the singing, now the breathing ivy," I muttered under my breath. "Get a hold of yourself, Ri."

I reached for the ivy again, and when that gust of air hit me, I mustered every last drop of my strength to keep from pulling away. I grabbed the leaves and reached further, beyond the flexible vines. I expected to touch the coarse brick wall beneath.

I grasped at air instead.

"You are not welcome here, little thief," a serpentine voice hissed. It overwhelmed my senses and clogged my pores; the fine hairs on my arms and the back of my neck stood on end like there was static in the air.

"Are...you the voice who was singing?" *Dumbass! What kind of question is that?!*

"Sssssssinging?" the voice crooned. It seemed to dance from one ear to the next. *"We do not sssssssing. But you. Oh, you can sssssssssing for usssss, little thief. Tell ussssss, what issssss your name?"*

I took a step back, holding the hand that had touched the ivy to my chest. My fingertips had begun to burn, like I'd dipped them in a kettle of boiling water.

"I'm not stupid," I shot back, unsure if the voice was in my head or not. "You're a Hollow. I'm not telling you my name."

The voice laughed, the sound echoing around me like nails on a chalkboard.

"Sssssssuch a clever little girl. Ssssssso clever. Ssssssssso sssssssmart. Tell ussssss your name, little thief," the voice continued. It seemed to be coming from *behind* the wall of ivy, but the resonating echo made it seem like it was everywhere. My knees buckled. I grabbed at the brick wall to keep from falling over. The skin on my fingertips had begun to blister and peel, blood spilling out and onto the brick.

Don't look them in the eyes, don't give them your name, I silently repeated over and over, until the mantra all but drowned out the serpentine laughter.

"Go away!" I shouted. "I'm not giving you my name! I've killed one of your kind before, and I won't hesitate to do it again!"

I bent down and grabbed a rock off the ground. Then, with all my might, I threw it at the ivy wall. It rippled, shuddering like a beast that had been struck by a bullet. Then, the voice let out an ear-splitting scream. Something hot trickled down the curve of my jaw. I fell to my knees, hands clasped desperately over my ears as I tried to silence the horrendous scream.

"YOU THINK YOU CAN OUTSSSSSSSMART USSSSSS, HUMAN? WE ARE GODSSSSSSS! YOU HURT USSSSSS! WE WILL NOT FORGET, LIT-TLE THIEF. KEEP YOUR NAME, FOR IT WILL NOT BE YOURSSSSSSS MUCH LONGER!" The voice had split into a dissonant tritone, the three mashing together in a clash that pulled a scream from my own lips. I squeezed my eyes shut, but it did little against the sudden blinding light that shot through the alley.

Then, like it had never happened at all, the screaming and the light and the voices stopped. Slowly, I opened my eyes. The wall of ivy was gone, replaced by another brick wall I could easily scale. The thick fog had faded, revealing the dreary city of Orinos. I pulled my hands from my ears. My palms were coated in blood, and the two fingers that had touched the ivy were now black, like I'd dipped them in ink.

I stood, my heart pounding hard in my blood-crusted ears. I rubbed my fingers on my shirt, expecting the black to rub off like soot. But it stayed, no matter how hard I tried.

Footsteps pounding against cobblestone pulled me from my desperate attempts. *Right! Those goons!* The bobbies had plenty of time to figure out where I'd gone. I grabbed the bricks, fingers finding decent holds in the gaps between mortar and stone and began climbing. I reached the roof just as the pair of goons rounded the corner and peered into the alley I'd been moments before. I sighed heavily and sank to my knees. Up here, squished between two buildings taller than the one I sat on, I had a bit of...peace.

I knew Hollows killed you if you looked them in the eye. If you gave them your name. I knew they sucked your soul from your body and left you as a withered carcass. But never had I heard of a Hollow doing...whatever it was that just happened. I stared at my fingers, trying to make sense of the whole thing.

Dread settled deep in my belly. They knew I killed one of their kind. And now, somehow, I'd hurt them.

I'd just made myself a walking target.

CHAPTER TEN

KORE

I ran the whole way home, my heart pounding impossibly hard against my ribs, with a fervent beating I feared would leave my chest bruised. Mother always said men were the scariest things lurking in the world, but clearly, she'd never met a Hollow.

My foot snagged on an upturned root, and I went crashing towards the earth. Only...

Only I didn't fall.

Something cool and slithery caught me, tendrils of vaporous ink curling around my torso and righting me. The root snapped in two, freeing my foot. The stillness that had gripped the forest before, when the Hollow had first come, didn't seem to blanket the trees. I could hear an owl hooting in the distance. The rustling of leaves in the canopy as a gentle gale pushed through. Still, I brought my hand up to shield my eyes, just in case.

"Relax, Little Star," came the Hollow's voice. It surrounded me, like there was a dozen of him all speaking at once in a whispered hush. "I have no intentions of hurting you. I only want to ensure that you make it home safe, but that seems to be difficult for you."

"Please," I begged, taking a step back. A branch snapped. In the distance, a flurry of wings sliced through the silence. "Please, I don't want you to hurt me. Coming out here was a mistake. I just want to go home."

"Oh?" the Hollow crooned. "And here I was under the impression that you wanted to flee your home. To flee the suffocating wrath of your mother."

How did he even know that?

"I –" my voice warbled. "I do, but..."

"But I am a *Hollow,* and I've come to devour your soul, is it?"

The Hollow chuckled. I took another step; my back hit the rough bark of a tree.

"Little Star," he continued. "How about we make a deal? If you meet me here again tomorrow night, I will make sure your mother never hears about this."

Something bright flashed in the corner of my vision. I peeled my hands from my eyes to see one of the six-petaled flowers that had sprouted in my presence floating in midair.

"I quite like these little things," the Hollow drawled. "If you return and grow a grove of these for me, I shall keep your secret. And, perhaps, I can teach you how to control your magic."

My magic. The one thing that both grounded and destroyed me. I'd always wanted to understand it. To learn how to better control it. To do *something* with it, other than use it to grow meaningless flowers that led everyone right to me. This man was a Hollow, but...

"Fine," I said, and looked up from the flower. There, shrouded in darkness thicker than honey, I caught the glimpse of deep blue eyes.

As I met the gaze of the Hollow, the world around me tilted, then went black.

I woke in my bed, my nightgown twisted around my body and my hair glued to my forehead with cold sweat. I sat up quickly.

How in the hells did I get back here?

"Kore!" came Mother's voice. I threw back my blankets and clambered out of bed quickly, barely managing to grab my dressing robe and pull it over my shoulders before the door swung open. Mother had one hand on her hip, the other pointing an accusatory finger in my direction.

"It is unlike you to oversleep like this," she scolded. *Did she forget about locking me in my room over some baseless rumor?* My cheek burned with a phantom sting, reminding me of the slap I'd gotten. Mother continued. "Your bed isn't made, your hair is a mess, and there are books everywhere. I did not raise you to be such a slob."

She went over to my bed and began yanking the sheets off, dropping them in a pile on the floor for me to deal with. Before she turned around, I caught sight of a twig stuck in my hair. Quickly, I pulled it free and shoved it into the pocket of my robe.

"If you thought you could turn into a filthy pig as an act of rebellion, I am beyond disappointed. I want all of this cleaned up." Mother turned, and when she approached me, it took all my strength to keep from flinching. She took my cheeks in her hands. There was nothing kind in her gaze.

"I apologize, Mother," I said.

"You know I only want the best for you, my dearest Kore. I only do this because I love you."

She hugged me. I forced myself to hug back.

"Clean this mess up," she said as she pulled away. "If you do it quickly, there will be breakfast waiting for you in the kitchen."

Mother left, closing the door behind her. I sank to my knees; all the fear having had turned my bones to jelly. *You faced a Hollow,* I reminded myself. *You faced a Hollow and* lived. *You do not need to fear your mother.*

I grabbed my discarded sheets and stood. They didn't need to be washed; Mother had only pulled them off to agitate me. I smoothed them out and began making my bed, making sure there wasn't a single wrinkle or crease to be found. When I finished, I splashed water from the bowl at my vanity on my face, dressed, and braided my hair.

There was a bowl of cold porridge waiting for me at the table when I finally went downstairs. Thicker than ink and seemingly inedible, I begrudgingly scooped up a gloopy spoonful and stuck it in my mouth. Hunger alone was the only thing that suppressed my gag reflex; I wolfed every last bit of it down. Mother watched disapprovingly.

"Clean the dishes," she instructed after I put the last spoonful in my mouth. "I have to run errands today. I want this house to be completely spotless by the time I return."

It wasn't an unusual chore. Mother made me clean the house until it shined at least once every other week. At least she wasn't going to be home to breathe down my neck as I worked.

As I trudged over to the sink to begin washing the dishes piled inside, I heard Mother's footsteps across the floor, then the creaky hinges as the door opened and shut.

A weight had lifted off my shoulders the second I was alone.

CHAPTER ELEVEN

SHASI

Mirza freed the shamshir sheathed at his hip. Without a proper blindfold or scarf, I hastily tore a strip of fabric off my clothing and tied it around my eyes. The fabric was thick enough that a Hollow wouldn't be able to see my eyes, but I'd be able to make out the vague shapes of my surroundings.

There were two rules with Hollows: never look them in the eye and never give them your name. The latter was easy, considering you just never gave your name to anyone. People relied heavily on nicknames when it came to meeting new people, a strategy Mirza and I had down to the tee. But the eyes... Hollows wore hoods and gauzy robes that made it impossible to tell what lurked in the shadows. Hollow hunters were some of the only people that had seen what they looked like, but Hollows turned to ash moments after they died.

"Well, well, well," came an unfamiliar yet heavily distorted feminine voice. I instinctively turned towards it, making out the blurred blob that was the Hollow. I slowly drew the dagger I kept on me, holding it at an angle meant to kill. "What do we have here?"

"Your demise, it seems," I shot back, even though I could feel Mirza's glare burning into my skin. "I'll give you exactly five seconds to explain how you got in here and why I shouldn't gut you and hang your corpse by your entrails for the falcons to feast on."

The Hollow chuckled. Mirza's slippers shifted on the ground; I knew he was going to attack. His shamshir would do little against the monster, but it would be far more effective than my skimpy dagger. *You seriously need to bring a pair of scimitars with you wherever you go, idiot.*

"Relax," the Hollow chided. Neither Mirza nor I relaxed. "I'm simply passing through. No harm, no foul. You let me through, I won't kill you."

"You can't kill us," Mirza said. "You'd need our names or our eyes to do so."

Once again, the Hollow laughed, and a sharp shiver surged down my spine. Dread puddled in my belly.

"Mir, we have to go," I hissed, but he either didn't hear, or he chose to ignore me.

"You humans are so silly," continued the Hollow. Their blobby form moved closer. I stepped back, the backs of my knees hitting the edge of the fountain. "I only need your names or your eyes to devour you. I can gut you without either if I so pleased. And you."

The Hollow, presumably, turned towards me.

"I know your name already. Shasi Dārayavahush. Crown Princess of—" the Hollow was cut off by a sick, gurgling choke.

"Shas, run!" Mirza yelled. He ripped his shamshir from the Hollow's chest, inky blood spurting free. It turned to ash before it could hit the ground.

The Hollow let out a shriek that made my ears bleed.

Mirza swung his blade, slicing through the robes of the Hollow. Ash spilled to the ground. In a blink, Mirza was on the ground, pinned by the Hollow who grabbed his scarf and tried to pry it off his face. Without thinking, I charged. My blade found purchase in the fleshy spot I assumed was the Hollow's throat. It screamed again; the statue in the center of the fountain cracked.

And then, as the Hollow recoiled, taking Mirza's scarf with it, an explosion sounded. Black blood spewed from the monster. It splattered against the ground in a sickening patter, not even turning to ash. I ripped my blindfold off.

A cloaked figure wielding what appeared to be a miniature cannon stood at the edge of the garden. The way they held themselves was enough to prove they weren't a Hollow.

"Sh-Shas, look..." Mirza said. I turned to see him kneeling by the Hollow. He'd peeled back the robes, exposing a face that looked...almost human. Its flesh was ashen and pale, lips thin and hair stringy. Its eyes were completely black, as if there weren't any at all.

I looked back up, expecting to see the stranger, but they had vanished seemingly into thin air.

"It's not turning to ash," Mirza's voice cut through the silence. He nudged the corpse with the toe of his shoe. "Who was that person? Where did they go?"

I shook my head, shock rendering me silent. Who were they, indeed? And what exactly had that weapon been? Was that why the Hollow was still corporeal on the ground, spindly body still made of flesh and bones?

To think, this creature was responsible for all the tension and strife and bloody massacres that had taken place. Seventeen years ago, they had come to this world and caused nothing but death and destruction. A bloody trail of soulless, withered corpses had been left in their seismic wake. Yet, there one lay, its mouth slightly parted and its eyes completely unseeing, and its body still very much *solid*.

"I want to study this," I said abruptly. Mirza whipped his head up to stare at me, his golden eyes full of confusion as if I'd just announced I'd grown horns.

"You know what?" he stood and brushed bits of ash off his pants. "I won't even ask. How do you propose we deliver this to...wherever you want it delivered, your highness?"

I stared at the body. Mother and Amma and everyone else in the palace would murder me on sight if they found out I'd dragged a Hollow corpse inside. I couldn't exactly bring it to the harem palace, either, knowing Amma would find out about it before we could even hide it.

"The stables," I finally answered. "We can just drag it over there. I want to study the wound caused by whatever that weapon was." What exactly had killed a Hollow on the spot and didn't reduce its body to ash?

I *needed* to know what that weapon was. And I needed to get my hands on it *now*.

CHAPTER TWELVE

Diora

"This is the library?" I asked once we were inside. The smell of old paper and leather and dust hit me all at once. Shelves stretched all the way to the ceilings, packed tightly with more books than I'd ever seen in my life. Tristan would have an *aneurism* here. What books couldn't fit in the shelves were stacked haphazardly on the floor, creating a clear path from the door to the semicircle desk where a librarian sat, typing away at a typewriter. The incessant *click-clack-click-clack* echoed against the massive shelves. The typewriter *dinged;* the librarian adjusted their page and went back to typing. They didn't even seem to notice me or Cas standing there.

"It is. Impressive, huh?" Cas boasted, as if he'd built the damn place himself. I refused to let him gloat.

"I was expecting more. It's..." I picked up a book from one of the stacks on the ground and stared at the dusty cover like it might hold the answers to all the important questions: who were the Hollows, how would we get to Svadaeva, why were men so aggravatingly stupid? "I mean, if you consider stacks of ancient books just on the floor to be impressive, I'm starting to seriously question your definition of the word." I dropped the book; it landed on a crooked stack with a dusty *thunk*.

The librarian finally noticed us and stopped typing away. "Welcome to the Welinas Library and Archives. Is there anything in particular I can help you find?"

"No," Cas said, just as I quipped, "Yes."

The librarian looked just as confused as the both of us. I shot Cas a glare, silently telling him to stop being such a human man and that I killed his kind for a living and looked back to the librarian.

"We're looking for books on Svadaeva. Travel brochures and encyclopedias and things of that sort," I continued. The librarian stared. They were trying to figure out why I was wearing a hood inside, I realized. But with my hair in braids, my ears would be noticeable, and my eyes would be on display. Without my hood, I was a walking, talking beacon inviting every human in Welinas to come kill me.

Try to kill me.

"Oh! Of course." The librarian rifled through the papers scattered across their desk until they found a blank bit of cardstock. "Are you two going on a trip? A honeymoon?" They picked up a pen oozing with gloopy ink and began writing on the card.

"No," I quickly answered, just as Cas chimed, "Yes."

We seriously had to work on our communication skills.

"Right, then," said the library. Cas hurried to the desk and took the card from the librarian.

"Oh, do you have any cards?" he asked, handing the note to me. I looked down at it, studying the librarian's studious script.

As I looked up, Cas was pocketing something and already heading towards the cramped wooden staircase tucked between more shelves of books. The steps were steep enough that I had to pick up my skirts to avoid tripping on them, cursing silently to myself the whole time. I would've already made it to the third floor if the library had been built by *fae.*

Damn humans.

"What was that the librarian gave you?" I asked, nearly out of breath by the time we made it to the third floor. Each staircase had nearly two dozen steps, and Cas walked fast for a human.

"Hm? Oh. Cards," he said casually. "That must be the cat."

We passed a red sofa pocked with mismatched patches. Dozing on an armrest was a grey tabby who eyed us as we walked by, her tail swishing silently. I reached out and scratched between her ears. She purred and nudged her face against my palm, silently demanding more attention.

Cas turned down an aisle of shelves. I touched my thumb to the cat's nose before hurrying after him.

The corridor between the shelves was narrow enough that we had to fit single file. Cas, with his bulky, human man muscles, couldn't fit unless he went sideways, lest he risk ramming his shoulders into the wooden shelves.

Alone, I pushed my hood off and shook my braids.

"What exactly do you need?" asked Cas as he pulled a dusty tome off a shelf. He flipped through it absently, then put it back.

"Anything with pictures or extreme details on what Svadaeva looks like," I said. To travel, I needed to visualize my destination with such excruciating detail that I sometimes forgot what my imagination was and what was real. The smells, the air, the temperature, the people, the pavement, the language, everything. If I couldn't distinctly picture what sort of stitch people wore on their embroidered handkerchiefs, I risked dropping us in the Nowhere.

Tristan had coined the term when we were younger, when we were taught that fae who didn't use portals correctly disappeared forever.

My heart ached when I thought about my brother. He was grown, but I never left for this long without sending word, especially after our fight. And I hadn't even completed a job, so I had no money to give to him. I could only hope he was coping on his own.

Hang tight, Tris, I silently prayed. *I'll be home soon.*

"Here. This should help." Cas shoved a book at my chest. I barely caught it before it could tumble to the ground. The spine creaked as I cracked it open. Black-and-white and sepia pictures filled entire pages. Rolling dunes of grainy sand gave way to a massive palace that stretched towards a cloudless sky. Another page showed a market with colorful tents blocking stalls full of fabrics and jewels and cones of *something* from the sun. Page after page revealed more of Svadaeva than I could've imagined. A moat hugging the palace. A massive cathedral with frescoed walls and ceilings. A throng of people wearing loose clothes and scarves walking alongside massive *beasts* with mountainous humps on their backs. As I stopped on a page with a sepia picture of what appeared to be various fruits I'd never even heard of, I realized I wanted to visit Svadaeva for my *own* reasons.

I slowly sank to the ground, drinking every photograph in, memorizing every detail until I could picture Svadaeva perfectly in my head, minus all the colors I knew it had.

"Mrrow?"

I looked down to see the grey cat rubbing her face against my knee, purring loudly.

"Do you fae just attract animals or something?" Cas asked. He reached out to pet the cat, but the cat shied away and wove through my legs to get to my other side instead. Animals never liked me, for some reason. They flocked to Tristan, soaking in every drop of his affection. The library cat was an anomaly.

I couldn't argue, though. Not when she began making biscuits on my thigh, kneading my leg through the filthy, torn fabric of my dress.

"What? Jealous that the library cat likes me more than she likes you?" I set the book down. "It's probably because you're big and ugly and smell like shit."

Cas frowned. "So do you."

"Not as badly as you." I picked the cat up and stood. As much as I wanted to smother her with kisses and take her on all my adventures, I had other priorities, and I knew she'd be missed. So, I let her climb onto a shelf and squeeze through the books and out of sight.

"You are a bitch. You know that, right?" he bent down and picked the discarded book off the ground, returning it to a random shelf.

"You should've realized that *before* you smuggled me out of jail."

With timing that couldn't have been more unfortunately perfect, a parade of footsteps came down the hall. I sucked in a breath, praying to the gods that they belonged to a group of people who decided to search for the library cat, or the acolytes supposedly on every floor.

"I sent them up here," came the timid voice of the librarian. "They were searching for books on Svadaeva."

Shit. *Shit.*

Cas and I locked eyes. With a slow, subtle nod, he began creeping down the aisle, slipping into the next one. I followed, barely turning the corner before a group of three bobbies stepped into the aisle we'd just occupied.

"They couldn't 'ave gotten far," came the tinny, nasal voice of a bobby. "Search for 'em. 'Ey are not to leave 'ere."

Cas sneaked into the next aisle, and I followed after. We got three rows of distance between us and the bobbies before he whispered, "how confident are you in getting us to Svadaeva right now?"

I thought back to the pictures. I could visualize the city in my head almost perfectly. Opening a portal shouldn't be a big deal. Worst case scenario, I accidentally dump us on top of a sand dune, but I'd rather face a desert than jail for the second time.

The problem was, I'd never transported a *human* before. I'd carried other fae with me, especially Tristan in the early days when he couldn't open portals on his own. But a human?

Would Cas even be able to survive the trip?

The bobbies drew closer; we were running out of aisles to hide in.

"Dio," Cas hissed, urgency bleeding into his voice.

I didn't answer. I didn't think. I just thrust out my hand, fingers splayed as wide as they could get, and opened a portal of blinding light and raw magic against a shelf of books. Sand glittered on the other side, though it was faint.

The bobbies rounded the corner. "There! Freeze! By the law of Welinas, you are under –"

I grabbed Cas's wrist before they could finish and pulled him through the portal.

CHAPTER THIRTEEN

KORE

There was little else in the world that I hated more than chores. With Mother gone, I had the urge to abandon my duties and run to the forest in hopes of finding the Hollow from the forest. As terrifying as he was, I hadn't felt in danger when I was with him.

I picked up the broom and began sweeping the wood floors, disturbing the microscopic flecks of dust that clearly bothered Mother. As I swept, I began to sing, just to keep myself busy.

"Asleep upon their earthen beds and tucked under the stars,
the gods of new do dream
and then they one day wake under Chaos's regime."

I swept the dust out the back door and propped the broom against the wall, grabbing a feather duster next. The windowsills and counters were all void of dust, but I still made the effort to clean them.

I clutched the feather duster tightly. Tiny vines sprouted from my palms and snaked around the handle. Instead of flowers, thorns grew. One sank deep into my skin, drawing a tear of blood.

"Ouch!" I yelped, dropping the duster. At once, the thorny vines turned to ash, creating a pile of dust that I'd have to sweep up again. I stuck my finger in my mouth, sucking on the wound to stanch the bleeding.

At least Mother isn't home to witness this, I thought, grabbing the broom once more and sweeping up the pile of ash. As I dumped the ash and dust outside, I glanced at the tree line, and I could just barely make out a set of vermilion eyes staring back at me.

I dried my hands off on my apron just as the door opened and Mother's voice rang out, "Oh, Kore! I'm home!"

She walked into the kitchen and set her basket of groceries on the table I had just wiped down. She didn't need to tell me to put everything away, since I already knew I had to. As she began inspecting the house to make sure I did everything correctly, I brought the basket to the kitchen. I carefully put the speckled eggs in a bowl and the block of butter next to it. I refilled the jars of sugar and flour and put the vegetables in the sink to wash for dinner.

"I'm surprised," Mother said as I scrubbed dirt from the purple carrots. "I was almost positive you would've been a rebel and ignored my instructions. The house looks adequate."

Adequate.

She couldn't even come up with a kinder word than *adequate*.

I gripped the carrot so tightly it snapped in two. I hurried to turn off the sink and get to work drying the vegetables.

Adequate.

I'd spent hours alone mopping the floors.

Adequate.

I washed all the linens and laundry and folded them once they were dry.

Adequate.

Nothing I ever did was good enough.

Tears burned my eyes, threatening to fall down my cheeks. I rubbed my face with my sleeve as I reached for the kitchen knife.

"Kore," she said, startling me. "Why are you crying? You have no reason to cry."

"The onions," I lied, gesturing to the onion I had begun chopping. Mother pursed her lips, considering this. She didn't respond, so I assumed she believed it.

Mother left me alone while I prepared dinner. As I chopped the vegetables and added them to a pot with broth noodles and mushrooms, I began to daydream, thinking of one of the stories I'd read in the limited books I had, hoping to at least distract myself from Mother's foul mood.

Before the sky was blue, the grass green, and the ocean full of salt, there lived three siblings: the goddess of nothing, Zina; the goddess of everything, Maulea; and the god of what lay between, Eemyr. The three lived alone in the vast nothingness, much to Zina's delight. But even she grew bored alongside her brother and sister with nothing to do and nobody to talk to. One day, Maulea decided to test her powers and create something out of the nothingness. She brought forth a sea of tiny lights that spread across the astral plane, creating outlines of people and creatures, drawing a map of the celestials. Stars, she called them, and with the stars she created Ora, the god to rule over them. Happy with her newfound abilities, Maulea left the astral realm to create more and more. As Maulea's powers grew, and with them her creations, Zina found herself aching to control the everything. There needed to be balance in the world, so she became Maulea's foil. Where Maulea created, Zina balanced. Maulea birthed deserts full of sand that stretched for miles and miles like a sea, and Zina revoked all life within them. Maulea filled the globe with water thick with salt and Zina removed all sunlight and oxygen and organisms from the depths.

While the two sisters created and balanced, Eemyr was left in the astral plane alone. As the god of what lay between, he had little power when it came to the rampant spree of creation and balance. So, he observed. He watched his sisters work with careful observation, memorizing each inanimate thing they made or balanced, each god or goddess they brought forth. Where there were once three, there were now more than a dozen deities ruling over the realms Maulea and Zina created.

And, as Eemyr watched with growing curiosity, he began to wonder. What created the astral plane where they had lived? Who had created them, and for what purpose? Maulea created Gausica to bring life to everything and Zina created Heela to extinguish it. But what purpose did a god of what lay between serve? Maulea created the fiery pits of hell while Zina created the celestial heavens. Was Eemyr supposed to create a purgatory to exist in between? The more he thought about it, the more his curiosity turned to confusion.

If Maulea had created the world and Zina brought balance to keep it thriving, was Eemyr supposed to destroy it?

But the gods of old would soon be forgotten, and with their memory, Eemyr's unyielding curiosity was, too, buried.

I stirred the pot lazily, the savory scents wafting into the air and making my mouth water. I scooped up a spoonful of broth and brought it to my lips to taste, then added a splash of crushed pink salt and an extra bay leaf to it.

Covering the pot to let the soup simmer, I busied myself with setting the table, making sure the bowls were perfectly aligned and the napkins didn't have a single crease out of place, lest Mother yell at me for *that.*

"Mother!" I called after pouring her a drink. Last minute, before she could come to the table, I used my magic to draw up a tiny valerian flower. I crushed it between my fingers, letting the nectar drip into Mother's cup. As I heard her footsteps, I shoved the plant into the pocket on my apron and went to serve the soup, hoping its savory smell would overpower that of the valerian.

Mother sat down and folded her napkin over her lap just as I finished dishing up the soup. I sat opposite of her and wordlessly began eating. I had no appetite, though. Not with the nerves that coiled up deep within my belly, giving me a restlessness that wouldn't relinquish.

I'd drugged Mother in hopes of getting her to fall asleep quicker. I'd done it so I could sneak out and meet with the Hollow, despite my better judgement.

The idea of mastering my magic was just too tantalizing to pass on. If I could master my magic, maybe I could prove to Mother its uses, and she wouldn't keep me locked away like some sort of prisoner whose only crime is existing.

I shoved a bite into my mouth, savoring the tender rabbit and crunchy vegetables. Mother brought her cup to her lips; I nearly dropped my spoon. She drank deeply. If she noticed the valerian, she didn't say anything, or even act surprised. She just set her cup down and scooped up some broth with her spoon.

"I read the newspaper today," Mother said, shattering the silence and feeding my nerves. This time, I did drop the spoon. Both our gazes fell to the spoon that had clattered on the floor. Quickly apologizing, I hurried to grab it and clean it off with my apron. The crushed valerian fell from my pocket, withered, and turned to ash, but I didn't notice it.

"Apparently, a new girls' academy has opened in Welinas," she continued as if nothing had happened. "Administration is currently accepting applications, and there is a hefty sum of scholarships just waiting to be used."

My stomach sank, the soup on my tongue turning to ash. I couldn't swallow
no matter how hard I tried.

"Mother, I'm twenty-two –" I began, but my protests were futile.

"I managed to get an application for you. I filled it out and posted it today."
She spoke over me, like she always did, drowning my weak voice with hers. It was
a power-play scheme; she always spoke over me whenever I tried to talk back.

"Isn't that illegal –"

"It would be so good for you to go," she concluded. "You can get a good
education and be away from the temptations of sin."

Whether that sin was my magic or the male species, I couldn't tell. Either way,
the thought of being shipped off to some academy like a trouble child being sent
to boarding school made my stomach sour.

Mother yawned and set her spoon down. She must've finished her drink
when I wasn't paying attention.

"I-I'm sorry," I blurted. "I'll clean up later."

"Kore, where do you think you're –" I didn't let her finish. Instead, I grabbed
my skirts and ran up the stairs to my room, slamming the door shut behind me.
Mother would punish me for that. She'd probably hit me or lock me in my room
for days. But I didn't care.

She's shipping me off to a school in Welinas.

I collapsed to my knees, tears burning my eyes and cheeks, splattering against
the wood floor like fat raindrops. Around me, those tiny white flowers that
followed me wherever I went began to grow, snaking around my ankles and
wrists, the pillowy petals kissing my skin.

I cried until I had no more tears left, and then I just sat on the floor, trembling,
and gasping for air like a fish out of water.

Mother's bedroom door opened and shut. I could hear running water, followed by the creaky springs of her bed that groaned whenever she climbed on.

I waited a minute. Two. Five. Ten, just to be sure that she was asleep. Then,
wiping away my tears with my sleeve, I stood and shed my apron, exchanging

it for a coat and boots. I pried open my window and carefully climbed out, heading into the Lavoisin Forest once again, this time purposely hunting for the Hollow.

CHAPTER FOURTEEN

AURI

There was a fae in this city, and I had decided that following her would be the first step to removing the dark stains on my fingers.

I had made it onto the tram, desperate to put some distance between myself and Orinos. And the Hollow corpse and ivy wall. I'd needed to find a new city to crash in for a while, with fresh pockets to pick, so I made it to the capital city of Welinas. As I stared out the window, fiddling with my fingers, a couple climbed onto the tram. A man and a woman, though the woman was nearly as tall as her companion.

And she acted like she had never, ever seen a tram before, despite this one having a routine schedule of running through Welinas every hour on a daily basis.

Curious, I moved to sit behind them, listening in on their conversation.

"You just need to find a book with, like, a map of Svadaeva so we can –" the man said. His voice was deep. Gravelly, like he'd just woken up or had his throat clawed out. They both looked like hell and smelled even worse.

"I never cared to learn your human geography." *Bingo.* "I know this city and a few others, and that is all I need."

I tuned them out after that, already having the one-word confirmation that I needed. The fae and her human companion got off the tram at the library, and I followed them, skulking in the shadows as I crept after them.

I never spent much time in the library. I liked its quiet, but there wasn't any food I could steal or people I could swindle, so I spent my time elsewhere. I could read, but I never understood why people devoted their time into reading books when they could be searching for money or food or odd jobs to make ends meet.

Then again, it seemed only the wealthy and educated spent their free time in the library. After all, they didn't have to use every drop of their leisure worrying about whether some other urchin stole their not-too-damp newspaper bed.

The fae and her companion took to the stairs. I waited until they had gone up a full flight before sneaking after. The warm sconces on the walls gave a low, comfortable light and plenty of shadows to hide in. Maybe I should spend more time in the library. It was warm, and even if it didn't offer food or money, it was a sheltered place to sleep.

On the third floor, the fae and her companion started stalking through the shelves. Stretching floor to ceiling, they would make for good escape routes if I needed to run from anyone. I passed by a grey cat and reached out to pet her, but she hissed and ran off.

Bastard.

I wove through the shelves, peering through the gaps in the books to watch the fae and the human man. The fae had sat down, a book balanced on her knees.

How boring, I thought. I stared at the fae, trying to see what she looked like under her hood. Thick braids fell over her shoulder, held together with metal cuffs instead of ribbons. My fingers itched to snag those cuffs to sell. Fae silver had to be worth a lot. Her eyes were gold, like pots of molten honey left under the summer sun, framed by thick, dark lashes.

The fae stood and began bickering with the man. I tuned them out, having little interest in whatever they had to argue about.

Just as I was about to slip through the shelves and confront the fae, since lurking in the shadows had gotten me nowhere, I heard a voice that made my stomach sink all the way to my feet.

The bobbies.

Fuck.

How could they have followed me here? I wove through the city, throwing them so off track that even I felt lost. I *fled* Orinos, yet... Yet they'd *found me!*

There was a blur as the fae and her companion tore past me. Without thinking, I got up and ran after them, keeping one shelf between us.

"There! Freeze! By the law of Welinas, you are under—" I heard one of the goons say. I peered through the shelves to see the fae and the human step through...

Through a *portal.*

My feet moved on their own, launching me through the shelves. I dove through the portal seconds before it snapped shut.

Sand filled my mouth and scraped against my palms. Blazing sun beat down on my back and neck, my hood having been thrown off. I choked, spitting out as much sand as I could.

"Aha! We made it!" came a female voice. I spat out another glob of sand-thick saliva and forced myself up.

Mountains of golden sand stretched out as far as the eye could see. In the distance, the dark outline of curved turrets and a bustling city stood out stark against the bright blue sky, gilded by the rays of the vicious sun. The rain that had soaked my clothes seemed to evaporate at once.

"We did not make it," a male voice said. "That looks to be Svadaeva there. We are *not* there."

"Well, *excuse me* for not getting the precise coordinates just right. Be grateful that I even got us here. Otherwise, we'd be in jail."

The black stains on my fingers burned. I rubbed them against my jacket. I took a step, instantly sinking in the sand that shifted and melted under my feet.

"Um, excuse me –" I started, trying to get the attention of the two. Without her hood, I could make out the pointed ears on the fae, and her elongated canines as she spoke. The man stared at her; his dark brows knitted in the center of his olive forehead. They were both pretty. Infuriatingly so.

"Where would you rather be; jail, or this hot fucking desert?" the man argued.

"You are the one who wanted to come here in the first place! Don't get mad at me; I did the best I could!" the fae shouted.

"Excuse me –" I tried again, but my words were drowned out by their arguing.

"Fuck me," the man grumbled. "I wanted to go to *Svadaeva. Sva-fucking-daeva.* Not the middle of the desert."

"Then walk, you man child!"

"EXCUSE ME!" I yelled. The fae and the man both turned to me, instantly forgetting about their argument.

"Cas," the fae said slowly, not once taking her eyes off me. Or, rather, she looked just past me, refusing to make eye contact. The man – Cas – stared at me dead on. "Who is this?"

"How am I supposed to know?" asked Cas. "Doesn't look like a bobby. Must've followed us through that shit portal of yours."

"My portal was not shit; I was *rushed!*" the fae argued. "Maybe they're a local. Are you a local? Can you direct us to Svadaeva?"

I looked at Cas – at his forehead, not his eyes – then at the fae. I'd always imagined fae to be these terrifying beasts with leathery wings and mouths full of too many too-sharp teeth. I imagined them to be reclusive, hidden from the sun and the world, unable to understand our language or consume anything that wasn't milk or honey or blood. The fae in stories were savage monsters with a thousand faces and a thousand ways to kill. They lurked in dark corners and conspired with the Hollows to take your name and eyes and soul. They could trap you in their realm forever with your name, and if you ate any of their food or drank any of their drink, you would never be allowed to leave. They would swap out human babies with changelings of their own, forcing the poor human parents to raise a monstrous devil of a babe until the fae returned to claim their own.

The woman in front of me was none of those things. If anything, she just looked irritated and slightly exasperated to be under the sweltering sun, suffocated by her cloak and heavy wool skirts.

"I'm Dio," the fae said. "This is Cas. Fae and human, neither of us are Hollows. He wears lenses over his eyes. I do not. Who are you? Can you get us to Svadaeva?"

I stared at the fullness of her mouth. Her lips reminded me of overripe cherries, the top ever so slightly more swollen than the bottom. Her voice was harsh on her tongue, her fae accent thick as she spoke.

"Hello?" Dio said, irritation lacing her tone. "We know you're not deaf."

"Ri," I blurted, giving the shortened version of my name. I had a million names, but I had too much attachment to them to offer them up to this fae, pretty as she was. My name was two syllables. Ah. Ri. There weren't many nicknames to get from it without dipping into my surname, so I chose the syllable that sounded the nicest on my tongue. Ri. The dissonant mash between the notes *re* and *mi*. The prefix of all the important words like *return* and *regain* and *remember*.

"What?" said Cas, breaking the silence that stretched across the desert.

"Ri. My name's Ri. I followed you through the portal because *you're* fae, and I need help." I began to pull my hand from where it was hidden in my pocket, only to be cut off by an ear-splitting screech. I jumped back, hand flying to my belt where my knife would've been, had I not left it in the Hollow corpse. In a blur of metal, Cas had two knives drawn, one in each gloved hand.

"What in the ever-loving fuck *is that?!"* Dio screeched. Cas and I looked down to see a cerulean blue...thing...scuttling across the sand. It was the size of my palm with spider-like legs, but a curved stinger the length of my finger. I took another step back, instinct telling me not to get close to the creature.

"That is our cue to get the hell out of here," Cas said, showing just as much disdain for the little monster as Dio and I. Dio hiked up her skirts and began awkwardly running along the sand.

The sun beat down on us as we ran, and the sand seemed to pick fights with us, slipping out from underneath us every now and then. As we headed towards the blurred outline of the city resting on the horizon, I explained between pants how I'd found the two of them and followed them, effectively jumping through the portal at the same time as them.

"Why – were you – running from – the bobbies?" I asked, breathless. The running and heat had sucked every drop of moisture from my body, and my lungs had to work overtime to keep up with the exertion. Running across haphazard dunes of sand was a whole different league of difficulty compared to the traipsing around the underbelly of Welinas that I was used to.

"Jailbreak!" Dio boasted proudly. She'd taken one of Cas's knives and shorn her skirts at the knees. We each took bits of fabric to wrap around our heads to protect our necks and faces from the garish sun. "I was arrested – wrongfully so – and Cas broke me out."

"Even *I've* never been arrested," I found myself saying. "And the bobbies have had me on their hit list for years now. Petty theft, not-so-petty theft, pickpocketing, loitering, solicitation, the likes. Oh, and I guess murder now, too, even though it was an accident."

Cas and Dio exchanged a look.

For some reason, my tongue decided to continue to run. "I killed a Hollow. Completely on accident."

Cas stopped dead in his tracks. I ran right into the solid wall of his back hard enough to make my eyes water.

"Did you just say you killed a Hollow on *accident?*" he demanded, the playful lilt that had been coating his voice up until now gone.

"Uh... Yeah?" I said slowly. My foot slipped and sand filled up my boot, much to my dismay. Whoever decided inhabiting a sea of sand was a good idea deserved eternal torment. The city in the distance didn't seem to be getting any closer.

"How?" Cas demanded. I eyed Dio, my smugness wiped clean and replaced by an uneasiness that crept up my esophagus. I still hadn't ruled out Dio having some involvement with the Hollows. After all, she had shown up right after I'd fled the scene, leaving the corpse of the Hollow behind.

My tongue weighed heavier than lead as I spoke. "I stabbed it. There was blood everywhere. It sort of just...collapsed into a puddle of its own blood and...died. I don't know. I fled afterwards, so I didn't really stop to check and make sure that it was, you know..."

"Ri," Cas spoke slowly now, as if I was nothing more than a toddler in need of scolding. "Hollows are damn near impossible to kill. And they turn to ash after they die. They don't bleed and their corpses don't linger. You couldn't have just stabbed one and killed it. Are you *positive* it was a Hollow?"

I thought to the inky thick blood that had coated my hands and boots. The blood that was far too dark a shade to belong to any human. I thought to the wall of ivy and the accusatory screams from a voice too dissonant to be real, like it had come from three different people speaking from three different telephones at once. I thought of the black stains on my fingers, where blood the same color had once been.

Maybe the body had turned to ash. I didn't exactly stay around to find out. I almost laughed at the possibility. If the Hollow *had* disintegrated away into nothingness, I had no reason to flee the scene, and I wouldn't have ended up with sand in my boots and a sinister sun beating my back.

"What color do you fae bleed?" I asked Dio.

"Red," she answered matter-of-factly.

I turned back to Cas. "Then it was definitely a Hollow, because its blood was practically black. The knife I used didn't belong to me. Maybe it was some magical anti-Hollow knife or something."

Cas considered the possibility, but I could tell the uncertainty of it irked him. He shook his head, dismissing the topic, and continued towards the distant city.

CHAPTER FIFTEEN

SHASI

Mirza and I stared at the corpse, which lay balanced on an old canvas cloth atop a mound of straw. We'd stripped it of its robes, revealing a rather uncanny humanoid body. Her – we determined it to be a female after uncovering her body – grey flesh stretched taut over angular bones, so tightly in some areas it looked translucent. Blackened veins ran under the skin, that same dark blood crusted around the circular wound from the strange weapon.

"Should we...touch it?" Mirza asked, glancing at the leather gloves on his hands. Still unsure as to whether the Hollow was dangerous to the touch, we decided not to risk it and wore gloves.

"What if it kills us?" I replied, nudging the corpse with my foot.

"It's dead, Shas," he said flatly.

"It's a Hollow."

Still, my curiosity was unsated, and I couldn't handle the suspense. Using my teeth to pull off my gloves, I knelt down and brushed my fingers against the Hollow's temple.

"Shasi!" Mirza yelped, grabbing my wrist, and yanking it away. "Are you an idiot?! What if –"

"Mirza, I'm fine," I said, prying my hand free. I flexed my fingers, examining them in the warm sunlight that spilled in through the slats in the stable's walls. Nothing appeared out of the ordinary. Nothing *felt* out of the ordinary. I crouched down and traced my fingers along the Hollow's harsh jaw, along her crested cheekbones and upturned nose. I turned my attention to the wound.

Now that the blood had coagulated into a gloopy, sticky crust around the hole, I could get a better look inside.

And there appeared to be something *stuck* in the scrambled mess of brains and skull. It glinted when the sunlight shone directly against it.

"Mirza," I said, not once looking up.

"Shit. Don't tell me you're infected and becoming a Hollow. Shas, you're the *heir*, and—"

"Shut up, will you?" I looked up. "Go get me a pair of forceps from the infirmary. And make it fast."

Not being one to disobey his princess – even if we were best friends – Mirza nodded and scrambled off to the palace.

The Hollow's anatomy was so like my own, and the longer I stared at her, the more uneasy I felt. I'd always assumed Hollows just spawned into existence, birthed from the darkness and shadows they shrouded themselves in. But this Hollow, thin as a wraith or not, had the body for growing and birthing a child. The body for nurturing a babe. For being a parent, whether Hollows fit into the standard mother-father parental roles. Did she have parents? Siblings? A life-partner and a family of her own? Did she have friends back wherever she came from waiting for her return; friends that would be devastated to learn she wouldn't be returning because her corpse lay on a pile of hay in the royal Svadaevan stables?

It bothered me more than ever at that moment to realize just how little we knew about Hollows.

Footsteps pulled my gaze up, and I was met with a pair of shiny forceps thrust out by Mirza. He panted, like he'd just run from the infirmary back.

I took the forceps. "Sorry for this," I whispered to the Hollow, even though I knew she was long dead and undeserving of an apology.

Then, I thrust the forceps into her skull.

As the heir to the throne, my mother had made me learn *every* skill imaginable. I could play sixteen instruments and kill a man a thousand different ways with poisons and knives and heavy shamshirs and wraith-like scimitars. I could name every city and town and hamlet, every river and hill and forest. I could paint and sew and embroider, even if I hated doing so. I could solve mathematic equations and recite poetry.

And I could perform surgeries if I absolutely needed to.

Thick, viscous blood oozed from the wound, lubricating the forceps, and causing them to slip. Without any light, save from that from the sun, I couldn't see what I was grabbing, if I was even grabbing at anything.

Metal scraped against metal, and the forceps found purchase. Squeezing tightly, to not lose whatever I'd grabbed, I slowly pulled them free. Mirza held out his hands; I dropped the blood-slick thing into his outstretched palms.

"What...is this?" he asked, using his tunic to clean the thing. He held it up for both of us to see.

The thing was smaller than my pinky nail, with one flat end and the other end appearing like a flower, with metal petals peeled back. I snatched it up and looked at it closer.

"This thing killed a Hollow?" I stared at the tiny bit of metal in disbelief. All this time we'd been struggling to perfect our swords and weapons to no avail, and *this* tiny thing killed one instantly?

"I went back to where the explosion happened." Mirza dug through his pockets and produced another slim bit of metal. This one was longer and cylindrical, no thicker than the base of the flowered piece in my hand. "Found this on the ground. I think maybe they might fit together."

He reached out for the flowered piece. When I gave it to him, he slipped it into the circular opening of the longer piece. The fit was snug, but they slid together like pieces of a puzzle.

"So...this is the weapon that can kill a Hollow," I said softly, taking the strange thing from Mirza.

We knew what could kill them.

Now, we just had to replicate it.

Mirza and I hid the Hollow under the canvas sheet, hoping to further study the corpse later. After bathing in jasmine-scented water hot enough to scald—and get the stench of death off—I dressed in the most casual clothes I could find – Amma had given me a second wardrobe full of common clothes because, as she said, *princesses always need an escape from the palace* – and met Mirza just outside the palace walls.

"I'm sure the souk has something helpful," he said, adjusting the scarf he wore over his head. While he bore no resemblance to the royal family, I still had the tell-tale features of the princess. I wore a silk scarf that covered both my curls and the lower part of my face. It wasn't an uncommon accessory, and it helped me look more like the people of Svadaeva than their princess.

Mirza and I visited the souk frequently. Mostly it was to spend our money on ornate knives and gaudy sheaths encrusted with fat emeralds and rubies, or to drink our weight in date wine and eat enough sugary foods that we got sick. This time, though, we had a mission to figure out if anyone knew anything about the metal flower, as we had taken to calling it.

"Even if they don't, I've been craving that manakeesh that one woman makes." My mouth practically salivated at the thought of the warm bread sprinkled with cheese and meat. The palace cooks couldn't ever get the ratios just right.

"Didn't you just have some, like, last week?" Mirza nudged my side with his elbow.

I rolled my eyes. "And? Don't tell me you've gotten sick of it."

"I could never." he grinned.

Before long, the wide streets had become congested with vendors yelling out at the dozens of passersby. Horses and camels pulled along by embroidered leads wove through the crowd. Tall cones of raw spices made my stomach grumble, and the wafting scents of bread and falafel and gloriously cooked meat did little to aid the hunger that gnawed at my insides.

Mirza, sensing my growing gluttony, grabbed my wrist and pulled me away from the food vendors and towards the row of stalls dedicated to jewelers and metalsmiths. Mirza and I frequented this part of the souk, since the best blacksmiths sold their knives and other blades here.

"You have the metal flower, right?" Mirza asked, approaching the tent of our favorite blacksmith. She was a burly woman with thighs that could crush a grown man's skull and biceps covered in scars. Despite her masculine body, she had a slim, girlish face with unruly curls and big, doe-like eyes framed by thick lashes and lines of kohl. She and Amma had been friends as girls, and even if she hadn't, I knew she still would've treated Mirza and me with the same motherly kindness she always showered us in. Amma had asked Mother to invite her to the harem once, but the smith had declined, saying she only had enough room in her heart for her forge.

"Mir! Shas!" the smith, Noor, exclaimed. She abandoned the blade she was polishing and scooped the both of us into a rib-crushing hug.

She finally released us and crossed her arms over her chest. "So, what brings you two here? How did those tulwars I lent you work out?"

I cringed at the mention of the swords. The swords that lay broken in half under my bed because I'd hoped nobody would bring up their existence ever again.

"Never mind that," Mirza interjected, saving me from having to explain why the swords had broken. "We need your help." He quickly explained everything that had happened – the Hollow appearing, the strange figure causing the explosion, finding the metal flower in the corporeal corpse of the Hollow. As he spoke, Noor beckoned us into her tent and had us sit. When Mirza finished, he procured the metal flower and showed it to Noor.

The smith took the small piece of metal and turned it over in her large, calloused hands.

"Do you have any idea what that thing is?" I asked, leaning forward. "Or what caused the explosion, or what it's made of?"

"I've never seen anything like this," Noor admitted, and my shoulders slumped with defeat. "But I'm just as curious as you two are. Do you mind if I keep this so I can figure out what it is? It's only fair, considering you still haven't given me my tulwars back." She eyed the both of us knowingly. Heat flooded my cheeks.

"O-of course," I stammered. "Please let us know what you find out." I stood and gave Noor another hug. I said my goodbyes and left the tent with Mirza in tow.

"She'll figure something out," Mirza said. "If anyone's a master when it comes to metals, it's her. Now, shall we get some of that manakeesh?"

As if on cue, my stomach grumbled. I fixed my scarf and began eagerly walking towards the manakeesh vendor.

When we arrived, a group of people stood in front of us, huddled around the cart. I could tell they were foreigners, as two of them had fair skin, and one of them wore wool skirts chopped haphazardly at the knees.

"How in the hells was I supposed to know to bring money with me, huh?" the dark-skinned female with the crudely cut skirts argued. "It's not like I had a lot of time to go home and count out my savings between getting arrested, getting bailed out, and traipsing across the desert. I swear, every time I feel a tickle, I think it's that weird blue thing. I wouldn't even have Svadaevan currency to begin with!"

"I mean, she has a point," the shortest of the three, a pale skinned female with even paler hair said. "Carrying around purses of coins is risky."

"I literally saw you snag a bracelet on our way here," the male said.

"Yeah? I can't exactly exchange that for water and whatever these things are. Look, the lady's distracted. I say we just –"

I cut the pale haired girl off by clearing my throat. The three spun around to face me. "If you steal, I will hunt you down and skin you. If it's food and drink you want, I'll pay for it."

They exchanged a look. I could feel Mirza's gaze burning against the back of my neck, rivaling the heat from the sun, but ignored it. Foreigners or not, these people were in my kingdom, and it was my responsibility to look after them.

Before they could make a choice, the woman turned back around. "Oh!" she exclaimed. "Such a big group!" With that, she began piling up stacks of manakeesh. The dark-skinned girl piped up, demanding drink as well. I wordlessly dropped a handful of coins on her cart. The woman passed glasses of water to the three travelers, who all greedily gulped it down.

When we all had our manakeesh, the three strangers started to walk in the opposite direction. I passed my bread to Mirza and hurried after them.

"No, you don't," I said. "I paid for your meal. You're going to explain to me who you are and where you came from."

The man sighed and rubbed his face with his gloved hand. "Is there somewhere we can sit?" he asked. I pointed to an open spot in the pavilion, right by the edge of a fountain. The fair-haired girl eyed the gilded statues greedily.

The four of us – Mirza hurrying to follow after – made our way to the fountain, sitting on the stone edge. The fair-haired girl thrust a hand into the cool water, grabbing a fistful of coins tossed in by children hoping to make a wish. I didn't bother stopping her, as I was too focused on what the man had to say.

He pointed to himself, the dark-skinned girl, and the little thief. "Cas. Dio. Ri. We're here on official business. We need to have an audience with the princess."

That caught my attention. I leaned closer. "What sort of business?"

"Hollow-related business."

Mirza and I exchanged a look. Hollow business? Did these three have anything to do with the metal flower and the Hollow corpse in the stables? I grabbed my manakeesh from Mirza and bit into it, chewing slowly so I wouldn't spill and tell them everything. The thief – Ri – was pale, but she didn't have the greyish tint the dead Hollow had. She was human, and so was Cas. But Dio... There was something about her eyes. Something about the way she stared at the manakeesh like it was poisonous, before handing it to Ri, who scarfed it down eagerly.

Cas continued, "I am a Hollow hunter. I want to work with the princess to eradicate them."

I curled my lips into a tiny smile. "Well, in that case. My name is Shasi Dārayavahush, and I'm the princess of Svadaeva."

CHAPTER SIXTEEN

Kore

The tiny white flowers that seemed to thrive whenever I visited the Lavoisin Forest trailed after me as I walked deeper and deeper into the woods. The border between Lysaen and Lavoisin rested in these woods; my fae blood had to be reacting to it, making my magic stronger.

I came across a mossy clearing, where the canopy was thin enough to let silky moonlight in. A nurse log full of tiny saplings and foxfire mushrooms that glowed green with bioluminescence made for the perfect bench. I sat, my little flowers snaking around my ankles. I began to pick them, creating a bouquet of snowy white.

"Hello, Little Star."

The deep voice caused me to jump. I nearly dropped my flowers. Inky shadows quickly picked up the flowers before even a single petal could fall. The Hollow stood behind me, his warmth pressed against my back. His shadows held the flowers out.

"Before you teach me how to control my magic," I began, "I need you to swear that you will not use my name nor my eyes to take my soul and kill me."

"Have you not already given me your name, Little Star?" crooned the Hollow. My ears flushed red. Etoile. He still thought that was my name.

"Semantics. You can't look me in the eye and suck out my soul or do whatever it is you Hollows do. And I deserve to know your name, too." Thorny vines sprouted from the earth and batted at the inky tendrils of shadow. The shadows playfully fought back, as if they didn't think the vines to be a threat.

"Aita," he breathed, and I knew he had given me a false name, too. "I swear upon my crown and throne that I will never take your soul from you lest you are willing to part with it."

"I want to see your face, *Aita,*" I said. I stood, the vines around me receding and returning to the dirt. When I spun around, there was nothing but shadows.

A hand slid around my throat, not harsh enough to choke me but enough to let me know it was there.

"If you're going to have rules, Little Star, it's only fair if I have them, too." Aita's voice was such a low whisper, so close against my ear, that harsh shivers raced down my spine, settling in a pool of fire within my low belly. Anyone with a shred of common sense would flee the area if a Hollow got that close to them.

Apparently, I had none.

I leaned my head back ever so slightly, until my curls brushed against the firmness of what I assumed to be Aita's chest.

"The first –" his chest vibrated as he spoke, and I melted into it, foolishly. "– You *cannot* see my face. And the second, since you have given me two rules, I don't want you traipsing through the forest late at night every time you want to be tutored. It's dangerous, and you've neglected bringing a light with you both times you've been out here."

I wanted to argue that the light of the moon was enough for me, but we both knew that was a half-assed lie at best. The damn moon didn't do a thing to alleviate the darkness shrouding the eerily still woods.

"Then how am I supposed to find you?" I asked.

"You call my name," he replied. "My true name."

Great. He wants me to summon him with a name he won't even give to me.

"Which is...?" I tried.

Aita chuckled.

Of course.

"Whatever," I grumbled, picking at the petals of my flowers. I really hadn't thought things through. Next time – because I was determined there would be a next time – I would bring a lantern with me.

Aita moved, sitting next to me. In the darkness, all I was able to make out was a blobby shadowy shape that ebbed and warped as the shadows moved. He wore them like a cloak, like a piece of armor, like a crown. They were a part of him just as much as they *were* him.

I had only ever seen Hollows in pictures and at a distance, safe with my eyes covered and my name kept locked up. Nobody had ever photographed one, that I knew of, and Lavoisin was too small a town to get regular visits, despite how close to Lysaen we were. I knew they wore shrouded cloaks of darkness to hide their features, but I think Aita took that a bit too literally.

"Your magic is an extension of you," Aita said, pulling me back to reality. Shadows caressed my hand, taking it into their grasp. "It is inside you just as much as it *is* you. Fae are trained early on to master their magic. All fae have it, though the potency varies from lineage to lineage. Two fae could both possess an aptitude for fire magic, but one can only summon small, cool-burning flames while the other can burn an entire factory down without batting an eye."

I wished I'd brought a notepad to write everything down. Instead, I tucked the precious bits of knowledge away, promising myself I'd write them down later. In just two minutes, I had learned more about magic than any of my books had ever taught me.

"You seem to know a lot about the fae, Aita," I mused. "Are Hollows fae?"

Aita chuckled. A flurry of white flowers sprouted from the earth, curling around Aita's shadowy form. My cheeks and ears flushed a red darker than my hair. Thank the *gods* for the darkness that shrouded the forest.

"I am not a fae, no," he answered carefully, picking each word like they were precious gems. "I am far more powerful than that. But you are fae. At least, part of you is. A powerful earth mage, it seems."

One of his shadows curled around the flimsy stem of a particularly affectionate flower, snapping it with ease. It brought the flower up and tucked the stem into my mess of curls.

He's a Hollow, Kore. Don't you dare get lewd thoughts!

"As interesting as the history of magic is, can you teach me how to better control my magic?" I asked, moving closer. Warmth emanated from his shadowy form; I couldn't help but feel drawn to it, like a moth to the flame. "Sometimes, I'm able to call upon it with ease. But it usually just...comes without me wanting it to, or without me realizing it. Like now. I have no control over these flowers, unfortunately. And it's only plants. I can only make plants grow, but never when it's convenient. It would be *great* to grow a magical garden so we wouldn't spend all our money grocery shopping, but *no*, I can only make thorny vines and flowers that are a bit too aroused –"

Aita cut me off with a deep, throaty laugh. One that made my insides turn to goo and my thoughts to a jumbled mess, like the print on a newspaper after being left in the rain. If I could get him to laugh like that again, I wouldn't hesitate to offer up my name and eyes and soul.

"They are quite affectionate, aren't they?" he chuckled. "Let's do this, then. I want you to think of a fruit. Any fruit your heart desires. And I want you to grow it. Just the fruit, if you can, but I won't be upset if you grow the entire plant, too. You can't have a garden if you can't manage one thing, right?"

I hated that he had a point.

I squeezed my eyes shut and focused on a fruit.

Years ago, before Mother seemed to hate my very existence, a foreigner from the kingdom of Svadaeva passed through. She wore the brightest colors, swathed in silks of gold and blue and green, and traveled with only a horse and a single bag. She was on a pilgrimage, she'd explained, heading to become the caretaker of some ancient temple or church. Mother had urged me to say hello, and when I approached the woman, I stumbled over my words so much, my cheeks turned the same color as the fat ruby she wore on her index finger.

The woman had chuckled and reached into her bag. "This is the food of the gods," she said as she produced a round, red fruit. I hadn't wanted to eat it, since the food of the gods shouldn't be wasted on a half-blood mutt like myself, but Mother cut it open, and tiny red seeds, swollen with juice, spilled out. They looked like tiny gems and made the sweetest crunch when I chewed on them.

I had no idea how the food of the gods grew, but my hands soon grew heavy. When I opened my eyes, the fruit rested in my palms.

"A pomegranate?" Aita asked. His shadows curled around it, prying the hard shell apart until the teardrop seeds spilled onto my hands. "They call this the food of the gods, you know." His shadows picked up a few of the seeds, swallowing them in darkness. I put one in my mouth, nearly moaning at the sweetness. It had been years since I'd had the fruit, but it tasted just the same. Better, even, now that it had been born from magic.

"Your magic seems to be stronger than you realized," he continued. I licked the sweet juice from my fingers. "You can only create what you know. You can't conjure things you haven't seen or tasted or felt before."

I looked at the pomegranate shell. Already, it was beginning to crumple to ash. Creating things didn't seem to be the problem. I could dream up plants without batting an eye. It was controlling when I created them, and how long they lasted, that was the problem. Most things I magicked into the world didn't last longer than a few minutes. I couldn't create a lavish garden that would last through the summer and fall. I couldn't create anything useful.

The last of the pomegranate withered to ash and slipped through my fingers.

"How do I make it last?" I asked, turning to look at Aita. The edges of his shadows blurred, straining my eyes. I had to look away. "The magic, I mean. Everything I create is gone within a few minutes."

"No," said Aita, and I looked at him again. An inky tendril of darkness held out a tiny white flower. "These don't seem to vanish. Not *everything* you create dies. But, Little Star, that's just the way of life. Everything born and whole dies eventually. Your plants, your flowers, you..."

"Even you?" I breathed.

Aita chuckled. "No, Little Star. Not me. Not anymore"

I didn't remember returning home, nor climbing into bed. I wore my night-gown again, though I had no recollection of donning it. When I sat up, my gaze landed on my nightstand. On top of a folded square of paper was a tiny black flower, identical in nearly every way to the ones I couldn't help but grow. I unfolded the paper and read it. Written in a neat, precise script were the words

I, too, can make things that do not die.
-A.

Heat instantly flooded my cheeks. I clutched the paper to my chest.

I dressed quickly and hid both the note and the flower under my pillow, where I hoped Mother wouldn't think to look. As I braided my hair, I hurried downstairs just in time to see Mother setting two bowls at the table.

"Kore," she said, voice taut, like saying the very name she gave me was a curse laced with poison. "I have to –"

"May I go to the library today?" I asked before she could finish. The Lavoisin Library was small, no bigger than the schoolhouse and full of outdated books barely worth the read. Most were textbooks or religious scripts, since not many dared part with their romance and horror novels.

Mother stared at me like I'd asked to skin a pig inside our house. "Whatever for?"

"I –" I paused. "I thought of a few recipes earlier and wanted to find a cookbook I could borrow and see if I could try them out. The mint in the garden is looking healthy... I could probably make a soup –"

Mother waved her hand flippantly, dismissing my words. "Fine, then. I will be speaking with the librarian, though, to see what you spent your time doing. If I hear you even looked at the same shelf as a boy, I will have you locked up until spring."

I swallowed hard. If only she knew about my midnight rendezvous with a *Hollow* of all people...

I ate breakfast quickly and cleaned up without having to be asked. Once the dishes were put away, I dried off my hands and hurried out of the house before Mother could change her mind.

It was late fall, and the smell of rain sat heavy in the cold air. The wind pushed through my hair, whipping my braid around my shoulders, and sending a flurry of red and orange leaves dancing across the sky. A pair of young women walked by arms linked, as they followed a small child who eagerly splashed in every puddle. I pulled my skirts to the side to avoid getting hit by the muddy water.

The Lavoisin Library sat by the post office, right on the corner of two streets. The aroma of fresh bread from the nearby bakery mixed with the petrichor emanating from the cobblestone road. Even though I just ate, the smell was almost too tantalizing.

I stepped into the library, greeting the librarian with a small incline of my head. Mother would be talking to them later, so I couldn't ask them for the books I needed.

I had little desire to cook with the mint in the garden. I always hated that plant.

Instead, I needed to figure out Aita's real name.

The things I knew about him were limited: he was a Hollow, he seemed to be a powerful one, he knew quite a bit about magic, and he supposedly couldn't die.

And he wasn't fae, but I was probably the only person who knew that Hollows existed in that grey area between humans and fae.

As I started to browse the shelves, looking for anything that might be interesting, I made sure to grab a few random cookbooks and books on botany, just in case. The books on Hollows, fae, and magic in general were so sparse that I grabbed all of them before finding a secluded spot to read. I set my stack aside and propped one of the books up on my knees, opening the leather cover with a satisfying crack.

"'*The History of the Lavoisin Forest,*'" a voice beside me said. I startled, dropping the book. Sitting across from me was a...boy. Or maybe a girl. Or neither, like the librarian. Their features were slim and delicate, a gentle mix between feminine and masculine. White hair curled over their alabaster forehead, and eyes so bright they looked like gems stared at me from behind thick, snowy lashes.

"Y-yes," I choked, reaching down to pick up the book. I glance around to make sure the librarian wasn't nearby. "S-sorry, who are you? Did you want to read this?"

They shook their head. "No. Just curious. Not many people are eager to learn about the forest, especially since it's so close to Lysaen."

Slowly, I closed the cover of the book. "Do...you know much about the forest?"

"Oh, plenty. Why? What do you want to know?"

I checked again, making sure the librarian wasn't around.

You've practiced magic with Hollows, Kore. You can handle a small conversation with a person who might not even be a boy.

"What about...Hollows...?" I asked slowly, testing the waters. I watched the person closely for any signs of a reaction, but if they were surprised by my words, they didn't show it.

"I know quite a bit," they responded.

"There is a certain Hollow whose...name I wish to learn. The name he gave me was...false." Saying the words out loud made the whole thing seem ludicrous. There was no way this person would even humor me and pretend to believe my words were true.

Instead of laughing in my face, the person reached into their coat pocket and pulled out a small leather book. They flipped through it carefully, as though the pages were made of silk.

"What was the name?" they asked.

I paused. In a voice barely even a whisper, I said, "Aita."

The person didn't look up, but their lips curled up into the smallest of smiles. "Ah. Aita. His true name was a tricky one to get."

When he looked up, there was an excited gleam to his eyes. "His name is Adonis. Adonis Nyx. And he is the king of all Hollows."

CHAPTER SEVENTEEN
CASSIEL

S ure, you are," I laughed. "And I'm the father of Medea's kid. You know, we could be Hollows. You could've just damned yourself for giving out your name."

The girl who claimed to be a princess exchanged a look with the man next to her. He was pretty, in the feminine sense, with a sloped nose and curved jaw and hair that fell in curls placed just right against his bronzed skin.

"You're not a Hollow," the maybe-princess said confidently. "And I can easily prove it. For one, you don't look like a Hollow. None of you do."

"And how do you know what a Hollow looks like?" Ri blurted. "Aren't they supposed to *turn to ash* when they die?" She gave me a pointed look that I couldn't shrug off no matter how hard I tried.

"Supposed to, yes," the pretty boy said. "But not always."

Ri *hmphed* and stuck her tongue out at me in the most *toddler way possible. You hunt Hollows, Cas,* I reminded myself. *Not annoying little thieves.*

It had taken us two days to trek across the desert, and I had spent most of that time silently *willing* Ri to be *silent.*

As if sensing my murderous rages, Dio spoke up, "Ri's right. How *do* you know what Hollows are supposed to look like? Because we could very easily be a group—a gaggle? A murder? –of Hollows, and you just gave us your name, *Shasi Dārayavahush.*"

The maybe-princess didn't even flinch at the words. Instead, her jade gaze shifted to mine. She looked me right in the eye.

A bold move for someone unaware of my sclera lenses.

"You say you're a Hollow hunter, Cas," she spoke slowly, with the grace of a princess. It occurred to me then that the people of Svadaeva did not speak the common Welinese language the rest of us knew. Yet, the maybe-princess spoke it with the accuracy of a native speaker, even though her accent was prominent. "If that's the case, then you must be Cassiel Jäger. I've heard of you. You have the highest kill count of Hollows amongst all the humans."

Well, shit.

She was good.

"Well, if we're giving out full names," came Ri's voice. She'd somehow, silently, managed to convince the pretty boy into giving her his flatbread. She finished it off in two bites before continuing, "Auri Luthien, and I also killed a Hollow, even though nobody believes me."

"You are all dumbasses," Dio muttered under her breath. "Dio Hyoscyamus. That's all you're getting."

"Mirza Issawi," pretty boy said.

"Okay, okay, backtrack," I said, holding my hands up. First Ri—Auri—claimed to have killed a Hollow with nothing more than a flimsy knife and now this most-likely-princess was confident in what dead Hollows looked like?

They looked like *ash.* Like piles of *dust* that blew away in the wind. They were so damn difficult to kill that it took me seventeen years to learn how to properly do it, and even then, I went into fights knowing it was more likely the Hollow would kill me.

So, what the hell did this princess know?

I opened my mouth to speak, but didn't get the chance, as Auri let out an ear-splitting scream. She leapt to her feet, standing on the edge of the fountain like the ground had turned to fire.

"It's that godsdamned blue monster!" she shrieked. Dio spotted it and lifted her feet, too, tucking them nimbly under herself. I reached for one of my knives.

Mirza freed his curved blade and used the end of it to pick the creature up. Then, with surprising gentleness, he tossed it to the side. The little bastard fell on its back but rolled over and scuttled off quickly.

"I assume you don't have scorpions where you're from," he murmured, shoving his sword back into its sheath.

Shasi stood and brushed her skirts off. She adjusted the scarf around her face. "We could sit out here all day but talking will get us nowhere. Come with us to the palace." Even with the lower half of her face hidden, she grinned, her eyes crinkling at the edges. "You will want to see this."

This turned out to be a horse stable, smelling strongly of hay and shit and...rot. I'd slept in plenty of stables before, but there was something especially off-putting about this one. I covered my nose with my hand. Auri, as unbothered as ever, waltzed right in like she owned the place. With the number of stolen coins in her pockets, she probably could steal the entire stable and get away with it.

Then, promptly, she screamed. Again

Dio and I raced inside, Mirza and Shasi following hot on our heels. Auri stood trembling with her back pressed against the wall and her hands clasped over her mouth.

There, strewn out on a pile of hay, partially covered by a canvas cloth, was a dead body. Its skin was ashen and grey, stretched tight over jutting bones. A massive wound split its skull open, the blood long dried.

That was where the smell had been coming from.

I gagged, swallowing back bile that rose in my gullet. I'd seen dead bodies before. But there was *something* about this one that was so much worse than ever before.

Seventeen years ago, the streets of Wallaekva had this smell. The smell of rotten flesh and iron and viscera. Each small piece of hay bleached white by the sun writhed in my mind, morphing into wriggling maggots fat from eating the corpse. Rigor mortis had set in and faded, leaving purplish blots on the underside of the body, where all the fluids had settled. Bloat had kicked in; if anyone tried to move the body, its back would tear at the seams and all the innards and gasses, and humors would spill out.

I did not want to stick around to smell *that*.

"Cassiel," the most-definite-princess said from beside me. I shot her a glance, but morbid curiosity pulled my gaze back to the body. Shasi continued smoothly, "How do you kill a Hollow?"

My response was automatic, robotic, rehearsed. "Hollows are nearly impossible to kill because you can't get too close, and their bodies are not human nor corporeal. The best way to do it is to behead them, if you're lucky enough to get a clean slice—"

Shasi held up a hand. "I asked how do *you* kill a Hollow?"

This is how you kill a Hollow, Jäger. Memorize these details because if you can't answer them correctly, it'll be your head on a pike.

I opened my mouth. Closed it. Opened it again, gaping like a damn fish. All eyes had turned to me, including the eyes of the horses and those strange lanky creatures with the lumps on their backs. I swore even the eyes of the dead *thing* were watching me carefully, waiting for me to make a mistake.

I spoke slowly. "My preferred weapon was a whip with barbs on the end. I say *was* because it was destroyed recently. It was effective for long-distance fighting. I would strike so the whip would wrap around their neck and the barbs would slice their head off. I've used swords, but they break easily. I think there's a corrosive in their blood that eats away at the metal. Knives can incapacitate them, but not kill them." I shot Auri a look; she flinched and turned her gaze back to the body. "If you could drag a Hollow to the guillotine, it would probably be the best way to kill them. But they aren't *corporeal,* and you can't just *stab one and watch it die* and when they do die, they *fade to ash.*" Each word caused Auri to sink deeper and deeper into herself until I couldn't tell where she ended, and her shadow began.

"So, the head seems to be the weak spot," Shasi said. Dio had inched closer to the body, crouching down to examine it.

"Isn't Hyoscyamus a poison?" "It's my preferred method of killing."

The grace and precision with which Dio Hyoscyamus examined the corpse wasn't that of a physician or doctor or surgeon or even a butcher. It was the grace and precision of a hitwoman who knew more about dead bodies than Heela, the goddess of death herself.

"What do you mean?" asked Auri, who still skulked in the shadows, her hood drawn tightly over her cloud of hair. "I don't care what you say, I know what I saw. I killed a Hollow with a knife, and it didn't turn to ash."

"I believe you," said Shasi. "Because Mirza and I watched someone kill a Hollow with a strange weapon we call the iron flower."

Shasi paused, then grinned a smile that screamed *eureka!*

"The iron flower is a strange explosive, almost like a cannon," she said. "It creates a massive hole for a wound. And that, my strange new friends, is the very-much corporeal body of a three-day-dead Hollow."

CHAPTER EIGHTEEN

DIORA

The Hollow had pointed ears and sharp teeth, though the body had begun to rot, leaving its mouth gummy and meaty, wet with blood and decay. *All* its teeth were sharp, I noted. Only my canines were sharp. I ran my tongue over my teeth. Hollows weren't fae.

But they definitely weren't human, either.

My hands itched to open a portal right then and there to flee back to Lysaen. To tell Tristan what I'd discovered. Hollows couldn't be human. They had to be something else. But *what?* My stomach cramped as I thought about Tristan. He probably thought I was dead in an alley somewhere after a job gone wrong.

Hang in there, little brother, I silently said. *I'll be home soon.*

I fixed my hood, suddenly worried about my ears. Cas had dragged my ass here to use me as a bargaining chip, but seeing the dead Hollow... How would Shasi react to me being fae? Would *I* be the rotting corpse in the palace stables, dead from some...some iron flower, or whatever they called the murder weapon?

I'd seen plenty of dead bodies in my life, starting with the corpses of my parents when I was little more than a child. Death scared me at first, and reasonably so. I couldn't sleep for weeks after seeing my parents' bodies, their wounds still gummy and festering. When I did sleep, I'd wake up screaming, drenched in sweat and urine and rattled with a bone-deep fear that simply wouldn't go away. Then, I began to kill. With each body that dropped, each coin in my purse, I became jaded. The death rattle that shook through every living being before they succumbed to their mortality no longer bothered me. The sticky stench of iron-thick blood as they coughed up their lungs and drowned on their own viscera didn't faze me. I opted for poison because of how clean it was, and how little death clung to my clothes after.

There was, though, something terribly wrong with this body.

"Cas," I said, speaking slowly so no one would see the tips of my canines. "I don't think Ri was lying about killing a Hollow with a knife."

"Oh, Medea's fucking *tits,* not this again!" Cas exclaimed. From her shadows, Auri grinned. Mirza and Shasi exchanged a look, and for a second, I envied them, for they hadn't spent two days trekking across the desert listening to Cas and Auri bitch about whether she killed a Hollow or not.

"Shut up, man baby," I snapped. "Look, what if she is right and she did kill one? I don't think Hollows are fae *or* human. What if they're evolving or something and can now be killed by stolen knives?"

"How *did* you kill a Hollow so easily?" Mirza asked, ignoring Cas and my groans. We'd spent two days stuck under the sweltering sun with no food and no water and no trust between us. Two days of listening to Auri tell Cas how she'd killed a Hollow and Cas telling her it was impossible. If I had to listen to the story one more time—

Auri peeled herself away from the shadows, skirting around the Hollow as she went to the stable door to stick her head out and breathe in a gulp of fresh air. "It bumped into me. Thought it was a thief or something. I meant to slash its side, but somehow misjudged my own strength and cut way too deep and then it was dead. There was blood everywhere and I ran." She lifted her slim shoulders in a weightless shrug. "Look, call me a liar all you want, but I *know* what I saw. That blood was black. The exact same color as the blood on that rancid corpse. It kept its form after it died, but I didn't touch it to see what it looked like."

She took a deep breath, steeling herself, before she turned around with a grin that didn't reach her eyes. I wanted to reach out and tell her that killing got easier, that you grew numb after a while, but her bright eyes turned glassy, and I couldn't bring myself to condone murder.

I'd cried after my first kill, too. And I was willing to bet that Cas had as well.

Shasi clapped her hands together suddenly, startling all of us. "How about we resume this conversation inside? I'll send for refreshments. The three of you look like you could use a bath." Beside her, Mirza straightened, going into guard mode. Desperate to get away from the stink of rot and death and decay, I followed the princess, heading straight for the gilded palace I'd only ever visited in my nightmares.

The inside of the palace left me speechless. Next to me, Auri's mouth was all but salivating at the sight of all the gold. Gilded marble floors gave way to gilded walls, melting into domed gold ceilings with heavy chandeliers hanging low. Massive windows painted intricately with bright colors to catch the sun swathed the corridors in a sea of rainbow. Mosaics made of precious gems lined the floors and walls where gold wasn't present. Auri shoved her hands deep into her pockets to keep from taking anything.

I *almost* reached out to grab a loose emerald off a wall mosaic.

Mirza broke off with Cas, leading him to a different part of the palace. Shasi brought Auri and me to a hallway with several arched doors. She stopped in front of one and opened it with a key she'd fished out of her pocket.

"These are our guest rooms," she explained, pushing open the door to reveal a room covered in extravagantly embroidered rugs. A four-poster canopied bed seemed to be the only thing *not* covered in rugs. "There's a bathroom through that door there. I'll send someone to get you when you're done freshening up so we can finish our discussion." Shasi gave a smile that made my stomach flop before sauntering off.

Auri slipped into the room, silent as a wraith. "Crowns or castles?" she asked, perching on the edge of the bed. The mattress was so huge it dwarfed her.

"What?" I asked, finally entering the room. I closed the door behind me.

"Crowns or castles." She pulled a coin out of seemingly nowhere. A Welinas shilling.

"Crowns," I said, thinking of the card game I had yet to play with Cas.

Auri flipped the coin in the air, catching it with one hand and slapping it down onto the back of her other. She pulled her hand away. "Crowns! You get first bath, then. Don't use all the hot water."

With that, she flopped onto her back and sprawled out like a star, taking up as much space as her small frame would allow.

Wordlessly, I hurried into the bathroom, closing the door, and locking it. There was a massive window overlooking a courtyard, but it had a heavy curtain, which I promptly pulled down.

Then, eagerly, I shucked off my dress and ripped off my corset, unfurling my wings with a shuddering sigh of relief. It had been days since I'd last freed them. They ached as much as my ribs did, sore and tender to the touch. I flexed them a few times to loosen my back muscles up before assessing the layout of the bathroom.

There was a claw foot tub, a rack of soaps, and a shower. As much as I wanted to sink into a scalding hot bath until my skin pruned up, the longer I stayed in here, wings and ears and fae heritage on display, the more at risk I was. So, I turned on the shower and stepped in, careful not to get my hair wet.

Using soaps that smelled of jasmine and plum and pomegranate, I scrubbed myself until my skin felt raw, and I couldn't find a single grain of sand nestled anywhere. The hot water soothed the pain in my back, even if just a bit.

I stepped out and dried off with a fluffy towel hand-embroidered with tiny lotus flowers, then begrudgingly put my clothes back on, making sure the special corset I wore concealed my wings. I pulled my hood on, despite the heat, and stepped out of the steamy bathroom.

"Your turn," I said to Auri. She groaned and sat up, her pale hair sticking up in every direction in a way that reminded me of my brother. She didn't even attempt to smooth it down, instead sliding off the bed and shuffling to the bathroom.

Tristan was the spy. He was the one trained in collecting intel, in blending in and not raising suspicions. My job was simply to kill the targets I'd been given. Here, I didn't have my pouch of poisons. I didn't have anything to defend myself with, to kill with. Unease twisted in my belly. I was a fae in a human kingdom. What would Tristan do? How would he avoid getting caught?

I paced the perimeter of the room, running my fingers over the woven rugs on the walls. Tristan probably knew what the symbology within the woven threads meant. He could point to the three squiggly golden triangles joined together by a red string my fingers rested on and tell me exactly what they were. Shasi and Mirza understood the common tongue well enough, but Tristan would probably be able to speak to them in their native Svadaevan language.

Tristan could probably do a lot of this better than I could.

I stopped before a tapestry depicting Medea in all her glory, palms facing the sky with rivulets of blood and gold spilling from either one. As usual, she wore only a skirt, revealing her full breasts and heavily swollen pregnant belly. Sheathed at her hip was a sword since she couldn't be the goddess of fertility without being the goddess of war. Creation and destruction; birth and death. The two went hand in hand, making her both the Mother and the Executioner.

The fae depictions of Medea gave her elongated ears and a set of leathery wings, but this one made her look human, with darker skin and a mane of wild curls, like Shasi had.

I brushed my fingers over the hand spilling blood. Nobody knew why she had blood and ichor spilling from her hands. Some stories claimed it was because she had slaughtered the gods of Old before birthing the new race of deities. Some said it was because she had killed the monsters that once raged the world and saved humanity. Some said it was simply because, as Mother and Executioner, she had more blood than anyone else had on her hands.

I wondered, not for the first time, if Hollows worshipped Medea, too.

My fingers moved down to the curve of her belly. Dark ink tattooed an intricate branching pattern just above her womb, stretched taut with pregnancy.

When we first met, Tristan had been alone, far too young to truly remember who his parents were. He'd cried about it most nights. All the orphans cried about missing their parents—some had been killed in accidents, some on purpose, some simply gave their children up or abandoned them. But Tristan cried the hardest. One night, I'd stolen a book from the small library within the orphanage and read to Tristan the story of Medea. When I finished the book and showed him the drawing of Medea, with her pregnant belly on full display, I told him she was his mother, and she'd given him to the fae because she was too busy being a goddess to care for him properly.

"Will she ever come back for me?" Tristan had sniffled, his chubby cheeks red and puffy from crying so hard.

I'd been nothing more than a child myself, ignorant to everything in the world. *"Yes,"* I'd told him because I'd already made things complicated by lying.

"I stole a painting of Medea once," Auri's sudden voice came from behind me, nearly scaring me out of my skin. I spun around to face her, my heart hammering against my ribs with adrenaline.

"Don't fucking do that!" I snapped, clasping my hand over my chest.

"What? Steal paintings of our Almighty Mother?" Auri shrugged, tossing her damp hair over her shoulder. Her shirt was wet from where her hair had rested against it, leaving it translucent. I looked away.

"That, and don't scare me. You're more silent than a mouse."

"Thank you!" she beamed. "Come on. Let's go see what the Svadaevan royals feed their guests. I want to dine like a queen while everyone proves I was right, and Cas was wrong."

The Svadaevan royals fed their guests a lot of meat, it turned out. The five of us—Mirza and Shasi included—sat at a low table in a room flooded with golden sunlight with a feast spread out before us. Some sort of meat marinated in spices that made my nose twitch, roasted vegetables in a whole rainbow of colors, oranges cut into tiny little slices, dates, nuts, a savory soup made of lentils with thick flatbread for dipping, and sweet wine that I was all too eager to taste.

"What's...in this?" I asked, pointing a silver spoon at the pot of soup on the table. Shasi looked up over the rim of her chalice.

"Lentils, potatoes, parsley, tomato, carrots, onion..." she trailed off. "Do you have dietary restrictions?" Shasi lowered her chalice, an emotion I couldn't read flickering across her features.

"I can't eat meat," I said. I knew I was only in Svadaeva because my fae heritage was supposed to be Cas's bargaining chip, but I still couldn't bring myself to admit to it.

Shasi's eyebrows shot up. "Oh! Goddess, you should've told me before. The soup is all vegetables. You can have that. As well as the bread and wine and fruits, of course. I can have someone make something—"

"It's fine," I said, and ladled a bowlful of soup for myself. I stirred it around with my spoon before scooping up a bite. Spices I'd never even imagined exploded on my tongue, a mix of sweet and savory and spicy. Eagerly, I ate another bite, and another. I almost wanted to ask for the recipe, since Tristan would love something like this.

We ate in silence. Cas and Auri wolfed down their food just as I did, the three of us still starving from our surprise trek across the desert. By the time we finished, and servants had taken everything but our decanter of wine, I was nearly too tired to talk about Hollows.

I eyed Cas nervously, waiting for him to share my secret. He didn't seem to notice, busying himself with gathering his damp hair into a knot at the nape of his neck. My gaze slid past him to Auri. She was grinning, her eyes wrinkling at the corners. I opened my mouth to ask Cas to switch spots with me so I could sit by her, but he spoke first.

"Do any of you know how to play Crimson Crowns?"

Oh, *Goddess*, not this.

Shasi tilted her head to the side. "The card game?" she asked. "Doesn't everyone?"

"We need coins," I blurted, my mind off Auri and onto the idea of cards. "I told Cas I'd teach him how to play with bets. That's how we do it in...my hometown."

Mirza grinned and pulled a pouch from his pocket, dropping it on the table. He spilled the copper coins out and began counting them into even piles. The pennies weren't worth much, just spare pocket change good for making wishes in fountains or giving to street kids. Or for placing cheap bets in a card game I was *definitely* going to cheat in.

Mirza pushed a stack of coins towards the each of us while Cas took the deck of cards he'd taken from the library in Welinas. He shuffled them smoothly, the cards flying between his hands. He dealt them out, giving each of us nine and putting the rest in the middle.

"The rules are the same," I said, picking up six of my cards, leaving the other three face down on the table. "Everyone starts with nine cards. The goal is to get as many crowns as possible. You can only switch out the six cards you have, leaving the other three face down until the very end. Pairs that aren't crowns get tossed into the middle. For every card you get rid of via pairs you have to draw a new one. We start off by giving a card to the person on our left. If you have no pairs, you have to take one from someone else at the table. You place bets based off your confidence that you'll win. If you lose, you give up all your coins. If you win, you get whatever's in the pot. We can start by putting one coin in the pot and raise the stakes each round. Make sense?"

Everyone nodded. I slid a single coin to the center before turning my attention to my cards. Three swords, a chalice, a wing, and a single crown. The swords were the least valuable and the ones I wanted to get rid of, but I had three so I couldn't pair them off. Instead, I plucked one and slid it towards Mirza, who sat on my left. Cas handed me his reject card, another wing. Grinning, I paired my swords and wings and threw them down, drawing two new cards to balance things off. A chalice and a crown. I paired my chalices, drew a new card, and slid another coin into the pot. I had at least two crowns now; eight were still unaccounted for.

Cas tossed in a pair of wings. "What did Ri's supposed murder and the iron flower have in common?"

"It wasn't supposed, dumbass. Give me that." Auri snatched up a card from Cas's hand, instantly scowling at what she got. Her turn was up, and she didn't have any pairs. Shasi calmly placed a set of polished swords into the pile, along with three coins. *Shit.* I looked at my cards again. Mirza took a card from Auri, whose scowl promptly turned smug. Still, he paired off his new card and tossed it in the pile.

"Nobody saw it," Cas argued. "What, you expect us to just traipse on back to Welinas to see this *supposed* Hollow corpse? Even if you are telling the truth, scavengers would've picked the body clean by now."

I snatched up a card from Cas, who protested incoherently. A crown. *Jackpot.* I pushed a few more coins into the pot.

"We're having someone look into the composition of the iron flower," Shasi said. She shuffled her cards around in her hand, her face so devoid of emotion that I couldn't even begin to imagine what she had. "I don't suppose you kept the knife, Auri?"

"Medea, no. I left it in the body and ran. Dio, give me the third card on your left – yes, that one." I handed Auri the card – a wing – and looked down at my hand.

What *did* the weapons have in common? Dread pooled in my belly. Iron was the only metal harmful to fae. What if it was *also* harmful to Hollows? The tapered ears and elongated teeth had made me uneasy, but now this?

No. It was impossible! Hollows killed fae. They sucked out our souls and claimed our names the same way they killed humans.

"There's no more cards," Shasi announced, drawing my attention back to the game. Silently, each of us drew up our concealed cards and looked them over. I had four crowns in my hand. Unless someone had five—or even the remaining six – I was as good as the winner. I didn't even *have* to cheat.

I threw my crowns down. One by one, everyone else did. Mirza had one. Shasi and Cas had none.

"Aha!" Auri exclaimed, tossing all five of her crowns on the table. "I win!" She scooped up all the coins from the pot, grinning wickedly the whole time. "Since I win, you have to pretend for the rest of the evening that I am telling the truth and that I did kill a Hollow. And the *strangest* thing happened after."

Auri folded her hands on her lap. She was hiding something. I needed to know what.

"I swear, after running away from the scene," she continued. "I heard this *song.*"

CHAPTER NINETEEN

KORE

Adonis Nyx. I snorted, trying desperately to hold back laughter. The King of Hollows? Taking an interest in *me?* I'd much sooner believe it if Medea descended from the heavens to kiss me on the mouth.

The pale haired stranger cocked their head to the side like a confused puppy. "I'm not joking," they said. "It took me quite a bit of time to get this name. Hollows are just as secretive with their names as we are. Why do you think they prey on our—"

The stranger stopped speaking abruptly. The soft clack of heels against wood approached as the librarian began making their way through the shelves. I turned towards the sound, and when I looked back a split second later, the stranger was gone.

"Miss Kore," the librarian said, startling me enough I nearly leapt out of my skin. I clutched my chest, trying to quell my hummingbird heart. The librarian eyed the stack of books. Thank the *gods* I had put some cookbook on the top. "Your mother is outside. She is requesting you join her."

I stood quickly, brushing the wrinkles from my skirts. For good measure, I grabbed the cookbook and clutched it to my chest, hurrying past the librarian before they could question me on the rest of my selections.

As promised, Mother was outside, her arms crossed and her frown so deep her wrinkles mimicked canyons. My own jaw ached at the sight. I hugged my cookbook tighter, as though it was a shield. Mother eyed the cover, one russet brow raised, then gave a shake of her head.

"Come along," she instructed. "I have a few errands to run and would like your company. I don't want you spending too much time around that librarian, as nice as they are. Their spouse was killed by a fae not too long ago."

That was code, I thought as I followed her, for *I don't trust you alone right now so I will be babysitting you even though you are a twenty-two-year-old adult.*

I bit my tongue to silence the quip aching to be said; *at twenty-two, Mother, you were knocked up by some anonymous fae man.*

I stepped over a puddle in the cracked cobblestone road. We passed the bakery, my stomach grumbling as I inhaled the sweet aroma of fresh bread once more. Ignoring me, Mother went into the post office.

I had never been inside the post office. Mother let me go to the library and the market on occasion, but never the post office. All our mail was delivered straight to our doorstep, usually nothing more than a few bills and the newspaper. A small bell above the door jingled as we stepped inside.

The post office was a small building with a counter and a wall of tiny mailboxes. Mother went straight to the counter, fishing a few envelopes from her basket.

"Ah, Miss Astra," the stocky old man behind the counter said. He had a round belly that jiggled as he laughed and penny-sized glasses atop a crooked nose. He emanated warmth. I wanted to soak it all up.

"I need these to be mailed today," Mother said sharply, her presence ice compared to the man's sun. He chuckled and took the letters, scanning over the addresses and making sure they were stamped. He put them in a crate.

"Anything else I can do for you today, Miss Astra?" the man asked.

I shifted away from the wall of tiny mailboxes and went to inspect a rack full of envelopes and postcards and little books of stamps so much prettier than the ones Mother used. Hers were the ugly brown of a coffee stain. These had paintings of miniscule flowers.

I thought of the flower under my pillow and my cheeks heated up.

"Come along, Kore," Mother said. If she'd answered the jovial man, I didn't hear. She grabbed my wrist harshly and dragged me out of the post office.

"Who were those letters for?" I wanted desperately to break the choking silence between us. The tension was thicker than the fog rolling in, leaving a sour taste in the back of my throat.

A pair of kids ran between us, splashing in a puddle that sent muddy water onto both my skirts and Mother's.

Great. I'd be washing those by hand later.

"No one of importance," she said coolly. I clenched my jaw tight. Well, that was that. Instead of stewing in the uncomfortable tension between us, my thoughts wandered to Aita. To Adonis Nyx, the shadowy Hollow who ate a pomegranate with me and made me a flower like the ones I'd made for him. Adonis Nyx, the king of all the Hollows, the man who helped me focus my magic because maybe he saw a spark of potential in me.

Nobody else saw that spark.

Mother was the only person who knew of my abilities, and she refused to let me use them. I supposed my father, wherever he was, would know I had them, since he was the one to give them to me. But Mother never spoke of him and as far as I knew, he'd vanished twenty-two years ago. When I was younger, I used to pretend he was off fighting some battle and he'd return to us one day. I used to imagine him coming home and melting away Mother's harsh exterior. He'd make her into a gentle, loving mother.

But that never happened, and I was starting to wonder if Mother somehow conceived me without outside help, as impossible as it was.

We made our way into the market. A girl, maybe five, had set up a makeshift table with carefully cut flowers strewn about it. Petals and stems clung to her messy ginger braids.

"Care for a flower, ma'am?" she gave me a gap-toothed grin. I glanced at Mother for permission, but she wasn't paying any attention.

"I haven't any money," I admitted. The girl's grin just grew wider. She plucked a red rose from the pile and held it out. The thorns had been peeled off, and judging by the bandages wrapped around her fingers, she was behind it.

"It matches your hair. Take it!" I glanced at Mother again, and when she didn't turn to face me, I took the flower and thanked the young girl.

I, too, can make things that do not die.

My cheeks flushed as red as the rose. I tucked it into my pocket and hurried to catch up with Mother.

Mother went from stall to stall, picking out a few things from some and arguing over prices at others. As we stopped at a stall selling hardware supplies, I realized Mother's basket wasn't full of fruits and meats like it usually was.

It was full of rope and bits of chain and hammers and nails.

Mother handed over a few crisp bills in exchange for a sack full of long screws.

"Mother...?" I asked. Dread, hot and burning, churned in my belly, turning to nausea that rose my gullet. My legs had turned into lead beams. My lungs filled with sand and my throat stuffed with cotton. I couldn't breathe. Oh, gods, I couldn't breathe. I wanted desperately to rip my dress off and peel my corset away from my skin just to get a damn *breath* in, because the realization of what Mother was doing was killing me by asphyxiation.

She didn't notice. Of course, she didn't notice because she never noticed any-thing important. When I didn't move because roots had quite literally sprouted from the ground and wrapped around my boots, keeping me in place, Mother grabbed my wrist and forcefully yanked me along with her. The roots dug into my legs, deep enough to bruise before they finally snapped.

"Don't play coy, Kore," she snapped, her words like knives burying one after the other deep in my heart. I stumbled as another thick root sprouted from the ground and wrapped around my ankle. "I know you've been sneaking out at night."

Everything I ever knew – everything I ever felt – condensed into a tiny glass ball that fell onto the ground and *shattered*.

Iknowyou'vebeensneakingoutatnightIknowyou'vebeensneakingoutatnightIknowyou'vebeensneakingoutatnight –

The world tilted and I tilted with it, stumbling over my feet – or maybe over the thorned roots that sprouted from the ground. What little control I had over my magic *snapped*. Thorny vines erupted from the ground, creating a cage around me. *Protecting me* from my own mother, who held with her the tools needed to make me a prisoner.

"Kore," Mother said, struggling to keep her voice even. It warbled ever so slightly as my name faded into the air. The town had gone silent – *too* silent. Dozens and dozens and dozens of eyes focused on me. On the magic gushing from every single one of my pores. The gap-toothed girl who'd given me the rose stared in abject horror.

"Kore!" Mother shouted. Cobblestone crackled, sending rocks spilling in a haphazard slide. Tiny white flowers grew around my feet, useless in their attempt to protect me. The ground rumbled. Mother shouted over it. "This is exactly why I have to do this! You have no control over yourself!"

"You don't get to control me, Mother!" I said. No, I yelled. My throat burned like I'd screamed the words over the tempests caused by the uncontrolled magic. The ground groaned, tremors splitting through it as a tree covered in thorns sprouted, larger than anything I'd ever created before. It oozed sap that wasn't sap at all, but hot blood that splattered against the pavement and onto the faces of the bystanders.

"Kore Astra, listen to your mother if you know what's good for you!" Mother screamed.

My limbs had become a separate entity. I had no control over my body, over the magic spewing out of it, turning the sleepy town of Lavoisin into a living, monstrous forest. A thorny vine whipped out, slashing Mother across the face and drawing welts of crimson blood. She didn't even *flinch,* but her gaze was filled to the brim with horror, raw and undiluted.

I had spent twenty-two years trapped inside my room all because of a mistake Mother made. She'd taken her own adultery out on me, punishing me because *she'd* slept with a fae and got knocked up because of it. I had no control over my magic because it took *twenty-two years* to get around to practicing it, and I only began practicing it when I had the help of—

Aita.

Through the torrents of malignant magic in a voice I couldn't even discern, I screamed, *"KING ADONIS NYX, I CALL TO YOU! HELP ME!"*

Time slowed, and with it the world, everything moving as though it had been stuffed into a brick of frozen jelly. Tiny drops of blood fell from the tree and from the bystanders slower than a snail. Then, shadows seeped up from the earth and cocooned my thorny cage.

Ahh, so you learned my name, Little Star. How clever of you.

And then, before Adonis Nyx's words could settle, the shadows enveloped me wholly and the entire world went black.

CHAPTER TWENTY

AURI

I'd cheated at Crimson Crowns. I always did. If Cas and Dio weren't going to believe me when I told them how I'd killed a Hollow, I would make them believe me by cheating at cards to get a sliver of leverage over them.

Mirza and Shasi exchanged a look. I'd never been friends with anyone longer than a handful of days, and even then, it had been friendships born out of convenience that benefitted me and me alone. I'd never known anyone intimately enough to have a silent conversation with them the way Shasi and Mirza spoke with just their eyes.

I reached for my goblet and brought it to my lips, only to find that it was empty. I frowned and set it down. Good wine was nearly impossible to steal, and I could steal anything. This wine was better than good. It was sweet and hot where it settled in my belly, leaving me lighter than normal. I bunched the fabric of my skirts in my stained hand. Shasi grabbed the ewer and refiled my goblet without a word.

"It seems like we all have information on Hollows," the princess said. She shifted, her bicep squishing against her bosom for a second that felt like an eternity. I couldn't pry my eyes away if I tried. "Except for you, Dio. What do you know about Hollows?"

Dio froze, her golden eyes flashing. They reminded me of polished coins reflecting gilded sunlight. Pretty. Expensive. Tantalizing. Very much not human.

When she spoke, her words were slow, like she had to translate them from her native tongue to the common tongue several times just to figure out what to say. "I know for a fact – one I am willing to stake my life and the life of my brother on—that Hollows aren't human, nor are they fae."

A muscle in Cas's cheek feathered.

"What do you mean?" Mirza butted in. I picked up my goblet and drank deeply, relishing in the sweet burn that slid down my throat. Oh, this was going to be interesting. Mirza and Shasi were oblivious to the fact that Dio was fae. I couldn't bite back the grin that tugged on my lips. If there was one thing I loved more than thievery and shiny things, it was spectacle, and the show brewing was going to be *delicious.*

"The teeth," Dio said with a nonchalant shrug. "Too many of them were sharp. Fae only have elongated canines. And the ears. Pointed, but not pointed the right way. And the eyes. And the lack of wings, obviously. All fae have wings. If they were cut off, there would be a disgusting scar on the back." She held up her fingers in a V shape, mimicking the shape the scar would be in.

"You know quite a bit about our fae neighbors," Shasi said. She said the word like it tasted rancid.

I knew for a fact that Hollows weren't fae. The fae had done nothing to make me dislike them. It wasn't their fault I was abandoned. It wasn't their fault the kingdom of Welinas was too dirt poor to offer me food or housing. It wasn't their fault I ran from the only home I'd ever known. It wasn't their fault I felt a thrill whenever I relieved someone's pockets of their belongings.

If anything, I hated the humans for the way they had chewed me up and spat me out, throwing me into an alley and pretending I didn't exist. For the scars on my back given to me by them.

I chugged the rest of my wine and grabbed the decanter without permission, refilling my goblet to the brim.

Cas and Dio glanced at each other. I finished my wine in just a few gulps, savoring the buzz that filled my head and made my body warm and numb.

"I came here to ask you for your help, Princess Shasi," said Cas. He scooped up all the cards and lazily shuffled them before stuffing the deck in his pocket. "Svadaeva is the leading kingdom in anti-Hollow advancements. I want weapons and strength—and support—to fight the Hollows. I brought with me my knowledge and abilities. This...thief who claims to have killed a Hollow. And I brought with me a fae."

Dio reached up and tugged down her hood, her dark braids spilling free. Tapered ears poked through her hair, adorning jewels and silver cuffs I longed to snag. Her golden eyes shone brighter without the shadow her hood cast over them, and when she parted her full lips, her teeth were sharpened.

Before I could even *blink,* Mirza had his curved sword drawn and pointed right at Dio's slender throat.

Dio didn't even flinch.

Maybe I'd had too much wine.

Nobody moved for what felt like an eternity. Dio stared down the blade of the sword. Cas reached for a knife at his belt, but one glare from Shasi caused him to drop his hands.

"How are we supposed to trust the word of a *fae?*" Mirza hissed, shattering the thick silence that blanketed the room.

"Mir, put the sword down," Shasi instructed. Her guard opened his mouth to protest, but slowly sheathed his sword, looking defeated.

"It has been seventeen years since the mass outbreak of Hollows," the princess said once no weapons were drawn. "For seventeen years, we believed the fae were the cause of them. Do you know how close the Svadaevan militia was to invading Lysaen to slaughter the fae we thought responsible for the fear that plagued our kingdom and the deaths we couldn't stop? You brought me a fae. I invited her to my home and hearth, and I dined with her. But she's *fae.* How are we supposed to know the Hollows aren't just some experiments they created to destroy our four kingdoms?"

Dio reached across the table to grab the decanter of wine. She gulped it down greedily, red rivulets falling onto her wool blouse.

"How in the hells am I supposed to trust that you humans didn't create the Hollows to destroy Lysaen, huh?" she snapped. "You did just admit to wanting to invade our kingdoms and kill us or whatever. You think the queens would be happy about that? I. Told. You. The Hollows aren't fae. If they were fae, how come *we* fear them just as much as you? They kill us too, you know. They steal our names and our souls too. So don't come to me with this bullshit. I came here to *help.*"

Dio stood, slamming her palms against the table with enough force to knock the decanter over, spilling wine all over the precious rug below. Fury blazed in her eyes, raw and unyielding. When she snarled, her fangs flashed in the warm light.

Cas reached out to touch her arm. She shot him a look that would've killed had he not been trained to survive. Then, she huffed and plopped herself right back into her seat, arms crossed over her chest.

"Dio is invaluable," Cas said. "I think we can all come to an agreement and work together. We all have a common goal after all. We need to figure out what these Hollows are and where they come from, so we can stop them from killing us all."

Dinner had been a disaster, and that was putting it nicely, but at least Shasi agreed to let us stay the night in the palace. My heart skipped a beat when Dio and I were led back to the same room we'd bathed in earlier instead of being dragged to the dungeons.

I'd spent a few nights in a jail cell, but never one in a guest suite at a royal palace.

There was one bed, but it was big enough for at least three people. If Dio was going to argue about who got to sleep in it...

Exhausted as I was, I was more interested in exploring the room. The tapestries on the walls were too big to steal, as valuable as they looked, but there had to be something else I could grab.

I found myself in front of the tapestry depicting Medea.

"You think Medea would know how to kill the Hollows?" I asked, staring at her woven eyes. Even made up of thread, she had an iron gaze that raised the hair on the back of my neck.

"The goddess?" Dio asked. I glanced over, watching as she tossed her cloak on the ground and kicked off her boots. She reached for the buttons on her blouse but stopped. Her brow furrowed.

"What other Medea do you know?" I turned fully and crossed my arms over my chest, leaning back until my shoulders hit the wall. "You can take your shirt off. Free your wings, or whatever. You *do* have wings, don't you?"

"Of course I have wings, thief," she snapped. With an angry huff, Dio worked on the buttons of her blouse, popping one tiny pearl bead after the other until she shrugged the shirt off. Her chemise and corset, both pale in color, stood out against her dark skin in a way that made me stare. I'd been leeched of color when I was born, leaving me with skin and hair so pale it was white and eyes like ice; a white chemise and corset would blend in with my features and make me look nude. Still, they tended to be the cheapest options, so I always wore them—at least, when I couldn't steal something nicer.

Dio popped the clasps of her corset and shrugged out of it, her chemise instantly taking away her shape. As the corset fell to the ground, Dio unfurled her wings.

They were so thin I worried they'd rip when she beat them twice to stretch them out, like a newborn butterfly would. Pale in color, the warm light from the sconces gave them an ephemeral glow, gold veining through the soft xanthous yellow of her butterfly-like wings. She folded them against her back, relief washing over her features.

"You're staring," she said.

"You're beautiful," I replied.

Her cheeks flooded with red. The tough, fearless Dio Hyoscyamus turned away, hiding her flushed face.

My words settled and I realized what I'd said. My face flushed even redder than Dio's. I looked away, trying to hide the embarrassment that surged through my body. I had not meant to say that out loud.

"I want the side of the bed furthest from the window," Dio said, her normally steady voice warbling. She stepped over her pile of discarded clothes and marched over to the bed, throwing herself down atop the plush mattress, her wings splayed out.

I quickly unbuttoned my blouse and peeled off my trousers, stepping out of the heavy fabrics until I wore just my chemise and socks. I felt oddly...naked. Usually, I wore all my clothes to sleep, in case I needed to make a quick escape. There was no reason for me to need to escape here.

Right?

I flipped off the lights and tip-toed over to the bed, slipping under the blankets on the side furthest from Dio. The warmth and weight of the duvet was foreign, almost uncomfortable; I squirmed a bit, trying to get comfortable.

"By the gods," Dio grumbled. "You're worse than my brother and he can't stay still even if it killed him."

I pushed back all but the thinnest of the blankets, though even that felt like I was being strangled.

"I'm not used to sleeping in a bed," I muttered, eventually yanking that blanket off, too. I curled in on myself, taking up as little space as possible.

"Where do you sleep, then?" the bed shifted, and even with my back to her, I could feel Dio's gaze on me.

"It depends," I said. "Sometimes on a pile of old newspapers. Sometimes under a bridge. Sometimes in the attic above the theatre. That's my favorite, even though it *reeks* of mothballs. The old costumes are comfy to sleep on, though."

Dio was silent.

I glanced over my shoulder, worried she somehow fell asleep, but her gilded gaze met mine, unwavering. Her dark brows pinched together.

"You really don't have a home?" she asked.

I turned back around, unable to face her.

"Yeah," I whispered. "Well, I did for a little bit. Though I wouldn't really call the temple a home. It was just a place to sleep at night. I ran – I *left* – a year ago.

"Why?" Dio's asked.

I swallowed the knot in my throat. I'd never talked about my eighteen years at the temple with anyone. The day I'd slipped from the window and onto the streets, never to look back, was the day I'd buried my past.

So, why was I talking about it now?

"It was a temple devoted to Medea," I whispered. "But the nuns and priestesses and all the holy Brothers and Sisters were sacrilegious. I *know* Medea did exist at one point, but after *eighteen years* of abuse in her name, it'd hard to see her as the hero." I laughed weakly; the sound forced.

"I was orphaned, too," Dio said after a pause. "Me and my brother. I took him in and kept him safe. Did your parents die, too?"

"No."

They'd left me in a box on the doorstep of the church with only a blanket and a letter I'd never read. The Sister who took me inside told me that I'd been cleaned of blood and fed only hours before.

When I was younger, I'd pretended my mother was a queen who would fetch me when I was old enough and full of knowledge on the common world. But as I grew older and learned that stories aren't real, I came to terms with the fact that my mother was probably some prostitute who got knocked up by a stranger and couldn't afford to care for me.

"Can you fly?" I asked, trying to get away from the topic of my absent parents. Exhausted as I was, my mind just wouldn't settle for sleep.

"No," she said with a sigh. "They're more of a defense mechanism. And they help with balance. You'd *think* fae would be excellent hunters, with our wings and heightened senses, but we can't even digest meat. We can just hunt...arugula. And berries."

Despite everything, I snorted. My hand flew to my mouth to muffle my laughter. Suddenly, the whole world didn't seem too big. The Hollows weren't a problem, and I wasn't worried I wouldn't survive the night. It was just me and Dio in this bed, laughing over the thought of a creature I once thought to be fearsome hunting for salad ingredients.

As our laughter died down, Dio whispered, "You cheated at cards, didn't you? There was no way you won by chance."

I couldn't help it. I grinned. "I did. Look, if you're going to tempt me with shiny things, be prepared for me to take them. A game of cards won't stop me from stealing all your coins."

"I knew it!" she exclaimed. The mattress dipped, but I couldn't bring myself to roll over. "You greedy little bastard! I should've known you'd be a cheater from the second I first saw you. You have to teach me how you did it."

It hadn't been hard. When the deck was being dealt, I snuck a few cards under my sleeve. While everyone was distracted, I'd swap my stolen cards with the ones on the table. It paid to be quiet during card games, especially when playing with people I'd never played against before.

"Ri?" Dio breathed after a moment.

"Hm?"

"Goodnight."

My cheeks burned. "Goodnight."

"And Ri?"

I gulped. "Hm?"

"For the record, regarding the Hollow, I believe you."

CHAPTER TWENTY-ONE
KORE

Mama? Why do we live so close to the forest if we can't go in?"

Six years old and I was already searching for loopholes in Mother's rules, flaws in her logic. Why build Lavoisin so close to the Lysaen border? The Hollows had swarmed a year prior, but Lavoisin had yet to see one up close.

"Because the fae are wicked bastards who will kill innocent girls like yourself in the blink of an eye," Mother said.

My hair hadn't been longer than my shoulders, wild strawberry curls that couldn't be tamed, much like the rest of me. With my vendetta against brushes and braids, my tapered ears were all but impossible to hide. I knew my ears made me different, just as I knew my habit of adding fresh blueberries to my oatmeal in the mornings even though they were out of season, and I had no access to them wasn't normal. Magic, I so eagerly exclaimed. A sin, Mother snapped.

"But why do we live so close?" I pressed. I'd seen a baby deer with its mother prancing through the copse of trees earlier, the fawn's coat still dappled with white snowflake spots. I'd wanted to chase after it, to prance and weave through the sword ferns and nurse logs the way it had.

Mother did not answer that question.

The first time I ventured into the woods had been a few years later. Mother chained me to my bed for two days as punishment.

Yet, she never deigned to move away from Lavoisin and the Lysaen border that called to me louder and louder each day.

I peeled my eyes open, struggling under the impossible weight of my lashes. It took three blinks for me to adjust to the low, warm light and four to remember what had happened.

I sat up so fast my head spun.

I was in an unfamiliar room, far more ornate and gothic than anything I'd ever seen before in my life. The bed was *massive,* and while I was atop the plush sheets, such a deep shade of indigo they were nearly black, I could tell I had been placed there with care. Across from the bed was a vanity with a horde of candles burning at varying lengths – some still tall with strong wicks while others were nothing but puddles of molten wax. A vase full of dark purple flowers – dead and dried – sat dangerously close to the candles. The arched window was paneled with stained glass so intricately beautiful it put the rose windows from the cathedral in Lavoisin to shame. Except, they didn't let in a phantasmagoria of colors since the sky outside was darker than pitch without a single star to be seen. On the table next to the bed was a glass of water and a folded piece of paper.

I reached for the paper and unfolded it, recognizing the handwriting instantly.

As if by magic, as soon as I finished reading the note, there was a knock at the door. Hesitantly, I slid out of bed and tip toed over, pulling it open just a crack.

"Miss Etoile," said the person on the other side. I opened the door further. The man – no, it had to be a boy, he couldn't have been much older than me – looked neither human nor fae – despite his pointed ears – with a floppy mop of dark hair and equally dark eyes and a grin that stretched just a bit too wide over skin just a bit too pallid. He was dressed smartly, with slacks and a buttoned shirt and a brocade waistcoat, but around his neck was a strip of leather plated with curved metal. A collar. My brow furrowed. Surely, Adonis wouldn't be keeping...*slaves?*

I remembered too late to advert my eyes before I could meet the strange boy's gaze, though his pupils swallowed his irises and his irises nearly swallowed the whites, so it was hard to tell where exactly he was looking.

"Ait—King Adonis Nyx must've sent you." I grabbed my skirts and sank into a curtsy.

"Unless there's another mysterious half-fae named Miss Etoile here, then yes. Donny sent me." The boy's grin grew, revealing two sets of twin fangs – one on top, one on the bottom; more than the single set of sharpened canines the fae had.

So, *this* was what a Hollow looked like.

"Oh, my manners," the boy quickly said, his voice thick with a lisp that I would've found endearing had I not been terrified of the Hollow before me. The boy stepped aside, giving me enough room to step into the ornate hallway.

"I'm Ceralis. I have many titles, but my current favorite is *Official Royal Bone Collector.* Made that one up this morning."

Ceralis's voice echoed against the tall marble walls, the barrel-vaulted ceilings giving his lisped voice more resonance. We passed a wall lined with portraits, all of men and women with the same washed-out complexion Ceralis had, as if something vampiric had sucked the color from their flesh.

Ceralis took a turn before I could see the end of the portrait collection, leading me now down a narrower hallway with electric sconces on the walls. Our shadows warped and distorted, becoming uncannily long and twisted. I took a step closer to the boy. Goosebumps erupted on my skin, despite it not being that cold. He was speaking, but I could hardly pay attention to his words, my focus instead on the split shadows dancing across the floor.

"– it was an unpaid vacation, really. But a vacation, nonetheless. I'd never been to Naia! I just lounged around all day while he, I dunno, expected me to perform tricks or something. He had this collection of furs from beasts he slew – slayed? I have yet to master grammar, but best believe I will do it one day... Oh! We're here." He stopped abruptly in front of a heavy ash wood door. He knocked once, then let himself in like he owned the place.

The room was small, the size of my bedroom at home, with covered windows and a fireplace with a fire that roared blue. Shelves were full of rocks and shining gems and bones. And there, standing before the fire, shrouded in shadows that made my tiny white flowers bloom around my feet, was Adonis Nyx.

"Well, have fun!" Ceralis said cheerfully. "I have work to do. Bones to collect. Grammar to master." With that, the young Hollow turned and left, leaving the door open for modesty's sake.

Adonis turned. Or, at least, I assumed he did, since it was difficult to tell with the shadows that clung to him.

"Little Star," he said. "I was waiting for you. Did Ceralis wake you? I was going to tuck you in, but you kept stirring every time I moved you, and I didn't want you to wake up terrified."

He didn't want to wake me...

I stepped over to one of the shelves and stared at the collection of gems there—fat emeralds, rubies the size of my fist, amethyst geodes oozing with sparkling purple clusters, diamonds in every color of the rainbow... I picked up a small gemstone. It looked purple—no, white. No... Green. Every time it moved, it shifted colors, from lavender to turquoise to aquamarine, like it was alive within my palm.

"Moonstone," came Adonis's voice. I nearly jumped out of my skin and quickly set the rock down. I turned to face him.

"He didn't wake me," I blurted. "I got your note."

My damn flowers, those little traitors, bloomed around Adonis's feet, snaking upwards as if they had plans to constrict him.

He simply chuckled. "You must have learned my title, Little Star, if you're acting this nervous around me. Please, there's no need to be afraid. I'm not going to hurt you, and neither will anyone else in Heladés. You're my honored guest. Have a seat. Are you comfortable? I do hope Ceralis didn't drag you around on an unabridged version of the palace tour..."

I swallowed hard, nodded, and sat on the velvet settee closest to the fire. The blue flames danced to a silent song, mesmerizing me. Adonis sat across from me, his shadows still swathing him in darkness, clinging to him.

"Ceralis... He didn't wake me," I said meekly. I cleared my throat, then pulled my feet onto the settee, hugging my knees to my chest. I felt...weightless. The severity – the reality – of everything hadn't quite settled in. This all felt like a dream, one I'd wake up from soon. Mother would scold me for sleeping in and avoiding my chores. Everything would be fine.

I took a shaky breath.

Everything was going to be fine.

When I exhaled, fat tears spilled down my cheeks, splattering against my knees.

Everything was most definitely not *fine.*

In an instant, Adonis had moved from his seat and knelt in front of me. He reached out and took my hand. Not his shadows, his flesh hand – though shadows still obstructed it from sight, I caught a glimpse of pale skin, of long nails stained black, of star-like beauty marks freckled here and there.

"Little Star?" he asked, rubbing my knuckles with his thumb. "Etoile, are you alright?" Concern laced his deep baritone.

I opened my mouth to speak, but a sob gripped my throat, choking me. All I could do was blubber incoherently as tears kept falling down my face, soaking my skirt.

Maybe abandoning Mother was the wrong decision. She'd only ever wanted to keep me safe, to protect me from the same fate she had. And yet, I'd summoned the king of all Hollows to whisk me away to his palace home because I'd thrown a *temper tantrum.*

I pulled my hand from Adonis's, fisting my skirts tightly. He didn't reach for my hand again, not even with his shadows. He moved, silent as a cat, to stand behind me. Adonis combed his fingers through my nest of wild curls, detangling them and pulling them off my forehead. As he began to braid my hair, he said, "I understand that this is scary, Etoile. I would be scared in your shoes, too. I will do everything within my power to make your stay here comfortable. If you want to leave, you just need to tell me. As long as you don't—"

I didn't hear the rest of what he said, as the pounding of my heart in my ears and my gut-wrenching sobs drowned his voice out. My head fell forward, smacking against my knees. The half-finished braid pulled free from Adonis's grip.

"I'm sorry," he whispered, sounding more like a man and less like a king. "I'm sorry I can't quell your heartache. I wish I could take the pain and sorrow from you. I wish I was better at comforting you, my little star."

For whatever reason, that only made me cry *harder.* I could feel him recoil.

Then, the settee dipped. When I looked up, I was met with shadows.

"May I touch you?" Adonis asked.

I didn't trust my voice, so I just nodded. He reached out with his inhumanly pale hand and wiped the tears from my flushed cheeks. More replaced the once he'd wiped away, but he cleaned those, too. His fingers were so thin and lithe, but they were soft, his palm gentle as it cupped my cheek. I leaned into his touch, whether by instinct or by desire for comfort.

"Do you ever wonder if maybe…maybe you were too stubborn to realize that you were actually in the wrong and you just royally fucked over the person trying to help you?" I croaked. There was little warmth in Adonis's touch, but the blue fire and the flush in my cheeks as the realization that a man was touching me set in kept me warm enough. I brought my own shaky hand up, placing it over top Adonis's. He stiffened in a way that made me think even he, too, wasn't used to this gentleness.

"Constantly, Little Star," he said in a voice dripping with regret.

I rubbed my eyes with the back of my hand. There was no point in crying right now. I could cry later when I was alone. Things were overwhelming now, and I knew they'd be overwhelming later if I didn't do something about it now.

"Where are we?" I asked, turning to look at the mass of shadows that was Adonis.

"This is my favorite private study in the palace. Of course, the palace is in Heladés which doesn't exist on the continent you are used to," he said. "You humans and fae are so naïve, thinking Hollows could spawn from either. Come, Little Star. Shall I give you a tour of the palace? The abridged version, of course. You can choose different chambers to room in if you don't like the ones I put you in."

I nodded, still sniffling. Adonis used his shadowy tendrils to open the door and hold it for me to step through. As I passed by, my tiny white flowers—those damned traitors—sprouted from the ground and hugged Adonis's legs. Hissing, I kicked at their stems to get them to leave before he could see.

I had seen grainy photographs and washed-out drawings of palaces before. There were three on our side of the continent: one in Wallaekva, one in Welinas, and one in Svadaeva—the three kingdoms ruled by humans. Living so far from any of them, I'd never dreamed of stepping foot inside a palace. All I knew were what glimpses I could steal; the palace in Wallaekva was gaudy and almost like a cathedral; the one in Welinas was long and tall, made of glass and stone and gold; and the one in Svadaeva was a gilded beauty with domed ceilings and marble archways.

But this...

This made the others pale in comparison. They didn't even come *close* to the beauty of Adonis's home.

Tall marble walls stretched to the heavens, pocked with heavy chandeliers humming with electricity. Portraits of men and women and people sat snug in gilded frames alongside paintings of fruits and dogs. Among a few paintings of a dark-haired woman was a painting clearly depicting Ceralis, with a wide grin and a tight collar.

As we walked down a sweeping staircase, Adonis pointing out the door that led to the ballroom and the door that led to the formal dining room, I caught sight of a small silver plaque on the wall.

"... anything here, or you'll be stuck – Little Star?"

Library

I reached out, brushing my fingers over the engraved word.

"Oh!" Adonis said, catching up with me in just a few short strides. "The library. Does this interest you? You are welcome to explore it, of course. The archivist will be more than happy to show you around. In fact, they would know where books on plant magic would be, if you are still interested in mastering your magic. Are you?"

I nodded quickly, hardly waiting for Adonis's approval before shouldering open the heavy ash door and stepping into the library.

CHAPTER TWENTY-TWO

CASSIEL

For seventeen years, I took pride in being someone who could fall asleep anywhere, no matter what. It was important since I never stayed in one place for very long. Since I needed to fall asleep quickly so I could get a few hours of sleep before I had to go kill Hollows. But here, laying atop a mattress that was too big and too soft in a palace I'd broken a fae out of jail to get to, I could not sleep. I tossed and turned for a while, trying to force myself to get comfortable. The room was too silent. There weren't any howling winds outside, no rain pelting against the window, as if even a *storm* could calm me down... If servants and guards paced the hall just outside the door, I couldn't hear them. Each time I moved, my hair would brush against the nape of my neck and my heart would skip a beat; those damn scorpions had *really* sucker-punched my ego.

I'd slept better in the desert, when Auri and Dio and I took shifts keeping watch. Two of us would sleep at a time, blindly putting all our trust in the other person whom we barely even knew. Each time I'd closed my eyes, I had little faith that I'd open them again. Yet I still slept better then, with sand embedding in my hair and in every crevasse on my body.

With a groan, I sat up. My eyes were heavy with exhaustion, but I just simply wasn't going to sleep. I swung my legs over the side of the bed and stood, silently pulling my boots on, and slipping out into the hall.

No servants and no guards stalked up and down the long corridor, though I wasn't surprised. Not with the lack of noise. The gilded sconces on the walls weren't lit, but I had relied on other senses besides my sight in much more hostile situations before. Clinging to the wall, I began walking down the hall.

If the palace was a maze during the day, it had transformed into a labyrinth at night. Without any light to guide me, I could only pray to Medea each turn I took wouldn't lead me to some restricted area. I shifted to the balls of my feet, silently gliding over the mosaic floors.

Cold air hit me after what felt like an eternity. I stopped, peering out an open doorway leading to an outside corridor. The night air was far warmer than anything I was used to but was cool enough to be refreshing. I stepped through the arch and into the pavilion.

Trees heavy with swollen fruits I didn't recognize lined the stone pathway leading to a fountain with rather promiscuous statues in the center. Near the fountain was a stone bench with floral patterns engraved in the sides, carved with such precision and care that it must've taken the artist years to complete. I sat on it, then lay down, my back against the cool stone. Leafy branches obstructed most of the night sky, but I could still make out a few sparse constellations and the heavy moon that sat proud in the sky.

I closed my eyes and began to hum.

"That song," came a voice so soft I nearly thought I imagined it until it spoke again. "I've heard it before."

I opened my eyes only to see a face mere inches from mine. I startled, sitting upright so fast black spots clouded my vision. Half a second later, I realized I'd taken my sclera lenses out and left them in my room inside.

Shit.

The person chuckled. Their voice was so airy and light, like if a cloud could talk. There was a certain deepness to it that could only belong to a male, but even then, I couldn't be certain.

"I'm not a Hollow," they said. I blinked a few times, finally taking their features in. Their face was elfin; slim with an upturned nose and lips curled into a whisper of a smile. Their eyes were wide, fanned by lashes that matched their snow-pale hair. *Auri...?* No, it wasn't the little thief.

"That's something a Hollow would say," I said. Pale hair wasn't uncommon amongst the fae. Auri wasn't the first white-haired girl I'd met, nor would she be the last.

Their whisper-smile grew, a tiny dimple forming near their mouth. "I'm actually here to spy on the Hollows."

"You must be a terrible spy, then, if you're admitting this to me." I gave them a pointed stare. They shrugged, stepping around the bench. They plucked a sunset-colored fruit from a tree and polished it off on their shirt.

"No. I'm actually the best spy there is. So many people waste all their efforts trying to hide the fact that they're spying. It makes them obvious targets. But now I've admitted my purpose to you. Or have I? You have no evidence. Nothing to back your claims up. Am I truly a spy, or am I pretending to be one? Am I actually the distraction?" From seemingly nowhere, they pulled out a paring knife and began skinning the fruit, letting shells of its skin fall to the ground.

"Who are you?" I asked, knowing I wouldn't get an answer.

They sliced a chunk of flesh from the fruit and speared it with the knife, holding it out towards me. It oozed thick, sticky juice, sinking low on the blade from how heavy it was. Curious, I took the piece of slippery fruit and stuck it in my mouth. Sweetness exploded on my tongue, a sort of tangy goodness I'd never tasted before. I licked the juices from my fingers.

"Tristan Edelweiss," they – he –said. He plopped down on the bench next to me and cut another sliver of fruit, holding it out for me to take again.

I hesitated. "Risky business handing out your name like that, Tristan Edelweiss."

He held the knife closer, the fruit slipping on the blade. I barely caught it before it could fall.

"You're not a Hollow either," he said with a nonchalant shrug. He stuffed a piece into his mouth and spoke around it, "Trust me. I'm the best at knowing everything. This here? This is called a mango. It only grows in the Svadaevan queendom. And I know you hunt Hollows."

I looked at the bit of mango in my hand. "Cassiel Jäger," I offered. "Though you can call me Cas."

"See, Cas?" Tristan grinned. "I am the best spy there is. I've known you for less than five minutes and I already know your name, I know you like mango, I know you favor your left hand over your right, I know you are not from Svadaeva and this is your first time visiting, I know you're not used to sleeping in such a nice bed, and I know you have an ego the size of the sun. Oh, and I know you hunt Hollows. See, that was just a guess when I said it a minute ago. Your face confirmed it."

I balked. He'd learned all that just from a few exchanged words? Either he truly was the greatest spy, or I was worse at keeping to myself than I thought.

I stuffed the mango in my mouth and wiped the sticky nectar off on my pants. Tristan tossed the pit over his shoulder; it landed with a soft thump in a bed of bushes. He licked his knife clean before slipping it into some concealed sheath I couldn't see.

"Fine, then," I conceded. Even in the dark, Tristan's face lit up. "You're right. I travel the continent hunting Hollows. I'm not used to sleeping in such a big bed, and I'm not used to the silence here."

"It does get rather quiet inside the palace, doesn't it?"

The corner of my lips quirked up. Spy or not, he was better company than Auri or Dio. "Do you play cards?"

"Who doesn't? My sister and I play Crimson Crowns constantly. Do you know Dancing Maidens?" Tristan moved closer, his knees bumping into mine. Even though he was wraith-like and lithe, he was still tall, with muscles cording his thin limbs. The way he held himself reminded me, strangely, of Dio.

I pulled the deck of cards from my pocket and absently shuffled them. I nodded. Dancing Maidens was an easy game that even children knew the rules of. Each of us got half the deck to start. We'd take turns picking a card from the other, gathering pairs until someone picked both joker cards. I cut the deck and handed half to Tristan.

He hummed as he fanned his hand out, picking through the cards with care. He gathered his matching pairs and set them on the bench near his thigh. "Let's raise the stakes."

I paired a couple of crowns and set them face-up on the bench. Dancing Maidens was a children's game – there was no way to raise the stakes. Placing bets was useless. Still, I cocked a brow and held my hand out for Tristan to pick his card, saying nothing to prompt him to continue.

He plucked a card, still humming as he added it to his hand. "For each pair you get, I have to tell you one secret. For each one I get, you have to tell me one in exchange. Deal?"

I faltered. What kind of information would a spy need from me? I had my fair share of secrets, some buried so deep even *I* didn't know about them, but nothing would be of use to this strange spy. But maybe I could coax some information from him. Something told me he knew more about the Hollows than he was letting on, and I desperately needed to know what.

"Fine," I said, taking a card from his hand. Wings. I tossed it and its pair down, glancing up at Tristan.

The spy groaned a very fake groan. He swung one of his legs over to the other side of the bench, so he was straddling it. As his pale eyes skimmed over the backs of my cards he said, "I am not human."

Then, with a simple wave of his hand, whatever seamless glamour he had concealing his features fell. His face stayed the same, but his ears tapered out to thin points, and his canines lengthened. Sprouting from his back came a pair of delicate wings, intricate and beautiful, like thin panes of stained glass stretched taut. They caught the moonlight, creating a shine of incandescent iridescence.

Artists always depicted the fae as monstrous beasts, with flesh-shredding needle-sharp teeth and grossly exaggerated ears and leathery bat wings sprouting from their backs. There wasn't anything horrifying about Tristan Edelweiss. I'd spent my whole life hating the fae, believing they were the ones behind my mother's death.

If the gods existed, they would have paled in comparison to the beauty Tristan Edelweiss emitted.

I nearly dropped my cards. He folded his wings neatly against his back, though every so often they twitched, moving gently. Tiny capillaries pulsed throughout the thin membranes, beating in tandem with his heart no doubt.

He waved a pair of cards in front of me, pulling me back to reality. Shit. He dropped the pair onto his ever-growing stack. I looked through my cards. I had one of the jokers. Maybe I could take Tristan's and win the game before I ended up revealing anything too secretive.

"I don't like storms. I'm not scared of them – I'm only really scared of snakes – but I don't *like* them." I plucked a card from his hand, cursing when it was a sword and not the joker I was looking for. He grinned and grabbed a card from my hand. I almost breathed a sigh of relief when he didn't put any pairs down. Secrets were a dangerous thing, and when I had more of them than there were stars in the night sky, I couldn't be too cautious.

I grabbed a card from Tristan. A crown – one that just so happened to match another I already held. I dropped them with a bit of triumph.

"My favorite color's red," he said smugly.

"That's not a very good secret," I said.

"I never specified how good the secrets had to be."

Tristan took one of my cards. Another pair. I sighed. "My favorite color is green."

"You absolute smartass."

This time, I was the one grinning.

We played back and forth late into the night, sharing the shallowest of secrets, though even those were secrets laced with more secrets. Layers upon layers of secrecy and hidden words exchanged as we dropped cards onto the bench. Soon, there were only a few cards left.

"If I win," Tristan said. He'd crossed his legs and propped his elbow on one thigh, chin nestled against his palm in a lazy, effortless way. "You have to answer any question I ask of you. If you win, I have to do the same."

I glanced at his cards. He had three. There was a one-in-three chance that I'd get the joker and win. I only had two cards – his odds were better. He held them all evenly, not favoring any one over the others. The backs of each card were identical, and since they were so new there wasn't any wear that would give the joker away. I grabbed one at random.

Wings.

Tristan yawned; I used his moment of distraction to shuffle the three cards in my hand around so he wouldn't know which one I'd just taken. I held my hand out.

Tristan took the joker without hesitation, as if he'd known where it was this whole time.

"Tell me, Cassiel Jäger," he said as he set the rest of his cards down on his messy pile. "What lengths would you go through for revenge?"

CHAPTER TWENTY-THREE

SHASI

The harem palace was still lively late at night, and I found a bit of sanctuary there, even with the smell of wine clotting the air and the sound of children yelping and playing numbing my senses. Mother had six jewels in her harem – three women and three men. While I was *her* only child, I had many harem-siblings born from the polycule the six jewels were in. Father was welcome to have a harem, but he preferred monogamy, unlike Mother.

Amma sat on a divan, working tirelessly at her embroidery. A pair of twins, the second youngest children next to the infant that had been born six months ago, ran circles around her. She looked up when I entered. She wore her hair loose and uncovered, and there were dark circles under her eyes. The only reason the twins were still awake was likely because the tiny baby was struggling to go down. It usually took all five of the other jewels to calm the little thing.

"Shasi," she said, as if surprised I was there. "What are you doing here tonight? I heard you had guests. I trust they are all settled and taken care of?"

"Yes, Amma." I sat next to her, squishing myself close. She set her embroidery down and turned to face me.

"Shasi, darling, what's wrong?"

The twins screeched. Amma shot them a look that made them mumble an apology. They went to the other side of the room to continue their game of chase. I picked up a spool of thread and rewound it, so it lay flat.

"Do you think I'm a good heir?" I blurted. Amma lowered her needle.

"Ali, Khalid, why don't you go to the other room and see if your mother needs anything?" Amma folded up her embroidery and set it aside. The twins exchanged a look but ran off, not wanting to disobey their Amma.

She turned to face me fully and took my hands within hers.

"Shasi, you are an excellent heir. Where is this coming from? Did your guests say something? Is this about the upcoming ball you're planning?" Her dark brow furrowed, her golden eyes searching mine.

I shook my head. "There... There was a Hollow here recently," I began to explain. "Mirza and I took care of it. But it's the first Hollow that's been in Svadaeva in ages. And it was in the palace gardens, no less. Would it be wrong to throw the party for my birthday? All the people in the kingdom will be gathered to attend; it would be an opportune time for the Hollows to attack. I don't want to worry the people, but I don't want to put them in danger, either. I... I need to figure out where the Hollow came from and why they're coming here. They've always avoided Svadaeva. Always."

Amma squeezed my hands tightly. The gesture made tears prick my eyes. I leaned forward and pressed my head against her shoulder. She pulled her hands away and slid her arms around my shoulders instead. She smelled of jasmine and honey, a nostalgic scent that shocked me right back to my childhood. Amma had always been the strongest and sternest person I knew, but she was also just as gentle and loving as my mother. Each time she hugged me, I cherished it, and sank as deep into her embrace as I could.

My emotions surged, creating a tidal wave of frustration and confusion deep within me. I had to know what the iron flower was. I had to know how to kill the Hollows. I had to keep my people safe.

"There's a book in the library," she said, her voice a low, lyrical whisper. "It has a brown cover with a gold stamp in the center, no title. Go find it. I will talk with your mother and cover for you. You're right, my little flower." Amma used to call me that when I was small, whenever I cried or was upset. "Your birthday is important, as is finding a spouse, but keeping your people safe is the most important. Nobody will bat an eye if you reschedule the celebration, but if a Hollow shows up at an event you're hosting, they will never forget it. It takes skill to kill a queen with a sword, but anyone can cut her down with rumors and gossip."

I squeezed my eyes shut, blinking away the tears that rolled down my cheeks. I nodded and pulled away. Amma kissed both my flushed cheeks.

"I love you, my little flower," she said. "You are a wonderful heir, and you will make a wonderful queen one day. I have faith in you."

"I love you too, Amma," I croaked out. She gave me a smile before waving me off with the impatient affection only a mother could have, even if we didn't share a drop of blood.

As late in the evening as it was, the library was almost completely empty, save for a sparse handful of acolytes busy restocking the shelves. I picked up a candle and lit it, holding it out in front of me as I walked.

Amma had never been good at relaying details, and by the time I made it to the second floor to scour the tightly packed shelves I cursed myself for not asking for better specifics. There were *dozens* of books that almost fit Amma's description; brown leather books with gold titles, dark leather books with no titles, colorful books with gold stamps...

I turned down another aisle, praying to Medea that I'd find the damn book soon so I could *sleep*, and promptly ran right into an acolyte crouched down close to the floor. The acolyte tumbled to the ground, dropping the book they were holding.

"Medea's asshole, are you okay?" I cursed, holding out a hand to help the acolyte up. She took my hand after a split second of hesitation and pulled herself to her feet.

"Y-your highness, I wasn't expecting you to be here. What are you doing here so late?" she brushed the wrinkles from her robe before bending down to pick up the book she'd dropped.

Dark leather. Gold stamp in the center of the cover. No title.

"That book," I spoke quickly, reaching out for it. The acolyte looked at the book, then at me. She handed it over.

"I was just returning it to its shelf. Someone had been reading it today," she explained nervously. I thrust out my candle, which she fumbled with before grabbing.

"Who?" I asked, thinking it was Amma.

"I'm not sure," she replied. "He didn't give his name, and he wore a hood, but he was a foreigner for sure Really unusual accent – one I'd never heard before. Very pale. Probably hasn't seen the sun much..." she rambled on for a bit before trailing off.

I cracked open the cover of the thick book, the musty smell of old paper and worn leather filling my nose.

The first page was blank, the second torn out, leaving only jagged edges behind. The third page had only a handwritten note scribbled hastily in the corner:

For my darling child,

I will find you again one day. The red string of Fate cannot keep us apart for long.

"What is this book?" I asked the acolyte. I traced my fingertips over the smudged words. The book had to be ancient – the pages were yellowed and curled, thinner than gossamer between my fingers.

"I believe it's a diary," she replied, handing the candle back to me. "You're welcome to take it back to your room to read. I'll make a note for the archivist."

I thanked the acolyte and tucked the diary under my arm. I hurried out of the library and skulked through the shadows back to my room.

I flopped onto my bed and opened the book once more. I passed the page with the message, flipping until I found a page full of text.

Svadaeva is a beautiful kingdom. I never believed anyone could build such a prosperous kingdom in the middle of the desert, but Svadaeva is a true oasis. The sun is overbearing, but the nights are cool, and the stars are incredible. They're the same constellations I see at home, yet they seem to be a thousand times more beautiful here. People in the north will claim women have no right ruling in a matriarchal way, but Svadaeva is a kingdom – rather, a queendom – more progressive than any other I've ever seen.

I skimmed the rest of the page. I'd spent my entire life in Svadaeva and while it was the most beautiful kingdom in existence, I could only read so much gushy nonsense before getting bored. I turned the page.

A knock sounded at my door.

I slammed the book shut, shoving it under my pillow. Amma *had* told me to find it and the acolyte *had* given me permission to check it out, but I'd been scolded by Mother and Father one too many times in the past for pilfering things they'd specifically told me not to touch, and I had a feeling this brick of a diary was one such thing.

The door opened before I could shut off the lights and pretend to be asleep.

"Oh, good, you're awake."

"Mirza?" I swung my legs over the edge of my mattress. Mirza stood in the doorway looking smaller than a wraith in sleeping clothes that dwarfed him. He stepped into my room and closed the door.

"Look, I... I'm worried about having a fae here," he blurted without preamble.

I stared at him, dumbfounded.

"I... I know the likelihood of the Hollows being fae is incredibly low now, but... We've been on the brink of war with them for seventeen years. *They* clearly seem to think *we're* responsible for the Hollows. Isn't it, I don't know, a bit risky to have a fae here?" He shuffled over to my bed and sat down without permission. He didn't need it. We'd been friends for ages; my room was just as much his.

I scooted closer and leaned my head against his shoulder. "Maybe it is," I said. "But she doesn't seem dangerous. She can't be much older than us. If anything, that Auri girl is the untrustworthy one. Something about her just rubs me wrong."

Maybe it was because she had cheated in cards. She hadn't exactly been subtle about it. Maybe it was the fact that her face seemed so...familiar. I couldn't place where I'd seen it, though. A newspaper? A magazine? Some wanted poster stuck in a window at the market? And then there was the fact that she'd killed a Hollow. It seemed too convenient. She showed up right after the iron flower blew the brains of a Hollow out...

Mirza let out a heavy, dramatic sigh and flopped down, his head hitting the pillow with a thud.

"Sonofa—" he started, sitting up quickly to rub the back of his head. His mess of dark curls grew messier the more he rubbed at them. Before I could stop him, he reached under the pillow and pulled out the book I'd hastily hidden.

There were hardly any secrets kept between Mirza and me. We practically told each other everything. So, when he pulled the diary out and stared at it, his dark brows raised all the way to his hairline, I could already picture the thoughts coursing through his head.

"Amma sent me to get it," I said, reaching for the book. Mirza held it above his head, just out of reach.

"What is it?" He flipped it open to a random page in the middle and began reading aloud. "'I visited the temple again today. They have started leaving offerings for the sleeping gods. I wish I had known about these new rituals prior, so I could've picked up some fruit from the market on my way.' Shas, this is *boring*. Your Amma had you get this? Why? Did she run out of steamy material to read in between visits with your moth—"

I threw a pillow at him. It clunked against his cheek, forcing his head to the side. He abandoned the book in favor of grabbing a pillow and chucking it right back at me. I narrowly dodged it. Mirza reached for another pillow from my mountainous hoard. I dove for the book, snatching it up before he could realize my scheme.

"I don't know why Amma sent this—hey!" Mirza threw another pillow at me. It landed smack in the middle of my face. He burst out laughing, doubling over, and clutching his stomach. I shot my foot out and kicked his thigh. "Pay attention, you scoundrel. I don't know why she sent me to get this, but clearly it was important."

A small scrap of paper fluttered out from between the pages of the book. Mirza caught it before it could fall on my bed. He scanned it before showing it to me.

Cameras were invented not even a century ago, and they hadn't become widely used until only a few decades ago. The wealthy still adored getting portraits done – something I could never understand, because I loathed sitting still for that long, listening to the rude comments from the artists about my body when they thought I couldn't hear – but photographs were so widespread they dominated everything else. The picture that had fallen from the book was not a photograph, but a drawing so detailed it could have been. If it weren't for the charcoal smudges that stained my fingers after I grabbed the picture, I would've assumed it *was* a photograph.

Sandy dunes like those in the desert surrounding my home reached towards an open sky. Though they were in greyscale, I could picture the reddish sands in my mind. Nestled in the middle, surrounded by a smothering of dunes, was a sandstone temple. It looked so out of place in the middle of seemingly nowhere, with a size so colossal it seemed only the gods could've built it. Endless stairs stretched up to gaping stone archways framed by massive statues on either side. A monolith stood before the temple, engraved with symbols I couldn't make out. Time had smudged them away to meaningless scribbles.

I flipped the picture over. In the same handwriting the diary was written in were the words

Temple of Medea, Svadaevan Desert
1702

"This drawing is nearly two hundred years old," I breathed. I loosened my grip on it, suddenly aware of the antique delicacy it possessed.

"What page was that stuck on?" Mirza asked, grabbing the book from me once again. He flipped through the pages, trying to find the smudges of charcoal from the drawing.

"Mir, I think... I think Amma wanted me to find this. I think the Temple of Medea might have answers," I said.

"There are dozens of temples for Medea out there," he said as he flipped through the pages a bit too fast for my liking. The last thing I needed was Amma – or the acolyte or, gods forbid, the archivist – scolding me for tearing the old book.

"Well, this is the first I'm hearing of this one. Didn't Medea slay the gods two hundred years ago?" No... That couldn't be right... I racked my brain, trying to remember that little detail from my history lessons. I barely paid any attention to classes that weren't on sword fighting or modern trends. Many years ago, Medea, along with the two other gods, banded together despite their hatred for each other to slay the Old Gods. It was then that she got her name the Executioner.

Mirza politely ignored my question and instead read from the diary, "'It seemed strange to build a temple in the middle of nowhere. The closest source of water comes from the ocean, but the monks and acolytes don't seem to mind. They tend to the temple with the same loving care and devotion a mother would have with raising her child. I was given a tour by the head monk. The temple is even bigger than I anticipated, with stretching archives and catacombs deep beneath the surface. The head monk told me about their prized collection, and the holiest item they possessed – the C –' The rest of the page is torn out. See?"

He held up the book. The page had been conveniently torn near the bottom, cutting the entry short.

"I think we need to find this temple," I said. I tucked the picture into the book. "Find this... *C* item. Maybe it can help us stop the Hollows."

"We?" he asked.

"You. Me. Dio and Cas and Auri." I knew he wouldn't be happy to have Dio come along, but Mirza didn't protest. Instead, he just inclined his head in a single nod, a silent agreement.

CHAPTER TWENTY-FOUR

KORE

Adonis led me to an elderly woman shrouded in the signature Hollow robes, who was hunched over a book thicker than my skull. She looked up; her eyes obscured by circular glasses with lenses nearly as wide as her book.

"Your Majesty," she said, closing the book. "Just the person I wanted to see. You see, your little guard dog came through here earlier and damaged three – three, I tell you – tomes of mine. Either get a leash for him or ban him from the library altogether."

Adonis simply chuckled. I drowned him and the woman out, trying to picture what kind of dog Adonis would keep. The baker in Lavoisin had a small lap dog who bit the ankles of anyone who got too close, and the farmer who always gave Mother a discount on vegetables had an old hound who couldn't herd cattle to save his life but could sniff out a treat from miles away. I couldn't picture either as being the *guard dog* for the king of the Hollows.

"Etoile?" Adonis asked, pulling me from my thoughts. "This is the head archivist, Loura. She said she'd be happy to deliver some books to your room."

Loura interjected, "It might take me a while to find books on your specific type of magic. But I will look and have someone bring them. Just keep them far away from that mangy little dog." She shot Adonis a glare so cold I half worried he'd freeze.

I nodded, grateful that I'd finally have something new to read. As Adonis turned to leave, I spun to face Loura fully.

"If I look you in the eyes, will you take my life?" I blurted.

Loura stared at me, though my gaze settled on the wall just past her. Slowly, so very slowly, I shifted my gaze to fully meet hers.

Her eyes were purple, so dark they looked black. Like Ceralis's. Pale lashes and a heavy pale brow gave her a grandmotherly appearance.

"Who started that?" she asked. "The humans or the fae? I've had a running bet going for nearly three decades now."

Three decades.

The Hollows only emerged seventeen years ago.

I blinked. Something snaked around my wrist, causing me to flinch. Adonis's shadows had pulled me closer to him. I didn't answer Loura, and instead followed Adonis out of the library. As I followed him down the marble hallway, I couldn't shake the lingering feeling of unease I got when locking eyes with Loura.

I'd met the eyes of a Hollow and I wasn't dead.

What does that mean?

Halfway through the tour of the palace, Ceralis appeared out of seemingly nowhere. He wore the same clothes as earlier, though the knees of his pants were grass-stained, and his shirt was muddied. His mop of black hair was even more disheveled than before.

"Cer, you know I hate when you track mud inside," Adonis said calmly. Ceralis ignored him, instead thrusting out a single white flower, identical to the ones that seemed to follow me everywhere.

"For you, Miss Etoile," he said, grinning from ear to ear. "I found it outside. Pretty, huh? We don't get many colorful things here. I mean, the River is kinda colorful, and so are the weird red flowers that grow by it, but I try to avoid – oh, Donny, ignore that. I don't avoid the River at all. Nope. Nuh-uh. I routinely check on it every day. Actually, that's why I'm here."

I hesitantly took the flower and tucked it into my hair. How strange that my five-petaled flowers grew here, in Heladés, where the Hollows lived. I hadn't tapped into my magic since coming here; it hummed in my core, though the buzz had dwindled, becoming less prevalent, more...manageable.

"—and I said *you absolutely cannot be here,* but *he* said *I have every right to* and I said—" Ceralis rambled on. He gestured wildly, creating an animated story as he spoke, walking circles around me and Adonis in a dizzying manner.

I looked down at my hands. Why had my magic shut up? It had *always* been there. I'd *always* felt the warm hum behind my ribs. *Focus...* I clenched and unclenched my fists, trying and failing to get a single flower to grow. No, I *had* used it. Back when I first woke up, a few hours ago. I just hadn't realized it. I never realized it when those traitorous flowers bloomed in Adonis's presence.

"—*the Goddess's sword will strike you down!* So of course, I just kicked him into the River, because he just would *not* shut up. *Anyways,* point is, I found these flowers growing by your rock garden, and I'd never seen them before, so I picked it and brought it to Miss Etoile because it was pretty like her and –" Ceralis finally stopped his rambling and pacing. His dark eyes went wide, and he grinned nervously. "Oh! Look at the time, I've gotta go."

Ceralis ran off just as an acolyte dressed in the library's robes stepped out from behind a pillar, holding a broom in his white-knuckled grip.

Adonis's shadows rippled, rising up to touch the small of my back, urging me to continue walking.

When I returned to my room later, exhausted from the walk around the massive palace, a neat tower of books sat on the vanity. I picked the topmost one and flopped onto the bed with it, cracking open the cover and flipping to the first page.

Magic had always been an incessant hum to me, a churning deep inside me that wouldn't settle no matter what. Maybe it had always been so loud because I'd always been so close to Lysaen, and my fae blood was desperately reaching out towards it. Maybe it was quieted now that I was in Heladés, wherever that was.

I groaned and flipped through the pages, already bored.

As I rolled onto my back to look at the ceiling, my mind drifted back to Ceralis's rambling. My tiny flowers had begun popping up by the rock garden. Adonis had pointed it out through a stained-glass window on the tour, not going into any detail as to what it truly was. But I knew where it was located, and maybe it would have more answers for me.

Adonis *had* said I could go anywhere I wanted within the palace, but I still found myself clinging to the shadows as I slipped from my room and made my way down the many labyrinthine hallways.

Recounting my steps and tracing the path we'd taken earlier, I found myself in that same hall with the wall of portraits. Curiosity got the best of me; I slowed my pace and took in each painting.

A woman with hair darker than ink spilling over pale shoulders, her doe-like eyes two different colors.

A woman with bright citrine-yellow eyes and a pale wings.

Ceralis, though lacking his usual lopsided smile, several years younger than he was now. His hair was much shorter, albeit still just as messy, and he still wore the collar around his neck.

The next painting was covered by a swath of black fabric. My fingers itched to pull it back, but I doubted my freedom of going anywhere in the palace included going beneath covered paintings.

The last painting was completely black, as if the artist only managed to prime the canvas before having to stop. My gaze drifted down to the plaque beneath it.

Adonis Aita Nyx

King of Heladés, Overseer of the River, Ferryman of the Hollowed

Hollowed? I scratched at the plaque. I'd never heard anyone call the Hollows *Hollowed.* If it had been a misprint, why display it on the palace wall, beneath the would-be portrait of the king himself?

I looked at the rest of the plaques, but the only other one that wasn't blank was Ceralis's.

Ceralis Ker Berethrou

The Flesh Devourer and Guardian of Heladés

No mention of his dozens of other self-imposed titles. Still, it was strange to think of Ceralis as a guardian, when he couldn't even finish a single train of thought without getting distracted.

I stepped away from the portraits before my curiosity could get me into trouble and continued down the marble hallway to find the rock garden.

148

The rock garden, it turned out, was a lot harder to find than I'd anticipated. By the time I finally managed to escape the maze of halls and stumble outside, I was exhausted.

The idea of having a garden of rocks seemed backwards to me. I always tried to get rid of the rocks when gardening, because they blocked the roots from growing deep and settling, and they got in the way whenever I tried to dig holes. You couldn't *grow* rocks, so why have a *garden* of them? Even flower gardens, which served no real purpose besides aesthetics, were pretty to look at. But a rock garden? It seemed rather...grey to me.

I did not expect the rock garden to be an *actual* garden.

I froze in my steps, eyes wide and mouth gaping as I stared at the sight before me.

The ground was soft black sand, mixed with bits of pyrite. Smooth stones created a path weaving between trees made of tiger's eye and rich brown agate. Leaves of aventurine and emerald shielded heavy fruits of ruby and garnet. Tiny flowers made of chalcedony and pearl were scattered around bushes of peridot and quartz. Larger, grey boulders were strategically placed throughout the garden, giving it a more natural feel. A bubbling waterfall sluiced over a pair of boulders, splashing into a pool filled with aquamarine and lapis lazuli. A bench carved from marble sat nestled in a brush of jade vines. And, of course, sprinkled throughout the stones were my little five-petaled white flowers.

I lifted my skirts, eagerly hopping from one stone to the next, making my way to the bench. I sat down, grinning.

"Pretty here, isn't it?" came a slithering voice. My grin faded instantly, my spine going rigid. I looked around, though there wasn't anyone there.

"Up here," came the voice once more. My gaze drifted to one of the gem trees. Lazing on one of the branches was a figure shrouded in darkness.

They leapt from the tree and pushed back their hood. Eyes darker than ink and hair just as black clashed with bone-pale skin. She wore a black dress beneath her cloak, the fabric hugging her curves nicely before spilling out into full skirts. When she smiled, her teeth were long and sharp, but she didn't appear malicious.

"So *you* must be the famed Etoile Cer wouldn't shut up about," she mused. She plopped onto the bench right next to me. She smelled woody and soft, like a fire long-gone-out. Her inky hair spilled over her shoulders in a mass of not-quite-curls, with two stubborn bits that stuck up like horns.

"Cer...alis?" I asked, still struggling to piece things together.

"The one and only," she confirmed. "Oh. Right. Mortals are so weird with giving out their names. I may be Hollow, but I have no desire to consume your soul. I'm Enodia."

I blinked once. Twice. "Etoile."

"Our names practically match. We're destined to be friends." Enodia grinned again, and my stomach fluttered. *Friends*. I'd never been allowed friends. I always thought of my plants as friends, and then Adonis. I supposed Ceralis would be my friend, too, but I'd never had anyone declare their friendship with me.

I nodded, unable to hide the smile that tugged at my lips.

"What do you think of this place?" Enodia gestured at the rock garden with a swoop of her spindly hands. "Adonis loves rocks and gems. He built this place himself. Guess he wanted a garden that couldn't die."

Something brushed against my skirts. I glanced down to see a small, thorny vine poking out of the ground. I raised my hand slightly, coaxing it to come up further. As it grew, little flowers the color of fresh blood sprouted amongst the leaves and thorns. Enodia noticed them, too.

The grin slid from her lips. "So, *you're* the one who brought that life here," she said. "How?"

How indeed.

I plucked one of the little flowers and rolled its stem between my fingers. Milky latex, thick and sticky, oozed from the broken stem and onto my hand. Not ash, like it would normally break into.

"My father was fae," I said. "I somehow inherited his ears and his magic." I dropped the flower and crushed it under my boot. The vine shrunk away, then crumbled to ash. I wiped the latex onto my skirts.

"Right. Only the fae have magic. I always forget that." Enodia heaved out a sigh and leaned her head back against the back of the bench. "The fae and the gods, you know."

"The gods are dead," I said without hesitation. Mother always preached that, saying Medea slew the Old Gods then withered to nothingness herself. I'd always fostered the grain of hope that Medea wasn't dead and would come rescue me, but that never happened.

If Medea truly did live, why did she let the Hollows come and kill everyone?

"The gods are most certainly not dead," she said, sitting upright quickly. "The old ones, sure, but not the new ones." Then, she slouched against the bench once more, waving her hand flippantly to dismiss the topic. "I digress. Adonis gave you a tour of the palace, didn't he? How's about *I* give you the grand tour of Heladés?"

CHAPTER TWENTY-FIVE

DIORA

"*For the record, regarding the Hollow, I believe you.*"

I stared at the ceiling, long after Auri had drifted to sleep, contemplating what I'd said. *Why* had I said that? I wasn't even sure if I *did* believe her. But after seeing the body of the Hollow in the stable, still corporeal and bloated, my stance started to waver.

Fae didn't bloat nearly as much as humans did after death claimed them, and they stayed in rigor mortis for a few hours longer, their bodies purpling as their muscles went taut. Their wings would crumble after a day or so, leaving a filmy membrane of dust on their bodies. Humans were just as disgusting within death as they were outside of it.

I thought of all the men I'd killed in hopes of getting information and money. I'd had a job to do, back in Wallaekva, but I never completed it. I never met the mark.

But I did meet someone who *looked* like my mark. Someone who seemed to be waiting for me so they could throw me into a cell.

I sat up quickly. Next to me, Auri stirred, but she kept snoring, deep in sleep. She hugged the pillow she'd been cuddling with for the past hour tighter.

Who was that man?

I reached a hand out, as if to open a portal, but stopped. Somehow, that man had known who I was and had known who I was supposed to meet. I couldn't go home to Lysaen.

Because someone in Lysaen had sold me out.

Tristan.

I could only pray my little brother was safe.

I flopped onto my back and returned my gaze to the ceiling. Auri let out a rumbling snore and rolled over. Drool slicked the side of her face, gluing her hair to her skin.

Without thinking, I reached out and tucked her hair behind her ear.

For the record, I believe you.

I didn't sleep that night. Auri's snoring kept me up, and my thoughts consumed me to the point of near insomnia.

Who was that man, and who sold me out?

Morning came with Auri falling out of bed.

Thunk!

I jolted, the sound nearly scaring me half to death.

"Auri?!" I peered over the side of the bed. Auri lay on the ground, tangled in a blanket, with her drool-stained pillow near her head. She spat out a chunk of hair that had made its way into her mouth and sat up.

"'M fine," she said with a yawn. "Did I wake you?"

You didn't let me sleep, I thought. I said, "No, I've been up."

Just then, there was a knock at the door. I hurried to yank a blanket around my shoulders to hide my wings, barely managing to cover them before the door swung wide open.

Shasi was dressed in loose trousers and a tight top, her hair and lower face covered by a silk scarf. "Wake up," the princess instructed. "We've got a lead. We're going on an adventure."

"Can't the adventure wait until after we've had breakfast?" grumbled Auri. She stood up and finger-combed her messy hair off her face.

"Nope!" said Shasi. "Adventuring waits for no one. Get dressed; we'll pick up something to eat at the market. I hope you two know how to ride camels, or at least horses."

"What in the hells is a camel?" Auri yawned. She shuffled over to her pile of discarded clothes, lazily tugging them on. She brought her hair over her shoulder and braided it.

"You'll see. Come on. Meet us in the front of the palace in ten minutes." With that, the princess was gone.

Auri stumbled over to the bathroom, leaving me alone in the room. I pushed the blanket from my shoulders and stood. I flexed my wings a few times, shaking out the last bits of tension. I folded them against my back and pulled my corset on. I tightened the laces and clasped the front, only huffing at the initial squeeze of whalebone against my ribs. Just as I pulled on my tattered skirt and buttoned my blouse, Auri came out of the bathroom. Her cheeks were flushed, lashes clumped and wet with water. She yawned again and walked out of the room. I tied my hair into twin braids and hastily followed her.

Mirza and Shasi greeted us outside. Already the sun was unforgivingly hot. I silently reminded myself to never willingly visit Svadaeva again.

Auri let out another yawn. "Where's that lumbering fool at?"

"If you're talking about me, you're going to regret calling me that," Cas said. He pulled a leather thong from between his teeth and scraped his hair into a bun. A few shorter pieces fell free and hung over his forehead. Dark circles sat low under his eyes.

I rolled my eyes.

"Good," Shasi said, clapping her hands together. "We're all here. Dio and Auri, you're going to come with me to get a few things from the market. Cassiel, you'll go with Mirza to ready the camels. Plan on meeting by the orange grove in two hours."

As Shasi turned and began walking towards the already busy town, I could feel Mirza's gaze burning into the back of my neck. I bristled, instinctively reaching for my pouch of poisons.

Only, I didn't have my poisons anymore.

I dropped my hands and shot the guard a look before huffing and trailing after the princess.

Despite it being so early, the market was crammed full of patrons and vendors, so much so that I had to squish myself against Shasi a few times to avoid being trampled by pesky humans *smaller* than me. I longed to free my wings, if only to strike some fear into the people of Svadaeva and get them to give me personal space.

"– a map, canteens, oh, you two will probably want better clothes. Maybe not you, Auri. You're so fair the sun will fry you skin right off." I caught bits and pieces of Shasi's rambling over the incessant chatter from the crowd. My palms slicked with sweat; I dug my nails into my skin to ease the itchy, anxious feeling I got when smothered by people. It was too busy. Too loud. There were too many opportunities for someone to yank off my hood or rip off my bodice, too many opportunities for some vengeful relative of one of my many victims to shove a blade into my heart. I clung closer to Auri who, despite being smaller than a waif and trained in disappearing into crowds, held herself above everyone else.

"Oh, here we are!" Shasi suddenly announced. She grabbed Auri's wrist, and then mine, and yanked us into a dimly lit shop.

A beast of a woman stood with her back to us, hammering away at a blade. My stomach fluttered, my traitorous heart skipping a beat as I watched her muscles ripple beneath the expensive fabric of her clothing.

"Noor!" Shasi said. The woman turned, her face lighting up for a split second.

"Ah, Shas," she said. She didn't even regard Auri or me.

Fine by me. No regards means I can stare without her catching me.

"I'm afraid I have bad news," the woman, Noor, continued. She turned around, digging through piles of metal – half finished blades and scraps that could hardly be recycled – then produced a tiny pouch. Shasi took it, glancing inside before stuffing it in her pocket.

Noor said, "I couldn't figure out anything about that iron flower. I'm not even sure it *is* iron. It has traces of black powder on it, but I couldn't figure out its origins or what it was used for."

Shasi lifted her shoulders in a nonchalant shrug, but the dullness of her pale eyes told a different story. "It's fine. Listen, we're about to go on a journey. Do you think you have a few blades you could lend us?"

Noor's face suddenly shifted into one that was stony and unforgiving. "Oh, no. Remember my tulwars? I don't care if you're Medea herself, I will not be *lending* you any of my blades, Shasi Dārayavahush."

"Then give me a few blades and send the bill to my parents – no, send it to Amma, my mother's consort. Dio, how proficient are you with a sword? Auri?" Shasi glanced at us.

Truthfully, I was terrible with a blade. I preferred poisons for a reason. "I could maybe handle a dagger," I admitted.

"I want something shiny and flashy and expensive," Auri butted in.

Shasi ignored her. "Two daggers," she said. "And a pair of scimitars. I think Cas could handle those well."

Noor went to a wobbly rack of weapons. She scanned them carefully before picking out two thin blades and two heavy daggers. She set them on the counter. "This is going to be expensive, Shas. I really wish you'd stop breaking my swords."

"I still have my shamshir you made for me. I polish it every night." Shasi handed a dagger to Auri, and one to me. I stared at the blade as she sheathed the swords and stuffed them into her belt.

The dagger was the size of my forearm, the blade wavy and dangerously sharp. The leather grip was smooth and cool against my palm.

I tucked it into my pocket. I'd have to find some poisons eventually. I was useless without them.

Shasi paraded us around the market, gathering dried food and canteens of water for our journey. She purchased a map, which she gave to me for safekeeping. She was smart to not trust Auri with such a thing. The thief had picked the pockets of a dozen people at least so far and she didn't seem the slightest bit concerned.

Weighed down with packs and dressed in the looser cotton clothing of the Svadaevan people, the three of us made our way to the orange grove to meet Mirza and Cas.

Cas leaned against one of the orange trees, warily eyeing the massive, slobbery beast that stood only a few feet from him. It stretched taller than the trees and had a protruding hump on its back that didn't look comfortable to ride on.

Shasi dropped her packs with a huff. She slid the sheathed scimitars free and thrust them in Cas's direction. "Weapons," she said breathlessly. "In case we run into any danger."

I turned my gaze to the camel closest to me, staring into its inky eyes. It gnawed on a bunch of grass, its jaw working slowly. With a snort, it dropped its head and tore another mouthful of grass from the ground.

Tristan would have loved these strange creatures.

"Dio?" Cas's voice pulled me from my thoughts. I looked over at the group. "The map?"

"Oh. Right." I shrugged off my pack and produced the map from its depths. I sat on the grass and unfurled it.

I recognized the jagged coastline of Svadaeva from books and maps I'd seen before but seeing the Svadaevan desert without the rest of the continent surrounding it was novel. There were no trees – no Lavoisin Forest, no Foloi, no greenery – and the only major city, the only city that was labeled, was Svadaeva itself. A few splotches of ink hinted at outposts or villages. People lived in the desert. They sought out oases and built their lives around pools of water and palm trees in the middle of a sandy nowhere. I'd grown up so close to the Lavoisin Forest; living somewhere so far from the shade the thick canopies of forests provided was absurd.

Shasi pressed a finger to the delicately drawn marker for the capital. "We're on this side of the city. Mirza said the diary – I'll explain that later, don't worry about it for now – said the temple we're looking for is in the middle of nowhere, and the closest source of water is the ocean."

The diary? I glanced at Mirza, but he refused to meet my gaze.

It dawned on me then that I had no idea what we were doing or where we were going. I knew it had something to do with Hollows and that iron flower, but...a temple? Every day I spent here, stuck with these humans, was another day I was away from home. Another day I wasn't bringing in that extra income to provide for me and Tristan. Another day where Tristan was left alone. He was the best spy there was, but I'd opened a portal to the clear other side of the continent without leaving a single clue behind. Even he wouldn't know where I'd gone. *I'd promised him I would never leave him.*

I needed to get that diary. Shasi was keeping too many things for us.

Mirza took a piece of charcoal from his pocket and circled a few spots on the map. Oases.

"This leaves the entire coast," Cas said. He took the charcoal from Mirza and traced a border around the jagged coastline.

"No, you idiot, you're forgetting these spots." Auri smudged the line he'd drawn with the pale green sleeve of her tunic. My heart ached at the sight of ruined fabric. She continued like nothing had happened, "Oasis here and here. And the river, duh. So that leaves only... Here, here, here, and...here." She drew circles the size of Medea's eyes over the four spots she deemed acceptable. Charcoal stained her pale hands. I didn't have the heart to stop her as she went to scratch her nose with the same hand, leaving a smudge of black on it. She kept her other hand tucked in the loose folds of her trousers.

She, too, was hiding something.

I reached up to brush my fingers against my earlobes, making sure my earrings were still there and that she hadn't swiped them.

"It would've been convenient if whoever drew this map included ancient temples in their legend," mumbled Mirza. He scraped a hand through his mess of curls.

"Well, we have four possible spots," Shasi said. I picked up the map and stood.

Part of me wanted to ask if there were any photographs of this temple so I could open a portal to it and save us time.

But the part of me that felt tiny and powerless under the scrutinizing gaze of Mirza bit down on my tongue and forced me to keep quiet.

I folded the map up and stuffed it into the deep pocket of my trousers. It weighed heavy against my thigh, not helping with the weight of the dagger I couldn't take my mind off.

The camel closest to me let out a snort. Shasi coaxed it onto its bony knees, low enough for me to grab the reins and swing myself onto the leather saddle.

I'd ridden a horse exactly once in my entire life. I found them pointless since I could just use magic to get places. They seemed even more pointless now that I knew about the tram system veining throughout human cities.

"Tilt your pelvis," Cas said from beside me. Just as I looked up to see him twice his normal height now that he was on his camel, mine stood. I gripped the reins tightly, squeezing my thighs into the camel's sides to keep from falling. The beast snorted again, unbothered by my touch.

"Your pelvis," Cas said again. "Tilt it. And press your thighs against the sides. Spine straight like you're wearing a corset made of iron – bad analogy, sorry. Like you're wearing a corset made of... Of solid steel."

Awkwardly, I shifted my hips, resting now on my tailbone. I straightened my spine, my wings screaming in protest at the sudden shift. The loose shirt I'd been given covered the corset I wore, keeping my wings completely hidden, but my ears exposed.

"What, you're an expert on riding horses now, too? Killing Hollows just wasn't enough?" I grumbled. The camel started walking, keeping a lazy pace as it followed the others. I gripped the reins with white knuckles. The clip-clop of the camels' hooves over the stone pavement created a droning lullaby that slowly, slowly, slowly dragged the unease from me.

"There aren't trams or trains everywhere and I can't afford one of those fancy autos, so, yes. I'm an expert at horseback riding." Cas looped his reins around the pommel of his saddle. With both hands, he fixed the messy bun his hair was in. He, too, had changed, his clothes matching Mirza's – a long, loose tunic over baggy linen pants. He kept his boots in favor of the slim sandals Mirza wore.

Autos were a human invention; one I'd come across in the library. Like trams, they were horseless carriages that ran on liquid fuel and could travel great distances in short periods of time.

I didn't doubt for a second, I thought smugly, that my portals worked faster.

"So," Cas said, shifting the conversation. Mirza and Shasi rode ahead of us, and Auri was busy muttering to her own camel like the beast cared about her problems. "You're an assassin. How'd you get into that profession?"

I tightened my grip on the reins. Suddenly the sun was too hot and my corset too tight. I owed Cas nothing. I'd upheld my end of the bargain. I could leave whenever I wanted.

So... Why didn't I?

Why did I find myself hesitating, mouth opening and closing like a fish gaping for water?

You owe them nothing, *Dio.*

"It's just me and my brother and I needed a steady income. It was assassin's guild, apothecary worker, or factory worker at the textile mill. I'm horrible with any plants that aren't poisonous, and I can only sew a basic stitch. A ladder stitch, too, but only sometimes, and only when I'm panicked it seems." I lifted my shoulders in a weak shrug. It wasn't the full truth but close enough to it that I didn't feel guilty. I left out Tristan's occupation. After all, what kind of spy would go around advertising that they are one?

"I guess assassin fits," Cas replied. "Who are your targets?"

You owe him nothing.

"Men," I said flatly. "Human men. Usually ones working for fae trafficking, or ones who we thought had ties to the Hollows, or general pieces of shit. Cheaters, liars, the likes."

Now that I knew the Hollows weren't a human creation, I realized I must have taken innocent lives. Innocent men – fathers, sons, husbands, brothers – who had no idea why I'd ended their lives so cruelly. As innocent as they could get, paying me as if I were a lady of the night.

"Not women?" he cocked a brow.

My camel snorted, tugging its neck forward. My heart fluttered; I yanked the reins close to my chest, focusing on keeping my pelvis tilted, my spine straight, and my thighs squeezed.

"I made it clear I wouldn't ever kill a woman unless I had proof she deserved it," I answered vaguely.

My gaze drifted towards Auri. Her hair was stuffed into a scarf a few shades darker than her pallid complexion. She hummed a song absently, caught up in her own world.

"What about you?" I turned my focus back to Cas. "What made you want to kill Hollows? Lose someone close to them?"

Something dark flitted across his gaze.

"I lost someone I loved when the Hollows first came. I had two people take me in. Hollows got them just a few years ago on a job gone wrong," Cas said, his voice taught. His jaw feathered.

More people than not had lost someone to the Hollows at one point or another. I was one of the lucky minorities, but every time Tristan went out on a job and was gone for days at a time, I worried I'd slipped into the majority.

The city of Svadaeva bled into the background as the camels passed through the gates and into that godsforsaken desert. A chill ran down my spine – phantom grains of sand itched in my scalp and burned my eyes. Every tiny movement in the corner of my eyes made me think of those evil little scorpions. The sand shifted, becoming loose as my camel put its whole weight on unstable areas.

"What's Lysaen like?" Cas asked. "Or are you from Caira?"

"I'm Unseelie," I said. "From Lysaen. My brother is Seelie originally, but he was brought to Lysaen because the orphanages in Caira all ran out of room."

The mass genocide from the civil war had left most of the children in Lysaen *and* Caira without parents.

I continued, "Lysaen... It's surprisingly a lot like Wallaekva. It's a big city – bigger than Caira because the palace is there. We don't have trams and rarely rely on horses. We don't eat meat, so there aren't any farms. Smells a lot better there. And our jails aren't rat-infested holes that lead straight to the sewer."

He chuckled. "I always imagined it to be this forest full of magical trees and houses up in the canopy. You don't live in a treehouse, do you?"

I thought back to my narrow flat I shared with Tristan. I thought of the table covered in dents and scuff marks, the worn path in the wood floor leading up the stairs to my room. I didn't even make my bed before leaving.

Gods above, I should have left a note for Tristan at *least*. I should have apologized.

"I live in a flat with my brother. It's squished between two buildings taller than it and its right downtown, but it's home. I have a garden on my roof where I grow my poisons."

Poisons that were probably dying now that nobody was tending to them. Tristan was even worse with plants than I was.

"I always thought fae were expert gardeners," mused Cas. His camel turned and nipped at mine. Mine, in turn, snorted and shook its head. I squeaked, tugging on the reins to get it to stop.

"Plant magic is extremely rare." I squeezed my thighs harder, earning an annoyed grunt from the camel. "So rare it's considered a myth. I think there's only been, like, one case of a fae having plant magic in the past century. Some exiled royal, maybe. I can't really remember the details. All fae can open portals, but other than that, we have limited magic. I can't do anything besides portals and the simplest glamours."

Fae learned magic from their parents since it was hereditary. My parents had died before my magic manifested, and the wardens at the orphanage couldn't have been bothered teaching several dozen fae children varying degrees of magic along with their basic schooling. I'd been saddled with arithmetic and reading and never had the opportunity to solidify my grasp on magic.

Which is why I'd turned to the assassin's guild instead of anything else.

And, as the sun rose high in the blazing cobalt sky, assaulting us with scalding heat, for the first time, I began to question my decision.

CHAPTER TWENTY-SIX

KORE

Seventeen years. People had been struggling to figure out where the Hollows had come from for *seventeen years,* and yet...here I was. I couldn't help but gape at the city before me. Enodia and I had taken a carriage – she didn't even bother asking Adonis, much to my dismay – to the heart of Heladés' downtown district. Tall buildings stretched towards a dark, starless sky. Gas lamps made from twisting metal lightened the city in a warm orange glow. Shops with massive windows boasted collections of hand-dipped candles, pipes and tightly rolled tobacco, hats made from everything from leather to velvet, and gothic dresses made from the same dark fabric as the cloaks I always saw the Hollows in. There was even a candy shop with a bunny-shaped sign welcoming the patrons in and tempting them with red-and-white swirled candies and rich dark chocolates.

A pair of smartly dressed children with billowing cloaks a size too big darted out across the cobble street in front of us, chasing after a shadowy cat who couldn't get away quick enough. A couple, the children's mothers, I presumed, watched from the sidewalk across the road.

Hollow *children.*

The entirety of Lavoisin was barely even the size of the main *plaza* here.

The world beneath my feet tilted, spinning me into a dizzy, unbalanced state. I grabbed Enodia's arm without realizing it.

"Adonis hates coming out here," Enodia said. She linked her elbow through mine and began walking, the square heels of her boots click-clacking against the street. "He's such a hermit, that damned king of ours. Always trapped behind his shadows."

I opened my mouth to ask why he always hid behind those shadows, when one of the children from before dashed out in front of us. He tripped over the hem of his cloak and fell to the ground.

Before I could even blink, a net of vines shot up from the ground, catching him before he could smack against the hard stone. The child rolled onto his back, stunned. Just as abruptly as they came, the vines turned to ash.

The other child and the two mothers stared, their inky eyes wide with shock.

Enodia pulled on my arm. "Come, Etoile. Let's go explore the city before it gets too late, and Adonis worries where you've scampered off to." She tugged me away from the scene before I could protest.

As she showed me around the downtown district, pointing out the best cafes and pâtissiers, the best tailors and the ones to avoid like a plague, I couldn't stop my mind from drifting back to the horrified expressions of the two women. Nobody else seemed bothered by my magic. Adonis was *teaching* me how to harness it better. But... The fear in their eyes made it seem like they were afraid I'd use my vines to *harm* their child.

" – usually sends me to this occult shop at least once a week," droned Enodia, her voice distant like my head had been thrust underwater. "Etoile. Etoile! Are you even listening to me?"

I startled, turning my head to face her. She crossed her arms over her chest and stared at me, one perfect brow cocked.

"I... No. Sorry," I whispered. I took a step back, tensing as I braced for a hit, a slap, something.

Though it never came.

"Etoile, I've barely known you an hour and you're already the strangest person I've ever met. And I know Cer, so that's saying something." She reached out – fast enough that I flinched – and tucked a loose curl behind my ear. "Come on. Let's go buy you a pretty dress. One I'm sure Adonis will love." She winked and continued walking. I blushed furiously, my cheeks turning the same color as my hair, and scurried after her.

Ten minutes later I sat on a plush velvet bench the color of fresh blood in the middle of what Enodia claimed to be the *best atelier in all of Heladés,* struggling to tell the difference between the two blouses the attendant held up in front of me.

"Which one was the lilac again? This one?" I pointed at the blouse on the left.

"No, no, no," the exasperated attendant sighed. "This one is lavender. *This* one is lilac."

The other attendants clucked their tongues and shook their heads, as if me not being able to tell the difference between two purple-grey blouses was the end of the world. They looked the *exact* same, down to the mother-of-pearl buttons spanning from throat to navel.

And, frankly, I didn't like either of them.

Enodia sat beside me, sipping on a blood-orange mimosa and alternating bites between chocolate-dipped strawberries and tiny sponge cakes the size of my finger. The way the attendants had poked and prodded at my stomach, shaking their heads when their measuring tapes stretched taut around my soft middle had killed my appetite completely.

"What about green?" she asked, her mouth stuffed full. "Try the sage. She'd look good in that. Oh, or gold and cream. Get her that."

Even if I wanted to protest, I couldn't, with how stubborn Enodia was. One of the attendants hurried to the rack of clothes and pulled out a few blouses. I groaned softly and stood in front of the mirror. The attendant held up a sage green blouse with a frilled neck and long, slender sleeves.

"Get that," chimed in Enodia. The attendant handed the blouse to another employee and held up another shirt to me.

By the time we finished, Enodia had purchased a dozen blouses, skirts, petticoats, corsets, and overcoats to be delivered to the palace. She had shoes in every color delivered, too, despite my protests that my boots were just fine. The clothes I wore now were fine, too, but every time she mentioned Adonis and how he'd love to see me all dolled up, I bit my tongue and went along with her antics.

Would Adonis truly like to see me in all this? I wondered, though as soon as the thought solidified in my mind, I vigorously shook my head to rid myself of it. Adonis was a Hollow, I had to remind myself. The king of the very creatures hellbent on killing humans and fae alike.

But...

I'd locked eyes with Ceralis. With Enodia, with Loura and the child who fell in the street earlier. I had no way of telling if I'd met eyes with Adonis. Did Hollows *really* steal the souls of their victims through *eye contact?*

Or were the Hollows here simply choosing *not* to devour my soul?

But Ceralis. That painting of him had dubbed him the *flesh devourer.*

A pang of homesickness wound its way up my core, gripping my throat with a slithery hand.

As Enodia held open the carriage door for me, allowing me to step in, I couldn't help but wonder if I'd traded one gilded prison for another.

"I've never been to the living realm," said Enodia as she adjusted her skirts to lay flat across her legs. She knocked on the carriage wall; the driver snapped his reins and we started to move.

She continued, "Well, not in a very, very long time. Where are you from?"

I found no harm in answering, "Lavoisin. It's near the forest that borders Lysaen."

She clicked her tongue. "Never heard of it." She spoke quickly – too quickly, like she was lying, or...hiding something, though I had no idea *what*. "So, you're from the human side of the continent, then? Have you ever been to Faerie?"

I tugged my curls over my ears, suddenly self-conscious of their tapered points. I used to imagine going to Faerie to find my father, to demand he claim me as his own and teach me magic, but as I grew older, I outgrew those ideations just as I outgrew my old dresses and boots. Lysaen had just become a far-fetched fantasy, a distant kingdom not unlike Wallaekva or Welinas or Svadaeva despite being only a forest away.

My silence, it seemed, was answer enough.

Enodia shifted the subject, talking with the same energy that plagued Ceralis about my new wardrobe and how we ought to throw a party to celebrate my arrival and how I was the first woman Adonis had brought to the palace in a long time.

"What do you mean?" I suddenly interrupted.

"Hm?" she cocked her head to the side.

"The first woman Adonis has brought here in a long time," I said. "What does that mean?"

Enodia glanced at the window, something dark crossing her ghastly features. I leaned forward. "Enodia?" I prompted. "What's it mean?"

She took a breath. "Well, it's not my place to say. But... If you ask Cer, he'll tell you. And Adonis won't get mad at him for sharing, but he *will* get mad at me, and I can't afford that right now."

I wanted to ask more, to pry more information from my new friend, but I bit my tongue. Around my ankles, my flowers sprouted, the vines like shackles keeping me grounded. I stared out the window, watching as Heladés faded from a bustling city into the needling spires of the palace. Enodia absently mentioned bringing the smaller packages we'd brought with us to my room – she seemed, somehow, to know exactly where I was staying.

I barely paid attention, determined even as I slid from the carriage and hiked up my skirts to walk faster to find Ceralis.

I found him crouched by a pond near the mouth of a maze made of hedges that had lost all their foliage, rendered to jagged, thorny branches that stretched higher than I was tall. His red boots and socks had been discarded haphazardly, his trousers rolled up past his ankles and his sleeves pushed up past his elbows. His messy hair was messier with little twigs entwined within the dark locks.

"Ceralis?" I asked, dropping my skirts as I approached him. He wobbled, nearly losing his balance, and toppling into the pond.

"Oh!" he exclaimed, sitting back on his heels. "Miss Etoile! There's something in the bottom of the pond and I absolutely *need* it. Do you know how to swim? Where'd you go? You smell like perfume and yew." His nose scrunched up. "I don't know why Miss Enodia loves those trees. They *smell*. Not bad, but not good either, and it's a very strong *smell* and you just wouldn't get – Oh! Right! *Can* you swim?"

I crouched down next to him, peering into the pond. The inky waters were eerily still. Ceralis was right, though. There *was* something glinting in the bottom of the pool. Something pale and white against the darkness of the still water.

"I can't," I said. "It doesn't look too deep, though. Can't you swim?"

"Well, I can, but Donny said if I track in wet footprints one more time, he's gonna ban me from playing out here, and if he does that, I think I'll surely die, and I don't really wanna die, Miss Etoile, not yet at least." He looked longingly into the pond.

"Well," I said gently. "How about you remove your clothes, so they don't get wet? I can fetch you a towel to dry off with when you get out. That way you won't get the floors wet, and Adonis won't even know you went for a little swim."

His eyes went wider than saucers, looking like miniatures of the pond.

"Miss Etoile, you are the smartest miss I've ever met." And, with that, Ceralis promptly unbuttoned his shirt, tossing it in the direction of his shoes. Heat rushed to my cheeks instantly. I turned away out of modesty, but not before I could catch a glimpse of silvery scars crisscrossing his thin body.

"I'll be back shortly," I said through my flustered state. I heard a splash and took that as my cue to leave. Picking up my skirts, I hurried back to the palace.

Tracking down a servant was easy, as I quickly learned every palace staff wore a delicate sheet of silk over their face, obscuring their features – and thus their eyes – from sight.

"Excuse me," I called to a maid passing by. She dropped into a deep curtsy instantly. Taken aback, I couldn't even remember what I was going to ask. It took me a moment to realize she must've been staring through her mask. I flushed and quickly said, "I need a towel. Please, and thank you."

The maid dipped into a low curtsy and hurried off without a word. I reached a hand towards her. Maybe she hadn't heard me, or maybe she chose not to fulfill my request.

Maybe you should follow her, I thought. *Go find a towel for yourself.*

But just as I started after her, the maid rounded the corner. She held out a black towel fluffier than spring clouds.

"Thank you," I said as I grabbed it. The maid, again, curtsied before going back to her duties. I raced back outside, just in time to see Ceralis, naked as the day he was born, dragging himself out of the pond and *shaking* like a wet dog.

I *threw* the towel at him, my face surely redder than my curls. I clapped my hands over my eyes. Ceralis dropped what he was holding to grab the towel, hastily drying himself off then, almost as if it had been an afterthought, grabbing his clothes and sloppily redressing.

"Did you get what you saw?" I asked, peeking through my fingers to make sure he was dressed.

"I did!" he exclaimed, bending down to pick up the thing he'd dropped. The second I lay my eyes on it, I recoiled.

It, much to my dread, was a skull, bleached by the sun with patches of slimy algae clinging to the bones. Its lower jaw was gone, but my gaze snagged on the upper teeth. The incisors were flat and thin, the rest of the teeth nearly the same. They weren't the sharpened teeth Ceralis had, with his canine-like jaw. But they weren't human, either. The lengthened teeth on either side of the front four gave it away, more than the sloped brow bone and sharp cheekbones, that the skull Ceralis had found belonged to a *fae.*

CHAPTER TWENTY-SEVEN

AURI

I could already feel the burn forming on the back of my hand and the back of my neck. I kept one hand tucked against the loose fabric of my trousers, the inky stain that had spread up past my first knuckles hidden from view. Years of dashing across rooftops and balancing on the narrow railings of bridges had homed in my stability and core strength, so staying atop my camel – whom I'd named Zina, after the ancient goddess of nothing – with only one had gripping the reins was a piece of cake.

Gods, I wished I had cake.

I also wished I had a tower of macrons in every color of the rainbow and chocolate cookies still gooey from the oven and enough fruit tea to fill a lake. I wanted more of what we feasted on last night – the wine in particular. My mouth watered at the thought of the sweet warmth of the wine – and more of what we ate at the market the day before. The unbearable hunger and thirst from my first desert traipse had left me untrusting of whether the packs attached to our saddles *actually* had food and water inside. I eyed the pack pressing against my thigh suspiciously.

"Plant magic is extremely rare. So rare it's considered a myth. I think there's only been, like, one case of a fae having plant magic in the past century. Some exiled royal, maybe. I can't really remember the details. All fae can open portals, but other than that, we have limited magic. I can't do anything besides portals and the simplest glamours." Dio's voice pulled me from my thoughts. I glanced over at her. She and Cas rode behind Mirza and Shasi. Curious, I nudged my camel closer to listen to the rest of their conversation.

"Glamours, huh?" Cas asked. "Can you make yourself look like someone else?"

Dio tugged on her scarf, hiding her ears. "I can. Sort of. I can hide my ears and wings, but that's about it. And it's draining, so I can't do it forever."

The saddle bag rubbed against my leg with each step Zina took. Even though the leather of the saddle was soft, and blankets were piled between it and her hump, my pelvis still ground against her painfully, my thighs aching with each movement. Gods, I was going to die when I finally got off.

"– the hells is *that?!*" screeched Dio. All of us looked at her. She clung to her reins tightly, color drained from her face as she tried to shy away from whatever scaly thing Cas held out.

"My sclera lenses," he said calmly, dropping the shriveled things into the sand. "They dried out, and I don't need them right now."

Dio gagged like he'd just gutted a fish in front of her.

Zina snorted. I leaned forward, patting her thick neck. I'd already survived one escapade through the desert with Dio and Cas; I could surely survive another.

Above us, vultures circled, creating black stains against the sky. A shiver ran down my spine.

Vultures were Heela's animals, as they symbolized the bridge between death and life, fitting for the goddess of death. To see more than one flying above was never a good sign. I closed my eyes against the heat.

We were taught a rhyme about birds at the temple. It was for children, mostly to help us learn how to count, but as the vultures circled above us, I couldn't help but think of it.

One for death
Two for mirth
Three for the daughter
Four for the son's birth

Five for happiness
Six for wealth
Seven for a secret
Eight for health

Nine for passion
Ten for bliss
Eleven for uncertainty
Twelve to be missed
And thirteen to beware of Chaos's rift

Eyes opened and straining against the bright light, I looked at the sky, silently counting the black smudges.

Three.

I shook my head. It was just a stupid rhyme the nuns made us repeat over and over again until we knew our numbers up to thirteen. It was just religious propaganda. Garbage. We were in the middle of the desert for Goddess's sake.

The damn birds probably just wanted to test their luck and find some rotting carcass to devour.

"– really matter if I can fly or not?" Dio grumbled. "I can't. They're really just for show and nothing more. Honestly, it would be a million times more convenient if the Goddess blessed our bodies with*out* wings, you know? I could sleep on my *back.*"

"Does anyone actually sleep on their back, though?" Cas shot back.

Dio paused. "I bet someone out there does."

"You liar. Nobody does."

"I bet *you* do."

"I do not!"

"Ha! You're in denial, you back sleeper!"

For the record, regarding the Hollow, I believe you.

I wet my dry, sunburnt lips with the tip of my tongue. Was the heat flooding my face from the sun, or from the warm shame filling my belly like magma? It *had* to be from the sun. Despite being named after the ancient god of the sky, Orinos, where I spent most of my time stealing and running from the bobbies – where I'd skipped over from to get to Welinas, only a fifteen-minute run away – was constantly plagued by a thick overcast that hung low in the sky and blocked out the sun.

So, it *had* to be the sun.

I looked at the sky again. One vulture remained, circling the sun like a messenger of death.

"Ri. Auri!"

I shook out of my trance-like state, turning to look at Dio and Cas. They stared a t me blankly.

"I'm sorry?" I blurted.

Dio rolled her eyes. "Told you she wasn't listening."

Cas just sighed. "I was asking if you're injured. You keep holding one hand close to your body. If you're injured, we need to treat it now before it has the chance to become infected."

Subtlety had never been my strongest suit. At least, not when it came to things outside of thievery. I could slip my hands into the pockets of anyone and steal everything but the clothes off their backs and the shoes off their feet, but I couldn't hide the stain on my fingers, I seemed.

Still, I kept it hidden. "No," I said. "I'm fine. Just a habit, really. Do you know how long it'll take to get to wherever we're going? I don't do well in the sun."

"It feels so nice," sighed Dio. "It's so warm."

"I have no idea," said Cas. "Shasi and Mirza are in their own little world up there. I doubt they'd be any help."

Still, I rationalized, being out here was a million times better than the fate that awaited me back north. I didn't do well in the sun, but I'd do even worse rotting in a jail cell.

At least I wouldn't get arrested for killing a Hollow.

At that, the stain on my fingers itched; I rubbed them against my trousers. Humans wouldn't punish me for my accidental murder, but the Hollows would.

Morning bled to afternoon and afternoon to evening before Shasi finally announced we'd be stopping and setting up camp for the night. I almost wept with relief when Zina knelt, and I slid off her back. My legs, however, gave out instantly. Throwing my hands out, I barely managed to catch myself before I took a mouthful of sand in my fall.

Dio laughed, but that laugh abruptly cut short when she, too, collapsed in the sand.

"We'll rest here for the night," said Shasi. "We'll take turns keeping watch. I doubt any Hollows would make it out here, but there are nomadic tribes that might not be happy with our presence. I'll take first watch. Any volunteers for second?"

"I can do it," Cas said. He sat down, legs crossed, and removed the scarf from his messy, dark waves. They tumbled down to his shoulders for a split second before he tied them back.

"I'll take third," volunteered Mirza. He glanced at Dio, who was too busy rubbing her inner thighs to notice.

Three volunteers seemed like more than enough. I didn't put myself out there, since I knew I'd likely just fall asleep instead.

Shasi opened one of the packs and took out two canteens. "We have to share to conserve our supplies. Try not to –"

I grabbed one of the canteens and greedily gulped its contents down.

"– waste it," the princess mumbled. Drips of water sluiced down my chin, rolling over my throat and splattering against the sand. I only stopped when someone – Dio – grabbed the canteen from me and whacked the side of my head with it.

"Thieving bitch," she muttered, bringing the canteen to her lips. "You can't take all of it." Her throat bobbed as she drank the rest of the water in deep gulps.

Mirza got to work building a fire while Shasi pulled out food from one of her packs. She passed bits of dried, salted meat around, along with strips of dried fruit. She handed over some of the fruit and some nuts to Dio.

After we ate in silence, I lay out my sleeping mat next to Zina. If I remembered anything about my first desert trek it was that it got *cold* at night. Zina snorted but didn't seem bothered when I curled up next to her.

Soon, the sun sank beyond the horizon and stars speckled the night sky. The stillness and silence that swept over the desert came with everyone falling asleep. Despite how tired I was, I stared up at the sky, finding the constellations I knew.

Orinos, with his outstretched hands bringing life to the sky.

Zina and Maulea, asleep for eternity in a speckle of light.

Ora, the watchful guardian of the stars, made of thirteen stars against a backdrop of green and purple.

The crane, with lanky legs and a stoic gaze.

The Cat and her Kittens; a set of playful stars taking the shape of a mother cat and three round kittens.

And the Hound, a mythical beast with three heads said to rule over the realm of the dead.

I closed my eyes, listening to the stillness of the desert. Zina's steady breathing acted like a metronome of white noise, lulling me into deeper exhaustion. I teetered on the edge of sleep, only to be pulled out by the soft singing of a woman.

Drift upon the waves
And the stars will align.
Until we reach the end
Just know that you are mine.

Instantly, I sat up, heart pounding hard against my ribs. Zina had stopped moving. She had become…distorted, like I was looking at her through water. The moon, a waning crescent, had inverted to a waxing crescent, and the constellations were…wrong. I couldn't recognize a single one of them.

"You," came a hissing voice, so unlike the gentle singing that had jolted me awake. *"You hurtsssss usssss. Why? Why would you take one of ussssssss?"*

"Who are you?!" I demanded. My fingers burned. I dared a glance, only to regret it instantly. The black stains had enveloped all five of my fingers and the upper part of my palm now, spreading further than it had before. I rubbed at it hastily with my other hand, as though it would smudge away like ink. It didn't budge.

"You hurtsssssss ussssss!" The serpentine voice screeched. *"You hurtssssss ussssss and he issssss not pleassssssssed with you! He will devour your sssssssssssoul. He will desssssssstroy you. He will hurtssssss you like you hurtsssssss ussssssss!"*

The voice let out a scream. I clapped my hands over my ears. Warmth tickled my palms, and I didn't have to look to know that it was blood. Iron filled my mouth from the blood trickling from my nose. My throat burned, and it took me a moment to realize *I* was screaming, too.

"YOU HURTSSSS USSSSS! YOU WILL PAY FOR YOUR SSSSSSSSINSSSSSS!" The voice came from every side at once, drowning me in the cacophonous screams of a creature in agony.

I curled into a fetal position, desperately trying to block out the screams. I tore at my hair and screamed back. The stars rattled in the sky, like little diamonds threatening to fall. Would we burn if they did? Would the screaming stop if they did? Shadows warped in and out of my blurred vision, creating vague humanoid figures that vanished just as quickly as they appeared. The sand dunes had sharpened into rocky mountains, stretching high into the wrong, wrong, *wrong* sky.

"LEAVE ME ALONE!" I screamed. I threw out my hand in a sweeping arc.

And, at once, the rattling stopped. The screaming stopped.

Slowly, I sat up, pulling my bloodied hands away from my bloodied ears.

A woman wearing tattered, bloodied clothes stood in the near distance. Her mouth didn't move as she spoke. "Daughter," she said, phrasing it more like a title than a motherly word of endearment. "You must hurry. Please. He is not happy with you, and He will not rest again until you are dead."

She paused, then said, softly, "Tell my son I miss him." And then, time and space and the not-desert around me sucked into a funneling vortex of colors so intense my eyes ached with the threat of exploding. It was over just as fast as it had begun.

I sat up, gasping, looking at the sky to make sure the stars were right. When they were, I nearly wept. It wasn't until I felt the sticky blood still oozing from my ears that my short-lived joy was shattered like glass.

The stain on my hand had spread just past my wrist now.

PART TWO

INTERLUDE

The Nurturing of Darkness

Many years ago, many things had gone terribly wrong. He had been but a child, but even a child could recognize the carnage that wrecked the continent, leaving a trail of wingless bodies and withered husks and blood blood *blood* in its wake. Perhaps it had taken witnessing the deaths of his parents to spark the darkness in his soul. Perhaps he had simply been born with the inky taint that spread throughout his body as days turned to months turned to years.

He was not a bad person, per se, just...cursed.

It was a curse that manifested on his soul in the form of an inkblot darkness; one he couldn't physically see but could taste, the stain like old coins and acrid smoke at the back of his throat. It tasted like the lingering cough he had after surviving consumption as a child, bloody and thick and wet.

The Shadow, as he took to calling the physical manifestation of his curse, started following him when he was a seasoned orphan. Nobody else could see the Shadow, but if they looked extra closely, they'd see that he had two gloomy penumbras following him instead of one, stitched to the soles of his feet and phobic of the sun.

He grew to loathe the sun, because the Shadow loathed it, but he wasn't quite fond of the suffocating emptiness the full dark brought, so his world became a perpetual dusk, his walls lined with sconces dimmed to the lowest flame, so the Shadow could thrive.

So the Shadow could nurture the darkness that grew inside of him.

You must trick them into thinking you are on their side, whispered the Shadow into his ear, a snake tempting him with mortal sin.

"And what do I get in return?" asked he, though the words clogged in his throat, and he couldn't seem to disobey.

There is something dark and twisted within you, and I only wish to nurture it.

He didn't like that answer, but his words had turned to asphyxia, and he couldn't get them out.

Too late did he realize it wasn't the words trapped in his throat like a blockade, but the thin, skeletal fingers of the Shadow wrapped around him, slowly choking the life from him.

Too late did he realize his soul had nearly turned necrotic, solid black and not his anymore. An evil-shaped *thing* stuffed into the body of a boy, unfitting, and contorted.

He vomited up blood until his esophagus burned and his stomach cramped, and tears streaked down his cheeks like rivers. When he slept, he slept like a bear in winter.

The Shadow was not pleased with his weakness, but it was pleased with the darkness it had been slowly cultivating for many, many, many years.

CHAPTER TWENTY-EIGHT

CASSIEL

Mirza decided the most effective way of waking me up for my watch shift was to throw rocks at me. Effective, sure. But an asshole move? Even more so. If I wasn't already pissed off about being yanked from sleep – even though I'd volunteered to take watch – being pelted with rocks did the trick. I cursed, forcing myself to sit up.

"Wake Shasi in two hours," Mirza said. He gave no further explanation, instead laying on his bedroll.

The silence was unusual. The cities where I spent most of my time never slept, even this late at night, and thick clouds of smog blocked off the true nature of the stars. The desert wasn't so bad, once I got over the blazing sun and the sand that got everywhere and those damn scorpions.

I checked under my bedroll twice to make sure the sudden lumps were from the sand and my overactive imagination and not those blue fiends burrowing beneath me.

When Mirza fell asleep – his snores shattering the peaceful serenity – I stood and drew my swords. They were light in my hands, but strange. So unlike the whips I preferred. Still, swords did the trick, and as I adjusted my stance, they fell naturally against my hands.

"You're holding them wrong."

I nearly dropped my swords. I spun around to face Tristan. He glowed against the inky backdrop of midnight, his pale hair falling over his mismatched eyes.

"Where did you –" I started.

"Scimitars are supposed to be wielded dually. You can't think of them as two separate swords. You have to think of them as one sword split in two." On silent feet, Tristan padded over. "May I?"

It took me a full minute to process what he was saying. When I did, I nodded and handed the swords over. He took great care not to touch the blades, or even the handguards, grabbing only the leather-wrapped hilts.

"Like this," he explained. "It's more difficult for me. These are solid iron." He swung both blades, slicing clean through the air with a *whoosh*.

"Where did you come from?" I asked, ignoring his little demonstration.

"Here. There." He shrugged. "Everywhere and nowhere and the empty spaces that lay between."

Trust a spy to not give straight answers when they matter.

Tristan handed my blades back. I took them and shoved them into the sheathes at my waist. Tristan, as if bored, sat on the sand with a groan.

"What are you doing all the way out here?" he asked, glancing over at the others' sleeping bodies. "I've known you for a whole of a night and a half, but I know you aren't the kind of person who enjoys traipsing across the desert."

That smartass little spy –

"I think we're looking for a temple," I said, recalling Shasi's plan. She'd kept a good chunk of information from us. Not like I wouldn't have done the same if I were in her shoes, but the point still stood.

"Oh." Tristan picked up a handful of sand, watching the grains slip from the cracks of his fingers and back to the ground. "Medea's old temple? How'd you find a map to it?"

I stared at him.

"What?"

"Medea's temple?" I asked. "That's where we're headed?"

He shrugged again. "I asked you. Where'd you get the map?"

Assuming the map Dio had, I pointed towards the others. "We bought a map of the desert in at the mark –"

"No, no, no, no, no." he dropped his handful of sand. "Not a map of the whole *desert*. A map leading to *Medea's Temple*. It shouldn't exist. Nobody has been able to find it in centuries. Trust me, I'd know. I've been *trying* to find it for *years* and I just can't."

"You can come with us," I offered. I sat next to him, picking up a handful of sun-warmed sand the way he had and let it slide through my fingers.

"Can't," he said. He didn't elaborate. I dropped the sand.

"I have to keep watch for two hours." I stood and brushed myself off. "Care to spar with me to kill the time?"

I drew my swords, holding one out towards Tristan. The corner of his lips quirked up; he took the blade.

"Swords aren't my weapon of choice," said Tristan. Despite that, he slid comfortable into a defensive stance, blade held at an angle to parry. "I prefer things that are more explosive."

"They aren't mine, either." And then, I struck. Tristan blocked my parry with speed I couldn't even comprehend. He slid his sword down the length of mine, pushing it away with enough time to spare to thrust his blade at my unprotected side. I barely managed to block the blow before he could gut me.

I swept my leg out, knocking Tristan off his feet. He tumbled to the ground but rolled out of the way just as I brought my blade down. He was up before I could strike again, inhuman speed aiding him. When he thrust his sword out again, I finally homed in on his patterns.

There were three types of swordsmen I'd learned: the ones who fenced for sport exclusively, the ones who had informal training, and the ones who had military training. Tristan was the latter. The deadly precision in which he struck, like he was a cobra and his blade his venom-laced fangs, only came with years of intense military training. He turned every variable into an opportunity skewed in his favor, even when I struck out, the tip of my sword nearly slicing through his carotid artery. In an instant, I stopped worrying about hurting him and started realizing that I simply *couldn't*. I'd been trained by two humans who had lost everything and decided vengeance was the only motivator they needed. My training was elementary in comparison to Tristan's.

He fought like Cora and August had.

He struck out, a blur of moonlight against the backdrop of night, and I felt the cold metal of his sword against my throat.

I dropped my own weapon, forfeiting.

Tristan sighed, dropping his blade, and flopping onto the ground. He hadn't even broken a sweat, hadn't even begun panting.

"For someone whose weapon of choice isn't a sword, you're good at wielding one," I said, lowering myself to the ground.

Tristan tipped his head back, face arching towards the sky. His throat bobbed as he swallowed, vulnerable and exposed, milky white under the light of the silvery moon. His pale hair fell over his forehead in messy locks and curled around the nape of his neck. My fingers itched to reach out and tuck a stray bit behind his pointed ear.

His hands were covered in raw blisters that hadn't been there ten minutes ago.

I sat up straighter. "Your hands," I said, like an idiot.

His neck relaxed, mismatched eyes – one was ever so slightly darker than the other. I'd only ever seen him in the moonlight, making it impossible to tell which colors they were – focusing on his hands.

"Ah," he said, like an idiot. "Yes. See, fae are allergic to iron, or something like that. It burns us like this, inhibits our magic. Only a few things can really, truly kill us, unlike you weak humans. Rowan, ash wood, a whole lot of salt, iron… Even with the grip on that sword, I guess it still got to me. Well." He stood. "This is my cue to leave, then, I suppose."

"Wait!" I rushed to say. Tristan raised a pale brow, urging me to continue. "I'm sure we have some healing salves with us. I could –"

"Oh, don't waste your resources on me." He waved a blistered hand flippantly. "I'll be fine. Until next time, Cassiel the Hunter."

He was gone in a heartbeat.

Shasi pitched a downright fit when I tried to wake her two hours later. I suddenly didn't blame Mirza for resorting to throwing rocks at me to wake me up. When she finally woke, cussing me out the whole time, I slinked over to my bedroll. Despite my exhaustion, sleep withheld itself from me. When it finally came, I didn't dream.

"Wake up, pretty boy!" Dio's voice was hardly enough of a warning, giving me no time at all to brace for the pack that hit me in the shoulder. I cursed, sitting up as the bag slid a few feet away.

"What is with you guys and your horrible wakeup methods?" I grumbled, shaking sand from my hair. My swords lay a few feet away from my bedroll. I sheathed them and got to work packing up.

"We tried more humane ways," Auri murmured apologetically. "But you wouldn't wake up. *I* tried to talk them out of it, for the record." She clutched her hand to her chest protectively.

After a breakfast of dry meat and hard bread, we mounted our camels and set off once more.

Dio nudged her camel closer to mine. While she still gripped the reins with a strength I envied, she was much more relaxed today than yesterday.

"We don't have a compass," she said in a low voice. "I get relying on the sun for directions or whatever, but don't you think we're going into this blind? We have a map and some...some diary they won't even share with us, and that's it."

It shouldn't exist. Nobody has been able to find it in centuries.

My throat had become cotton-stuffed, impossible to remove no matter how hard I swallowed.

"We need to get that diary from them," I whispered, my voice barely audible over the steady footfalls of our camels. "Before we get to wherever we're going."

It shouldn't exist.

Trust me, I'd know.

My gaze slid over to Shasi's back. She and Mirza were deep in an animated conversation, unbothered by the sweltering sun.

"Auri," Dio hissed. The little thief looked up quickly. White, cloudlike curls escaped from her scarf, brushing against her pinkened skin.

She urged her camel closer.

"Do you think you can steal something for us?" asked Dio. Auri's entire face lit up. The pieces clicked into place.

"Mirza and Shasi have a book," I said quietly. "It's probably old. I don't know. We need you to get it."

Auri grinned like never before, her whole face crinkling and her pale eyes vanishing into tiny crescent moons.

"Oh, abso*lutely,*" she said.

Her over eagerness to steal should've put me on edge, but I couldn't shake Tristan's words.

Shasi and Mirza were hiding something from us.

CHAPTER TWENTY-NINE

SHASI

The sun was almost unbearably hot. Sweat glued my shirt to my back, creating a second skin that was wet and itchy and uncomfortable. With each minute spent under the sun, I daydreamed about chopping my hair off just to get the heat off my scalp and neck. Beneath my headscarf, my cheeks were flushed pink with the promising beginnings of sunburn and my forehead was so wet with sweat that I practically had an oasis on my face.

"It's *autumn*," I hissed, keeping my voice low enough that only Mirza could hear. His full lips tugged up into a grin and he shook his head.

"Shasi Dārayavahush, you have lived in Svadaeva your entire life and you're *just now* realizing we don't have any seasons besides summer?" he clicked his tongue. "Shame on you."

I repeated his words back to him, pitching my voice to make it seem mocking. He snorted, doing that thing he always did when he tried to hold back laughter where he bit his tongue and held his breath.

When we were younger and took lessons together – etiquette, mannerisms, this whole *finishing school* course Mother hired a tutor from Welinas to proctor – Mirza and I made a game out of trying to get the other to laugh without getting caught. Our tutors – the old hag from Welinas especially – were stricter than Amma and had shorter tempers than a moody camel and wouldn't hesitate to whip the backs of our hands with rulers if we acted distracted. We learned to be sneaky about it, embroidering phallic designs sneakily amongst our lotus flowers, writing lines of poems about sexual acts disguised by flowery prose. Even now, grown into our roles as princess and guard – though only one of us had a career change over the years – it seemed some things never changed.

"I wish we could find an oasis," I mused dreamily. "I'd give anything to go for a swim right now."

"And get my legs eaten off by a crocodile?" Mirza huffed. "No way. My legs are one of my greatest features."

"And what's *the* greatest? Your charming personality?" I raised a brow.

"That's second. My ass is first." He flashed me a grin. If I wasn't holding my reins, I would've thrown something – anything – at the bastard. He tipped his head back and laughed that deep belly laugh that made my insides twist and flutter and my cheeks warm.

"You *are* an ass," I shot back to cover up my embarrassment. He just lifted his shoulders in a nonchalant shrug.

"We should be nearing an outpost by noon," he said, switching the subject quickly. He raised his voice to his normal speaking tone, allowing the three others behind us to hear. "We can stop there and refill our canteens. See if any of them have directions for where to go."

I looked down at my hands. Right. We were relying on an unmarked map and a two-hundred-year-old drawing that may or may not even be legitimate. Shame churned in my belly. I was the crown princess, only a few years from becoming the powerful ruler of the most influential kingdom in the continent. Mirza was right. I'd lived my entire life in Svadaeva, and yet I didn't even know what the lands outside the main city looked like. I knew the capital was an oasis of its own in the middle of the desert, and I knew there were nomadic tribes and outposts scattered throughout, but... That was it.

A veinous river snaked around the capital, feeding from one ocean coast to another. Centuries and centuries ago, Svadaeva had been built on the fertile soil next to the river, the founders claiming Gausica herself had birthed such a perfect place to live in such an imperfect biome. But the river was long and wide, and there had to be other cities built on its banks besides the capital. How else could Svadaeva be the largest and most influential kingdom in the continent if it was comprised of one city and an endless desert?

But Mirza didn't seem to have an outstanding knowledge of the kingdom, either so either our tutors went over those details on a day we weren't paying attention or neither of us had been taught Svadaeva's geography.

Around noon, when the sun had reached its zenith, the sandstone buildings of the outpost were finally visible beyond the crests of the sand dunes. I nearly wept with joy as we led our camels into the tiny village. Tattered canvas coverings stretched from one old, decrepit building to the other. Birds rested atop the fabric, eyeing us warily with beady eyes. As we passed a building that looked to be little more than just a pile of bricks, I caught sight of a cheetah lounging in the sun, her tiny cubs playing with her lazily swishing tail.

"Where is everyone?" Dio asked from behind me. "I thought outposts were supposed to have a few permanent residents. At least, the outposts where I'm from are that way."

Mirza's eyes narrowed; I shot him a look that said *don't you dare say anything rude.*

"They're like that here, too," Cas supplied. "So, unless the residents turned into vultures and spotted cats, everyone must've left."

At once, like dust settling heavily after a storm, we seemed to all draw the same conclusion.

Hollows.

Unease, thick as syrup, clotted my veins. I urged my camel towards a wooden hitching rail that had seen far better days. It snorted and sank to its knees long enough for me to slide off and tie the reins to the rail.

"There are animals here," I said as I fixed my trousers, which had glued themselves to my inner thighs with sweat. It was the single most un-princess-like thing I had ever done in the presence of others, but the chafing on my thighs was too much for me to care about anything else.

"So, there must be clean water somewhere," Mirza said at the same time Cas quipped, "There has to be food here."

"Let's split up," I said. "Into teams of two. One group will look for food and water, the other will look for supplies and signs of people. Even with Hollows, people don't just disappear into thin air. Mir, you're with me."

"I'll go with them," Auri volunteered. Dio rolled her eyes. She'd dismounted her camel and stood as far from it as possible, glaring at the creature the same way the cheetah had glared a me.

"Mirza, Auri and I can look for people. Diora and Cassiel, can you look for food and water?" I asked. Neither of them protested. With that, I beckoned for the others to follow me as I led them into the belly of the outpost.

The shade from the canvas tarps did little to block the scalding assault from the sun. My curls were soaked with sweat, clinging to the back of my neck desperately enough that I strongly debated taking a knife to them.

Auri suddenly cursed loudly, causing both me and Mirza to jump. Mirza yanked his blade free, ready to cut down any foe that stood before us.

The foe, it turned out, was a scorpion scuttling across the sand.

Mirza sighed heavily, sheathing his sword, and holding an arm out for Auri to take. "They're harmless creatures, you know. There's a cheetah family back there just a way. I'm surprised *they* didn't freak you out."

"I can handle cats," Auri said as she puffed out her chest. She slid her arm around Mirza's, though, clinging to him tightly. Heat blossomed in my chest, turning the back of my throat sour. I barely paid attention to her as she said, "I can't handle creepy creatures with that many legs. Oh, you're surprisingly buff. I feel much safer now."

I dug my nails deep into my palms and walked ahead of them. I couldn't stand watching Auri grope Mirza's bicep for a second longer.

The outpost was a ghost town, and the further we ventured into it, the more evident that became. Vultures watched us closely as we poked around each abandoned building in search of anyone living there. The stone buildings were crumbling, as if they'd been abandoned for decades. There were no signs of life at *all*.

No dishes set out on tables.

No wardrobes full of clothes.

No curtains hanging from the windows or carpets adorning the floors.

It

Was

Empty.

The sun started to sink beneath the horizon by the time I finally decided to give up. We'd passed the same family of cheetahs three times and I didn't want to walk by a fourth time and risk them getting hungry. Still, the place seemed safer than out in the open to set up camp.

Dio and Cas were playing cards when we found them right where we'd parted ways hours earlier. A few canteens were neatly stacked by the fire they'd build.

"Ha!" Dio cried, throwing her cards down. "I win *again!* Goddess, you *suck* at this game! Pay up, big boy."

Cas grumbled incoherently and dropped a few coins in Dio's outstretched hand. Pocket change, really. Still, she beamed as she shoved it into her trousers.

"Did you find anything?" Auri asked, pulling away from Mirza to join them.

"We found a well," Cas said.

Dio began picking up the cards, shuffling them a few times before handing the deck to Cas.

"The water's clean," she added. "We tried it. Filled as many canteens as possible. But no food. Found a couple chicken bones, but that's it. This place looks completely abandoned."

I sat down, my tired legs practically weeping in relief, and grabbed one of the canteens. I took a deep gulp. The warm water was stale, but better than nothing. I took a few more gulps before setting it down.

The outpost was within my kingdom, and I had no idea what had happened to its occupants. Did Mother? How many more outposts and villages had been abandoned like this one?

"What do you know about the gods?" I blurted out. Everyone turned to face me. I toyed with the hem of my shirt awkwardly before saying, "Like, Medea and the old gods. We're all from different places. How true are the stories we've been told?"

Silence fell over the group as shame filled my belly.

Finally, Mirza – ever my savior – spoke up. "Medea was the daughter of Orinos and Gausica. She was created to cleanse the world, and both punish the sinners and praise the saints. When she fought the Old Gods – her parents and Heela and... Oh, I always forget the last one. Kain? Kale? I don't remember – she was pregnant with the child who was prophesized to follow in her footsteps once the gods rose from their sleep. Before them, though, there were two gods. Maulea and Eemyr or something?"

"No, there were three gods," Auri butted in. "Maulea, Eemyr, and Zina. Zina created Heela and Maulea created Gausica and Ora. Ora and Gausica birthed Orinos. They obviously had a bunch more children, but that's not the point.

Medea was *not* one of the two. She had a sibling who she tasked with guarding the tomb she locked the gods in, and then she went to sleep."

She huffed grumpily and grabbed a handful of dried mangos, stuffing it in her mouth.

"I didn't think you were religious, Auri," said Cas.

"'M not," she said with her mouth full, and cheeks stuffed. "But I *did* grow up in a temple, so I know everything about religion."

Dio looked up from where she was busy drawing in the sand with her finger. "Our stories are different," she said carefully, ignoring the look Mirza gave her. "Along with the gods and all the creatures of the world, Maulea and Zina created the humans and fae. Zina created creatures made of clay and earth, giving them hearts and strong bodies and minds that were unbreakable. She made them out of love, supposedly, though they were flawed. Maulea copied her idea, though she made her creatures out of stone and moss. She gave them wings and breathed some of her own magic into their little bodies. You know, in *our* stories, all the gods and goddesses have fangs and wings and elongated ears. Just saying."

"Where I'm from," Cas said, "Medea wasn't ever pregnant. And she was the only goddess, and she was the goddess of war. She struck down her enemies and slew monsters that crawled up from the depths of hell. She was a savior, but she abandoned us when she returned to the earth."

In the distance, one of the cheetahs chirruped, the sound sending shivers down my spine.

I glanced at my bag, which held the diary. Medea *had* been real. She had to have been. There were too many relics of her reign left behind for her to have *not* existed.

"What if," I said slowly, not taking my eyes from the bag, "Diora's mythology is correct? What if Zina created the humans and Maulea the Fae, and Eemyr created the Hollows?"

I just couldn't wrap my brain around the Hollows, no matter how hard I tried. If they were neither human nor fae, what were they, where had they come from, and why, after centuries of silence, did they emerge seventeen years ago?

The iron flower safely tucked in my pocket had turned leaden, growing hot and heavy where it rested against my thigh.

"But they existed millennia ago," protested Dio. "Like, thousands and thousands and *thousands* of years ago. Why create something that just now came into being? And how would they fit into the whole *everything* and *nothing* and *what's in between* thing the old gods had going?"

Cas reached for a cloth bundle of nuts and popped a handful in his mouth. He chewed slowly, thoughtfully, and swallowed before saying, "Well, Maulea gave the fae *everything* – wings and magic and lengthened lifespans. Zina gave us *nothing*. But I guess that doesn't answer how the Hollows are *everything in between*."

I stared at my bag. Something just wasn't adding up, and it itched the back of my head. I wanted desperately to submerge my hand through my skull to prod at my brain and relieve the scratch.

"When were cameras invented?" I asked.

There was a silence, followed by another, thankfully more distant, cheetah chirrup.

"I think around the 1780s," Cas said. "But darkrooms have been around since the 1500s."

Mirza nudged me with a canteen. I took it and drank deeply, though part of me wished it was wine inside and not water. That damn itch wasn't going away, and sobriety wasn't helping.

With a groan, I flopped onto my back and stared at the inky sky above, picking out all the constellations whose names I knew.

Why did the author of the diary draw the temple if they were able to take a photograph of it? Why wasn't the temple ever mentioned again?

Where did the people of this outpost go?

CHAPTER THIRTY

KORE

Ceralis beamed, his chest puffed out with pride. He beheld the skull like it was a priceless trophy while I stared at it in abject horror. Bile tickled the back of my throat, persisting no matter how hard I swallowed. How did a *fae skull* end up in a *pond* outside the Hollow palace?

Ceralis must've noticed my fear, as his grin slipped. He cocked his head to the side like a confused puppy, wet, inky tendrils of hair catching in his dark eyelashes.

"I *told* you I'm the Official Royal Bone Collector," he said, as if that would ease my fear. It didn't. If anything, it did the *opposite*.

"Ceralis, *what* kinds of bones are you sent to collect?" I asked, my tongue heavy and my throat thick with unrelenting bile.

I regretted the question as soon as I'd said it.

"I can show you," he answered, as nonchalant as ever. "I have to keep them in the catacombs, and Donny gets *so* mad when he goes down there and it's messy, but *I* know where everything is, and I think that's the only thing that really, truly matters. I'll show you. I have to bring this one there anyways."

He picked up the skull like it was a ball and began marching towards the palace. I spared the discarded towel a nervous glance – someone would surely come and fetch it before it grew thick with mildew – before picking up my skirts and hurrying after Ceralis.

Ceralis wove through the narrow palace halls, leading me down steep staircases that brought us deeper and deeper into the bowels of the castle. The further down we went, the colder the air grew. I wrapped my arms tightly around myself, wishing I'd brought a coat or a shawl with me. Ceralis, despite having soaked hair that seeped into his shirt, didn't seem bothered by the lack of heat in the slightest.

He also didn't seem to mind how dark it had grown.

Before I could ask if there was a light or a lamp or even a torch, Ceralis pushed open a door that had been previously shielded by shadows.

Tiny lights, almost like fireflies, hung from the arched ceiling, creating a warm glow to the room. Tall cases stretched towards the lights, glass panels protecting their insides from harm. A table was in the middle, covered in papers and saws and other surgical tools I couldn't name. Littered amongst the tools were jars and bowls and old crate boxes.

Ceralis grabbed a cord hanging from the ceiling and tugged on it, illuminating more lights.

The room was *filled* with bones.

Skulls filled the cases, femurs and long bones hung from hooks along the walls, ribs and pelvises were haphazardly balanced on metal rods and stacks of boxes. The jars and bowls were filled with tiny bones and teeth – gods, there were so many teeth. Some were small, like the milk teeth from a child, while others were dangerously thin and needle-sharp.

"My catacombs!" Ceralis said proudly, arms spread wide. He'd set the fae skull on the table, seemingly forgetting about it.

"What is this?!" I hissed before I could even stop myself.

His smile fell instantly. "I told you, Miss Etoile. It's the catacombs. I'm the Official Royal Bone Collector, remember? I have to collect bones that end up down here when they're not supposed to and clean them up and keep them here. I think Donny studies them sometimes. I don't know why, but he always locks me out when he works down here. I think – Miss, Etoile, are you all right? You look paler than a sheet. Oh, don't tell me you're scared of bones. They're just *bones.* You got a whole skeleton inside you, you know. It's not like I kill these people. I just find their bones and clean them up and try to give them a bit of honor back."

I took a step back, choking down vomit. Death had never scared me. How could it when it was such a natural thing that happened to everyone? Everything I created died, turning to ash, and vanishing in the blink of an eye. I had wished for my own demise more than once over the years. As such, bones didn't scare me, either.

But seeing this...this catacomb of bones that were just *found* rubbed me wrong. There were children's *teeth,* and some of the skulls looked far too small to belong to a fully grown adult. There were no animal skulls, either, only human and fae.

And no Hollow skulls, either.

It was the shocking unknown of it all that made my knees buckle and my stomach flip.

"Ceralis, what do you mean you *find* these bones?" I asked slowly.

Ceralis, for once, was silent. He stared at his newest collectible, as if it would have the answers. I opened my mouth to ask the question again, but he beat me to it.

He said, "I mean I find them. Bones just end up here, all over Heladés. I don't know why. I think Donny studies them so he can figure out why. He just tells me to find the lost bones and bring them here. Sometimes people have to call and say they found a femur or a rib or a humerus or something and I have to go fetch it. Donny probably has all the answers. He usually does. Or the library might, I don't know. Do you need to sit down, Miss Etoile?"

I shook my head. How *naïve* I'd been, thinking Adonis was this perfect man, this kind and gentle soul who only wished to help. Who had I run into the arms of? He collected *bones* and wore shadows and was the king of the damn *Hollows*.

Maybe Mother was right. Maybe I should have stayed with her and accepted my punishment for traipsing around with the *King of the Hollows*. Maybe this was my divine punishment for disobeying her one too many times.

"Come, Miss Etoile." Ceralis took my hand, ignoring me when I flinched at his sudden icy touch. "Let's get you back inside. If we can find Donny, I bet he'd be willing to answer your questions."

Unable to argue and unwilling to stay, I wordlessly followed as he retraced our steps, bringing us back to the main floor of the palace.

I glanced at the collar around Ceralis's throat. Had he put that there himself, or was that Adonis's doing? Why would he need to wear a collar meant for a dog?

"– *really* mad after his sister basically banished him, but I don't have sibl – okay, that's a lie, I *do* have siblings sort of, but they technically don't exist, and I haven't seen them in *years* but that's beside the point. *Anyways,* as I was saying – oh, look, there's *Enodia.*" Ceralis dropped my hand and covered his nose instead, just as Enodia walked across the hall. A pair of servants with their faces covered by black lacey silk trailed after her. She turned in our direction and gave a smile before walking off.

And then, before I could remember to ask Ceralis about the previous women brought here, the familiar feeling of Adonis's shadows slithered around my ankles, and a hand shrouded in darkness grabbed my jaw.

His warmth pressed against my back, and in a low voice he said, "there you are, my Little Star."

CHAPTER THIRTY-ONE

AURI

Stealing a diary was amongst the easier things I'd done in my life. I'd volunteered to go with Mirza and Shasi in hopes that they'd mention it or allude to where it was, but they didn't. So, I waited until we got back and watched the two of them. And when Shasi began staring at one of her bags, I knew exactly where it was. It would've been much harder if Dio and Cas weren't on my side, since then I'd have to slip the book out without being noticed by *four* people instead of two.

The second Shasi looked away to take the canteen from Mirza, the two of them distracted, I grabbed Shasi's bag and switched it out with mine, the two identical in every way except for their contents.

Finished drinking, Shasi looked back at her bag – *my* bag – none the wiser. I pretended to rummage around mine, thankfully finding some of the same nuts Cas was eating inside. I pulled them free, not after brushing my fingers against the familiar leather binding of a book.

Bingo.

"I can take first watch tonight," I volunteered, knowing damn well I wasn't about to do it.

But I needed the others to *think* I was willing.

"No, that's okay," Mirza quickly said. I had to bite the inside of my lip to keep from smirking. Men were always such naïve dumbasses. Mirza knew I was a thief, and likely thought I'd use the guise of night to steal from all of them. That I was eager to keep watch so I could steal their rations and expensive clothes for myself.

And, just like that, I'd bought myself an alibi.

Because how could I possibly steal the crown princess's precious book if I was asleep the whole night?

"I can take the first watch," Cas said, because he wasn't as big of an idiot. "I don't mind. I doubt I'll be sleeping much anyways with those big ass cats just down the way."

"I'll take second, then," said Shasi, foolishly. "Mir, do you mind third?" When her guard shook his head, my plan solidified.

I'd figure out what they were keeping in that book, swap our bags back, and sleep like I hadn't just committed a crime.

We finished eating in silence, then prepared our bedrolls for sleep. I used my stolen bag as a pillow, curling up and closing my eyes to pretend to sleep.

I counted to a hundred, then two hundred, then three hundred before the steady breathing of everyone around me signaled me to open my eyes and sit up.

Only Shasi and Mirza were asleep.

"Did you get it?" hissed Dio, her voice quiet as to not wake the others.

I grinned, pulling the book from the bag. Cas and Dio crowded close as I cracked the cover open.

"'For my darling child, I will find you again one day. The red string of fate cannot keep us apart for long,'" I read. "This is literally just a diary. When do things get good?" I flipped through the pages. A small scrap of paper fluttered out.

Dio grabbed it. "Ah," she said. "I think *this* is what they were looking at."

She showed us the picture. It was a drawing of a temple nestled between dunes of sand. The temple we were likely looking for.

"'Temple of Medea, Svadaevan Desert,'" she read from the back of the picture. "It has a number, but it's smudged. It either says *102* or *702*. Or something like that. I know neither of you have eyes as good as mine, but here. See if you can figure it out."

Cas took the paper, and I leaned close to look at it.

702. There was no number in front of the date. Meaning this drawing was *a thousand* years old.

I *almost* dropped the journal but didn't. It didn't feel ancient. It felt like a few decades old at most, if even that. The leather had grown soft over the years, and the pages had yellowed, but it hadn't withered into a decrepit state. Either the archivists at the Svadaevan Library were masters at their craft, or this thing wasn't really that old.

Or, I realized with a sinking sensation, it was magic.

Dio and Cas bickered over the drawing, as if figuring out the date on the back was the most important thing in the world. I looked down at the book, suddenly feeling guilty as I flipped through the pages. I stopped towards the end.

I scattered the Relics across the continent in hopes that nobody would ever wake them. Though, my dear child, I have left clues at each site that will make it easy for you to find them if the time is right. It's no secret what the Relics are, but in case that knowledge has been lost to history, I have listed them here: the Lyre, the Sword, the Chalice, the Bolt, and the Mausoleum. Find them and use them if malevolent powers threaten this world once again. Should these Relics fall into the wrong hands, the world as we know it will fall to chaos. He should never wake, but if He does, only these Relics can stop Him as they did once before. My time is

Tears prickled my eyes for reasons I couldn't even begin to comprehend. I slammed the book shut before my crying could ruin the ancient pages. Dio grabbed it from my hands and shoved the drawing into a random spot.

"Put it back," Cas hissed. "They could wake at any moment with how loud Dio's being."

"Me?!" Dio smacked his arm. "You're the loud one, you massive oaf!"

They bitched back and forth, showing no signs of stopping. I stuffed the book back into Shasi's bag and quickly swapped it back with my own. As I lay down with my head against the bag, staring at the stars that were *right,* I tried to quell the aching in my heart.

Why had I felt like those words were written for *me?*

I dreamt of a desert of snow and vultures when I finally managed to fall asleep that night. I skipped breakfast before we set off the next morning, unable to bring up my appetite. The unease I'd felt when reading the journal had followed me like a shadow, and I couldn't quite shake it away.

Zina seemed to sense my discomfort as she snorted and slowed her pace. I loosened my grip on her reins, muttering an apology as I did so.

We rode through the morning and stopped at noon to look over the map and eat. The whole time, I couldn't quell the unease that boiled in my stomach. There was no way a diary from a thousand years ago would have been written for *me.* I was an orphan who took to living on the streets, who used soggy newspapers as blankets and drank from puddles if I got desperate enough. I was a lowlife thief, not some...some fantasy protagonist whose legacy predated the decade I lived in.

After letting our camels rest, we climbed back on them and continued towards the first spot on the map.

It came into view when the sun was low in the sky – not quite sunset, but somewhere close – and the air was hot and dry. Mountains of sand reached for the clouds, almost concealing the temple. Sandstone weathered by the years made up the foundation of the massive structure. Two statues stood guard outside, standing on the crumbling steps.

The same temple from the diary.

Shasi was the first to dismount once we got closer. She tied the reins to a collapsed pillar thin enough to withhold the knot.

"Well," she said once we were all on our feet. "Now is probably the best time to explain this to you. I found this hundred-year-old diary in the library, and it talked about *this*. The Temple of Medea. If we're to find any clues on how to kill the Hollows, they'll be here."

I swallowed thickly, forcing down the lump that had built in my throat.

Not a *hundred* years. A *thousand* years.

My legs felt like gelatin as I forced myself up the steps and into the temple. Instantly, the temperature dropped, the sandstone and marble blocking out most of the intense heat from the sun.

Statues lined the walls, alternating between pillars made of marble veined with gold. Each was so goliath I couldn't even make out the features on their faces, but the lack of shirt and swollen belly led me to believe most were of Medea. The others were of a male with long hair that looked soft even though it was carved from marble.

Paintings and carvings on the walls depicted the same god and Medea, along with a triple-headed dog and a figure wearing a cloak eerily like the ones the Hollows wore. I shivered, walking past the carvings quickly.

I passed a corridor as I hurried to catch up with the others when the tantalizing glint of gold caught my eye. I stopped and stepped backwards. The others were so caught up in the temple that they wouldn't miss me if I slipped away, right?

I followed the gleam of gold until I came across a sunspot. A crack in the ceiling let in just enough molten sunlight to illuminate and bathe a crooked painting in gold.

I blanched, my stomach turning sour.

Painted against a backdrop of night with diamond-like stars and a milky moon was a woman. Her inky hair spilled over one shoulder, her mismatched eyes – one blue and one brown – fanned by thick lashes. She had a smattering of beauty marks across her face and décolletage. Her doe eyes stared at mine in a way that made me sick.

That was *my* face.

What was a painting of me doing in a thousand-year-old temple?

I stepped closer, scouring the painting for a signature, a name, *anything* that could tell me who had painted this and *why*.

"Ri!" Dio called, her voice faint and echoey from wherever she was. "You coming?!"

I wet my lips with the tip of my tongue. "Just a second!"

That face... It's mine.

It's mine.

There is a portrait with my face in the Temple of Medea thousands of miles from where I'm from.

I stumbled back until my shoulders hit something. I spun as it clattered to the ground. Another painting.

Dread froze my veins like ice as I picked up the painting and turned it over. My hands shook like the earth during a quake.

It was the same woman, though she wore no shirt. In one hand, she held a chalice. In the other, she held a sword. Her pale skin glowed blue from the flash of lightning in the back, and on the ground was a golden *thing,* and though I couldn't make it out – the canvas, unfortunately, had been ripped – I knew it was a lyre.

The woman was heavily pregnant, the way she was always depicted.

I dropped the painting, letting it fall face-first to the ground, catching sight of a few scribbles and four letters I knew better than anything.

AURI.

I collapsed to my knees, clutching my mouth as if that would keep back the acrid vomit I kept choking up. The stain on my hand *burned* like I had dipped it in fire, and my core almost *tugged* me towards the painting. I hardly even registered that the nonsensical scribbles on the back resembled a map.

No, I was too preoccupied with the *fear* that came with the realization that the goddess Medea simply *had* to be my mother.

CHAPTER THIRTY-TWO

KORE

The second I felt his heat against me, I completely forgot about the mysterious other women Adonis had brought to Heladés. I forgot about everything really, from the way the mothers in town stared at me in horror to the catacombs lurking beneath the palace floors. I melted like ice cream on a hot day.

"I just went into town," I said, squishing some of the naughty flowers that had grown around my ankles and were rubbing up against Adonis's legs like overly affectionate cats. "With Enodia. And Ceralis showed me his...ah..."

"My collection!" Ceralis butted in. Adonis pulled his shadows away ever so slightly. "In the catacombs. Miss Etoile helped me find a skull, so I showed her where the bones are. And then we found Miss Enodia, but you can always tell where she is because she smells *so* much. And then you –"

Adonis chuckled, reaching his shadows out to ruffle Ceralis's hair. "Thank you for showing Etoile around. I am sure she appreciated it. Do you mind if I steal her away for a bit, Ceralis?"

My heart damn near fell out of my chest. I was starting to understand why my traitorous flowers felt so affectionate towards him.

Ceralis beamed and nodded so fast his hair became a dark blur. He said something that might have been a goodbye, but his words came out faster than I could decipher.

"You must have questions," said Adonis as I watched Ceralis scamper off, chasing poor Enodia like she was a cat. "Especially after seeing the catacombs. I promise you; I do not play a role in harvesting those bones. They appear, sometimes in ponds, sometimes on lawns or in the middle of the street. I have Ceralis fetch them because he is quite good at smelling death."

I *did* have questions, but the catacombs weren't where I wanted to start.

"Can we sit?" I asked. Thorny vines sprouting tiny flowers had begun creeping up the walls, and while their faces were concealed, the handful of servants in the hallway with us had stopped and were clearly staring in shock.

Not at all unlike the women in town.

Adonis's shadows curled around my torso, giving me a squeeze before letting go. "As you wish, my little star." Like a blot of ink shifting across a page, he started walking, and all I could do was follow, leaving a trail of tiny flowers in my wake.

He led me to the same sitting room that I'd gone to when first arriving. The fire was roaring, casting an orange glow that danced across the various rocks and gems he had on display. The coffee table had been mostly cleaned, though a few chalices half-empty sat strewn about, and a bowl full of ripe pomegranate seeds sat in the middle. I sat down, grabbing a few seeds, and rolling them between my fingers, testing how plump and full of juice they were.

"I will answer your questions provided you do not inquire about three specific topics: my past, my present, and my future." Adonis closed the door and sat down, his shadows swirling about him and drinking up the light that dared to venture too close.

I squished one of the seeds, the juice exploding on my fingertips. His past, his present, and his future. They were such vague terms, but they ruled out any questions about Adonis himself. Asking him to remove his shadows might fall under the *present* category, or the *past* category if he was hiding old scars – whether physical or not – with the inky tendrils. Asking about the bones was futile, since it seemed he, like Ceralis, had no idea from whence they derived from. I rolled the remaining seeds between my fingers absently. I could ask about the catacombs – what purpose they served, what experiments Adonis did when he locked Ceralis out. I could ask about Ceralis and why he wore that collar, though I quickly shot down that idea. If I wanted to know, and I did, I would have to ask Ceralis himself. The parameters I'd been given took away most of my options, simple as they were.

Adonis leaned to pour the contents of his abundance of goblets into one, clearing up some of the clutter. I popped three seeds into my mouth, crushing them with my teeth.

"Are the Hollows afraid of magic?" I asked.

His shadows moved, indicating that he'd looked up. "Pardon?"

My cheeks flushed. I hastily wiped the pomegranate juice off on my skirt. "Enodia and I went into town earlier. This little boy tripped and fell and without thinking, I used my magic to create a net to protect him. He was okay, but his mother... She looked terrified. And just a moment ago, one of the servants was staring at my plants like they'd never seen it before."

Somewhere beneath his shadows, Adonis chuckled. "Oh, little star. It isn't the magic they're wary of; it's the life. Things do not grow down here. They do not understand your gift. They don't know what to make of it."

I let go of the breath I'd been holding since seeing that woman glare at me. It was as if a weight had been lifted from my shoulders.

"Your servants," I continued, switching to another question that hopefully didn't fall under the categories of *past, present,* and *future* Adonis. "Why do they wear facial coverings? Why make that a part of their uniform?"

He brought the chalice into his shadows, the golden cup disappearing into a fog of black. It reappeared a moment later when he set it down. "Perhaps we should make this a game, little star. For each question you ask, and I answer, I get to ask a question in turn. We will each be allowed to pass on answering three times." Three shadowy tally marks appeared hovering just above where his shoulder would be. They vanished moments later.

My stomach churned. I wasn't used to talking about myself. Mother often forbade it, claiming narcissism was a curse just as anything else.

I set my jaw, nodding once. "Your guidelines also apply." Even though I had no way of knowing the future.

Could Adonis see *the future?*

"Clever, Little Star." I could hear the grin in his voice. "How did you come about my name so quickly?"

I thought of the strange pale-haired boy at the library with his book of Hollow names. I trusted Adonis, but... Something tugged on my insides. I couldn't just give that up. I had no idea who that strange boy was, yet I found myself defending him, keeping his identity a secret.

"I found it in a book," I said, and it wasn't a lie. "At the library. 'Adonis Nyx, King of the Hollows.' Unless there was another Adonis Nyx who also went by the alias of Aita, I figured it was you."

His shadows stilled, and my stomach sank, the pomegranate seeds I'd eaten turning fermented. Had he realized I was lying? Would he punish me now? I diverted my gaze quickly, making sure he couldn't lock eyes with me to consume my soul. He still didn't know my true name, right?

"How strange that humans would keep such a precious thing in a book," he mused. "To answer your earlier question, I don't force my staff to wear the masks. But since I'm shrouded in anonymity, it only makes sense that the employees here are, too. They can see through the fabric just fine. Our eyes are extremely sensitive to light, so the coverings protect their vision."

Hollows were always seen wearing dark cloaks, their faces hidden. Was that because their eyes were sensitive to the sun? There wasn't a sun here; it only made sense. Enodia's and Ceralis's eyes were like pools of ink, all pupil, and no iris. That *had* to make them so incredibly sensitive to the light.

"You creatures of the living have seasons," said Adonis, already moving on to his next question. "Summer, spring, winter, and fall. Which is your favorite?"

"Spring," I said without a beat of hesitation. His silence only prompted me to continue, the excited word-vomit spilling out before I had the chance to stop it. "Mother always insists on doing spring cleaning, which I can't stand, but I love everything else. We have a garden that starts to grow when the days get warmer, and all the baby animals are born. One of our neighbor's barn cats had kittens last spring and she brought them to sleep in the flowerbox outside our kitchen window. And the ducks in the pond in the forest all have ducklings and sometimes the mother ducks will let me hold them. And the flowers! All the flowers bloom in spring. Cherry trees, roses, gardenias, all of them! I know I can grow flowers whenever and wherever I want, but there's just something so special about watching little daisies and marigolds pop up and bloom on their own. And the weather is warm, but not too warm, so I can go outside barefoot. And when it rains the rain is warm. I can't stand the fall and I loathe the winter even more."

My cheeks and ears warmed as I continued to babble on. Mother rarely let me out of the house, but most of my fondest memories were of the springtime. Whenever the cold of winter faded away, I felt stronger, too, like my magic had become more powerful. It weakened during the fall, and even more so during the winter.

Adonis's shadows had become hazy, but I still couldn't make out the figure beneath them. His posture had relaxed, his spine curved as he leaned forward with curiosity.

But my excitement slowly faded when I looked at the shelf behind Adonis, the shadows from the fire making the rocks look like yellowed skulls. The empty chalices on the table could have been filled with milk teeth and I would've been none the wiser. The pomegranate seeds in my hand reminded me too much of bone shards; I let them tumble to the ground and roll under the settee and coffee table.

"Where exactly *is* Heladés?" I asked slowly. Then, to clarify, I hastily added, "Like, on a map. It doesn't seem to fit anywhere on the continent."

If the Hollows were truly fae like I'd always been led to believe, Heladés would have to be somewhere in Faerie, but I'd never seen room for it on a map. But it couldn't fit amongst the human kingdoms, either, since all three of the monarchs were greedy when it came to land and wouldn't spare even a square inch of space for the King of the Hollows. I knew there had to be more continents out there, somewhere beyond the stretch of sea that blurred into a glimmering line that met the sky. There were islands with nomadic peoples, and even old fae stories about cities underwater. Had Adonis somehow brought me to a different continent – one without sunshine or plants or natural life – when I called his name?

And what, if not human nor fae, exactly *are* the Hollows?

"Heladés is a city-state," Adonis explained. I bit my tongue to keep from saying that I didn't ask what the geo-political state of Heladés was. He continued nonetheless; "Roughly the size of half your continent. Maybe a third. I digress. Heladés is... It's basically what you humans and fae consider to be Hell. We exist on a plane slightly below and to the side of your continent, skewed as if you crossed your eyes and looked at a map. There are places where the lines blur – your Lavoisin Forest, for example."

He paused, then said, "Now would probably be a good time to tell you that Heladés is not a realm of life. It's quite the opposite, really. I believe your stories referred to this place as the Underworld."

The nausea that struck me after learning where exactly I'd fled to was so sharp and so sudden that I retired to my room before Adonis had the chance to explain himself any further. Forgotten were all the other questions I had for him – the other women, the purpose of the catacombs. I had forsaken myself, damning myself straight to hell to avoid being *grounded.* Mother wouldn't know where to look for me.

I had, undoubtedly, messed up beyond my own comprehension.

I should have known. The lack of life, the darkness and death that shrouded the Hollows, the sunless sky reminiscent of a cave, sans stalactites.

I sat up from where I'd flopped down on my borrowed bed, clasping a hand over my neck, frantically searching for my pulse. When I found it, my heart fluttering like a hummingbird's wings, I let out a shaky breath. I wasn't dead.

But did that mean the Hollows *were?*

For seventeen years, we'd been trying to figure out what the Hollows were. What if they were just the lost souls of humans and fae?

But there had been children in town, children who clung to mothers. It was impossible for that many blood relations to die at the same time, right?

Unless...

The massacres from seventeen years ago had been devastating. I'd caught glimpses of old news clippings and sections in books recounting the thousands and thousands of deaths wrought by the Hollows. I'd heard Mother whisper about it when she thought I wasn't listening, describing the slaughter with the details of someone who had experienced it first-hand. I'd only been a child, my memories of fire and carnage and screaming hazy at best.

I lay back down, my vision blurring as I tried not to focus on the ceiling.

Ceralis and Enodia had heartbeats. They had lungs that filled with air and stomachs that required food. Dead souls didn't need any of those things. Maybe... Maybe *Underworld* was simply a mistranslation.

I rolled onto my side, curling up against my pillow.

Adonis was keeping far too many secrets from me, and he, I decided, owed me nothing less than the truth.

CHAPTER THIRTY-THREE

DIORA

I gathered my hair up, tying it into a messy bun to keep it off my neck. The temple was considerably cooler than the scalding desert outside, but even the hottest summers in Lysaen couldn't compare to the Svadaevan heat. I could only hope that the air would be cooler and less stale behind the massive, gilded door we stood before.

Sometime between entering the temple and finding the door, we'd lost Auri.

I wasn't too worried. She was a competent adult, and she was a thief inside an abandoned temple practically made of solid gold. The only thing that could rival her excitement would be a child in a candy shop where there were no limits to what they could take.

Still, it had been a while, and the temple was massive. She could've easily gotten lost.

I turned my gaze back to the door. It stood taller than both me and Cas combined, arched, and etched with carvings depicting some story I didn't know.

A fae with feathered wings. A girl surrounded by vines. A dog with three slobbering heads. More nonsensical drawings I didn't care to interpret.

On each of the corners were carvings that piqued my interest. A stringed instrument that looked like a harp. A jagged bolt of lightning. A sword leaning against a tree. A decrepit building that almost resembled the temple but in miniature. And on the center of the door, sliced perfectly in half, was a chalice.

"Ri!" yelled Cas. "Where the fuck are you?! You can't steal everything; we have to carry it all back!"

I bit my tongue, deciding not to ruin his argument by saying I'd open a portal to take us back.

"Auri, you can't steal!" shouted Shasi, her voice frantic. She stepped away from the door, slippers barely making a sound against the crackled marble floor. "This is a holy temple! I don't care if you're atheist, you can't steal from a goddess!"

I didn't doubt Auri *had* stolen from a goddess before. It seemed like the type of petty shit she'd do, especially after fleeing the temple she'd grown up in.

Shasi grumbled to herself before shouting for Auri again. I turned towards Cas.

"I'm not saying we should peek at what's behind this door, but I'm definitely saying we should peek at what's behind this door," I whispered. After Auri had put the journal away, I'd stayed awake to peek at it again. There was an entry about a set of relics, and this door pictured all of them, assuming the miniature harp-thing was a lyre.

I had no idea what a lyre was.

I'd felt like Tristan, though, in that moment where I snuck out the journal. A thief like Auri. A spy like Tristan.

"Sorry," came Auri's ragged, panting voice. She stumbled to a halt, bracing her hands on her knees – though one was conspicuously hidden by her sleeve

– as she gulped in breaths of air. Her pockets didn't bulge or sag. Pride flitted across my heart at the thought of Auri resisting her temptations to steal.

"Oh!" Auri said suddenly, her lungs miraculously filled with air. "This door! We have to go through it." She put her hand over her chest and took a step closer. I stepped aside to give her access.

She reached out, brushing her fingertips against the chalice carving. The door groaned, hinges wailing as it slid open.

And the floor promptly gave way beneath our feet.

Someone screamed – maybe it was me – as we tumbled into sheer darkness, a mouth-like pit that swallowed us whole. I thrust out my hands, trying to open a portal or use some sort of magic, but the light only sputtered before giving out completely, like iron manacles had been clamped around my wrists. I clawed at my corset, as if I could use my wings to fly, to avoid being crushed like a measly insect.

But our wings weren't for flying. Centuries upon centuries had led us to forget the true purpose of our wings, and as I tumbled helplessly though the air, my wings as useless as wet paper, I cursed my ancestors.

An eternity passed in the span of a second before I hit the ground. *Thud!* The air escaped my lungs, red-hot pain searing through my body. I was alive.

I sat up, groaning as I did so. One of my ribs poked painfully against my lungs. My corset, as much as I loved it, did nothing to help with the pain.

Screw propriety at this point.

I blindly yanked on the laces, ripping the corset free and letting it fall to the ground. It was dark, so dark that I couldn't see my hands in front of my face, but I fumbled with my tunic and managed to rip two very uneven holes in the back. I pushed my wings through, the thin membranes stretching out in a way that brought tears to my eyes.

"Who's dead?!" yelled Cas from somewhere in the dark.

"Goddess, I *wish* I was," shouted back Mirza. A loud groan from Shasi confirmed she was alive, too.

"I'm here," I croaked. I stood on wobbly legs, teetering like a newborn foal. I grasped blindly at the dark, trying to find purchase to keep from falling over.

"Ri?" Cas said. "You alive?"

Silence.

"Auri?" I called.

"Guys," came her soft voice. "You should come see this."

It would be great if I could see anything, I thought. Still, I forced one foot in front of the other, following her voice.

She was humming. I didn't know the song, but the melody was familiar. It drew me right towards her, guiding my feet through the inky darkness where I would have otherwise wandered aimlessly.

Then, slicing through the darkness like a fire-doused blade came light. I squinted against it, nearly running into Auri as I stepped from the cloistered darkness into the vestibule. Marble columns with gold veining kept the arched, frescoed ceiling in place, not unlike the columns in the other part of the temple. Only, these weren't as worn and cracked; time had yet to touch them.

At the very end of the lengthy nave was a pedestal, and atop the pedestal was a single cup, made of iron or silver or some other grey metal without even the simplest of detail work.

"Holy shit," breathed Auri.

"This is a sacred temple," chastised Shasi. But even she let out a low breath when she saw the *holiness* surrounding the dingy old cup.

"You don't think—" started Cas.

"I'm going to steal it," cut in Auri.

"Don't you dare," scolded Mirza, but even he didn't make a move to stop her as she stepped forward.

In an instant, arrows sprung out of seemingly nowhere, striking the space Auri had just been standing in. They would have impaled her had Cas not tackled her to the ground first. Auri stared at him, pale eyes wide.

"Your wings," she said, her gaze landing on me.

And then the others looked at me. I shrunk into myself, wishing I hadn't torn my corset off.

"Pretty," said the Svadaevan princess, who had looked at me like I was a monster when I revealed my bloodline. "Any chance you can fly over there and inspect what that cup is?"

She... Has no idea what that thing is, I realized.

"We can't fly," I said. "Our wings are too flimsy. I think this place is booby trapped –" I ignored Auri's immature snicker "–so getting to the chalice isn't going to be a walk in the park."

Goddess, I wished Tristan were here. He'd be able to deduce where all the traps were just by taking a cursory glance around the vestibule. He was better suited for this heist. For this entire scheme. Why had *I* been the one to get dragged all the way to Svadaeva? I was an *assassin;* he stole information.

But... This whole thing wasn't safe, so maybe it was for the best that he was back in Lysaen, far from the horrors of the temple and the desert.

"Ri stepped here," said Cas. "So, if I step here..." he gingerly placed his foot onto the tile adjacent to the one Auri had triggered. We all tensed, waiting for something to happen. Nothing did. I breathed a sigh of relief.

Cas reached into his belt and pulled free a handful of rubble he must've picked up when exploring earlier. He tossed the rocks onto the path, letting them scatter across the tiles.

Arrows sprung free from every direction, slicing through the air faster than I could process.

"Plan B," said Cas. "We just fucking make a run for it."

CHAPTER THIRTY-FOUR

SHASI

Cas grabbed Diora's wrist and pulled her as he began running, ignoring the maelstrom of arrows raining down on us. Dio just barely managed to grab onto shell-shocked Auri.

I grabbed Mirza's hand and ran after them.

Arrows nicked my arms and cheeks, shredding my clothes as I ran. Blood dribbled down my forehead, mixing with sweat that I couldn't spare a second to wipe away. Each wrong tile we stepped on released another flurry of arrows that aimed to kill. One struck me in the ear, tearing through cartilage like it was paper. I didn't even have the breath to spare to scream.

An arrow pierced right through the thin, gossamer membrane of Dio's wing. She yelped in pain, stumbling over her own feet, and nearly collapsing against Cas. Bright blood welled up like a carnation, dripping down her twitching wing and staining the jade limb red.

And then, just when I thought it would take us a century to reach it, the arrows stopped pummeling us and the podium was within reach.

The cup was so…anticlimactic. It looked no special than the cups we used at home, if not less than that. It glinted silver, though age had dulled its shine to a drab grey. The rim was chipped.

Auri bent over and vomited all over the ground. She choked, furiously pushing her hair out of her face only for it to frustratingly fall back. I took a step closer.

But Dio beat me to it. She grabbed Auri's mane of curls and tied them with the leather thong she'd used in her own hair. Auri dry heaved, unable to force the bile out of her throat. Dio patted her back, ignoring the gaping wound in her wing.

And I couldn't even do a damn thing.

"You okay?" Mirza panted beside me. He looked up through his thick lashes, pale eyes full of worry.

I put on a smile that didn't quite reach my eyes and said, "I'm still alive, aren't I? Now, let's see what all this fuss was about."

I reached out, fingers sliding around the warm – *warm?* – metal of the chalice, pulling it off the podium.

Click.

The sound was so faint I didn't hear it until it was too late.

"Shasi Dārayavahush, you never think before you act," my mother, goddess bless her, used to scold me. *"You sleep through your classes, you don't care to learn dances, you are loud and clumsy when you sneak home at night – and yes, I know you sneak out into the city at night, don't you dare play dumb with me. I am your mother."*

"Shasi, my love, you are a brilliant young lady, a wonderful heir, but perhaps you should take a moment to think before you act," said Amma in the gentle tone that was somehow harsher and scarier than when she yelled.

"My darling girl, you wouldn't have gotten into this mess had you paused to think about the consequences to your actions first," my father said. "You always rush into situations that could have been solved much easier if you had thought things through first."

"Shas, you know I love you, but maybe if you thought things through before rushing into this head-first, you wouldn't have gotten hurt," Mirza scolded as he wrapped the bandage around my arm, where I had injured it in a skirmish earlier.

The wall across from us slid open, and a *creature* emerged from the darkness. It seemed to be made of sandstone, its body hard and yellowed like the temple exterior. Its bottom half was made of thick, rippling muscular legs, each one as wide as my entire torso, and I didn't have a slim figure. The upper half was a bovine, though still humanoid in some features. It dragged a mace twice as long as I was tall.

"What in the ever-loving fuck *is that thing?!"* shrieked Auri as she scrambled to hide behind Dio, who looked just as terrified. Her wings fluttered helplessly as she reached for her pocket. Something flitted across her face – disappointment? Realization? – and she pulled free her dagger.

"Whatever it is, I think it wants to *kill us!"* Cas shouted.

And he charged right towards the thing.

Cas swung his sword, the metal slicing against the monster's torso. Sparks scattered as metal met stone. Cas stumbled back, but rebounded quickly, striking the creature in the back of its knees in hopes of slowing it down. The creature let out a roar that caused the room to tremble. Its ruby-like eyes narrowed into furious slits.

It turned on Cas, swinging its mace and just narrowly missing Cas as he rolled out of the way. He stood and thrust his blade.

The metal shattered, bits of shrapnel raining down dangerously.

I took a step forward, stopping only when I felt a hand on my arm.

"Don't," breathed Mirza, concern filling his gaze. "Shas, don't."

"I know how to fight, Mirza." I ripped my arm free.

"You know how to fight skirmishes in the fucking training ring! Shasi, this is real life!" each word grew more and more desperate, his voice cracking as it rose higher in pitch. He reached for my arm again, but I stepped away before he could touch me.

"Take care of this," I said, tossing the cup into his arms. I slid my sword from its sheath and ran towards the monster.

The beast towered over me, though all its focus was on Cas, who stood with the hilt of his broken sword gripped tightly in one hand, blood spilling down his cheeks from the bits of metal that had cut him.

In a second that was both an eternity stretched out and a blink gone too fast, I was on the ground, a hundred feet away from the monster.

I rolled onto my side, vomiting up blood and bile. The sharp, acrid taste stung my sinuses, making my eyes water. The back of my head throbbed; I reached to touch it.

When I pulled my hand away, my fingers were slick with blood.

I realized then that my ears were ringing. I could no longer hear the roars of the beast, the screams of my friends.

Huh, I realized with a strange sense of calm. That serenity spread throughout my limbs, replacing the adrenaline that had only been there moments before. *I'm going to die.*

Death didn't scare me, but maybe that was because I never really experienced it up close. The people of Svadaeva died every day, whether by natural causes or more malicious means, or from the Hollows themselves. My grandparents passed away when I was a child far too young to remember. I had a whole harem of mothers and fathers atop my birth parents, and I had no friends except for Mirza.

I never thought about what happened after death. Would the goddess of death, Heela, come to take my soul? Would I be brought to a plane of eternal paradise?

Or would there simply be nothing?

I sucked in a raspy breath, as if my throat had been replaced with a porous straw. Iron-thick blood wet my tongue, turning it leaden.

I didn't get to say goodbye to Mother or Father. Only Amma knew where I'd run off to.

I'd never get to drink date wine and eat street food again.

I'd never hug Noor again and endure her lectures.

I'd never dance at another ball or spar with my guards in the training arena.

I'd never tell Mirza how much I hoped we'd never wed so we could be together, because I'd liked him since the day I met him, when he wasn't even Mirza but a timid little thing drowning in boys' clothes three sizes too big.

I choked on more blood-bile, coughing it out a moment too late. It spewed from my nose and mouth together, adding to the puddle soaking through my clothes.

Through fuzzy eyes speckled with encroaching black spots, I watched as Cassiel grabbed something from Dio – her daggers. He charged the beast again, though with strength I couldn't comprehend, he launched himself up, digging the daggers deep into the ruby eyes of the monster.

It might have roared in pain.

The ceiling trembled as if it had, but I couldn't hear a damn thing.

Cas twisted the knives before yanking them free, pulling out the skewered eyes. He grabbed the monster by its horns and swung himself around, legs wrapped around the beast's thick neck.

He twisted, *hard,* until the monster's head snapped to an angle no living creature could survive. There was a lull, a pause, a tense moment of stillness before the monster's knees buckled and it fell to the ground. Cas leapt away just before he could be crushed by the thing.

My friends are safe now, I thought as I finally let my eyes close. *I can rest.*

And then, the world faded to black.

"–si. Shasi. *Shasi!*"

I awoke with a jolt, eyes wide and heart pounding. I looked around the room, panicked.

Cracked columns, arrow-littered ground, crumbled ceiling.

Corpse of a monster.

"Shasi Dārayavahush, you are *not fucking allowed to scare me like that!*" Mirza slapped me across the face with a trembling hand. Tears rolled down his dark cheeks, his bottom lip quivering as he tried to hold back his tears.

"What—" I croaked, but Mirza smacked my cheek again before I could finish that sentence.

"You almost died," came Diora's nonchalant voice. I turned in the direction of her speaking. She sat on the ground, knees pulled to her chest and wings tucked neatly behind her back. Her dark hair frizzed out around her, loose from its usual braids. Her black skin had a pallid sheen to it.

"The monster hit you," whispered Auri, who clutched the chalice like a lifeline. "*Smack.* You flew clear across the room."

Dio swallowed thickly. "Can... Can I see that iron flower?" she asked softly. I blinked, and she continued as if to clarify. "I need to test something. I have a really strong feeling, especially after all of...that."

I looked to Mirza who nodded, and gently reached into my pocket. He pulled free the iron flower and dropped it into Diora's hands. She tensed, as if expecting it to hurt, but nothing happened.

"I knew it," she whispered. "This is made of the same stuff as the chalice. It's not iron."

Auri's eyes went wide, as did Cas's.

Dio continued, "it's *silver.*"

I'd broken three ribs, according to Cas. My eardrums nearly ruptured and a canyon-sized split stretched from the base of my skull to the tip of my ear. I hadn't even lasted thirty seconds against the monster, and yet I was expected to rule over an entire kingdom. I was expected to protect my people, to lead them into war should that ever happen.

It was a group effort to find the exit of the cavern, and even more of an effort to drag me out. This was a temple after all, so there was a chamber designated for acolytes and scholars to sleep in. Auri found it and led us to it. Mirza helped me onto one of the board-stiff cots.

"What even was the point in all of that?" he muttered as he tugged off my shirt, leaving me in only my underclothes. He had a thick roll of bandages he'd snatched from one of the packs. "Sit up," he instructed. I did so, begrudgingly, and sat as still as I could while he wrapped my torso tightly.

"A-ah," piped up Auri. "I think I might know…"

She reached into her trousers and pulled out a folded piece of canvas. I caught a flash of paint – a woman – as she flipped it over to the other side.

The canvas was old, yellowed with age, but the scribbles were as clear as day: five drawings scattered across a map of the continent, lyrical words creating a border around it.

Auri recited, *"Five relics from the days of old, to slay the gods with blood of gold. A lyre to create and to unmake, unto death it shall betake. A sword of silver to cut through all, through moonlit mirrors thine gaze shall fall. A chalice of poison to corrode from within, to drink shall be a mortal sin. A bolt of light fled to the skies, for it once was the god's demise. And at the end a tomb will lie, and he who enters is bound to die."*

Mirza tightened my bandages harshly.

"A chalice of poison to corrode from within, to drink shall be a mortal sin," mumbled Cas. He rubbed his stubble, brow creasing in the middle of his forehead as he mulled over the words. "That's great and all, but the cup is *empty.*"

Mirza tightened my bandages again.

"I'd like to *breathe,*" I hissed, squirming as I tried to get the wrap loose. He muttered an apology and loosened the bandages.

"The poison could be in the metal," said Dio. "It could be painted in, or the silver could've been tainted. Poison isn't always a tangible thing, you know." Her wings fluttered, catching stray bits of light.

I grabbed my shirt and pulled it over my head. "What about the map?"

Auri pulled the canvas close. "There are five drawings placed around the continent. There was a mark drawn over the desert here. I *think* if we follow it, we can locate all the relics."

"But why?" Mirza asked, stealing the words right from my mouth.

Auri's pale gaze flitted to the side. Then, she tapped the bottom corner of the page before whispering, *"Asleep upon their earthen beds and tucked under the stars, the gods of old do dream. And then they one day wake under Chaos's regime. The gods of old and the gods of new and the gods bound by a string will one day vanish. And never look back lest you find your soul gone. Chaos will sink your boat and your flesh he will banish. From whole to shell, souled to Hollowed."*

CHAPTER THIRTY-FIVE

CASSIEL

*M*ama?" I asked, climbing onto my mother's lap to play with her curls of dark hair as she recited a bedtime story. The fourth bedtime story, mind you, but I was never satisfied unless I had at least five. My mother smiled, hiding the dark circles that kissed the underside of her stormy eyes as she did.

"Yes, my angel?" she asked, carefully prying my fingers from her plait.

"Where are the gods? Are they sleeping in beds like mine? Do they have mamas to tell them stories and kiss them goodnight?" I paused, stealing a glance at the small lantern on my nightstand. It had a glowing orb of fae light, something my mother said my father had given her. It gave off a soft green light. "Do they need nightlights, too?"

My mother kissed my hair. "Silly boy," she cooed. "The gods sleep on beds made of earth with blankets woven from stars. They don't need nightlights because they have the night sky to keep them safe. And the gods don't have mothers, not like we do. But I'm sure they would be happy to hear a bedtime story."

She picked me up and carried me to my bed, setting me down amidst the fluffy blankets and pillows.

"Don't turn off the light," I said quickly, grabbing her sleeve.

Mother gave a soft smile. "I won't, my angel. How about this: when you feel scared, tell the gods one of your stories. Maybe they'll be happy to hear it and send some bravery down to you."

I nodded and rubbed my sleepy eyes. "Yes, Mama."

She kissed my forehead. "Goodnight, my little angel. I love you."

I'd slipped out of the temple, where we decided to stay for the night, unsure of how Shasi's frail body would handle the travel, and made my way to the turreted roof, finding a smooth expanse of sandstone to sit on so I could watch the stars.

"Long ago," I began, my voice soft enough that only I could hear it. "A farmer and their wife welcomed a child into the world. Their crops had failed the season before and they had to sell one of their cows, but they were overjoyed to have their son. As the seasons passed and the boy grew, the farmer's health began to decline, and on their deathbed, they called their son to them and asked him to watch the farm and to take care of his mother. The boy could hardly comprehend what was happening, but he vowed to give his mother a life worth living. His parent died shortly after, his mother perishing from heartbreak only a few months later, leaving the boy an orphan. Alas, he did not forget his promise to his parent.

"The boy worked day in and day out, all through the nights even to tend to the farm. He built a community with his neighbors, and soon everyone loved and praised him. Until one day, the old gods came and unleashed hell unto the farm, destroying it. The villagers were angry, but the boy – a man, now – only knelt before the gods and begged for forgiveness. His friends meant no harm; they were only upset that their homes had been taken from them. Pleased with the boy's response, the gods restored the land, only instead of farmland, they built a kingdom. And thus –"

"And thus, King Heinrich Welinas became the first monarch of the Kingdom of Welinas," concluded a familiar voice.

I turned to see Tristan standing on the ledge of the temple, lithe and wraith-like, as if he were a pale cat reflecting silver against the moonlight. His lips curled into a half-smile.

"The story of King Heinrich," he supplied, silently stepping of the ledge, and padding over toward where I sat. "Any particular reason why you're reciting human history alone out here?"

I glanced at the sky, thinking of my mother and her bedtime stories. It had been seventeen years. Her voice was a distant, hazy memory now. I could hardly remember what she sounded like, even if my last memory of her was of her voice.

Dark, dense clouds had rolled in, obscuring most of the stars and shielding the moon. A shiver spidered down my spine.

I hated storms.

"Any reason why *you're* suddenly out here?" I stood, brushing the stray bits of sand from my clothes. I knew fae could open portals, but Tristan had the strange habit of just showing up.

He shifted from one foot to the other. "I wanted to see you," he admitted.

Thunder rolled in the distance, but I could hardly hear it over the thump-thump-*thumping* of my heart pounding in my ears.

He took a step closer. I took a step back.

"Tristan, you do know I was hellbent on killing your kind only, like, a week ago, right?" I spoke. My voice was scratchy, my throat clogged with cotton.

He lifted his shoulders in a nonchalant shrug. The wind had picked up, whipping his pale hair over his face, his mismatched eyes shining in the dark night.

"Are you –" I started, then stopped because the question burning on the tip of my tongue like hellfire was so damn *stupid* that I couldn't get it to vocalize.

He chuckled. "Between my sister and I, one of us likes women, and one of us likes men. I am not the former."

I could kill Hollows. I could split them apart with my whip, I could end the lives of the unkillable, the soulless. I slept outside more often than not, relying on the donations of townsfolk for food and board when things got especially dire. I faced certain death every single damn day for the last seventeen fucking years and yet...

And *yet*

When he stared at me, lips curved into a whisper-smile, my mortal enemy in the form of pure, radiant light

I

Fell

Apart.

He stepped closer and I froze, turning to stone as if I were nothing more than a gargoyle to decorate the temple's roof.

Tristan sat, patting the empty space next to him. Wordlessly, I sat, too, because there wasn't anything else for me *to* do.

"Have you ever heard the story of the Sister Goddesses?" He turned his face up towards mine. A constellation of freckles kissed the bridge of his nose, so faint I could hardly tell they were there.

Without waiting for an answer, he continued. "The Moirai sisters. They were the daughters of one of the Old Goddesses, before Medea supposedly slew them all. Most of their stories are useless. Nobody ever remembers their names, or even their existence. I think their mother tried *extra* hard to pretend they didn't exist. Whether it was to protect them from Medea or because she was ashamed, I don't know. The important thing about them was they were the ones to create fate. More importantly, the red string that personifies it."

My heart skipped a beat. *The red string of Fate and the kiss of Destiny. I'll be with you again, in Time, just wait and –*

The last words my mother ever spoke, seventeen years ago. It was a lullaby, or perhaps a love song, she used to sing constantly. *"Your father used to sing it,"* she would say, her eyes going glassy as she stared off into the distance, perhaps remembering the times before my father turned into a deadbeat sack of shit who left in the middle of the night.

"I've always had a hard time grasping the concept of fate," mused Tristan, pulling me from my memories with the eloquent gentleness of his voice. "Or, maybe I'm just too selfish to believe that three nameless gods, who we really only know them as Fate, Destiny, and Time, were capable of predicting my entire life and death hundreds of years before I was born. I lost my parents when I was young, so maybe I'm just angry at the Sisters for taking them from me. Then again, if they never died, I wouldn't have met my sister, and in a roundabout way, I wouldn't have met *you.*"

Fate. Destiny. Time.

I'd only known my mother for eight years, but it dawned on me just how little I *actually* knew about her. My father left when I was too young to remember, and she never spoke of him in detail, only when it came to that song. That song that was, apparently, about the triplet daughters of some ancient goddess.

He pulled his knees to his chest, his shoes scraping against the sandstone roof.

"Silver kills Hollows," he said. Then, he reached into his pocket and pulled out a small box, no bigger than a matchbox. It was old and worn, but he handed it over with pride.

I took it, carefully, and slid the top off. Nestled inside was a length of red string and a silver chain coiled around itself.

"How did you—" I started.

"I told you, Cas," he said. He turned his head, resting his cheek against his knees. "I'm a spy. The best one there is. You can kill Hollows with normal weapons, but it's a hell of a lot harder. Silver kills them instantly. Their bodies don't fade to ash."

My focus, though, wasn't on the chain. It was on the bit of red string. The corporeal representation of the metaphor of Fate, tying me with Tristan henceforth.

I snapped the lid of the box shut and stuffed it into my pocket, its weight settling familiarly against my thigh.

"Why King Heinrich?" asked Tristan. Like Auri, he didn't know when to be quiet. Unlike Auri, I found his voice endearing.

"It was the first story that came to mind. Someone I was... Someone I was close to once liked to say she was a distant relative of King Heinrich, even though nobody believed her."

My heart ached, the knife of memory slicing clean through it. *August. Cora.*

Goddess, they would throw a *fit* if they saw me now. They'd been firm believers, right until their deaths, that the fae were behind the Hollows. While they never directly attacked, or even entered Faerie, they refused to support anything fae-owned or fae-made. When August got drunk, he'd rant about how the continent would be better without any fae around. Cora wore jewelry made of coffin nails, pure iron through and through, which she'd subtly brush up against anyone close to her, to make sure they weren't hiding any fae blood. Though it was usually easy to tell – glamours were easy to break if you knew how to. Half breeds weren't as common as they were centuries ago; I always doubted the statistics that said there had to be at least *one* out there.

I lowered myself down until my back was against the sandstone. The stars were completely obstructed by the heavy clouds now, pregnant with rain threatening to fall. I absently rubbed my thumb against the silvered scar on the inside of my wrist, the puckered flesh slightly raised.

Ever since Cora and August died, I'd isolated myself. Why bother getting attached to people if their own mortality would rob you of them? I'd settled with working alone, killing Hollows, and scraping together as much money as I could to survive, determined to never let anyone in again.

And then Dio came along, with her bitchy attitude and smart-ass nature, stuffed in a cell meant to hurt her.

And then Auri, with her non-stop talking and sticky fingers and penchant for picking fights she knew she couldn't win.

And Shasi, who only wanted to protect her people, who put herself in harm's way over and over and over again just to keep this ragtag group of strangers safe.

And Mirza, who was as secretive as a shadow but wicked talented with a blade, with his obvious one-sided pining for the naïve princess.

And... Tristan.

Tristan, who always appeared out of nowhere.

Tristan, who ate mangoes and played cards and laughed with his whole body, his mismatched eyes glinting like stars.

Tristan, who sparred with me even though holding the blade had hurt him and told stories to me and gave me the answer I'd been searching for for *years*.

He brushed his fingers over mine, his touch whisper-soft like a butterfly kiss.

"Fate has a vendetta against me," he whispered, lowering himself to the ground so he could lay parallel to me. "She's had my string measured out since the day I was born, and the odds were never in my favor. But I think that maybe... Maybe there was a bit of kindness in her heart when she drew out that string, because against all the odds, she led me right to you."

For the first time since starting our journey, we didn't sleep in shifts. Exhaustion had kicked our asses, and with the locking door and lack of windows, we felt relatively safe. Despite the booby-trapped arena housing a giant monster.

Morning came, and as we breakfasted on dried meat and fruit, we looked at the map Auri had found.

"That damn poem is about as helpful as a surgeon in a library," muttered Shasi. "Meaning, it's *not*. What in the hells does *betake* even mean? I don't think that's a real word."

"It is a real word, and if you'd paid attention in your lessons, you'd know that," Mirza retorted. "It means, like, *to bring.*"

"You didn't pay attention either, Mister I-sleep-through-every-lecture."

Dio tapped a finger against one of the marked spots on the map, a tiny four-pointed star drawn over a forest. She said, "this is Lysaen. It's the Foloi Forest. I've been to the border of it a few times. I could easily open a portal to bring us there."

"You can *do* that?!" blurted Mirza, his jade eyes the size of saucers. A scarlet flush creeped onto Dio's cheeks as she slowly nodded.

"We have no idea *what* Relic is there," said Auri. "But... I felt a strange *pull* to the chalice. I bet..." she stopped herself, biting down on her tongue. She toyed with the tight bandages she'd wrapped around her hand sometime in the night.

Auri was hiding something.

She grabbed the map and quickly rolled it up, shoving it into her pocket.

"You guys gather up the supplies." Dio stood and brushed stray sand and dust from her clothes, her wings fluttering softly before she folded them against her back.

Dio continued as she walked towards the wall, "I'll open us a portal to the Foloi. I'll warn you now, we don't usually venture too close to it. There're rumors of the forest being haunted or housing some sort of unknown beast."

The matchbox suddenly felt like lead in my pocket.

"Silver is what kills Hollows," I said, as if it wasn't already clear. "See if you can find any here before we go. I think we'll need it."

CHAPTER THIRTY-SIX

KORE

Ceralis Ker Berethrou did not understand the concept of personal space. I managed a full twenty minutes of solitude of wallowing in my conflicted feelings while strangling the life from my pillow as I hugged it tightly, before my door burst open and in waltzed Ceralis, dragging a canvas bag behind him. He heaved the bag onto my bed with a *thunk,* startling me into a sitting position.

"Donny wanted me to bring you a map of the courtyard so you can figure out where to put your garden," he explained. He dug through the bag, pulling out a rolled-up piece of paper. When he flattened it out, a map of the palace from an aerial view was drawn on it.

Right. I was supposed to create a flower garden for Adonis – to bring *life* into the *Underworld.* The task had seemed manageable at first, but now it was damn near impossible.

"And I also brought you some things because your room is, well, it's sad." He dug out a few more things, tossing them onto the mattress one by one.

A chessboard, but no pieces.

A cracked vase with carvings of dogs on it.

A shimmery rock that I quickly recognized as the moonstone from Adonis's parlor.

A book titled *Medea and Kaos.*

A stick that looked like it had been chewed on.

A jack.

A box of mostly used watercolors and a frayed paintbrush.

A sepia photograph of a burly dog lain in front of a fireplace.

A picture frame cracked and without a photograph.

A... handwritten note?

I stopped paying attention to Ceralis as he unloaded his treasures and picked up the note, scanning over the elegant script carefully.

A,

Things were not adding up, so I did some research, and I regret it completely. There were not thirteen Old Gods. There were fourteen. And while the Old Gods are, for the most part, dead and New, that fourteenth is still alive. I do not trust her, brother mine, and I believe she is poisoning your mind. I have killed deities before, but I do not think I could stand against her in a battle, so for now, I must pretend like I don't know anything. I have traced her lineage back and it seems she is the sister of Fate, Destiny, and Time. That makes her a half sibling of you-know-who.

Also, congratulations. You're to be an uncle.

-M.

"– and then *I* said, '*if you're going to try to get in here, you're gonna have to go through me,*' and he just laughed, so I kicked him out for good. Donny had to put a ban on him. No idea why some fish man would want to hang out down here. There aren't any fish in the Rivers. Trust me, I'd know. I tried swimming through one once and Donny got *so* mad at me. I have never seen anyone that

239

mad before in my entire life, and I've lived a very long –" Ceralis cut himself off, inky eyes turning to land on me. "Miss Etoile? What's that?"

I hastily folded the note and shoved it into my pocket. The *A.* the letter was addressed to had to be Adonis. But... Who was *M?* Adonis's...sibling?

Goddess, I really knew nothing about him. The thought made me seethe, anger boiling over like tea in a kettle. I dug my nails into my palms.

"Ceralis, is Adonis married?" I blurted. "Is he courting anyone?"

He blinked once. Twice. I opened my mouth to repeat the question – no, to tell him not to bother answering – but he was already talking again.

He said, "No. I'd know if he was married. He *was* courting someone once. Miss Hedy. He got really angry with her, though, and I haven't seen her since."

I had no right to the jealousy I felt. This Miss Hedy clearly wasn't around anymore. But the fact that Adonis was keeping so much from me only added fuel to the anger I felt, white-hot and scalding as it coiled tightly around my core.

"Cer," I whispered, reaching out to touch his freckled cheek. He flinched, shying away from my touch in a split second that lasted an eternity.

"Why do you wear a collar?" I continued, dropping my hand onto my lap.

He cocked his head to the side, touching the strip of leather around his throat as if just then realizing it was there.

"Oh," he said, the usual enthusiasm dripping from his tone gone completely. "It's to control me. So I don't split into thirds and destroy the world again."

Adonis summoned me to his rock garden later that evening. The summons arrived in the form of a neatly written note in a pristine envelope with a tiny black flower sealed into the wax. I wanted to ignore it. With the catacombs and the shadows and this *Miss Hedy* person and Ceralis's collar and every other little secret he kept from me, I felt justified in ignoring him.

Still, I found myself buttoning the last few buttons of my new blouse that had arrived only an hour prior. The green brocade hugged my waist, mother-of-pearl buttons stretching up the bodice. Taffeta and lace sleeves draped over my arms like vines, the same fabrics creating an overskirt atop the matching brocade. I fought with my hair, trying to pin it up, but eventually gave up, my arms far too tired to continue the battle. I settled for braiding the mess of curls as I walked down the hall, following the familiar path to the rock garden outside.

Adonis sat on a stone bench, his shadows swirling protectively around him.

"Little star," he said calmly, and I almost – *almost* – forgave him for all his damn secrets.

"Why did you summon me?" I asked. Adonis pat the empty bench space beside him, but I crossed my arms, declining his request.

"I wanted to see if you've figured out where to create your garden. You didn't forget our deal, right?"

I hadn't forgotten. I had a sketch in my pocket of where I wanted the garden to be, along with a list of *what* I wanted to grow, besides my signature flowers. It had seemed feasible when he first proposed the idea, but now that I knew Heladés was the Underworld, I had my doubts.

"Let's play a game, Adonis," I said, ignoring his question. I curled my hands into fists, knuckles turning white, then relaxed. Crescent-shaped pockmarks lined my palms from where I dug my nails into them. "A truth for a truth."

His shadows – his head – cocked to the side. "A truth for a truth, mm? Fine, then. You know my rules."

I grit my teeth together. "I hardly think that's fair."

"What's there to be unfair about it? My past is mine, my future is unknown to me, and my present is being shared with you."

This infuriating man!

I sucked a breath through my teeth. "Do you have a sister?"

The shadows stilled.

"Who told you that."

I hesitated, like a meek mouse before a cat. His tone was ice cold, voice sharper than a blade. I took a step back, my slippers doing nothing to protect my soles against the rocks.

"Nobody," I stammered. "I just... The... There's a portrait. Of a woman. I'm guessing family or lover, but since there's no lover here... Unless that's Hedy..."

The shadows had stopped moving completely. I'd never seen them go so still. It was as if Adonis had become encased by a brick of solid ink, unmoving and uncanny. I took another step back.

"Enodia or Ceralis," he said flatly.

"W-what?"

"Enodia or Ceralis, Little Star. Who told you about Minniva?"

My throat threatened to close. "C-Ceralis. He mentioned a *Miss Hedy.*"

The shadows twitched, but otherwise remained still. My heart sank to my feet. Was it too much to hope for Ceralis or Enodia to come rescue me? Damn it, why had I accepted the summons?!

"Minniva Hedy was my consort many, many, many, *many* years ago," he said slowly. "The woman in the portrait is not her."

"Your sister, then," I pushed.

"My sister," he begrudgingly answered. "My turn, then, Little Star. I know Etoile isn't your real name. What is it?"

Oh, Kore, you are in trouble.

"I can't tell you," I said, because it was the truth. King or not, Adonis was still a Hollow. I might've been able to look Hollows in the eye, but there was no telling what might happen if I gave up my name.

The shadows twitched again. "I was hoping it wouldn't come to this, Little Star. You see, I just wanted to hear *you* say it. I already know it. I know the names of most everyone. I promised I wouldn't use it against you, remember?"

I squeezed my eyes shut. He *had* known a lot. He knew about my mother, about how I snuck out, about how angry she would be if she caught me. And she *had* been angry. Just as he'd predicted.

"Kore," I squeaked. "Please... I can't stand that name. It's... It's so ugly."

He repeated it anyways, the single syllable rolling off his tongue in a way that sent shivers racing down my spine. My stomach flopped, my legs turning liquid for a second that lasted an eternity.

Thorned vines sprouted from the rocks, twining around my legs like barbed wire. The thorns bit into the thick brocade of my skirt, tearing at it like kitten claws.

"Adonis," I whispered. "Why do you collect bones? Why... Why are you Hollows killing us?"

The shadows faltered, and for a split second, I caught the sight of pale skin and dark clothing beneath them.

He spoke slowly, carefully, as if each word were a vial of poison, he had to deliver gingerly to avoid death. "There are only three people in Heladés capable of crossing the two outermost rivers – Archyr and Styxia – Kore, and I am the only one who has stepped foot outside of them. Nobody else can leave here because everyone else is dead."

CHAPTER THIRTY-SEVEN
DIORA

S hasi, despite still being stuck in bed, mummy-like with the bandages wrapped around her, scolded Auri for defacing the temple when Auri shoved *everything* off the wall I'd pointed at.

"You can't just *throw* stuff on the ground! This is a holy space!" scolded Shasi. Mirza braced his hands on her shoulders to keep her from getting up.

"And I'm an atheist," Auri said with a shrug. She kicked an idol of some three headed being to the side, and Shasi nearly had an aneurism.

"I don't see why you have to *destroy sacred artifacts* to open a portal," the princess muttered.

"You didn't need a blank wall back at the library," chimed Cas.

"It works better if it's against a flat surface, and since I'm opening a portal to Lysaen, which is *far away,* and I need to transport *five people,* it's best I do this as accurately as possible."

I'd opened portals to Welinas constantly. When I was too lazy to walk from our flat to the grocer and back, I'd open a portal. It was the only magic I was any good at, even if I had dumped us in the middle of the desert.

Still, as I splayed my hands out, palms facing the wall, a sweat broke out on my forehead, and I couldn't *focus* long enough to draw the magic in my blood to my fingertips.

Five people. The most I'd ever transported was three and I'd messed up then, leaving us stranded in the desert for two days.

I knew Lysaen like the back of my hand. I'd been born there, raised there. My entire life had been confined to the kingdom of Unseelie, and yet – and *yet* – I couldn't bring myself to open a portal home.

I was bringing humans with me.

The queen and all her subjects still believed humans were behind the Hollows.

"It didn't take this long the last time," said Cas.

I whipped my head around to glare at him. "I could do it a hell of a lot faster if you *shut up* for once."

He held his hands up defensively.

Grumbling, I looked back at the wall.

"Any day now would be *great,*" Auri chided.

"Literally just shut the *fuck up,*" I snapped.

I opened the portal, swirling whorls of chartreuse and cerulean breaking up the dull yellow sandstone. Beyond the wispy edges of magic were the blurred masses of blue-green firs and twisting oaks, a darkness bleeding into my vision.

The Foloi Forest was massive, taking up most of the eastern part of Lysaen. Tristan and I had gone a few times, though we never ventured further than the first few trees. Even though we were beings with magic in our blood, the forest was never to be trusted.

"I... Can't hold... It open forever," I hissed through gritted teeth. Sweat spilled from my brow, my concentration faltering.

Cas grabbed Auri's wrist and yanked her through the portal. The surface rippled, shimmering scales of pearlescent light refracting as it settled back down, the two of them successfully on the other side.

"Go," I barked. Mirza, hesitant as ever, just stared at the portal.

Shasi clambered out of bed, stumbling ungracefully towards the portal. Mirza watched as she vanished to the other side.

"How do I know you didn't just kill them?" he asked slowly, reaching for his curved blade.

"Oh, for the love of *Medea!*" I cursed.

I grabbed Mirza's sleeve, giving him no choice but to follow as I jumped through the portal.

Cold autumn air assaulted me, the wet smell of petrichor and fallen leaves and freshly cut grass slamming into my senses all at once.

"How do you live like this?!" Shasi whined, rubbing her exposed arms to keep warm. Neither Auri nor Cas seemed bothered by the foggy air, their northerner blood already used to the chill.

"Well, proper clothes would do the trick," I said. "There's a village not too far from here. I'm going to get us some clothes and supplies."

"Who died and made you boss?" Auri muttered.

"Ri, you're coming with me."

She cursed, loudly, but dropped her bag and shuffled over towards me.

"Cas..." I glanced at him, hoping he'd read what my eyes tried to say. He inclined his head in agreement.

I turned on my heel, shoes squelching in the mud, and began walking towards the distant town.

"We have no money, you know," Auri piped up after a mile of walking in silence.

I stepped over a broken fence. "I know," I said. "We aren't going to the town. I'd feel too bad stealing from them. I just wanted to get far enough away to open a portal."

I didn't want the others to see how exhausted I'd become after the stint I pulled getting us here. I just had to open a portal to the city, to my flat, and back to the forest. I stumbled over my boots, one foot squishing through a rotten pumpkin.

With a shaky hand, I cast another portal in the empty air before us. Grabbing Auri's wrist, I led us through and

into my living room.

It was almost identical to how I'd left it. Dried mud clung to the wood floors. Decorative pillows were thrown on the floor. Dishes were piled in the sink. I stepped over one of Tristan's discarded boots, silently cursing my little brother for picking up on my slobby tendencies.

"No stealing," I warned, heading for the stairs. I hurried up them, pausing in front of Tristan's door. No light bled out from the crack beneath it. He wasn't home. He always kept a candle burning or a lamp on, even when he slept.

My shoulders sagged. It wasn't unusual for Tristan to be gone for weeks at a time, but...still. He had to have been worried about me, right? I was never gone for a day at most, and even then, I'd leave a note.

I shook my head and passed his door, shouldering open mine instead.

I went for my wardrobe first, peeling off my Svadaevan clothes and discarding them on the floor as I walked. Throwing open the oak doors, I rifled through my clothes until I found something suitable; a blouse and thick, wool trousers meant for riding but practical for traipsing through the magical forest. I preferred skirts, but the trousers still hugged my minimal curves nicely. I grabbed an overcoat and shoved my arms into it, then stepped into my leather boots.

I kept most of my money in the bank, but I never put all of it in my vault. I dropped to my knees next to my bed and fished under my mattress, pulling out a leather purse. I stuffed it into my pocket quickly and hurried out to find Auri before she could ransack the place.

"Is this your brother?" she asked as I descended the stairs. I paused.

Auri stood by the fireplace, holding a frame in her hands. I knew that picture. It had been taken the day Tristan and I left the orphanage. Despite our hardships, we were grinning as the photographer snapped the picture. We'd made it. We hadn't been adopted, but we hadn't been separated, and that was all we truly cared about. I'd worn a yellow dress that day, even though the sepia tint of the photograph didn't pick that up.

"Tristan," I said, finally giving him a name. "Tristan Edelweiss, my adoptive brother."

"How old are you here?"

"Eighteen," I said without hesitation. Tristan had been fifteen.

"Ah," she whispered. "A year younger than I am now. I'm guessing the orphanage wasn't the life of luxury?" she set the frame down. "The temple wasn't, either."

I paused. The orphanage wasn't...terrible...but maybe that was only because I had Tristan. If I'd been alone, I never would've survived those early years after my parents died. There was a certain pain that came with watching the others get adopted, leaving with a brand-new family to love them forever and fill that empty void their birth parents had left behind.

"It doesn't really matter. Not anymore," she said suddenly. "Let's get our supplies and find the others."

I glanced at the photograph once more before nodding and marching out the door.

Rain pelted us instantly, the skies so unreliable in the fall. Fat raindrops splashed against the pavement. I tugged my hood over my head.

"There's an atelier just down the block," I said. The clothes there were cheap and sturdy, good for work and everyday use. When I didn't have any extra money to spend on the frilly, prettier dresses I adored, I shopped there.

We hurried through the streets, finally stopping before a small red building, a warm orange light spilling out from within. I shrugged off my jacket under the shelter of the awning and held it out to Auri.

"Wear the hood," I instructed. She did just that, hiding her curved human ears.

The bell above the door jingled when I pushed it open. A round woman with eyes and hair the color of autumn leaves looked up from her ledger.

"Welcome in," she chirped. "Let me know if I can be of any assistance to you. We're running a sale currently; half off all blouses and shirts."

I shot Auri a *don't-you-dare-think-about-stealing* glare before going to one of the racks of shirts.

Auri was about my size, only a handful of inches shorter. Shasi was a size bigger, maybe two, and Cas... He could fit into fae clothing easily, that tall bastard. Mirza was like Tristan in build, though his hips were closer to mine. I gnawed on my inner cheek as I rifled through the clothes.

"Ri." I pulled an off-white blouse from the rack and held it up to myself, checking the length of the sleeves.

Auri hastily pulled her hand from her pocket and skipped over.

"Hold these for me," I said, shoving the blouse into her arms. Best to keep her hands busy so she couldn't steal anything further.

Auri stood patiently as I loaded her arms up with more clothes – blouses and jackets and vests, pants and socks and boots that would definitely bite into my savings. A pair of gloves for Auri since the shoddy bandages on her hand drew more attention than anything. A handful of hair ribbons in a rainbow of colors.

I led Auri to the counter. She dumped her armful of items, causing the woman to startle, her wings twitching at the blatant disrespect for her merchandise.

"Will you be paying up front, or shall I charge it to your bank?" asked the woman. She flipped to a new page in her ledger, scribbling down the items and prices in the neat lines.

I brushed my fingers against my pocket where my purse sat.

"Charge it to my bank," I said.

The woman, not once looking up from her ledger, slid a slip of paper and a fountain pen towards me. I picked up the pen, writing my name and account details.

"Would you like me to have these delivered to your residence?" the woman snatched up the paper, scanning over it before tucking it into her ledger.

"No, thank you. We'll take them now."

The woman pursed her lips but began folding the clothes and tucking them into a bag. She handed it to me and said nothing as we left.

"What did you steal?" I asked, fishing out my new coat from the bag, balancing it awkwardly against my hip with one hand as I slid the warm fabric over my arms.

Auri glanced at the ground, suddenly very interested in the moss growing between the cracks in the bricks.

"Auri."

With a sigh, she reached into her pocket and pulled out a pair of earrings. They were shaped like teardrops, jade green in color with flecks of gold threaded throughout. They had to be worth more than my entire purchase alone, if not more.

"It's too late to return them," she hissed, shoving them back into her pocket. "So, I won't. It's not like she needed the money. And *you* clearly have money."

I stopped in my tracks.

"What?"

"You're loaded. You just bought all of that like it was nothing."

"Auri, this was probably most of the money in my bank account," I said slowly, struggling to pick the right words. "Believe it or not, being an assassin doesn't really pay well."

"Uh huh. Sure. You get to sleep in a bed every night, in a house, with food and warm clothes and a family who loves you." She pulled her hood over her face, and I knew it wasn't just to keep the rain out of her eyes.

"My parents are *dead*," I snapped. "They were killed *right in front of me*. Not by Hollows, not by humans, but by my own *kind*. Their wings were *ripped out*."

My voice broke. More than anything, I loathed talking about the civil war between kingdoms, the war that took my parents from me and left me to die alone.

"My mother is alive," Auri blurted. She spun around to face me, tears staining her cheeks. She yanked her bandaged hand from her pocket. "She's alive. I know who she is. But I probably won't ever get to meet her because I *fucked up* and now, I'm *cursed*."

Auri ripped off the bandage, revealing a hand blacker than ink. It consumed her fingers and palm, her wrist, most of her forearm.

"I *told* you guys I killed a Hollow," she choked, voice thick with tears she furiously blinked back. "I killed a Hollow, and then there was this *song,* and when I followed it, I touched a wall and now they won't *leave me alone!*"

I grabbed her wrist, the untainted one, and dragged her into an unoccupied alley, safe from the rain and watchful eyes. I dropped my bag and pulled out the leather gloves I bought, thrusting them out towards Auri.

"And I believed you," I said. "I've killed dozens of people, Ri. I believed you. The knife you stole was probably silver, and that's how you did it."

She broke.

Auri started to sob, clutching the gloves to her chest. Tears clung to her pale lashes like tiny diamonds, her cheeks flushing pink.

I stepped around the bag, over a puddle, and stopped before her.

Auri sobbed and sobbed, and I took her into my arms, hugging her fiercely. The gloves fell to the ground; she gripped the back of my jacket with all her feeble strength, sobbing into my shoulder the way an infant would their mother.

"You're okay, Ri," I whispered against her hair, her hood having had fallen off. "You're okay. We'll figure out what this...curse is, and we'll stop it. And we'll find your mother. I'm going to yell at her, though. No mother should ever abandon her child, much less offload one at a temple."

She let out a sound that was a wet mix between a sob and a laugh.

"Let's go get some food and weapons," I said, slowly peeling myself away. I ignored the wet spot on my shoulder, instead bending down to pick up the discarded gloves and hand them to Auri.

"Okay," she whispered. She pulled the gloves over her hands, flexing her fingers to stretch the leather.

During the spring and summer months, an outdoor market would stretch along Main Street, vendors offering their goods at cheaper prices. But the rain that came during the colder months drove the market into hiding, leaving us with only the indoor market, which was, much to my dismay, clear across the city. I tapped into my well of magic. I had just enough to get us back to the Foloi Forest before I'd need to rest.

A few years ago, the Queen had commissioned a glass convention hall meant to display technological advances and historic artifacts. After the exposition had ended, though, the Queen allowed local vendors to set up their shops inside when it was too rainy to hold a proper market.

I suddenly found myself wishing we had the trams the humans had.

"Keep your ears covered, Ri." I pulled her hood over her head and picked up my discarded bag. "We're going to have to catch a cab, and there aren't going to be many out because of the rain."

There weren't many public cabs in Lysaen to begin with. Most people opened portals to get from place to place or used whatever magic they were able to harness to get them around.

I had no such advantage.

Auri laced her fingers with mine, the leather of her gloves warm to the touch. I stumbled over my boots, my cheeks heating up like flames.

Calm down, Dio, I silently chastised myself. *It's good she's holding your hand. It means she's less likely to steal.*

Before long, a dark coach drawn by horses double the size of those found on the human side of the continent – though, now that I saw them, they were only a bit bigger than the camels in Svadaeva – rolled down the cobblestone road. I thrust my arm out, waving it down. The coach came to a half, the horses whinnying and stamping their hooves.

The coachman hopped down and opened the door for us. "Afternoon, ladies. Where to?"

Auri climbed into the coach first. I began up the steps, taking the coachman's hand delicately and tossing him a sweet smile. The smile of an assassin who used seduction to her advantage.

"The Glass Pantheon," I said, saccharine dripping from my voice. The man's dull eyes lit up beneath heavy brows. He nodded and closed the door once I'd sat down on the leather seat, worn, and cracked with age.

The coach lurched before it began moving. I pulled the cotton drapes around the windows closed.

Auri reached over and yanked them open.

"Y'know, I never really expected Lysaen to be like this," she said, never once taking her pale eyes off from the window. Brick buildings blurred as we passed by, the steady *clip-clopping* of the horses' hooves lulling me into ease.

"Like... A normal city?" I snorted.

"It looks a lot like Welinas or Wallaekva, just... The people are taller and the streets less clogged with trams and autos. The air feels cleaner, too."

"Cas thought we lived in magical tree huts." the corners of my lips tugged up into a smile. Auri chuckled, the sound like music. "It's a lot better than Svadaeva at least, right?"

"A million times better. I can't *stand* the heat. The food there is good, and there's lots of marks I can steal from, but I'd choose Lysaen over it any day." She tucked a stray curl behind her ear.

"Have you ever been to the Isles?" I asked. Surrounding the continent were a handful of islands, seven to the north and six to the south. The Southern Isles were more tropical, with crystal-blue waters and shallow reefs and warm sand the color of snow. The Northern Isles were made of sharp rocks and steep cliffs and massive seabirds that battled the mountain-sized waves. I'd never been to either, though.

She shook her head. "I've seen pictures. Have you been? Are there really trees with leaves the size of your body?"

"I've never been. But I want to go," I said. "I bet there probably are trees with massive leaves. I've heard Ia is beautiful year-round." Ia was the largest of the six Southern Isles.

"Maybe… Maybe we can go after all of this," she whispered, toying with her gloved hand absently. "All of us. We need it."

I stared out the window, watching as raindrops streaked down the glass.

I didn't even know what *this* was.

I was supposed to help Cas get Shasi on his side so he could figure out how to kill the Hollows. But that was *before* Auri found the map with its ominous poem leading us to the very relics Medea used against the Old Gods.

Are the Hollows gods?

It wasn't my responsibility to stay, to help the others enact whatever vengeance they sought. I could jump out of the coach and run home to make sure Tristan was okay.

Yet if the Hollows were *gods,* there was nothing I could do to keep him safe other than help track down these damn relics. The Hollows had taken nothing from me, but I'd be damned if I let them touch my baby brother.

At least, I rationalized, *if you help kill the Hollows, maybe the queen will give you a generous stipend. Then you can buy as many gowns as you want.*

The coach came to a halt, the coachman rapping on the wall to let us know we'd arrived. He pulled open the door, holding his hand out to help each of us down. I put a generous handful of coins in his outstretched palm, a silent thanks, before hurrying after Auri.

The Glass Pantheon was a building half the size of the palace but twice as magnificent. Made completely of glass, its insides were completely visible from the outside. A rooftop greenhouse added a sudden splash of green against the dull greys and browns of the city, even though its glass windows were foggy with condensation. Two statues stood guard outside the revolving door – Medea in all her motherly-and-executionary fashion, and Queen Elizabetta the Third, the current queen of Lysaen and the commissioner of the Pantheon.

I always found it a bit egotistical, but if the queen wanted to have a massive, hundred-foot-tall statue made of solid marble of herself next to the goddess, so be it.

"I can't glamour you," I whispered, taking Auri's hand within my own and leading her through the throng of people. "So, you have to keep your ears hidden. We're just here to get some food and water and weapons. Nothing more."

Auri's gaze lingered on the statues until I pulled her through the revolving door.

At once, the smells wafting from different vendors and the incessant chatter of the shoppers hit me. I was overwhelmed with the scents of fresh bread and hand-dipped candles and something spicy that reminded me of the market in Svadaeva. There was the sticky-sugar smell of sugarcloud, the savory smell of roasted vegetables sautéed with olive oil and flaky salt. My stomach grumbled loudly, betraying my hunger to everyone within earshot.

"Let's get something to eat, first," I muttered, and I pulled Auri towards a covered booth.

The vendor, a fae only a handful of years older than me, smiled at us.

"Welcome, ladies," they said. "Anything I can help you with?"

Think of the stipend, Dio. Think of the stipend.

"We'll take two of the sugar-cherries. Pitted, right?" when they nodded, I continued, "and two of the roasted chestnuts. Ri, you want anything?"

Auri was busy staring at the massive fountain in the center of the Pantheon to answer. I squeezed her hand gently.

"And two plum pastries." I fished out my coin purse, handing over some coins. The vendor wrapped everything in old newspaper and handed it over with another grin.

As we walked away, I gave Auri her share.

"Let's sit by the fountain," she said, stuffing one hand suspiciously in her pocket.

We sat down on a bench close enough to the fountain to feel its spray. A handful of children squealed, running laps around the fountain as they chased after each other. One of them had a shock of pale hair that reminded me of Tristan. My heart ached at the thought of my brother.

I bit into my sugar-cherries, the crunchy sugary shell shattering against my teeth as it gave way to the juicy cherry beneath.

We ate in silence, my focus on the kids. One of them tripped and fell, scraping his knees against the marble floor. His father rushed over in an instant, picking the poor child up and cradling him against his chest.

I could hardly remember my father's face. His memory had been reduced to a fuzzy outline – dark locks, a clean beard, wings the color of jade.

I couldn't even conjure up his voice if I tried.

I licked sugar off my fingers and absently toyed with the newspaper while I waited for Auri to finish. It wasn't unusual for vendors to use old papers as wrappers for their goods.

Suddenly, I caught sight of the headline on one of the crumpled papers. Frowning, I smoothed it out and scanned over the words.

BREAKING NEWS:

I stared at the words as if that would force them to make sense.

War.

War.

The sugar-cherries I'd eaten threatened to rise up my throat again.

We were going to *war.*

CHAPTER THIRTY-EIGHT

AURI

Hundreds of eyes were on me.

Well, maybe not *hundreds,* but it sure felt like every single person in the Glass Pantheon was staring at me, even though my ears were hidden.

I'd devoured everything Dio bought, licking the sugar off my fingers when my gaze finally settled on her.

She was staring at a piece of newspaper on the ground. Curious, I bent down and scooped it up, reading the headline that seemed to have caught her off guard.

War.

War?

I frowned. "Dio," I said slowly. "Why can't Shasi just, I don't know, use her political power to explain to Elizabetta and Wilhelm that the Hollows are their own thing, and that silver kills them?"

She looked up, her gold eyes wide and wild.

I'd never really cared for politics. Why get caught up in something that will never involve me, anyways? Politicians didn't care for the street rats, the vagrants, the thieves, even if their campaigns said otherwise. To them, I was just a dirty stain on their perfect city, one that belonged behind bars because the rich and well-off didn't like when someone lesser scraped the top off their coffers.

Already I'd stolen a pair of earrings, a pocket watch, a ruby ring, a pearl and jade bracelet, and a bottle of perfume that I *thought* was going to be something far more interesting. Its flowery smell was overbearing. I'd tossed it into the fountain when Dio wasn't watching.

Normally, I'd pawn my goods for food or money, or save the more valuable ones just in case. But nobody in Welinas would take fae items and nobody in Lysaen would strike a deal with a human.

A...demigod.

I reached my hand into my pocket to brush against the earrings. I'd stolen them because they reminded me of Dio – gold eyes, green wings, beauty that couldn't be summarized into any words I knew. I didn't even know if her ears were pierced, but she was beautiful, and the earrings were beautiful, and I just –

My cheeks burned hotter than flames. I smacked my face a few times to calm them down.

"Ri?" Dio asked, cutting herself off from whatever she'd been saying. "Something wrong?"

I shook my head quickly and stood before she could reach out to touch my shoulder. If she did, I wouldn't be able to handle it. I'd simply combust.

She's just being nice.

"Let's get what we came here for," I grumbled. She nodded and folded up the newspaper, stuffing it into her pocket for later. Her motions were hesitant, as if she wanted to say something, but she held back. As she picked a direction to walk in, her shoulders slumped, and her golden gaze became fixated on the ground.

Buying food and toiletries was the easy part. Dozens of shops sold nuts and dried fruits and dehydrated vegetables alongside glass bottles full of water. Soon, we were weighed down from all our bags.

We should've brought a couple of Shasi's packs, I thought, loathing the hindrance our shopping caused.

Our last stop was at a small, nondescript shop that sold both hunting knives and dried herbs amongst other things I couldn't name. Dio went straight to the counter and began talking with the shopkeeper.

"Dio!" the man greeted. "It's been quite a while since I've seen you or your brother."

Dio's voice was taught behind a fake smile when she spoke. "We've been busy. Look, I need a few things. A couple of knives and some herbs."

The shopkeeper's smile was just as forced. "Which herbs? Pick out the knives while I prepare them."

She rattled off the names of a few plants. I recognized a few, but the rest went over my head. "Hyoscyamus, solanine, belladonna, nightshade, strychnine, and if you have it in stock, some laudanum would be *great.*"

The shopkeeper turned to dig through the bottles and jars on the shelf behind him. Dio took the opportunity to pick out a few knives. She tested the weight of each, checking the tags before adding them to her pile on the counter.

Silver. She was checking to make sure they were silver.

Bored, I turned my attention to the glass case next to me. Inside was a velvet cushion, and atop it was a strange…thing. It almost looked like an *L*, though big enough to fit in my hand with a mother-of-pearl grip and a silver barrel. Next to it was a box of silver…*things.*

They almost looked like the un-blossomed version of Shasi's not-iron iron flower.

The shopkeeper was busy measuring out liquids in tiny glass bottles. Dio was busy assessing the lengths of two knives.

The case wasn't even locked.

I slowly slid my hand under it, grabbing the box of iron flower buds. They didn't even rattle as I gripped it tightly, yanking my hand free and shoving the box into my pocket. The shopkeeper set one of the vials down and moved on to the next.

I waited a full minute before reaching for the *L*-shaped thing. Just as my fingers curled around the hilt, the shopkeeper turned around. I froze, praying to any god that would listen *(hello, Mother, care to acknowledge me for once?)* that nobody would notice.

The shopkeeper didn't. He instead began calculating the price of everything. He put Dio's goods in a black box, which she slid into one of her many bags. As she reached for a piece of paper to write her banking information on, the shopkeeper looked up.

And locked eyes with me.

Well, fuck. Thanks, Mother.

I grabbed the weapon and shoved it into my pocket.

"Hey!" the shopkeeper yelled. "Thief! Stop! You can't take that!"

I picked up the bags I was tasked with carrying, holding them in one hand, and ran right out of the shop. The man continued to yell, and the familiar tinny bells alerting the bobbies – damn it, they even had *bobbies* in faerie land – ringing out.

Someone grabbed my wrist, and I spun around, ready to crack my fist against their jaw.

"Ri, it's me!" Dio yelled.

"Open a portal!" I screeched. Boots thumping against marble rounded the corner.

"Freeze!" the fae bobbies yelled.

Dio blanched.

"Now!" I yelled.

Dio waved her hand, the blues and greens of the portal ripping through the air. She shoved me through, jumping in after. We

tumbled onto the muddy ground, rain pelting us instantly as the cold air bit at my nose and suddenly exposed ears.

"Medea's teeth!" Cassiel cursed. I groaned, rolling over and pushing myself into an upright position. Cas, Shasi, and Mirza ran over.

"Dio –" I mumbled, searching for her. She'd landed a few feet away, in a patch of grass that wasn't muddy at all. Her wings twitched, flicking away drops of rain.

She sat up. Blood dripped from her nose, but she hastily wiped it away.

"I specifically told you *not* to steal!" she scolded instantly, her golden eyes narrowed into a glare. "Why would you do that?!"

The metal thing was lead in my pocket. I didn't dare reach for it. Instead, I stood and picked up my discarded bags. "We should find somewhere dry to change and pack. I can't feel the pull of the Relic, so we're going to be wandering for a while."

"I need to rest," Dio said. She struggled to pick up even a single bag. "Let's go to the village. I'll get us a couple of rooms at the inn. Ri, you and I are going to have a *talk.*"

Half an hour later, the five of us were cramped into two rooms – one for Mirza and Cas, the other for the rest of us. Dio had divided the clothes and weapons and supplies we'd bought, sending everyone to get dressed and packed. Shasi, showing little modesty, stripped out of her soaked clothes to put on the new ones, admiring the soft fabric and the way it clung to her curves.

Dio flopped onto the bed with a groan.

"What did you steal." Her voice was muffled by the pillow she had smothered her face against.

I reached into my pocket and slowly pulled out the weapon.

Both Shasi and Dio stared at it.

"What in Medea's name –" it would never stop throwing me off to hear my *mother's name* as a curse "– is that?" Shasi asked.

I shrugged, setting the thing down and taking out the iron flower buds. I said, "I think these are the iron flowers. Silver flowers, I guess. They sort of look the same, just not... Exploded?" I struggled to think of the right word to describe the blossom shape the iron flower made.

Dio let out a groan and pulled the thin blanket over her head. "What did you mean earlier? When you said you can't feel the pull of the Relic."

I returned both the iron flower buds and the *L*-thing to my pocket.

"I don't know if it has to do with my curse or –"

"Curse?" Shasi butted in.

I ignored her and continued, "Or something else, but I can feel a pull towards the Relics. The chalice, at least. And the map. And basically, everything else that has proven itself to be useful. It's like there's a string inside me *pulling* me towards these things. I can't feel it right now."

Shasi sat on her knees. "Do we even know which Relic is here?"

I shrugged. "That damn poem wasn't helpful in the slightest."

The princess was quiet for a moment. Then, she grabbed her bag and pulled it close, digging through it until she procured a familiar book.

"Maybe," she said as she flipped through the ancient pages as if they were brand new, "there's something in here."

Without thinking, I snatched the journal from her. "This thing is ancient. Careful."

"It's only a couple centuries old."

"Cent – It's a couple *thousand* years old!" The picture fluttered out, as if on cue, and I grabbed it. "See? Look at the date. It's *ancient.*"

Shasi took the picture, her brow furrowing as she studied the smudged numbers. She muttered, "how do you know?"

Dio snapped at us to shut up so she could sleep.

I flipped through the pages of my mother's diary carefully, until I saw the familiar words *Foloi Forest.*

The Foloi Forest is an ancient place, were Gausica lay down to sleep. I am forever grateful that I did not have to slay my grandmother. I would not have been able to handle it. Gausica went to sleep centuries before. I hid one of the Relics amongst the trees, deep in the earth and rocks. If you, my dear, are lucky, you will be able to harness the Bolt as well. Only someone worthy of wielding it may reach into the skies during a storm to grasp it, and what better place to free it to the skies once more than the forest where my grandmother sleeps?

Beneath the entry was a drawing, in the same charcoal style as the one of the temple; a stone boulder covered in moss deep within a copse of trees. Mushrooms dotted the mulchy ground around it.

"Hey," Shasi whispered, handing the picture back to me. I carefully tucked it into its place. Medea – my *mother* – had left this journal for me; the least I could do was treat it with respect.

I glanced over, one brow raised.

"I... I'm sorry. For the way I treated you and Dio. I... I was scared of Dio because I'd spent my whole life believing the fae were behind the Hollows. I didn't believe someone as…well, as small as you could kill a Hollow on accident. That was cruel of me."

People didn't apologize to me. I was a thief. A scoundrel. An overall bad person. I didn't deserve apologies, especially not ones from *princesses.*

She continued, as if not noticing my silence. "I was convinced that monster was going to kill me. I realized there's so much in life I still want to do. So many places I want to visit, people to meet. It's nearly my birthday. I'm supposed to get married. I… Mirza's been my only friend for as long as we've known each other. I'm not really the best with people."

I snorted. "Neither am I. I just see people as marks. But you – all of you – have really helped me with that. I was abandoned at birth; I've never really been able to connect with anyone. Goddess, jumping in that portal after Cas and Dio was the dumbest and best thing I've ever done."

She giggled. Dio shifted, causing both of us to snap our heads in her direction. She let out a snore, cuddling harder with her pillow.

"Maybe we should let her sleep," Shasi whispered. "Let's go find the guys. Maybe we can play cards. I was *just* about to hand Cas his ass in Crimson Crowns before you two came barreling out of the sky."

I couldn't help the grin that tugged on my lips. Nodding, I stood up, and followed Shasi out of the room.

We found Cas and Mirza in their room next door, both of them sitting on the floor trying to figure out who got which knife of the two Dio had given them.

I sat down cross-legged near Cas. He sighed through his nose, pocketed a knife with a jade-green hilt, and pulled out his worn deck of cards, the edges frayed from use. Without hesitation, he shuffled them and dealt the deck.

"Where's Dio?" Mirza asked, eyeing the door as he dropped a pair of wings onto the floor.

"Asleep," I said. I slid three of my cards – all crowns – into my sleeve and took three more from the deck as a replacement. One crown, twin swords. I dropped the pair onto the floor. "Her magic wiped her out."

"Maybe if you didn't steal something and force her to open a portal when she had no strength, she wouldn't be asleep," muttered Shasi. Her brow knit as she focused, her plush lips pursing. She rearranged her cards before snatching one of Cas's. Whatever it was, it wasn't something she wanted, as she cursed under her breath.

"What *did* you steal?" Cas asked. He took one of my cards – a single chalice.

My stomach flipped as I thought of *the* Chalice, tucked away safely in my bag in the other room. I could feel a tether pulling me towards it, my fingers itching to grab it. Only a thin wall separated me from the Relic, but it felt as if it was clear across the continent.

I plucked a card from Shasi and dropped my pair of swords onto my pile. Then, I explained everything – the Glass Pantheon, the shops, the weapons shop, the *L*-shaped thing, and the iron flower buds that weren't iron at all, but *actually* silver ("How do you *know* they're silver?" Mirza asked. I said, "A proper thief can identify silver just by touching it.").

As I flipped over the three cards, I'd swapped out for the ones hidden in my sleeve, I won the game. We hadn't bothered with bets, but I hated losing.

I pulled the thing out of my pocket.

Shasi and Mirza exchanged a look, Mirza's eyes wide.

Mirza said, "That's the weapon that killed the Hollow back home."

CHAPTER THIRTY-NINE

KORE

Before the sky was blue, the grass green, and the ocean full of salt, there were three gods; Zina, goddess of nothing; Maulea, goddess of everything; and Eemyr, god of what lay between. Maulea's creations, Orinos – god of the sky – and Gausica – goddess of the earth – birthed three children: Okeon, god of the seas, Reiner, god of the mountains, and Eo, goddess of storms. From his blood, Okeon created twin gods – Archyr and Styxia. They are river gods. When they went to sleep shortly before Medea's slayings, they became the rivers that guard Heladés. Only three people can cross them – Ceralis, Enodia, and myself. Even in sleep, they are helpful. They keep the Hollowed from getting out and mortals from getting in." Adonis leaned back in his seat; feet propped up on the coffee table. He'd given me no time to process the fact that the Hollows were *dead*, instead jumping straight into a theology lesson.

"I don't really see how that's relevant," I muttered. "And I've never heard of Archyr and Styxia."

Adonis inhaled sharply. "That's because, Little Star, mortals tend to ignore those who didn't play a pivotal role in their history. Medea didn't battle the river gods. They were asleep before she usurped the Old Gods. It *is* relevant."

My fingers had grown sticky with pomegranate juice, only becoming more uncomfortable when I tried to wipe it off on my brocade skirt.

"Your rivers are faulty, then. Because the Hollows have been killing people like mad up there." I crossed my arms over my chest. "You can't give out your full name or look them in the eyes, or they will devour your soul."

"Do you know where that term comes from?" he asked. *"Hollow?* It refers to how they are hollowed shells. Their souls have departed from their mortal vessels, leaving a hollowed spirit behind."

"But –"

He cut me off. "All the Hollowed in Heladés are accounted for. Not a single one, save for myself – though I technically don't count – has left Heladés in the past *century.* Ever since Archyr and Styxia went to sleep guarding Heladés, nobody has been able to get out."

"Yes, but –"

He kept talking, ignoring my pointless protests. "There has also been a considerable decline in Hollowed arriving here, especially considering the fatality rate your Hollows seem to have. That means, Little Star, the Hollows and my Hollowed are two *very* different things. It also means that those who are killed by the Hollows don't end up in Heladés. I don't know where they go."

I paused, mulling the information over. The Hollows – Hollowed, as Adonis kept referring to them as – here looked human, save for their pallid complexions. They acted human, going shopping and indulging in pastries and playing with their children. They lived in homes and had lives within the afterlife.

Yet...

"If this is the underworld and everyone here is dead," I said slowly. "Why can't you figure out where all the dead are going? Aren't you the king here?"

"The king, yes. But I'm not the goddess of death. That's Heela, and she was slayed by Medea centuries ago."

I shivered. Was the goddess of death really dead herself? If so, how were the deceased ferried to the afterlife?

Unless...

Unless her death sparked the flood of Hollows who consumed souls and left nothing to be brought to the afterlife. Unless Medea's usurpation triggered a cataclysmic event ending in the massacre of thousands and the fear of handing out your name.

Unless Medea, our supposed savior, our Mother, and Executioner, was the reason behind the Hollows.

I swallowed a wave of nausea.

Wetting my lips with the tip of my tongue, I asked, "Why *did* Medea slay the Old Gods?"

Adonis chuckled. "Now you're asking the right questions."

"But you're giving me no answers."

"To understand *why*, you must first understand the circumstances leading to Medea's upbringing."

His shadows flickered, dancing like flames about to go out.

"Eo, the goddess of storms," he began, "had fallen into an affair with Eemyr's sole creation."

My brow furrowed. I could barely even remember who Eemyr was. I hadn't ever heard of him having a creation, like Maulea and Zina.

Adonis, not seeming to notice my confusion, continued, "It was a glorious affair, burning brighter and hotter than the sun, but lasting no longer than the spark of a match. Their nebula was bigger than their love and the fallout was catastrophic. It is not easy for gods to become pregnant – most gods reproduce asexually, you see – but Eo fell pregnant with twins. Now, it should be known that Eemyr's creation threw Eemyr into an exile of nothingness, reducing him to mere atoms and rendering him as dead as gods can be. Because of that, his

269

creation feared his own offspring would do the same. So, while heavily pregnant, the creation banished Eo to the Isle of Storms. Eo was in labor for a year before she birthed her children. Knowing that the birth was successful, the creation ventured to the Isle of Storms where he *devoured* the first-born twin. Eo hid the second, replacing her with a rock which the creation swallowed. Then, alone on the Isle, Eo raised her daughter to enact vengeance on her father, and to slay the Old Gods who simply sat back and watched as Eo's first-born was devoured and Eo left for dead."

"Medea," I whispered."

Adonis's shadows flickered, revealing a sliver of pale skin for a split second. "The one and only."

But Medea had slain Heela. She had disrupted the natural order the gods brought about, and then... Then the Hollows came.

"Do you know how much time had lapsed between Medea going to sleep and the arrival of the Hollows?" Adonis asked.

The Hollows had arrived seventeen years ago. I shook my head no.

"Two years. Do you know what happened in those two years?"

Again, I shook my head. My heart palpitated with anxiety. With the realization and revelation that everything I'd thought I'd known was a twisted truth, the victor's history, the sugar-coated version of the violence Medea had endured.

"Medea's child," he said, "was veiled, and those who wanted her dead could no longer locate her."

I swallowed twice, forcing back vomit that rose up my gullet. The pieces clicked into place like a puzzle, like the oiled gears of a clock.

Medea had given birth to a child. She went to sleep. The child was veiled. And the Hollows who wanted to find and exterminate the offspring of Medea – their greatest threat – could no longer locate her. So, instead, they turned to genocide, killing everyone and everything in their path to hunt down the child of the Executioner.

The killings had never been aimless. They'd been executed with a single goal in mind; track down Medea's child and kill her before she could turn around and kill them.

I sucked in a breath. "What about Medea's twin? What ever happened to them?"

The shadows stilled.

"When Medea slew her father with *Titanomachy,* she found her twin deceased within his stomach, cut to pieces."

I frowned. There was no way that was it. Her long-lost twin was just...dead? Where did gods even *go* when they died?

But Adonis wasn't finished. "Medea was distraught when she found her brother dead, so she called on one of her Relics, the Divine Lyre, to revive him. She'd only used the Lyre to unmake, but with it, she played one final chord and *created.* She revived her brother from death, putting him back together like a crude puzzle, though she couldn't fully bring him back. Half of his soul was gone, lost to the stars. But it was enough. She had her brother back and ruled with him until she went to sleep."

I sank into my seat, overwhelmed.

"The bones," Adonis continued, going back to my original question, "Just appear here. Some of them are only a handful of months old, but others are centuries old. I have Ceralis collect them so I can figure out where they're coming from and *why.*"

I curled my hands into fists, my tiny white flowers blooming around my knuckles like rings. Their thorns bit into my flesh, drawing crimson beads of blood.

"Medea's...daughter," I whispered. "Do you know where she is? Is she still alive?"

"Yes," he said without a beat of hesitation. "She's alive. I don't know where she is – she's still veiled – but I know she's alive."

I opened my mouth to ask another question, but the door was thrown open and in tumbled an exasperated Ceralis.

"I tried to stop her," he panted. "But she wouldn't take no for an answer. Donny, you have to get rid of her. She's throwing a tantrum. She threw paint over the walls, and she won't stop until she gets an audience with you."

In the distance, a feminine voice screeched, *"Adonis Nyx, where the* fuck *are you?!"*

Adonis released a breath. He whispered, "Ah, fuck. Speak of the devil. Kore, I beg of you, go hide yourself. She will *not* be pleased to see you here."

"Who?" I asked, nervously.

Adonis's shadows twitched. "Minniva Hedy. It seems speaking that bitch's name all but summoned her."

CHAPTER FORTY

CASSIEL

I took the weapon from Auri – much to her reluctance; it would've been easier to steal a fish from a feral cat – and turned it over in my hands. It had a weight to it that I hadn't expected, but it felt...nice. I rubbed my thumb over the mother-of-pearl grip. It felt almost like the whip I favored.

A cardstock tag had been tied to the u-shaped cutout branching off the grip. I turned it over, reading the handwritten note.

Silver, ivory, mother-of-pearl
.40 silver bullets, 6 cartridge barrel
Wilcox Revolving Pistol
c. 1893
G100.00

"One hundred – Ri, are you crazy?!" I hissed, nearly dropping the revolving pistol. A hundred gold could purchase a section of the damn Welinas *palace,* and I'd *still* have enough left over to live comfortably for the rest of my life.

She lifted her shoulders in a bored, nonchalant shrug, as if to wordlessly say *I am.*

"We could sell it," she said. "I found it, so I get the biggest cut."

"We are not selling it!" Shasi grabbed a handful of discarded cards and threw them at her. "This thing can kill Hollows *fast.* Before they even have the chance to attack us. We *need* this thing. We just have to figure out how to use it."

I looked at the revolving pistol again, fitting the rounded part of the grip against my palm. I pointed the elongated barrel at the wall, my finger curving over the u-shaped appendage.

Bang!

An explosion filled the room, leaving behind the smell of smoke and the powdery smell that lingered after fireworks. The wood wall splintered, leaving a fist-sized crater that went all the way through, allowing sunlight in.

I stared at the weapon.

"I think..." I said slowly. "I might have figured out how to use it."

Auri eventually slunk back to her room to see if Dio was awake so we could start our journey into the Foloi Forest. She returned only a few minutes later.

"Well," she said, dramatically draping herself over the rickety wooden desk chair, "looks like we will be staying here overnight."

Shasi and Auri returned to their room after eating the dinner a bellhop brought us ("it comes with the rooms," he'd explained when I tried to say we didn't order the bowls of stew, nor did we have the money for it. "Don't let it go to waste. I'll eat it if you don't want it." Shasi, much to Auri's protestations, gave Dio's portion to the boy and told him to enjoy it.). I let Mirza take the bed, since I had no plans to sleep.

Once I was sure he was fast asleep, I slipped out the window and clambered onto the slanted roof. The tiles were still slick from the deluge of rain earlier – it had slowed to a drizzle. Annoying, but nothing I couldn't handle. I'd slept in worse conditions before – but I centered myself, muscles flexing so I wouldn't fall. I had my silver knife and the box of iron flower buds – bullets, I'd assumed they were called after reading the tag again – in one pocket, the pistol and Tristan's matchbox in the other. I pulled the matchbox out and plucked the red string from it, twirling it around my fingers. The ends had begun to fray, the string growing softer the more I toyed with it.

"I'm glad to see my gift brings you entertainment." Tristan sat down next to me. There was no moonlight to illuminate the sharp planes of his face – the slope of his nose, the cut of his cheekbones, the edge of his jaw – but I could see his features perfect. His eyes, jade green, and myrtle blue, stared at the village below us, unblinking until a fat raindrop splattered against his pale lashes.

"How did you know I was here?" I asked, curling my fingers around the bit of red string. I stuck my hand into my coat pocket to protect it from the rain.

"I'll always know where you are," he whispered. "So don't go somewhere I can't follow. Don't leave me behind. Promise me, Cas."

My heart skipped a beat. I found myself grabbing his hand. I found myself brushing my lips against his knuckles, for once not worried about the unevenness from the scar that split through my mouth. I found myself vowing to never go where Tristan couldn't follow in a silent kiss to his hand. A vow to defy Time and Fate and Destiny if they did anything in their power to pull us apart.

I'd only seen Tristan a handful of times, but I felt like I'd known him my entire life. I found comfort and familiarity with him, as if our souls had been forged together by the gods themselves.

I let go of his hand, but he reached out and grabbed mine again. We were nearly the same height, yet his hand felt so much smaller in mine, so much more fragile, as if his bones were made of fine china and glass.

The rain began to pick up, splashing against the roof. My hair clung to my forehead. Tristan's lashes clumped together.

"Technically this doesn't count as a storm," he breathed.

I chuckled. "Technically you're right."

"Technically," he scooted closer until his thigh was pressed against mine, "I could still keep you safe if you feel uneasy. It is a lot of rain after all."

"Technically you could."

I reached out and brushed a stray clump of wet hair from his face, tucking it behind his pointed ear.

"We're in Lysaen, you know." I let my fingers linger for a whisper longer before pulling them away. "Why don't you show off your wings? Isn't it uncomfortable to keep them hidden?"

"Exceedingly so." He stretched his arms above his head as if to prove a point. "It's like having your arm bound to your body tightly – with a corset three sizes too small cinched up *all* the way. It hurts, but I hate my wings. They're... Hideous."

"Tristan, I find that absolutely false. There isn't a single hideous thing about you," I said flatly.

He shifted uncomfortably, drawing his knees to his chest. "Fae only have monochrome wings. One color. Mine are multicolored. Like my eyes."

"So?"

"So, they're hideous. I don't like drawing a lot of attention to myself, either. It sort of defeats the whole purpose of being a spy."

I was positive nearly everything Tristan did defeated the purpose of being a spy, but then again, I was a hunter. I struck first and asked questions never. What did I know about being a spy?

What did I know about anything?

For seventeen years, I'd been determined to kill Hollows, yet it took me that long to learn what they were – rather, what they *weren't* – and how to really kill them. I'd been slicing their heads off with razor blades when a silver dagger would've done the trick.

When a silver dagger would've kept August and Cora alive. My *mother* alive.

In the distance, thunder rumbled. My spine went rigid.

Tristan tightened his grip on my hand. "Where'd you get that scar?" he asked, pointing at the thin one slicing through my lips.

He's distracting you.

"I wish I could say I got it fighting, but I got it when I was young and still learning how to control my whip." I ran my tongue over the indent. August had thought giving a ten-year-old a whip was a good idea. When I inevitably hit myself in the face with it, Cora switched between coddling me and yelling at August, who'd thought I'd been faking the injury until Cora made *him* give me sutures.

He ended up having to buy me a set of custom glass straws since I couldn't drink anything without crying from the pain for weeks after.

"What about this one?" Tristan touched the thick scar that curved over my cheekbone under my eye.

Thunder clapped again. I sucked in a breath through my teeth.

"A Hollow," I said. "It got too close. Swiped at me with its claws. I still hadn't mastered fighting blindfolded, and I got too close, and..."

And when the Hollow pinned me to the ground, poised and ready to rip off my blindfold and treat me to the same death my mother had faced, August stepped in. He didn't walk out of that fight alive. He didn't walk out of that fight at *all*.

Tristan seemed to notice my discomfort, as he moved to point at a thin silvery scar on my neck. "This one?"

"A human, surprisingly," I said breathily. "I was arrested for loitering. Soliciting? I don't remember what they said. I was sleeping on what I *thought* was an abandoned porch, but it wasn't. The bobbies in Orinos are cruel bastards in case you were thinking of sleeping on a not-abandoned porch there. Held a knife to my throat. I saved that same ass from a Hollow less than three months later. He didn't even remember me."

Tristan's lips quirked up into a smile. "He must've been quite the idiot to forget you. You're rather memorable."

When the thunder struck again only seconds later, I didn't even hear it. Tristan leaned against me; his head pressed against my shoulder. My heart pounded so hard and fast that the booming of the thunder in the distance couldn't keep up.

I'd never allowed myself to get close to anyone, not after Cora and August died. I knew I wouldn't be able to handle the heartache that followed their inevitable demise, so I just pushed everyone away. I never entertained anyone romantically for longer than a week, maybe two if I was staying in one city for a longer time.

Tristan touched his fingers to my ear – to the ripped bit of cartilage just above the silver hoop I wore. "This one?"

I said, "Hollow. It stretches all the way back along my skull. My ear just took the brunt of it."

"I've killed a few Hollows before," he said, stretching his legs out. "I also have a list of Hollow names."

Hollow names? Did their names hold power, as ours did? Could we kill Hollows with their names, too?

He continued, "This strange girl came to me asking for the name of one of the most powerful Hollows recently. I wonder what happened to her."

I shifted to face him. Storm be damned, I was finally *getting somewhere*.

"What do you mean?" I pressed.

He sighed through his nose. "Hollows often have two names. Their name, and their true name. I was able to dig up some of the true names. The girl – she was a half breed, you know. Probably the first, and only one in our lifetime

– had the name of the King of the Hollows, but not his true name. Goddess knows why she needed that."

King of the Hollows. They had a *king*.

If I could track down that king and kill him, maybe the senseless massacres would finally stop. Maybe they were like wasps – if I killed the monarch, the rest would come crumbling down.

Tristan continued, "I had to trade something rather personal to get that name. I'm curious as to why that half-breed was poking around the king. What did she want with him?"

He reached into his pocket and pulled out a small leather-bound book, no bigger than his palm. He flipped through the delicate pages until he landed on the one he'd been looking for.

"'Aita, king of the Hollows. True name is Adonis Nyx. Hides himself in shadows. No records of what his face truly looks like,'" he read. Then, before the rain could destroy his work, Tristan shoved the book back into his pocket. "Some rumors say he's a god. Some say he's absolutely hideous and that's why he hides himself. I find it strange, though, that he is tucked away safe in his kingdom and all these other Hollows are out here killing people. And why did that girl need his name?"

I had the same questions myself, but no answers. Instead, I said, "Aren't you the spy? Isn't getting answers your whole job?"

He groaned loudly. "You sound *just* like my sister right now. Wasn't getting the names good enough? I'll just have someone else get the answers. I don't get paid enough for this."

He spoke dramatically, dragging out his vowels and adding a whine to his tone.

Something told me he definitely had answers but was omitting them on purpose for whatever reason.

"What do you know about Medea's Relics?" I asked, deciding to change the subject since Tristan wasn't keen on giving me any straight answers.

He cocked his head to the side, as if he was a confused puppy. "Well, it depends on what you want to know."

I sat up straighter. "What are they? Where do we find them? What do they do?"

His lips quirked up into a lopsided grin. He flopped onto his back, letting fat raindrops splatter against his pale face. He looked...angelic. Godly. Absolutely *divine.*

"The Relics were what Medea used to slay the Old Gods," he explained.

I frowned. How was a *cup* supposed to kill an ancient *god?* It hadn't seemed particularly special. If anything, it was cheap. Simple. Something that a low-level gentleman's club would use over and over again to quench the thirst of their patrons. Something found in a bar or tavern, dented, and rusted after being used again and again. It hardly seemed worth the trouble we'd gone through to get it. It hardly seemed worth Shasi's life.

"We found one," I said. "A...cup. It was in the Temple of Medea in the Svadaevan Desert. Any idea what that thing is supposed to do?"

He opened his eyes and looked in my direction. "The Chalice? Stories say that whoever drinks from it will be rotten from the inside out. It doesn't matter if you fill it with an elixir of immortality, you'll still decay."

The inexplicable trust I felt for Tristan obviously wasn't reciprocated. He wasn't telling me everything.

"What's the catch? Medea wasn't *over*powered. So, what's the catch? What happened when she used the Relics?"

Tristan's hand found mine once again. He laced his lithe fingers with mine, his thumb rubbing the back of my hand affectionately.

"She's asleep, isn't she? She's been asleep for nearly two decades. I don't know what would happen if a mortal used the Relics, though. Medea was a goddess and she still had to go into hibernation. Have you used the Chalice yet?"

I shook my head. Lightning lit up the sky, illuminating Tristan in a bath of celestial light. The dark circles under his mismatched eyes looked nearly black.

"Not yet," I said. "Tristan, do you want to come inside and rest? You look exhausted."

He waved his hand flippantly. "No. But you'd better get inside soon. The storm is getting closer. The last thing I'd want is for you to get struck by lightning."

I opened my mouth to respond, but the warmth of his hand suddenly vanished, and he was gone. The red string in my pocket felt heavier than lead.

The inn didn't have any baths in the room, but after pulling my hood over my ears and talking to the concierge at the front desk, I was pointed to the common bathroom on the first floor of the inn. Since it was so late, it was, much to my delight, empty. I filled one of the copper tubs with warm water and peeled off my soaked clothes. I lay them over the radiator to dry.

I'd bathed in public places like this before. While I hated how vulnerable I felt being fully naked and at the mercy of anyone who walked in, I couldn't complain about having a free bath, especially one with hot, clean water.

I stepped in, letting myself sink until the water was up to my chin.

If there was one thing humans could learn from fae it was how to make bathtubs big enough for my entire body to fit in.

I washed quickly, getting the rainwater and dirt and stubborn grains of sand off my body. The soap was cheap, made of olive oil, but did wonders to get the remaining bits of sand from areas that had no business hosting the vestiges of my desert adventure. I scrubbed my scalp and washed my face twice. I desperately needed a shave – the rough stubble I usually kept maintained had grown wiry, not quite a proper beard but longer than normal stubble – but that would have to wait. I rubbed the olive oil soap over my cheeks, trying to clean up the gentle acne that had formed there.

Goddess, I deserved some sort of reward payment from the kings and queens of the entire continent if I somehow managed to put an end to the reign of Hollows. I would use the cash to take a vacation to the Southern Isles. I'd book an entire grand hotel for myself and dine like a king. I'd bathe in gilded tubs and have the prettiest of men massage my aching muscles and –

I sank my head under the water, blocking out the world and the rest of my thoughts.

When my lungs ached and I emerged from the water, I heaved myself out of the tub, using one of the scratchy terrycloth towels to dry myself. My clothes were mostly dry – my coat and stiff boots were still damp, so I forgo putting them on – so I dressed and slipped back upstairs to my shared room.

I dreamt of lightning, holy and bright, that night.

Morning came with the same bellhop as the night before bringing us break-fast ("is the other miss awake to eat?" he'd asked softly when he pushed the cart full of bowls of porridge into our room. He looked relieved when Shasi, who was busy brushing her mane of curls into a manageable shape, said she was).

The porridge was bland, even when I sprinkled brown sugar and dried fruit over it, but I was hungry and desperate enough to not be picky, so I ate it all in just a few bites.

The five of us met outside the front of the inn, everyone bathed and fed and dressed.

"I think Dio should handle the Chalice," I said once everyone had gathered.

Auri frowned. "Why? I don't want to give it up."

My lips formed a tight line. "I... Found out that the Chalice basically poisons whoever drinks from it. If anyone should carry it, it should be the assassin who literally named herself *after* a poison."

Dio opened her mouth, presumably to ask me *how* I knew that, but Auri spoke before she could; "Fine." She dropped her bag and dug through it, pulling out the silver cup. She thrust it out to Dio, who snatched it up quickly.

"I want the next Relic, though," Auri huffed. She pulled her bag over her shoulder and started walking towards the tree line.

"We don't even know what Relic that is!" Shasi shouted after her.

"Don't care!" responded Auri in a singsong voice. "It's mine!"

Please, Medea, I silently prayed. I followed the others towards the Forest. *Let the Relic be something so heinously boring that Auri stops whining for* five minutes.

The forest loomed before us, oak trees stretching up to scrape against the cloudy sky. Intermixed throughout were spindly cypress trees and ancient, gnarled yew trees. There was a strangeness to the thicket, a fog that seemed to ooze out and beckon us in. Magic, I assumed, unlike any I'd ever felt before.

Dio stepped into the copse of trees first. When she didn't instantly combust on the spot, Auri followed, then Mirza. I followed Shasi in. The temperature instantly dropped a handful of degrees. I was thankful my coat had fully dried after I'd left it on the radiator all night.

"Welcome," Dio said, sweeping her arms widely, "to the Foloi Forest."

CHAPTER FORTY-ONE

KORE

With nowhere to go and little warning, I stood and hurried to the book-case where Adonis kept his rocks. There was just enough behind the chair next to it for me to squeeze myself.

Why had I been given plant magic when something like Adonis's shadows would've been a million times more useful in this situation?

Closing my eyes, all I could do was listen to the chaos outside the room.

"*Adonis!* You know it has been *far* too long! I was in the area. I just *had* to visit you." Her tone had changed; no longer was it full of seething fury. Instead, she spoke in a high-pitched squeal that made me want to claw my ears off.

"Not long enough, Minniva," grumbled Adonis in response.

She ignored him completely. The sharp *clickety-clack* of her heels against the marble floor drew far too close for comfort. I held my breath, as if she could smell my fear like a hound.

"I'd been waiting for you to write to me, Adonis dear. I checked the post every day to see if there was a letter from you. You used to write me love letters, don't you remember?"

I stiffened. *Adonis* wrote her *love letters?*

I could see his looping script on a piece of thick paper, pouring out his heart for this...this Minniva *bitch.*

Thorny vines sprouted from between my fingers, curling around my knuckles and wrists. Crimson blood spilled down my flesh and onto my skirts, but I hardly even noticed.

The voices suddenly stopped just outside the door of the room I was in. Minniva said, "Why's this door closed? I miss this room. We used to make love –" the doorknob jiggled. Panic seized me by the throat. I swallowed hard.

I had to get *out.*

I stood, grabbing onto the bookcase for support.

The bookcase shifted, nearly sending me tumbling to the floor.

A draft hit me in the face, coming from... *behind the bookcase.*

The doorknob jiggled again. I shoved all my weight into the bookcase. It slid over, revealing an opening just big enough for me to slip through. I pushed the bookcase back into place just as the door opened.

Darkness enveloped me.

Damn my fae blood for giving me *plant* magic and not *light* magic.

I blindly felt around the dark, trying to assess my surroundings. Cold, stone walls, close together and claustrophobic. Stairs – narrow, judging by how I nearly slipped down one.

I lowered myself down until I was seated against one of the stairs. With one hand pressed against the wall, I began scooting down. Each bump caused my teeth to clash together, but it was better than tumbling down the stairs to goddess knows where.

Think of plants, Kore, I told myself as I slipped down two stairs at once. *Those white flowers that follow you everywhere.* Another step.

Vines, sometimes with thorns, sometimes with flowers, sometimes with both or neither. Another step. Another.

Pomegranates, shared with Adonis in the moonlight. I slipped down two more steps. Fuck.

Garden vegetables that don't crumble to ash if I stop thinking about them. Another.

Fungi that irritate Mother, even though they're pretty, and sometimes glow green. Another, another, another.

Unruly bushes that – wait.

I stopped, my heart in my throat. The glowing mushrooms. I had no idea *what* they were or how I'd created them, but...

I held my hands together and focused, just as Adonis had taught me to. *Focus, focus, focus...*

Then, birthed between my palms, a tiny green light began to glow. It grew and grew, illuminating my surroundings until it was the size of my fist. The mushroom's stalk was thin, its cap drooping and heavy. The light flickered as the mushroom – *foxfire* – threatened to turn to ash. I cupped my hand around it protectively, refusing to let it burn out.

I was in a stairwell, almost like the one leading to the catacombs.

Standing, I picked up my skirts with my free hand, holding the foxfire out with my other to light up the curved stairway as I slowly, slowly, slowly made my descent to the bottom.

A narrow stone hallway lined with long-emptied sconces opened before me. Holding my foxfire tighter, I tiptoed down the hall.

Every now and then, I'd stop and look at the stones on the walls. Most were old and weathered, but some... some held tiny carvings.

A three-headed dog standing before an iron gate.

Three women – one old, one young, one heavy with child – knelt before a river.

A woman with wings dipping a wingless child into a second river.

A sword, a bolt of lightning, a goblet, a stringed instrument shaped like a horseshoe, a mausoleum barred with thick columns.

A vast swirl of stars, some making constellations I knew – the Crane, the Cat and her Kittens, Ora – while others were scattered about to create the illusion of night.

A man and a woman, hand in hand.

My foxfire flickered again, so I picked up my skirts once again and hurried down the rest of the hallway.

The narrow walls finally opened into the mouth of an antechamber. Even my foxfire couldn't light all the corners. I clutched it to my chest, walking slowly into the belly of the room.

In the far corner, a glowing blue stone caught my attention. I hurried over to it, clipping my hip on something solid. I hissed in pain but didn't stop to see what had attacked me. The blue glow was *pulling* me to it. My hand itched, desperate to *touch* it.

I reached out, slowly, slowly, achingly, and pressed my palm to the blue glow.

And the room *exploded*.

Light flooded the antechamber – which wasn't an antechamber at all, I realized – bathing the smooth stone walls in a pale blue glow. I'd expected them to be made of stone, but *no*.

They were covered in frescoes, perfectly preserved save for a few chipped and cracked areas here and there. I spun in a slow circle, taking in the story told through ancient ceruleans and vermilions.

A shadowed creature with red eyes standing beside a woman with hair so pale it looked white and eyes so purple they looked red.

The woman conjuring up a storm cloud, bringing rains down on a dried field. *Eo*.

Eo and the shadow figure, taller than mountains, fighting a battle that razed cities and cracked the earth into canyons.

Eo, her stomach swollen with a child – no, *children.* Her consort, the shadow figure, banishing her to a desolate island with rocky shores and steep cliffs and stormy skies. *The Northern Isles.*

The consort swallowing the first-born child and a rock.

Eo raising her child – a girl with dark hair and mismatched eyes, one bluer than the oceans she was born looking at, one as brown as the earth she'd been birthed onto.

Medea with a chalice, pouring it into the mouth of a pale-skinned, dark-haired woman. The liquid left the chalice blue but turned red as it spilled into the woman's mouth.

Medea with a bolt of lightning nocked against a bow like an arrow, piercing it through the chest of a god with ocean waves for hair.

Medea with a sword, slicing through the consort until he was nothing more than minced chunks of flesh.

Medea locking the remnants of her father in a mausoleum shrouded in darkness.

Medea strumming the lyre, calling back the soul of her brother.

The Relics being scattered – to a forest, to a lake atop a mountain, to the skies, to a temple in the desert, to a dark pocket of nothingness.

I turned once more, trying to catch the end of Medea's story, but it was gone. Someone had slashed up the frescoed wall, leaving a cliffhanger to the goddess's life.

Then, I caught sight of what exactly I'd hit my hip on. In the center of the room, which was not an antechamber, but a *crypt,* was a marble casket. Hesitantly, I stepped towards it and brushed away the thin coating of dust on top of it.

FROM STORMS AND CHAOS WAS SHE BORN,

FOR REVENGE, HER SOUL WAS SWORN.

THROUGH DEATH AND DEMISE,

The tugging sensation returned, my palms *itching burning aching*.

I grabbed the lip of the casket and *pushed*, the marble scraping with a sound that sent harsh shivers racing down my spine.

Through the blue light, I was able to make out a sliver of the cadaver resting there. Only, it wasn't a skeleton. It was a...fleshy body, with cheeks still flushed with life. She had soft brown curls that tumbled over lithe, albeit muscular, shoulders. Her lips parted slightly, as if she was still breathing. Beneath her thickly lashed eyes were two beauty marks on the highest point of one cheekbone. Her hands were clasped over her chest, holding a bouquet of the same little white flowers that followed me. Her chest that rose and fell gently.

She didn't even need to open her eyes for me to know, without a doubt, that they were mismatched – one stormy blue, one warm brown.

I took a step back.

I'd just stumbled upon the final resting place of the goddess Medea.

I didn't fix the slab of marble covering the Mother and Executioner in her sleep. I didn't go back to the blue stone to extinguish the light. I gripped my foxfire tightly, as if it was my lifeline, and dashed up the stairs. I'd rather face Minniva Hedy than stew in the fact that Medea was not only *alive,* but asleep beneath the Underworld palace.

Did Ceralis know? Did Adonis know?

He *had* to know. There was no way he wasn't aware of a *goddess* sleeping beneath his home. After all, the only entrance had been in his parlor.

I soon found the backside of the bookcase blocking the entrance to the tomb. I put my hand on it, then stopped. There were voices coming from the parlor.

"Are you going to make her your queen?" Ceralis. He had to be referring to Minniva Hedy. Jealousy coiled deep in my stomach.

"I don't know, Cer," sighed Adonis. "I don't. I know I need a queen, but..."

"Well, if he's returning, you probably should get a queen. I doubt he still thinks you're dead."

There was a pause before Adonis said, "If my father does return after all these centuries, I doubt a queen will do any good to stop him."

"But," drawled Ceralis in a sing-song voice, "reinforcements. Surprises. He wouldn't expect it."

Adonis sighed again. Was he really thinking of making Minniva his queen?

Finally, Adonis said, "I suppose I will bring the topic up."

"Good," said Ceralis. "I know you don't want to, but it would be good. After all, maybe she can finally track down the other half of your soul."

PART THREE

INTERLUDE

To Kill a God

To kill a god, one must not only destroy their flesh vessel, but they must also extinguish their soul. For every god has a soul (though some have multiple), and their souls are what tether them to the corporeal realm. The Shadow was not a shadow, though that was the form he took, but a corrupted soul of a god thought to have been slain many centuries ago. Even Titanomachy could not slice through the intangible essence of an immortal being. Without a vessel, the Shadow latched onto him like a predator on prey.

The differences were subtle at first. He no longer liked certain foods. Certain smells made him sick. He burned more easily in the sun.

They became more noticeable as the years went on. After he'd given the Shadow his first taste of blood – rich with the flavor of earth – after centuries of fasting.

The Shadow became insatiable, and he could not keep up with the hunger pains that twisted his stomach into knots and left him starving for more, no matter how much he ate.

Earth blood was salty and nutty in flavor, leaving the aftertaste of petrichor in his mouth.

Iron blood was coppery and warm, and while it burned like cayenne, it made his stomach feel warmer and fuller.

He longed for the mixed earth-iron blood that coursed through the veins of a single soul, but he resisted the Shadow's urges, for he was not that kind of monster.

Yet.

To kill a god, one must burn the corpse, for dicing it into cubes and locking it away will not prevent them from returning.

He hunched over the toilet of the rundown inn he'd crashed at, coughing up bile that looked like ground coffee and pink foam. His twin shadows danced against the wall, flickering in time with the oil lamp he'd knocked over in his desperation to get to somewhere decent to empty his stomach.

You are weak, chided the Shadow.

You picked me as a vessel, he shot back. Then, he gripped the lip of the toilet and heaved until his stomach cramped and ached and he couldn't do anything but spit globs of pink saliva out of his dried, burning mouth.

He flushed, whisking away his vomit down the septic pipes and out of sight. He slumped to the ground, clothes dangerously close to the kerosene. Perhaps he would be lit aflame. Perhaps he would be doused in fire that would crumble his body to ash and free his soul from the decay tainting his insides. Perhaps he'd finally be rid of the Shadow.

You shall never be rid of me, said the Shadow. The lamp was moved, just out of his reach.

To kill a god, one must first give it a body, and the Shadow had been cultivating the body of the boy before him for many, many years.

Because to kill a god, a god must first be *alive.*

CHAPTER FORTY-TWO

SHASI

The damp air clung to me like a second skin, chilling me to the bone despite the heavy wool jacket I wore over my woolen trousers and high-necked sweater. Dio had helped me put my shirt on backwards and my coat on the right way so the holes sewn into the back to accommodate fae wings wouldn't overlap and make the cold air even more unbearable.

"How exactly are we going to find the Relic?" I asked, toeing a strange greenish mushroom with my boot. It crumbled easily, leaving a stain on the once-pristine leather.

"It's this way," said Auri. She hopped over a fallen log. I glanced at Mirza, who was too busy studying a blue moss that clung to the trunk of a cypress tree to notice. I grabbed his hand, giving it a gentle squeeze to pull him back into the present.

The others didn't complain and simply followed Auri as she began traipsing through the woods like this was a game.

She *always* acted like this was a game.

I was nearly killed by the monster in the temple – my body still ached from the remaining bruises – and all Auri could do was steal weapons and whine about getting a Relic to herself and hop over logs like she was a child.

I dug my nails into my palms to keep from saying anything.

Mirza nudged my shoulder with his own. "You know, I don't actually hate this place. It's damp and muddy, but at least I won't be waking up with sand up my ass for once."

"Mir, you have never once woken up with sand up your ass," I shot back, unable to keep the grin from my face. "You get to sleep in a nice bed inside."

"Only because I'm your personal guard," he said.

"You got to sleep in a nice bed when you were my lady-in— my…" I bit down on my tongue.

He just chuckled. I'd slipped up more than once over the years, but he always laughed it off. He treated it like it wasn't a big deal, but I knew it ate away at him.

"I *was* your lady-in-waiting, Shas," he said. "A *long* time ago. I don't even think it technically counts, since we were both gap-toothed kids. And I'm your guard now, so I don't care."

I grabbed one of his unruly curls – made even unrulier by the wet air – and gave it a tug. "My point stands. Anyways, I have no idea how you can even stand it here. It's too cold and too wet."

"I didn't say I *stand* it. I just don't hate it. It's a nice change of scenery for once."

"Well, I hate it. And I hate these clothes, too." I tugged on the waistband of my trousers. I wasn't used to clothes that constricted my body. I hated the way the trousers cinched my stomach and pressed into my hips, making me feel like a loaf of bread stuffed into a pan two sizes too small. I was overly aware of the soft bulge my belly made against my jacket, and the rubbing of my navel jewelry against the waistband of my trousers drove me insane.

"Shas." Mirza squeezed my hand. "You're beautiful. You know that, right? The fae and us Svadaevans have different beauty standards, but neither are wrong. The clothes here probably have to be thicker and stiffer to keep people warm, just like ours have to be looser so we don't melt."

I glanced down at myself. He did have a point. I would've frozen into a block of ice if I'd stayed in my regular clothes a minute longer. The wool was scratchy, but it did keep the rain from seeping into my bones and kept me warm.

Mostly warm.

I stepped on a twig that broke with a *snap* that sent my heart into my throat. Even though I had my sword still, I couldn't help moving closer to Mirza, as if he could keep me safe.

We walked in silence for a few hours, following Auri as she either led us to the Relic or to our doom. At least we had Dio, who could open a portal and get us out of here if things went sideways.

I decided to break the silence. "How old are all of you, anyways?"

There was a pause. I quickly jumped in by saying, "I'm twenty-one. I'll be twenty-two in less than a month. Mirza is two months younger than me."

He scowled, as if two months were truly all that important.

Auri piped up, "I'm nineteen."

"Twenty-two," mumbled Dio.

"Cas?" Auri prompted.

Cassiel grumbled something incoherent before huffing, "Twenty-four."

Auri burst out laughing. "You're *old!*" she managed to choke out through laughter so loud it shook the canopy above us.

Cas scowled. "You're practically an infant. No wonder you have to resort to cheating in Crimson Crowns; you're too young to grasp the concept of the game."

Auri fake-gasped, clutching her gloved hand to her chest. "I do *not* cheat!"

"There's no way you can win that many games in a row without cheating," he said pointedly.

Auri bent down and grabbed a hunk of mulchy moss. She threw it at Cas, who barely managed to dodge it.

It hit Dio instead, striking her right in the chest with a wet, squelchy *smack*. Her wings twitched, and in an instant, she had her knife drawn. Auri screeched, tripping over a rock as Dio ran after her.

"So childish," I muttered under my breath.

Mirza squeezed my hand. "She's still young, you know. And maybe acting childish is how she copes. After all, she's probably just as scared as the rest of us."

We walked and walked and walked. Even with my thick socks, my boots ate blisters into my heels and the sides of my toes. With the thick canopy blocking out the sky, it was damn near impossible to tell what time it was. The timepiece Cas had stopped working the second we stepped into the Foloi Forest. Whenever anyone asked Auri how close we were to the Relic, she'd just hug her hand to her chest and mutter, *"close."*

Eventually, Auri stopped dead in her tracks.

"What –" Cas started.

She held up a hand. "Shh. Do you hear that?"

I glanced around the dark copse of trees. I couldn't hear...anything. No wind rustling the branches, no birds singing, no rushing of water...nothing.

The forest had gone completely silent. The only question was... How *long* had it been silent?

"The singing?" urged Auri. "Does anyone hear the singing?"

I narrowed my eyes. Even if I strained hard, I couldn't hear anything other than my own breathing. I sure as hell didn't hear *singing*.

Auri started to hum what I could only assume was the song she heard.

Cas blanched. "That song," he said. "I know that song. It's what my mother used to sing."

Auri didn't hear him. At least, she didn't acknowledge him. As if in a trance, she began walking – almost as if she was floating – towards a rock formation smothered by moss and vines.

"Auri!" Dio called after her. But Auri didn't hear.

She grabbed a handful of vines and pulled them aside, revealing an opening in the rocks. Then, she fell to her knees, hands clamped over her ears as she *screamed.*

She screamed and screamed, as if in agony, the sound tearing at her throat so harshly it made my own vocal folds ache.

"YOU HURTSSSSSS USSSSSS, SSSSSSO WE HURTSSSSSSS YOU!" screamed Auri. Her voice had split into a dissonant trifecta of voices that weren't her own. It sounded like nails against glass, like metal clanging against metal.

Above, there was a fluttering of feathers. A murder of crows – thirteen, blast that unlucky number – had taken flight from their watchful posts.

"Cut it off!" Auri screamed, her own voice bleeding through the cacophony of dissonant thirds. *"Diora, cut it off* please!"

Dio reached for her knife but stopped.

"Shut up! Just shut the fuck up!" Tears rolled down Auri's pale cheeks. Dio forwent her knife and rushed to Auri's side instead, crashing to the ground and pulling the girl close in a smothering hug.

My gaze skirted past the two of them to the mouth of the cave Auri had revealed. An incandescent glow cut through the abysmal black expanse, gleaming golden, like a miniature sun had been stuffed inside the rock formation.

I took a step closer. *Would Medea really hide a Relic in plain –*

Out of the cave stepped a monster.

Auri had stopped screaming, her lithe body curled around Dio as if the assassin could protect her from the otherworldly beast that had emerged. Cas drew his knife, holding it at an angle to throw. Mirza freed his sword, taking a step to stand in front of me.

The monster was even more heinous than the beast in the Temple of Medea. Where that one walked bipedal, this one crouched on four feline legs. It had the body of a large cat – not unlike the cheetahs in Svadaeva, only bigger and without any spots – though from its back sprouted a pair of large, feathered wings.

And, most disturbingly, its face was that of a woman. A *human* woman.

It bared its human teeth, chapped lips curled into a snarl. The monster stepped closer, its head twisting and twisting and twisting until it went in a full circle.

I gripped my sword tightly, the hilt slipping in my sweat-slicked grip. My heart pounded so hard and fast in my throat I worried less that my insides would bruise and more that the beast would hear it.

"There are two sisters," the monster spoke, its voice even worse than the earsplitting mess that had spilled from Auri's mouth earlier.

Its head went in a full circle again before it continued, *"When one gives birth to the other, the other gives birth to the first."*

What?!

The beast prowled closer, circling Auri and Dio. Dio clutched her close. She reached for her bag, presumably to get the Chalice.

"There are two sisters. When one gives birth to the other, the other gives birth to the first," the monster repeated. It wasn't phrased as a question, but it wasn't a statement, either. The monster's head spun again, the gnashing of its bones drawing nausea up my gullet.

Not a question. Not a statement.

A...

"Riddle!" I blurted out. Four pairs of human eyes landed on me. One set of inhuman, monster eyes stayed on Auri. It was as if I hadn't even spoken. The monster circled the two again.

"It's a riddle," Mirza supplied when my explanation – or, rather, lack thereof – got nowhere. "It's a riddle! We have to figure it out!"

"Well, I'm fresh out of ideas," Cas said, giving up already. "I didn't go to school, so I don't know how to solve riddles."

"They didn't teach us how to solve riddles at the assassin's guild," muttered Dio.

Auri choked on a sob. The monster let out a low, predatory growl that churned my insides.

"There are two sisters. When one gives birth to the other, the other gives birth to the first," the monster hissed again.

"Not helping!" Dio snapped. The beast didn't acknowledge her.

I tightened my grip on my sword. I should know the answer. I had the best education out of everyone here, save for Mirza who had attended every single one of my classes since the day he became my lady-in-waiting.

Think, Shasi, think! The cave likely held the Relic, since the last time we faced a chimeric monster like this one, it had been when we found the Chalice. The beast before us had to be some sort of guardian appointed by Medea herself. A guardian entrusted to protect the Relic with its life.

The riddle would have to be something Medea knew the answer to, but also something that wouldn't be impossible to solve. Auri still had both the journal and the map in her bag, and with the monster prowling around them like a predator stalking its prey, there was no chance I could get close enough to grab either.

"There are two sisters..."

I squeezed my eyes shut, my brows knitting together. There were plenty of famous sisters throughout history. There were Fate, Destiny, and Time, the children of Heela and masterminds behind all our lives, but they always came as a set of three. There were Christine and Raven, twin sisters who ruled over Wallaekva several hundreds of years ago, before they were killed in battle. There were –

"When one gives birth to the other…"

I shoved my sword into its sheath and began pacing, almost as if mimicking the monster. The blisters on my heels were an afterthought, as I focused all my attention on trying to solve the riddle.

I thought back to my theology and history classes, hoping to scrape a clue or two from them.

Medea was a goddess who, after witnessing the death of her mother, went out to kill her father. She ended up slaying all the Old Gods, had a child, then went to sleep somewhere. Did she have two daughters? Two sisters who, imbued with the godly power of the Mother and Executioner, could somehow birth each other, like morning did to night did to morning?

I stopped, nearly tripping over my own feet.

Morning and night. Night and morning.

"The other gives birth to the first."

Night and day! The answer had to be night and day.

"It's night and day!" I shouted, hoping the monster would acknowledge me this time. It had crept too close to Auri and Dio, its mouth salivating in a way no human mouth should.

The beast didn't respond. It opened its mouth and repeated the damn riddle again.

That had to be the answer. It just *had* to be. So why wasn't the monster responding? There was no specific goddess of the night – Orinos was god of the sky and Ora was god of the stars – and no goddess of the day.

The monster lunged, feinting just before its jaws could close on Auri's throat. It was targeting *her*.

"Auri, you have to answer!" Mirza said, catching on only a second after I did. "It's night –"

"Zina and Maulea!" Auri screeched just as the monster lunged again, this time aiming to kill.

It fell short, collapsing to the ground on all fours. Then, with a blood curdling cry, it burst into flames. It writhed, screaming in agony that was both human and monstrous. Chunks of burned flesh and fur peeled from its body, dropping to the ground in hunks of smoldering ash. The only thing worse than the screaming was the *smell* that permeated the air, drowning out the scents of petrichor and earth that previously dominated the forest. I gagged, choking down bile.

The monster's lower jaw snapped, falling to the ground. Stringy ligaments, torn and burnt, splintered, and broke, boiling blood splattering against the ground in crimson rivulets of gore. The screaming didn't stop, not until the hellish flames ignited the flesh-fur throat of the beast, eating away at its trachea and vocal folds.

When it finally collapsed, the fire dying into thick plumes of black smoke, there was nothing but charred bones left.

I turned and vomited.

Auri did the same. Cas covered his nose and mouth with the collar of his jacket. It did little to hide the greenish pallor to his face, slick with a sheen of sweat.

Auri coughed, spitting out yellowish bile and thick strings of saliva.

"How –" started Dio, only she was cut short when Auri heaved again. Patiently, Dio scraped back Auri's pale tresses, braiding them into a single plait while she emptied her gullet once more.

"G-goddess of nothing," choked out Auri, her voice hoarse and scratchy from the stomach acid she'd regurgitated. "A-and ev—" she dry heaved, clutching Dio's arm tightly. Tears and snot ran down her face.

Cas silently slipped over to them, removing his jacket and draping it over Auri's shoulders.

"Burning flesh is disgusting," he said, his version of comfort. "It's not something you ever get used to trust me. It's not something you'd *want* to get used to."

"N-not the first time," croaked Auri. She wiped her mouth with the back of her hand.

My feet moved on their own accord, bringing me closer to the two of them. I stepped over the pile of bones, still smoking with bits of meat stuck to them, and knelt next to Auri.

"Maulea gives birth to everything," I said slowly, rationalizing the answer to the sadistic riddle. "And Zina destroys it all, creating a blank canvas for Maulea to create with."

Auri tilted her head up, her pale eyes blurred with tears. I choked back tears of my own. I was a princess, and while I was hundreds of miles from home, these people before me were my friends. I had a duty to keep them safe. To put their needs first and comfort them before I could comfort myself.

I brushed my thumbs under Auri's eyes, ridding her snowy lashes of crystalline tears. She leaned into my touch ever so slightly, a shuddering breath escaping her lips.

"The Relic," she gasped, "is *mine.*"

I flicked her nose.

"No shit," I said, un-princess like. "It's yours. You can fetch it once you feel okay enough to stand."

"What was that thing?" Mirza asked. He toed the bones with his boot before shifting his gaze to Dio.

Dio frowned, her mouth a thin slash against her face. "How am I supposed to know?"

"You're from here." Mirza shrugged.

"I didn't ask *you* what that bull-man-thing in Svadaeva was," she said pointedly. Mirza kicked one of the bones away. It crumbled to ash almost instantly – far too fast to not be something otherworldly.

"Fair," he mumbled. "So, it wasn't fae. Does that mean it was... Hollow-made?"

"I was thinking Medea-made," Cas said exactly what I was thinking. "Just like that thing in Svadaeva. She must have put these...beasts wherever she hid her Relics. Otherwise, what's stopping someone from stumbling upon one and taking it?"

Auri gripped Dio's bicep, using it as leverage to stand. She stumbled, Dio quickly steadying her. They exchanged a look that lasted no longer than a second but seemed to span an eternity between them.

I knew that look.

I gave Mirza those looks when he wasn't looking. He gave the palace staff – kitchen girls and stableboys and anyone in between – those looks.

One foot at a time, as if she was an infant learning to walk, Auri stumbled towards the mouth of the cave. Dio followed closely behind, leaving Cas, Mirza, and me to trail behind.

The cave was pitch dark inside, save for that twinkling light of gold. The rock formation seemed, strangely, much bigger on the inside than it was on the outside. We followed the light, going deeper and deeper into the igneous cavern.

A lifetime seemed to pass, the darkness becoming thick and suffocating, like congealed blood had filled the air, before the golden light no longer twinkled as a gentle glow but became a gilded beacon.

Auri approached it, and we let her.

She brushed her fingers against the light, turning the incandescence into something corporeal and physical. The light dimmed, no longer blinding but tolerable enough for me to make out what exactly Auri was holding.

A lyre, solid gold with yew leaves and tiny flowers engraved in the soft metal. Seven strings made of the same gold were strung taut, ready to be plucked.

A lyre to create and to unmake, unto death it shall betake.

Auri chuckled, the sound rasp and hoarse. "Gods damn it, I got the *worst* Relic."

And then, without warning, Auri collapsed to the ground.

CHAPTER FORTY-THREE

KORE

I shoved the bookcase aside without hesitation. I had no reason to be jealous. Adonis wasn't mine. He was just... a friend. A friend dedicated to helping me. It shouldn't matter if he wanted to marry Minniva Hedy and make her his queen.

But still, jealousy burned through my veins, hotter than magma and brighter than the sun.

Adonis and Ceralis both turned to face me. Shock was plastered on Ceralis's face. Adonis's shadows twitched, betraying no emotions.

"There you are, Little Star," Adonis said calmly. "I was wondering where you'd run off to. Clever hiding spot."

Did... Did he not know about the crypt behind the bookcase? Did he not know that Medea lay asleep in a casket beneath the palace, beneath our very feet?

I curled my nails into my palms.

"I want to go home," I said.

It wasn't what I meant to say. I wanted to call Adonis out on all his secrets. I wanted to tell him to marry Minniva Hedy and make a queen out of her. I wanted to demand answers. But all I could do was ask to go home.

Tears burned my eyes. I blinked furiously, refusing to let them fall. Refusing to let Adonis see me cry.

Mother was right. I was nothing more than a child – a weak and pathetic *child.*

"You can't go!" cried Ceralis. "I don't want you to go! Donny don't let her. Make her stay!"

Adonis's shadows shifted. He said nothing.

Ceralis grabbed Adonis's arm, tugging on it like a child having a temper tantrum would do. "Don't let her leave! Don't make her go back! *Please!*"

My heart twisted, aching at the sight of Ceralis on the verge of tears. I opened my mouth to tell him it would be okay, but Adonis spoke before I could.

"If that is what you wish, little star, then so be it."

His shadows enveloped me. In an instant, I could feel my magic flare, building up like a spark within me. It swelled until it nearly burst. A flurry of petals and flowers and vines with thorns erupted around us, a violent storm of pure magic I couldn't control, seeping from every pore of my being, as if my soul itself was leaking out in the form of amaranth and hyacinths.

The darkness of Adonis's shadows smothered me. There was a flash of blue, like the darkest depths of the ocean come to swallow me.

Then, there was nothing.

The darkness had become eternal, stretching for an infinity in each direction until all I could see was ink.

Then, a flash of gold.

"You are not meant to be here," hissed a feminine voice.

From the shadows stepped a woman. Her skin was black as night with twin-kling constellations of gold stars splattered across her flesh. Her hair was just as black, tumbling over her shoulders in a series of thick coils and blending in with the loose black fabric of her ancient-styled dress. One of her eyes was inky black all the way through. The other was shot through with a gold iris, the same color as the stars on her skin, the same color as the paint across her thin lips, the same color as the clasps and beads strung through her hair.

"What are you doing here, Child of Ceres?"

Ceres. My mother's name.

I opened my mouth to speak. No sound came out.

Another figure appeared seconds later. She was the antithesis to the first in every way possible. While the first woman had skin the color of obsidian, the new guest was the color of moonlight, a white so bright it was blinding against the swath of darkness around us. Her hair was thin and mostly straight, the gentlest of waves curling the ends that brushed against her full hips. While the first woman's right eye was solid, this new one's left was opaque white, the other with a silver iris. She wore the same ancient tunic-styled dress, the loose fabric hugging her hips and full bosom. Her lips were full, painted silver, and the stars on her skin were the same color.

"A child of Ceres," the new woman purred. *"Your birth predates even our own children."*

I wet my lips with the tip of my tongue. Where was Adonis? Where was *I*?

"Who…" I started.

The first woman spoke over me. *"I am Zina, Goddess of Nothing."*

The second woman said, *"I am Maulea, Goddess of Everything."*

When they spoke again, it was at the same time, a dissonance that almost blended into harmony. *"Do you know how to kill a god, Child of Ceres?"*

"Do you slice off their head and leave them for dead?" Maulea said in a sing-song voice.

"Do you burn them at the stake and wait for death to take?" chimed Zina.

Spider-like shivers raced down my spine, pulling the fine hairs across my body to stand on end.

"You must take their soul…" Maulea said.

"… And destroy it. Are you a soul eater, Child of Ceres? Are you Hollow?" Zina asked.

Both goddesses reached up and unclasped the pins at their shoulders, letting their dresses fall to the ground in puddles of black and white. Across their bodies were thick scars, crisscrossed like lines on a map. Each one was deep enough to be a fatal blow, even to a god.

"The child of our children did this to us," Zina hissed. *"The child of our brother's spawn destroyed us. She thieved our souls and went to sleep."*

Maulea continued, *"We have no qualms with the child of our children. But she did not kill our brother's spawn. She did not destroy him the way she destroyed us. She did not rid the world of his soul, and he is not happy."*

"He is hungry," Zina rasped. *"He is hungry, and he is restless, and he will not stay satiated for long. He will return, Child of Ceres, and you must be there to put an end to him."*

I took a step back. Where was Adonis?! My heart thrummed against my rips, palpitating an arrhythmic beat that left my lungs aching for a full breath of air.

"You must find the child of Medea," the two said in unison. They closed their solid-colored eyes, the twin irises of gold and silver staring unblinking at me. *"You must find the child of Medea, Child of Ceres, and destroy the spawn of our brother before he can obliterate the world. He thirsts for revenge, and Medea will not wake in time."*

Their crisscrossed wounds began to weep blood, gold for Zina and silver for Maulea.

"You ate the Fruit of the Underworld," Maulea accused, not unkindly. *"You must stay to take your rightful place. You must find the child of Medea. You must find the vessel of Kaos before his transformation is complete."*

The goddesses began to fade.

"Wait!" I cried. "How... How do you know my mother?!"

Maulea's silver lips curled into a smile. *"Ceres Astra, the rightful heir of Caira, banished from her throne after laying with a human. We knew her well."*

Just as suddenly as they appeared, the two goddesses blinked out of sight.

The darkness left my vision slowly. I blinked a few times, the sudden light from a low-hanging gas-powered chandelier blurring my surroundings.

"–oile! Miss Etoile?" Ceralis's disjointed voice slowly sucked me back into reality. I wasn't in my home. I wasn't even in the center pavilion of Lavoisin, or the Lavoisin Forest. I was in the same parlor as before, in the same spot as before, not having moved an inch.

I sank to my knees, gasping for air. Ceralis crouched by my side, touching my cheek with his knuckles, as to not scratch me with his claws.

"She's burning up," he whispered. His gaze shifted to the murky blob of shadows that hovered above us both. Adonis.

Without waiting a second longer, Ceralis picked me up with surprising ease despite his lanky, slim figure.

His face blurred.

I ate the fruit, I thought.

Or maybe I said it out loud.

I couldn't tell. Thinking became too difficult, my body too heavy. I closed my eyes and welcomed the sweet embrace of unconsciousness.

I opened my eyes to an unfamiliar ceiling. Frescoes donned the entire expanse, decorated with paintings of black flowers and twisted trees and clouds dyed red from the setting rays of the oil-painted sun.

This was not my room.

I rolled over, smushing my cheek against the silk pillowcase beneath me. It smelled woodsy, like ash and cloves and funeral dirt and smoke. Adonis's smell.

I sat upright so fast my head spun.

On the black velvet chair beside the bed sat Adonis in his shadowy glory. His shadows twitched.

"You're awake," he said.

Something wet plopped against my legs. I glanced down to see a folded towel still damp with cold water. It must've been on my forehead.

"How... What?" I breathed, my voice hoarse with disuse.

"You had a fever," he explained. "You were in and out of consciousness for the entire afternoon. It's about three in the morning now. How are you feeling?"

I lay back down, staring at the vines adorned with black flowers that circled the ceiling. My head ached and my stomach cramped with hunger, but I didn't feel sick. I sure as hell didn't feel feverish.

"You ate something here," he continued when I didn't answer. "Didn't Ceralis tell you? If you wish to leave Heladés at one point or another, you cannot consume anything here."

I thought to the pomegranate seeds I'd eaten. I'd had no more than a handful, and now... Now I was trapped.

"Why?" I whispered.

"Because everyone here is either dead or divine and none of us have any real need for food. A guest who is neither dead nor divine will be forced to stay if they consume something here. Those were the rules Archyr and Styxia set, the rules I have no choice but to enforce." His shadows slumped, as if he slouched his shoulders. "I can't take you home, Little Star. I'm sorry. I shouldn't have trusted Ceralis to relay that information to you."

I toyed with the damp rag, twisting the terrycloth corners absently. If I was trapped, how was I supposed to track down Medea's child? Adonis said she was still alive, so there was no chance she was in Heladés. And if I couldn't leave...

I rolled onto my side. "Well," I grumbled, "if I'm stuck here for good, can I have something to eat?"

"What would you like?" he asked.

I squeezed my pillow to my chest. I'd give anything for a bowl of Mother's soup right now.

"I don't care," I replied. "Surprise me. I'm not picky. I can't eat meat, though."

The chair creaked as Adonis stood. He said, "I'll return shortly, then." His footsteps echoed across the wood floor. The door squeaked open, then shut with a slam.

I finally let the tears spill down my cheeks. I gripped the pillow tighter, sobbing into the no-doubt expensive satin. I'd always thought my house in Lavoisin was a prison, but it was *nothing* compared to this. I could never leave. Adonis was going to marry Minniva Hedy. I had *no one*. For the first time in my life, I was irrevocably and undeniably *alone*.

As my shoulders shook and trembled with each new wave of sobs, Maulea's words finally donned on me.

Ceres Astra, the rightful heir of Caira, banished from her throne after laying with a human.

Caira, the Seelie capital. A *fae* city.

My mysterious father wasn't my faerie parent; *Mother* was.

The door swung open moments later, and in stepped Adonis. His shadows acted as extra limbs, carrying trays piled high with what looked to be an entire kitchen's worth of food. He set them down, one by one, on the bed. I sat up and rubbed away my tears to get a look at the spread he'd brought. Fresh bread fluffier than clouds alongside dishes of sweet jam – I'd have to ask Adonis later where he managed to find the fruits to make it, since nothing could grow here without my help – and clotted cream; porridge topped with cinnamon and cloves and nuts; rich brown tea and a dish of cubed sugar; and, of course, a bowl of pomegranate seeds. Hungry as I was, I reached for the seeds first, forgoing the tiny silver spoon next to the dish and plucking a few of the jewel-like seeds with my fingers. I popped them in my mouth, crushing them against the roof of my mouth with my tongue.

Adonis returned to his seat next to my – *his* – bed, his shadows angled towards me.

I tore off a piece of bread and piled it high with jam and more seeds, nearly moaning when I sank my teeth into it. The only thing that could beat warm homemade bread, it seemed, was bread made for a king. I finished it quickly, devouring it in just a few bites. I went to the porridge next, eating it quickly despite how hot it was.

"I'm sorry," I said between mouthfuls. "It's been ages since I last ate anything, and I only had a couple pomegranate seeds."

Adonis chuckled, the sound sending warmth deep into my belly. He said, "Don't apologize, little star. All living things must eat, and you are still alive. We eat for pleasure here; the chef was ecstatic to hear someone would be eating their cooking for necessity."

I plopped two sugar cubes into my tea, sticking a third one into my mouth and letting it melt on my tongue.

"Where did you get the pomegranates? And the fruit for the jam?" I sipped my tea, hissing when the scalding liquid burned my tongue. Setting it down, I opted to simply stir it with the little spoon.

"There is this *darling* market in Renavalon – you've heard of it?" Renavalon was a small city just outside the capital of Lysaen, known for its artisans and craft guild. "I visit there once a week to get things for the kitchen that we can't grow here."

I tried to imagine Adonis, swathed in shadows, standing at a market vendor's stall, bargaining for fruits and vegetables.

Somehow, the idea of it was enough to distract me from my momentary stresses. I snorted, unable to hide it.

He continued, though there was a slight lilt to his voice, as if beneath the darkness that cloaked him, he was smiling, "Though, perhaps with you here, that can change. Most of the people in Heladés haven't had fresh fruits or vegetables since they were alive, and for most of them, that has been a long time. You will have to fight Cer for anything sweet, though. Almost all the fruit here gets devoured by him before any of us can touch it."

I lifted my cup again and took a sip, the tea cooler now. The malty goodness settled in my stomach, warming me to the core.

Adonis picked up the trays now that I'd finished eating, using his shadowy tentacles to move them to the oval coffee table near the roaring fireplace. I held my teacup in my hands, the warmth seeping through the bone china and into my palms.

"My mother is a long-lost fae princess," I blurted.

His shadows stilled. "I know."

"That makes me – wait, you *know?*" I nearly dropped my cup. I quickly gulped down the rest and set the empty cup on the bedside table. Turning toward Adonis I said, "What do you mean you *know?*"

"I know that your mother is Ceres Astra, Little Star," he said simply. "I just didn't know she had a daughter until I saw her with you at the market when you called for me. Though, now that I've made the connection, I must say, the resemblance is uncanny."

Self-conscious, I reached up to tug on one of my red curls. Mother's hair was more of a russet auburn, much tamer and more humanlike than my fiery tresses.

"Her ears are round," I protested, as if that could somehow make the truth different. "And she doesn't have magic. She always said..."

Except she didn't. She'd never specified that my father was fae. Only that he left her when she was pregnant, and she never bothered to hunt him down. I'd always *assumed* he was the one behind my fae blood, but Mother never said otherwise. She never corrected me, but she never offered the truth.

She hated the fae, though. That was no secret. Despite living right next to the border of Lysaen, Mother never kept her prejudice a secret.

Except, she was prejudiced against humans, too. And if her own people disowned and abandoned her, she'd have every right to loathe them. It was no secret that the Seelie and Unseelie fae had tensions – after all, the civil war between them nearly two decades ago had left a scar that never quite healed right. Mother was Seelie, and we'd lived on the border of Unseelie.

Mother had a strange knowledge about my magic, too. More knowledge than someone who'd slept with a fae once would have. She'd been the one to teach me how to conceal it – though I'd never quite severed the tie my emotions had on my magic – as if she herself had been forced to hide her own magic. And, I realized with a frown, she never let me into her room while she slept. She kept the door locked from the inside.

"A glamour," I whispered. "She kept her true form hidden with a glamour. She pretended to be human all these years and…"

"If she's truly from the royal bloodline, her magic would be extremely powerful. She would have no problem holding a glamour that long," he finished for me. "I should have guessed it just by looking at you. The Demetria line is known for their red hair."

Demetria. The surname I would've inherited had Mother not been shunned.

"But the Demetria family doesn't have plant magic," he said. "I don't know *where* that came from. It's almost as if you share *some* blood with Gausica."

"We knew her well."

If I truly did share blood with the goddess of the earth, it would have been the least shocking revelation I'd come to in the past day.

I flopped onto my back, my gaze finding the tiny flowers on the ceiling fresco once more.

"Adonis," I whispered. "Why do you keep yourself hidden by those shadows?"

He didn't answer right away. I turned my head to ask again, but he spoke before I could. "Because, Little Star, until I am whole once more, I am cursed."

CHAPTER FORTY-FOUR

DIORA

I crashed to my knees, grabbing Auri by the shoulders and shaking her, trying to wake her up. When she didn't stir, I pressed my fingers to her throat. Her pulse was there, faint, and fluttery like the wings of a butterfly.

"She's alive," I said. "Just unconscious. Cas? Can you help me pick her up?"

Cas said nothing as he slid one arm under Auri's knees, the other under her neck, and picked her up. I grabbed the Lyre, clutching it to my chest.

"What happened?" Shasi asked, the golden glow from the Lyre casting her in a heavenly light.

"She grabbed the Lyre and collapsed," Cas said. He carried Auri out of the cave and set her on the ground. The bones were gone, completely crumbled to ash.

"Dio grabbed the Lyre, too," Mirza pointed out. If I wasn't so scared for Auri's life I would have made a snarky remark about how he finally used my nickname.

I looked at the divine instrument in my arms instead. I hadn't passed out like Auri had. Was she unworthy of wielding the Relic? No, that couldn't be. All of us had held the Chalice at one point or another and none of us had been rendered unconscious because of it.

I folded myself onto the mossy ground. Auri's chest rose and fell steadily, but I didn't feel relief at the sight. *What if she never wakes up?*

The Lyre warmed on my lap. My fingers itched to strum the golden strings; I dug my nails into my palms instead.

"Where the hell did the bones go?" Mirza asked. He frowned at the pile of ash. "Last I checked, bones don't just...vanish."

Cas kicked at the ash. "This is what happens when a Hollow is killed. It turns into dust like this. Are we *sure* that cat-bird-lady thing wasn't Hollow-made?"

"Why would Medea entrust a Hollow to guard her Relic?" Shasi, ever faithful to her goddess, said.

"I don't know," Cas said. "I'm a Hollow hunter, not a Medea's-guardian-monsters hunter. I'm just saying, when I kill a Hollow, it usually looks just like that."

"Not if you kill one with silver, apparently," Mirza mumbled.

"Oh, you're right," Cas said, throwing his hands in the air. "Let me just revive the cat-bird-lady monster and shoot it with silver."

"I was just saying," grumbled Mirza.

I pulled Auri's upper body onto my lap, her head resting on my thigh. Her hair had tumbled free from its braid, creating a snowy halo around her. I brushed a few curls off her forehead. Her breath hitched, her pale brow knitting, creating a V-shaped dimple in the middle of her forehead. I pressed my thumb against it, rubbing away the tension. Her pale features were common amongst the fae – Tristan had the same white hair and fair skin – but it was unusual amongst humans. Her almond-shaped eyes led me to believe one – or both – of her parents came from one of the Southern Isles – Ia, maybe – but the people there had darker skin and pin-straight black hair. I brushed Auri's hair away from one of her ears, revealing the curved shell. No scar tissue to suggest she *was* fae marred the flesh there. Not to mention her flat teeth and her ability to eat meat.

Her eyes flew open seconds later, her pupils so constricted they resembled tiny pinpricks against the pale blue of her irises. I pulled my hand away as she jolted upright. She scanned the area around us frantically, only loosing a breath when she spotted the Lyre. She snatched the Relic up quickly.

"Ri are you –" I started.

"The next Relic," Auri cut me off. "We have to find it now. We have to get it before the war comes. Before the humans and fae become so damn divided that the Hollows will kill us all. That's what he wants. That's what he's aiming for. He wants unrest and chaos so severe that we won't be able to fight the Hollows when they come again. The next wave will make the one from seventeen years ago look like a mercy."

She turned, grabbing the front of my jacket, and pulling me close. Her eyes were wide and wild with fear. She whispered, "They're looking for me, Dio. They're looking for me and they won't stop until I'm dead, and I *don't want to die.*"

I grabbed her wrists, gently prying her hands off my jacket.

"Nobody is going to kill you," I assured her, but doubt filled my tone.

She pulled away from me, going for her bag instead. She furiously dug through it until she pulled out the map. Her hand trembled as she pointed to a line in the poem. *A bolt of light fled to the skies, for it once was the god's demise.*

"This one," she hissed fervently. "We have to find this one."

Cas peered at the poem, trying to make sense of it. *"The skies* is pretty vague. Which mark on the map does it belong to?"

He asked it rhetorically, but Auri still slid her finger over to a mark on the map – a mark that covered the *whole of Lysaen.*

How did she know this...?

"She came to me," Auri said, as if she'd heard what I was thinking. "And she told me that only the worthy can call down the light when the tempests plague the skies, and the blood is fresh."

Clearly the she *is the same person who wrote that damned poem, since nothing can ever be anything but vague.*

"Am I the only one who has no fucking idea what that means?" asked Cas.

"No, I second that," Mirza piped in. "Look, I know I'm really only here because it's my duty to keep Shas safe, but I don't think *preventing a second genocide* and *following some crazy poem* that may or may not be *fake* was in the job description."

Shasi muttered something under her breath that earned her a glare from Mirza.

I sighed. He had a point. I hadn't signed up for any of this, either. I'd agreed to go to Svadaeva with Cas to help get Shasi devoted to his Hollow hunting cause just to avoid imprisonment. I never once thought I'd be roped into this whole mess of gods and Hollows and *genocide.*

And the war brewing with the correspondence between Queen Elizabetta and King Wilhelm. The Hollows were a plague, but if they infested the continent like they'd done seventeen years ago again, the war that would inevitably break out would be beyond devastating.

I hadn't volunteered to stop a war. I hadn't volunteered to stop a genocide. I hadn't even volunteered to face the Hollow-Medea-creation monsters. I just wanted to keep Tristan safe, but that was starting to look impossible.

Tristan.

My heart ached at the thought of him. Was he safe? Gods, how would he react to all of this? Could I even *tell* him anything? Or would he take it to the queen, sparking the final piece to fall into the plan for war? Queen Elizabetta would push the blame of everything onto King Wilhelm. Forget the Hollows, the war that would break out across the continent would kill us all.

Just like the civil war that killed my parents, leaving them wingless and mutilated, leaving me an orphan in the wake of it all, left to enter the assassin's guild and seduce men into giving up information in exchange for their pathetic lives.

Mirza was right.

I hadn't wanted to do any of this.

I wasn't some hero sent to put an end to this all. This was real life, not some fantasy novel. I wasn't a hero. I was supposed to be a background character, an extra who just blended in and lived my life without any adventure or anything.

But... But the tip I got was wrong. The man I was sent to kill was wrong. Someone knocked me unconscious, and Cas found me.

I frowned. Something was missing; some vital piece to the puzzle that was the past few weeks.

Who was the target, and why did the job go so wrong so fast?

Who knew I was going to be there?

Shasi sat down, peering over Auri's shoulder to look at the map.

"Let's try to think this through," she said. Her voice wobbled but she swallowed it back and added, "When tempests plague the sky, right? That must mean a storm. A bolt of light must mean lightning. So somehow this Relic that's a bolt of lightning can only be accessed by the worthy during a storm here in Lysaen?"

She pointed to the spot on the map overtaken by the marking. "But what did you mean by *when the blood is fresh?*"

Auri stared at the map shellshocked. I slid an arm around her shoulder and tugged her close.

When Tristan was little, he used to have night terrors. Since we shared a room, it was always my job to calm him down and quiet him before the warden came and scolded the both of us for being awake. He never told me what the terrors were about – I always assumed it had to do with witnessing the deaths of his parents – but they were bad enough to scare a toddler into thinking he was going to die. If we were lucky, he'd drift back to sleep after climbing into my bed, but we were rarely lucky. I found two things that calmed him down; a special *potion* – warmed milk with honey, lavender, and cinnamon – and pulling him close, limbs squished at his sides so he couldn't move.

I didn't have our special potion, so I decided to use the latter. I hugged Auri tight, squeezing her arms so they were stuck to her sides. Reluctantly, she lowered her head until her forehead smushed against my shoulder.

She took a deep breath, her entire body melting when she exhaled.

"Auri," I said softly, in the special voice I reserved for comforting Tristan during his night terrors and panic attacks. "I know you feel some weird pull towards the Relics, but do you think you can figure out which of us the woman you spoke to deems worthy? I'm going to open a portal back to the inn we stayed at last night and you're going to get some rest."

Her shoulders shuddered when she took another breath. I loosened my grip on her just enough for her to lift her arm and point.

Right

At

Cas.

CHAPTER FORTY-FIVE

CASSIEL

Dio waved her hand, prying open a portal.

"Well, Mister Worthy," she said. "I'm taking Auri back to the inn. Who wants to come, and who wants to stay? I'll come back in about...five hours to bring you back."

I spoke before either Mirza or Shasi could. "Both of you go. I can do this by myself."

I wanted to do this by myself. I couldn't lose anyone else. I couldn't risk them getting hurt. It was better if I was alone.

"Go," I urged. Mirza and Shasi exchanged a look. Mirza grabbed Shasi's hand and pulled her through the portal.

"Fresh blood," whispered Auri, her hand clutched tightly to her chest. "Fresh." Then, Dio shoved their bags through the portal and slipped through moments later, carrying Auri with her. The portal blinked out of sight, leaving me alone in the forest.

Now would be a great time for you to magically appear, I thought, touching the matchbox tucked safely in my pocket.

Of course, the one time I asked for it, nothing happened.

I cast one last cursory glance at the pile of ash before hoisting my bag over my shoulder. I had five hours to figure out what Auri's words meant and five hours to pray, for the first time in my life, for a storm to appear.

The forest was far too quiet, and it put me on edge. Hollows brought silence with them, a preternatural stillness that followed them like the black shades they wore around their bodies. Forests fell silent when predators stalked amongst the trees, and I was nothing more than an outsider here. Prey.

"Don't wait for them to strike first," Cora had said once, many years ago when I was still small. She'd stood behind me, waiting for me to strike the hay dummy she and August had put together the night before.

"Why?" I'd asked, taking my eyes off the target for no longer than a split second.

August had been hiding behind the dummy, jumping out the second I was turned away and tackling me to the ground.

"That's why," he'd said, tickling my sides until I laughed so hard, I threw up.

I slid my silver knife from its sheath at my hip. I preferred long-distance attacks, but Cora and August had taught me well; I could wield any weapon if I needed to. As I walked, I tossed the knife back and forth between my hands, keeping myself busy and on high alert.

I walked for an hour and a half, trying to find a clearing where I could see the sky. I eventually found a rocky incline that breached the canopy. Hiking up it took longer than anticipated, but I finally reached the summit of the hill.

A thick fog covered the top of the forest, creating an ocean of grey that stretched for miles and miles in every direction. The treetops created spires that resembled the teeth of some leviathan beast. A cloying dampness weighed in the air, clinging to everything it touched. I scraped my hair off my forehead and the back of my neck, tying it into a messy bun.

At least the sky was overcast with heavy black clouds.

"I think it's sort of a divine irony that *you* were chosen to wield the storm-weapon."

I spun around to face Tristan, who had appeared, once again, out of nowhere. He wore a brown coat with a fur collar, which he nuzzled his lower face into. His white hair curled around the elongated points of his ears and fell across his mismatched eyes. His hands were stuffed deep into the pockets of his jacket.

"I think it means Medea hates me." I sat on a mossy rock, regretting it instantly because the dewy dampness seeped into the seat of my pants.

"Oh, nonsense." He waved his hand flippantly. His buttery leather gloves creased, squeaking as he flexed his fingers. He stuffed his hand back into his pocket.

"Regardless." I sighed and tipped my head back to gaze up at the sky. The clouds swelled with rain, heavy with the anticipation of precipitation that had yet to come. "Do you want to stay with me until the storm comes? It might be a while. My... Friends are going to come back in a couple of hours, so I could..."

I trailed off. I didn't need company. Company – *friends* – were a weakness I couldn't afford. Mother's death had devastated me, but the deaths of Cora and August tore the last broken shards of my heart from my chest and annihilated me. I tried – goddess knows I tried – my best to keep from getting close to Dio, then Auri, then Shasi and Mirza.

But Tristan. *Tristan.* Maybe it was because Fate and Destiny and Time had tied us together with that metaphorical red string. Maybe it was because his soul was so much like my own that it was beyond familiar. I couldn't not push him away. I found myself pulling him *closer because* I *couldn't* stand being apart.

Tristan sat on the ground, seemingly unbothered by its dampness. He nuzzled deeper into the cocoon of his coat, looking more like a ruffled bird than a man. The wind around us picked up, whipping his pale hair off his forehead.

"When I was little," he started, "my parents brought me on an adventure to the top of one of the mountains down in southern Caira. Not one of the steep ones; just a small one that could be summited in a day. I was really young, but I remember the way the sun felt on my cheeks. I remember my mother feeding me seedless berries she squished between her fingers so I wouldn't choke. It was summer. My father held me on his chest, and I fell asleep like that. At least, I must have, because the next thing I knew, I was back at home. I don't have very many good memories of my parents, but I'm glad I have that one."

I slid off the rock. I was already wet, so it didn't bother me as much as it should have when I sat on the mossy ground next to Tristan.

"I never knew my father," I sighed. "My mother would alternate between saying he was the greatest man alive and the scum of the earth. Though she usually only criticized him when she thought I couldn't hear. I don't know where he is or if he's even alive. There was a point, right after my mother died, where I wanted to track him down. I was furious. Mother had died while protecting me, but she didn't *have* to die."

She didn't have to open her eyes when the Hollows came. She could have taken me and run. She could have hidden her gaze until the Hollows left. But she didn't. She looked at them and they devoured her soul for it.

I almost hated her for it.

I continued, "I was taken in by this couple. Cora and August. They were barely older than teenagers, but they didn't hesitate to help me. They gave me a place to sleep – most of the time – and food to eat and they trained me to be the hunter I am today. I wish I had more memories of my mother, but I think I'm content with what I've got, because I was lucky enough to get a second family after my first was taken from me."

He tipped his head back. The first few raindrops the clouds had been teasing fell. It wasn't a storm, though; not yet.

"My parents were killed during the civil war," he said. "I was four. They were slaughtered right in front of me. Their wings were ripped from their bodies. They were still alive when that happened, choking on their own blood from slit throats. They told me to run. I didn't. And then, I was taken to Lysaen, because apparently amends had been made and my parents had been killed for nothing all because the queen of Caira and the queen of Lysaen thought the other was hiding the Hollows."

I'd heard about the civil war in rumors and hushed whispers shared by August and Cora and the other Hollow hunters we worked with. Queen Elizabetta of Lysaen and Queen Marilee of Caira had gone for each other's throats when the Hollow attacks surged. Elizabetta had thought Marilee was behind the attacks, and Marilee thought Elizabetta was responsible. It made my stomach twist thinking about how unnecessary blood had been spilled.

Tristan rested his cheek against his knee. His face and ears were flushed from the wind. The rain had begun to pick up.

"That's when the voices started."

Lightning streaked across the sky, followed by a clap of thunder that shook the earth and sent my heart into my throat. Panic, hot and wire tight, gripped me by the throat. I tried to swallow but the lump of lead that had formed kept me from doing so. Blackened hands grabbed my lungs, wringing the air out of them.

Tristan grabbed my face – I grabbed his wrists, whether to pry them away or pull them closer I didn't know – and kissed me.

The storm stopped. The rain was no longer cold, the winds no longer howling, the sky no longer screaming with thunder and lightning.

It was just Tristan.

His lips were warm and soft, and when I kissed back, he gasped into my mouth. It nearly sent me spiraling. The too-tight wire of panic coiled in on itself, growing tauter and tauter until the fear gave way to something else. Something warmer and far more welcomed.

I brought a hand up, grasping the snow-white strands of hair, pulling Tristan closer until our bodies were flush. I parted my mouth; he did the same, accepting it with a soft groan when I pushed my tongue against his. Tristan's pulse thrummed like a hummingbird in his throat, but he didn't pull away. He didn't break the kiss, not even to get air. He just breathed into my mouth, stealing my breath as if it belonged to him. And it did, because his soul was mine and my breath was his and if we cut open our wrists, they would bleed the same blood.

I finally pulled away, watching as the strings of saliva that kept us together for a split second longer snapped.

And then it dawned on me. Fresh blood.

Tristan said, "Gods, I didn't... I should've asked... I just –"

And I ignored him, focused solely on pulling free the silver dagger from my belt. Tristan's mismatched eyes went wide.

"Cas, wait –" he reached out to grab the blade, but I'd already swiped it across my palm, drawing a well of blood so hot it burned. I held my hand towards the sky just as thunder rumbled again, a heavenly army marching over Lysaen.

The flash of lightning that came was blinding, far brighter than it should have been. I looked away, shielding my eyes with my arm. The heat on my palm burned hotter and hotter until it was *scalding,* as if my viscera had been swapped with sweltering magma.

"*Cas!*" shrieked Tristan. He grabbed my arm and tugged it away from my eyes.

It wasn't magma pouring from the wound on my palm. The bleeding had stopped completely, leaving behind another scar, another story, another imperfection that I'd have to deal with until death took me to the afterlife.

No, in my hand I held the gilded hilt of a whip made of pure lightning.

The storm vanished almost as quickly as it had appeared, but the whip of lightning stayed. It lay coiled across my lap, warm and tingling as it hummed with raw godly power. I'd returned to the rock formation where Auri had found the Lyre, sitting with my back against the stone as far from the ash pile as I could get.

Tristan left with the storm. He didn't say goodbye. He never did. My lips were still warm with the vestiges of his kiss.

A flash of green appeared in my peripheral, followed by a *hiss*. I turned to see Dio standing on the other side of the portal. Dark circles lined the underneath of her golden eyes, and her braids were undone, leaving her hair a curly, frizzy mess that tumbled over her shoulders and down to her waist.

I clipped the whip to my belt, the familiar weight of the weapon something I hadn't realized I'd missed. I stepped through the portal and into the same room we'd rented from the small inn the night before.

Shasi and Mirza were laying on the ground, scribbling alternatively on a piece of paper. Auri sat on the bed – she took up the entire thing. It wasn't a massive bed, but Auri wasn't a massive person, and the bed could've easily fit two – flipping through the diary.

"So…" Dio murmured, her gaze flicking to the whip. "That's it?"

The other three instantly abandoned what they were doing in favor of swarming me to get a better look at the lightning bolt.

"Medea really used that?" Mirza asked.

"It looks like a fancy skipping rope," Shasi said.

"I want it," Auri said. Of course.

"You already got a Relic," Dio snapped. "And you're the one who said only the *worthy* could wield this."

"Is it hot?" Shasi asked.

"How are your clothes not burning off?" Mirza asked.

"Ew, why would you want to see him without clothes?" Auri stuck her tongue out.

"It's kind of…unimpressive. I thought it would've been bigger," Dio said.

"I bet it gets the job done," cackled Shasi.

"She's right," snickered Mirza. "You can't judge something based off size alone. I bet it's got a great personality."

"Any bigger and it would be *too* catastrophic," snorted Auri.

Dio smacked her palm against her face and muttered something about how *this is why she can't stand men.*

I rubbed my thumb over the hilt. It shivered in response, as if it was alive. It was strange to think that Medea had killed the Old Gods with this very weapon. Had it taken the form of a whip, too?

And why had *I* been the worthy one?

"So," Dio said. "How did you do it? How did you call down a literal flash of light, Mister Worthy One?"

I loosened my grip on the weapon and told them the story. I left out the details of Tristan, of course, focusing instead on how I'd sliced open my palm and reached for the sky, about how there was a flash of light and heat and then the lightning bolt was in my hand in the form of a whip.

Auri stood and shuffled over to the bed, where she promptly flopped down and picked up the diary again. She flipped through the pages absently.

"Dinner was delivered about a half an hour ago," Shasi said, gesturing to a covered plate on the desk. My stomach grumbled as if on cue. I settled into the desk chair and began eating the cold stew.

"Did you have to fight a monster?" asked Auri. I looked up from my bowl when she repeated the question.

I swallowed. "No. I just cut my palm and the bolt came to me. Though it is strange. We had to fight beasts for the other two Relics. Maybe I didn't have to because I am the *worthy one,* or whatever."

Auri frowned. "Maybe whoever defeats the beast gets to harness the Relic."

"But Dio has the Chalice, and if I remember correctly, Cas killed the bull-monster," said Mirza.

But I'd been the one to tell Dio to take the Chalice. I had been the one to give it to her. With only two Relics left, according to that damned poem, there was only one chance to figure it out, and we had a fifty-fifty chance of getting the last useful Relic by picking a random spot on the map.

We just had the silver sword and the tomb remaining, and I doubted a whole tomb would do us any good in fighting off the Hollows.

"Shasi," I said. "You need to fight the next monster and kill it. If you can do that and wield the Relic, then maybe Auri is onto something. We still don't know anything about these Relics or what good they'll do against the Hollows. Haven't you guys noticed how weird it is that we haven't run into a single Hollow since leaving Svadaeva? No, listen..." I held up a hand to silence Auri before she could say something unhelpful. "That outpost in the desert was completely abandoned like something came and took everyone away unexpectedly. It *had* to have been the work of a Hollow, right? And I *guess* it makes sense that Hollows wouldn't be roaming the desert or the woods because there isn't easy prey there, but you'd think we'd have seen at least *one* by now, right? But we haven't seen any, except for that dead one in Svadaeva."

"That's not true," whispered Auri when I finally paused. "I've been hearing the voices of them following us since we left for Svadaeva in the first place. They just know how to stay out of sight. They aren't happy, you know. They keep going on and on and fucking on about how *he* isn't happy and how *he* is going to be waking up again soon."

Dio frowned, her golden gaze flicking to Auri's gloved hands. She said, slowly, "Ri, what are you hiding from us?"

Auri clutched her hand to her chest.

Dio breathed, "What are you running from?"

CHAPTER FORTY-SIX

AURI

There were, admittedly, many things wrong with me. My mother was a goddess – the same goddess I grew up loathing more than anything. There was a curse-stain on my arm that was up to my bicep now. The hissing voices of the Hollows screaming that I'd hurt them followed me into my damn dreams. When I wasn't hearing the screaming, I heard the singing. There was a thread in my chest pulling me towards the Relics and a voice that filled my head ever since I'd grabbed the Lyre, instructing me on what to do. The voice was pretty. Soothing, soft, a gentle lisp that only added to the motherly tone. I knew, without a doubt, that it belonged to Medea, and somehow my mother, who was asleep and missing, was communicating with me telepathically.

And that was only scraping the surface of the more recent things.

I glanced down at the passage I'd been reading.

There are many things I wish I could tell you, but by the time you are old enough to read this, I will be long gone. I wish I could guide you and help you through your trials. I have decided that, when you come, I will entrust you to my priestesses, since they will teach you all the things that I cannot.

I snapped the journal shut. The priestesses Medea had entrusted me to had abused me to the point where I refused to believe the goddess even existed. I carried physical scars from the torment I'd endured, and my mind was riddled with the lashings and pain I spent eighteen years dealing with.

I hated Medea.

"We need to focus on finding the next Relic," I said, ignoring Dio completely. Why did she have to be so nosy? I'd already showed her the curse-stain on my hand; what more did she want?

Shasi pinched the bridge of her nose. Nothing about the way she sat slumped on the floor, spine curved into a slouched position that was about as regal as I was pointed to her being excited about being the one who had to fight the next monster.

Wait...

I snatched the journal again, flipping it open and leafing through the pages. Was it too much to ask for Medea to write something *useful* in here?

As I searched for the word *monster,* I stopped.

There was a drawing of a mountain, the charcoal edges sharp and defined against the backdrop of a night sky, the moon full and heavy and shedding its silvery light against the harsh planes of the mountain. Beneath, in Medea's perfect script, were the words

A sword of silver to cut through all, through moonlit mirrors thine gaze shall fall.
Titanomachy, upon Olympus, in Avernus.

Shoving the journal aside, I grabbed the map. Of the two markers left, one was placed directly atop a jagged ink splatter – no, not an ink splatter: a *mountain.*

I drew my gaze down to the writing – which I knew to be Medea's now – at the bottom of the canvas. *Asleep upon their earthen beds and tucked under the stars, the gods of new do dream. And then they one day wake under Chaos's regime. The gods of old and the gods of new and the gods bound by a string will one day vanish. And never look back lest you find your soul gone. Chaos will sink your boat and your flesh he will banish. From whole to shell, souled to Hollowed.*

And, next to it, was my name.

The nuns had found me in a cradle with a blanket and a tag that said my name, because at least Medea had bothered to give me that.

Unless my unknown father had given me that name, but I loathed him more than I loathed Medea.

It was a surreal thing, seeing my name printed on an ancient painting of my mother. I wanted to flip the canvas over to study Medea's face like I'd done a dozen times already. Was that what I'd look like if I hadn't been born with the disorder that sucked the pigment from my body, leaving me with the pale coloring of a fae? Would I have mismatched eyes in place of the pale ones I had now? Would my hair be inky black instead of snowy white? Or, perhaps, I would've taken after my father, a thought that did little to comfort me.

"Olympus," I said, finally looking back at the map. "Does that ring a bell for anyone? It looks like it's in... Caira."

All eyes went to Dio, who groaned.

"Look, I've never been to Caira before. Need I remind you, I'm from *Lysaen,* and the people I was hired to assassinate all came from the *human* kingdoms?" she rubbed her face with the heel of her palm. "I've heard of Olympus, though. It's close to where my brother was from, supposedly. I think his parents liked to climb it, back when they were – oh, that's irrelevant. If I can get some books and photographs of it, I can open a portal."

Cas and I exchanged a look. The last time Diora had opened a portal to a place she'd only seen in photographs, we ended up in the middle of the desert without food or water for three days. By some strange miracle, we'd survived, but every time my hair brushed against the back of my neck wrong, I instantly thought those damn blue scorpions were crawling over me.

Dio shot both of us a glare. "If I'm not *rushed,* I'll be able to get us there more accurately. As long as no bobbies are chasing us down, we'll be fine. There's a library in town. I can go and find some books. Ri, Cas, you're coming with me. I need all the help I can get, and you two look the most fae."

"Fine by me," Shasi said. "Mirza and I will pack our things and get us ready to go first thing in the morning." The tension in her voice relayed what she didn't speak out loud: *she was scared.*

I slid the journal and the rolled-up canvas into my bag, exchanging them for my coat, which I tugged on and pulled the hood over my head to hide my rounded ears. Cas coiled his blindingly bright whip, hiding where it rested against his hip with his jacket.

It was raining outside; the sky dark as heavy clouds obstructed the sunset.

"Is the library even open at this hour?" Cas grumbled, pulling his coat tighter around his body.

"The libraries here don't close," Dio explained. "At least, in Lysaen. I don't know about Caira. But Queen Elizabetta wanted us to have access to knowledge at all hours of the day. What if it's three in the morning and someone has a burning question they need to research right then and there?"

Cas mumbled something incoherent in response.

Before long, we had arrived at a small building no larger than the inn we were staying at. Warm orange light spilled from the front windows, casting the sidewalk in a gentle glow. When Dio pushed open the door, a small chime rang out to announce our presence, but nobody came to greet us.

"Books on Caira will be in the nonfiction section," she muttered to herself. "Which will be upstairs. I trust both of you – okay, well, I trust you, Cas – know how to use a library system. Find as many books on Caira – ones with pictures – as you can. Ri, no stealing."

As she walked away, I said, to no one in particular, "I actually *do* know how to use the library system, thank you very much."

Cas snorted. "Well, I guess you learn something new every day. Come on, Miss Capable. You're going to explain some things to me while we look."

I suddenly found myself wishing I'd stayed behind.

Cas led the way upstairs to a windowless floor stuffed full of shelves and piles of books that didn't seem to fit anywhere. He picked a row and began scanning the spines for anything useful.

I didn't tell him that the placard on the end of the shelf had read Nat Sci A-D.

Cas pulled out a random book and flipped through the pages like it might be useful. It would have been useful if we were looking for books on the types of moss found in the Lavoisin Forest, but we were miles and miles away from there, and Lavoisin was about as relevant to our mission as moss was.

"You don't happen to have a fae sibling, right?" he asked.

"Not that I know of." Medea wasn't said to have an affair. As far as I knew, she went to sleep after I was born. Unless my father had a one-night stand with a fae woman, leaving me with a half-sibling, I had no one.

Even then, half-bloods were so rare, they were more myth than anything.

He put the book back and moved further down the aisle. He said, "Are you from the Southern Isles? Ia?"

I shrugged. "Not that I know of," I repeated. Maybe my father was from Ia, but I have no idea where I came from. Only that my mother was a sleeping goddess who abandoned me at a temple filled with priestesses and nuns who hated me. Who never bothered to hide their disdain for me.

He went down the next aisle, only this time, when he saw the placard, he backtracked and skipped the next few rows until he found one labeled Geography A-F. He turned down that one and began perusing the books.

I grabbed a book titled *A Guide to Exploration on the Eastern Continent*. I flipped to the index in the back. When I found a section titled *Mountains and Mountain Ranges*, I turned to those pages.

"How do you know so much about the Relics?" he asked.

I found a grainy sepia-and-white photograph of a mountain labeled *Olympus.* I tucked the book under my arm.

"I..." I sighed. "I don't know. I hear voices and they like to tell me things. I think it's my – Medea. I don't know how else to explain it. I don't really know anything. Only that some Old God is waking up and we have to find the Relics to stop him, or something. Medea, or whoever, said that you were the worthy one and the only one who could call down the Lightning. I don't know, okay? I never wanted to be here. I'm not a hero. I just... I didn't want to get arrested. A lot of people don't like me and would pay good money to see me hanging from the gallows, so I did the only thing I know how to do – I ran. I ran because I'm a coward who doesn't want to die, except it looks like that's inevitable, because I'm cursed."

Cas slowly set down the book he'd been looking at. "What do you mean you're *cursed?*"

I used my teeth to pull off the leather glove hiding the black stain. It had fully consumed my hand, turning my fingers and nails and palm into a void.

"I touched this wall after killing that Hollow and this happened. It's been spreading ever since, and with it, the voices are getting louder."

He stared at my hand, frowning. His own hands were the same warm tan as the rest of his skin, meaning that *he* didn't get cursed when he killed Hollows. I tugged my glove back on and grabbed another book, just to busy myself.

"Does it hurt?" he finally asked.

I shook my head. "My fingertips feel numb, but it doesn't hurt. Well. It hurt back in the Foloi. It hurt so bad I wanted it cut off. It felt like my entire arm had been doused in oil and set on fire, like my whole arm had died, leaving rotting flesh behind. It hurt, Cas, but now it doesn't, and that's what scares me. What happens when it spreads across my entire body? Will it hurt then? Gods, if it does, I want you to kill me. Use that revolver pistol thing and kill me."

He sighed. "I'm not going to kill you, Ri."

"Please," I begged. "I don't want to deal with that pain again."

His hand stilled, hovering over the spine of *Topography of Lysaen and Caira*. His dark hair fell over his face, obstructing his eyes. His other hand absently touched his coat pocket. I instantly looked there. He had something important stuffed in his pocket. My fingers itched to reach in and grab it. I dug my nails into the cover of the book I held.

"I can't, Auri," he whispered. "You're my friend, and I... I can't lose anyone else."

The leather spine cracked as I dug my nails deeper into it.

"I'm not asking," I said. "I... Cas, you're the only one I trust to do something like that, and if this curse turns me into a Hollow or something, I *need* you to do it."

His throat bobbed. "Fine."

Dio chose that moment to pop into our aisle. She exclaimed, "How have you only found *three books?*"

Cas and I both turned towards her. She had an armful of at least a dozen books balanced haphazardly against her chest, her gilded eyes barely visible above the pile.

"Between the two of us, apparently only one of us knows how to use the library system," I said, tossing my hair over my shoulder as I strode out of the aisle and towards a reading nook I'd seen earlier. "And it's not Cas."

I folded myself onto a worn leather chair near a lit fireplace – the flames were pale green in color and definitely fueled by magic – and opened *A Guide to Exploration on the Eastern Continent*. Finding the section on Olympus, I began folding the corners of each page with pictures of the mountain.

"Do we know what a *Titanomachy* or an *Avernus* is?" I asked, setting *A Guide* aside to look through the second book I'd found.

Dio shook her head. Her curls were even more wild now that her hood was off, and they were damp from the rain. I stared at her, trying to figure out why exactly she looked even prettier without her braids. The curved slope of her nose, the purse of her lips, the way her ears poked through her mane of hair even though it was massive...

My cheeks burned hotter than the magical fire; I buried my face in the book.

"Never heard either of those words," Cas said. He dogeared a few pages in his book before grabbing one from Diora's stack. She murmured a thank-you.

I sucked in a harsh breath.

Right. Because someone as pretty as Dio would obviously have a lover. Because she would obviously choose *Cassiel* as her partner.

I stared over the edge of my book, having abandoned the prospect of reading completely. As Cas went through each book, he'd look up at Dio, his steel eyes crinkling at the corners ever so slightly before he set the book down and grabbed another. She gave him little looks, too. Her lips would quirk up into a smile, she'd curl a coil of hair around her finger before tucking it behind her pointed ear, her body would shift so she was sitting closer to him on their shared settee.

I had no right to be jealous.

Just because Dio was nice to me didn't mean anything. Just because she'd believed me about killing the Hollow didn't mean anything. Her hugging me in the alley meant nothing. She'd only brought me along then, and to the library now, because I vaguely resembled a fae.

Salt filled my mouth; I hadn't realized I'd been crying until the tears slid between my lips. I pulled my feet onto the chair and hugged my knees to my chest, using the book as a shield to hide my face. I squeezed my eyes shut in a desperate attempt to stop the tears, but it only seemed to make them fall faster.

You have no right to be jealous, I scolded myself.

Dio and Cas didn't even look over. They didn't even *notice*. They just kept reading, laughing quietly as they exchanged books, as if they'd been the best of friends for decades.

And I... I was just the awkward third wheel. The one dragged along because they could use an extra set of eyes, an extra pair of hands. I was never anyone special. I was just... Auri. Luther, the thief who stole because they could, because they were hungry and alone. The offspring of Medea, the unwanted baby who never knew what a family was, who decided sleeping in the attics of theatres was better than being hit with a cane because they couldn't pray right. Auri, the immature, annoying tagalong who wasn't allowed anywhere alone because she'd steal and cause problems and not take things seriously. Why was Auri allowed to hunt down Relics? Why was Auri here to help stop the Hollows? All she did – all *I* did – was fuck up and make things worse.

I killed a Hollow and that wasn't enough, so I got cursed.

I broke the law one too many times and I wasn't a problem enough, so I butted into someone else's life.

I ran away from the only home I ever really had because it wasn't good enough, and *I* wasn't good enough, so I turned to destructive habits because I didn't know better.

Auri, who made phallic jokes about a Relic.

Auri, who couldn't handle stress and fear, so she made poorly timed comments.

Auri, who wasn't trusted to keep a night shift because all she did was steal.

Auri, who stole coins from a fountain because she couldn't help herself.

Auri, who stole a weapon because she *wanted to*.

Auri, who had no reason to be here, who just jumped after two strangers because the unknown seemed better than the gallows, except now...

Now I wasn't quite sure I'd made the right choice.

I dropped the book and stood. I didn't know where to go, but I had to get away from Diora and Cassiel. I had to. I ran through the maze of shelves, finding a secluded corner mostly hidden by books. I crashed to the ground, pulling my knees close, and began sobbing as quietly as I could.

I was a thief.

A scoundrel.

Unwanted.

Unloved.

A failure.

A mistake.

A child.

Worthless.

So *fucking* worthless.

I bit down on the fleshy skin where my thumb and forefinger met to keep from choking on my sobs. It was easy to suffer in silence, easy to simply curse the darkness around me.

What was the point in even trying anymore? Why did I even bother trying to find the Relics?

Becausssssse we needsssssss you to. Becaussssssse you owe ussssssss after hurting ussssssss, hissed the voice that had been following me since I killed the Hollow.

I bit my hand harder, desperate to silence my sobs. Iron filled my mouth; the sting from piercing my own flesh with my teeth didn't even register.

You dessssssserve thisssss, the voice hissed. *Atone for your sssssssssinsssssss and the pain will ssssssssssssstop.*

I wanted the pain to stop. I wanted it all to stop. I wanted to beg Cas to wrap his lightning whip around my throat and end all the misery that had been building up and up and up since the very first time one of the nuns cracked a cane over my bare back, splitting flesh and drawing blood and scarring me for the rest of my life because I said a *prayer* wrong.

A prayer to my own fucking mother, no less.

The voice of the Hollow was right. I did deserve this. I deserved nothing but misery.

Let go of the sssssssshield. Let go and give in and let the pain sssssssssstop. Letsssssss ussssssss in and letssssssss ussssssssss free, the Hollow growled, its voice low and guttural and utterly grating against my eardrums, as if someone was scraping two chunks of metal together.

My shoulders shook with each sob. My blood burned beneath my skin, itching, and aching for me to scratch at it and let it flow free. I sank my teeth deeper deeper deeper into my hand. I had no idea what *shield* the Hollow-voice was talking about. I didn't care, because all I cared about was getting my blood out of my veins because it was sweltering like magma, and I couldn't *handle* it.

I choked on a wet sob.

And then...

And then, "Ri?"

I opened my bleary, tear-heavy eyes. Dio sat crouched before me; concern plastered over her features like a mask. Next to her was Cas – Cas, who held my wrist and had tugged my hand away from my mouth, revealing the bloody, saliva-slick wound I'd given myself. His stoic, expressionless face held a hint of worry; his thick brow creased in the center of his forehead, his scarred lips were turned down, his steel eyes narrowed.

"Ri, it's okay," Dio said in a voice that was too gentle to belong to an assassin.

"Is it the curse?" asked Cas. Dio shot him a look of confusion that lasted for a split second, no longer, before she looked back at me. Her eyes were like fireflies. I wanted to trap them in a jar and hold them close forever.

I couldn't shake my head no. I couldn't even nod my head yes. All I could do was sit there and wail like a toddler. Cas didn't let go of my hand. Instead, he did something unexpected. Something very un-Cas-like.

He pulled me into his arms, hugging me ferociously, tightly. His heart thumped steadily beneath the jacket and sweater and muscles covering his chest. I pressed my ear against it, the steady metronome quelling my tears. His scratchy, stubble-covered cheek rested against my hair. I never had a father, or even a brother, but I assumed this was what being hugged by one would feel like.

As he tightened his grip, flattening my arms against my sides, my shoulders slowly stopped shaking, my tears stopped flowing, and my lip stopped trembling.

When Cas pulled away, I lingered for a second longer, then sat upright. I scrubbed at my eyes with my sleeve.

"Do you want to talk about what happened?" Dio asked. She reached out to tuck one of my curls behind my ear. I flinched. I couldn't help it. I had grown so used to touch that was unkind that even the *kind* ones scared me.

She dropped her hand.

"I don't want to be a hero," I said, my voice nasally from my congested nose. I sniffled, then laughed sharply, because I had to look ridiculous with tears wetting my cheeks and snot running from my nose. I wiped my face with my sleeve again, but that only seemed to make things worse.

"Ri, I guarantee the only person between the three of us here who wants to be a hero of sorts is Cas, but I think this whole Relics-and-ancient-gods-and-weird-poems thing is way above his paygrade." Dio smiled. It didn't reach her eyes. "I didn't sign up for this. I was supposed to be a bargaining chip for Cas to use to get Shasi on his side. It was that or the guillotine – or whatever – and I quite like my head where it is, thank you very much. Look, the point is, nobody wants to be here. Not really. I want to be at home with my brother where it's safe. I bet Shasi misses her parents and her home, and while Mirza is happy wherever she is, I bet he misses his routine and shelter, too. I could kill for a hot bath with good soap and my brother's soup right now.

"I became an assassin because I needed money and killing men in exchange for information was a good gig. The Hollows have never taken anything from me. But they might. They could take my brother from me one day. My friends. Being a hero is scary. It's not all glorious like the folk songs claim. I'm downright terrified, you know. But the Hollows are stronger now, and *we* know how to stop them. *You* are the only one who can lead us to the Relics, Auri. The continent needs us. We need you. I... I need you." When Dio reached for me again, I didn't flinch away. She cupped my cheek with her warm hand.

Cas spoke before I could. "I don't want to be a hero, either. I just want to kill all the Hollows because they took three very important people from me. But Dio has a point. We need you. Curse or no curse, you are the most important person right now. We can't do this without you."

They're lying, screeched the Hollow. Liarliarliarliarliarliarliarliarsssssssssssss! They do not needsssss you! They wantsssssss to ussssssssse you! Ssssssssssset usssssssssss free!

I pushed Dio's hand away and stood. I scrubbed at my face again, trying to get the lingering tears gone.

I said, "Did you find anything useful?"

Noticing my shift in tone, Dio sighed and said, "We found where Olympus is. I can get us there in the morning. I don't know where on the mountain we need to go, but a small hike should be nothing compared to what we've already endured."

I wanted to throw up at the possibility of climbing a mountain, but I swallowed my scorn and nodded stiffly.

Cas picked up my discarded glove. I tugged it back on, ignoring the scrape of leather against the open wound.

"Let's go back to the inn," he said. "Get some rest."

I nodded again, my tongue too heavy to speak. I couldn't even hear myself think over the screaming from the Hollows.

Dio insisted I take a hot bath to soothe myself. I didn't want to, but as soon as I sank into the warm water, I gave up all protests. Tipping my head back and closing my eyes, I tried desperately not to think about how the black curse stain had spread up to my bicep and showed no signs of stopping. No matter how hard I scrubbed at it with the block of olive oil soap, I couldn't get it to budge. Eventually, I gave up and washed my hair and picked the dirt out from under my nails.

Drop the sssssssssshield.

Alone in the bathroom, I said, "No."

I didn't even know what shield they were talking about. I was as vulnerable as I could get, completely naked and half-submerged in lukewarm water.

I opened my eyes and stared at the ceiling tiles. My fingers had completely pruned up and the water was starting to chill. With a groan, I heaved myself out of the tub and tried off hastily, dressing in the same rain-damp clothes as before and returning upstairs to my room.

Dio and Shasi were sitting on the floor – Dio with her wings out and hair in a messy bun, Shasi with her hair in a thick braid, an oversized shirt over her soft trousers – looking through one of the library books. They both glanced up when I slipped in.

I was always silent when I walked. I knew how to creep around without making a sound. Maybe... Maybe I had closed the door a bit too hard, making sure the squeak of the hinges was audible enough to announce my presence.

"I'm... I'm gonna sleep," I said. I didn't go to the bed. I grabbed my bag instead and tucked myself into the far corner of the room. I held the Lyre close to my chest, its thrumming warmth steadying my heart and lulling me into a deep sleep.

The sky was wrong when I opened my eyes. Wrong wrong wrong. And the woman with dark hair and sad eyes greeted me with a smile.

She said, "There will be a door waiting for you, Auri Luthien, daughter of Medea. Do not open it. For if you do, all that is evil will be unleashed."

I opened my mouth to call after her, but only silence came out. As the woman turned, her loose dress swishing around her ankles, she began to sing.

Drift upon the waves
And the stars will align.
Until we reach the end
Just know that you are mine.

Two coins for your fare

For the boat at the dock.
We dance this revelry
On the shores of the loch.

The red string of Fate
And the kiss of Destiny.
I'll be with you again
In Time, just wait and see.

CHAPTER FORTY-SEVEN

KORE

Cursed. I almost didn't believe it. If I hadn't just stumbled upon Medea's sleeping body and the incorporeal forms of the two original goddesses, I would have laughed in Adonis's face, because curses simply could *not* exist.

I slumped back against my pillows, feeling strangely defeated.

"Is Ceralis cursed, too?" I asked. I'd wanted to ask Ceralis himself, but the question came out before I could stop it.

Adonis's shadows shifted. "In a sense, yes. Ceralis... Well, Cer is technically the youngest in a set of triplets. He... He was the only one born with a body. The rest were Hollowed. They followed Ceralis around, speaking words only he could hear until he went insane. I found him and gave him the collar, trapping all three souls into one un-Hollowed body."

I blinked once. Twice. So that was what he meant when he said he'd split into thirds... He literally had three souls within one body.

"Ceralis, Ker, and Berethrou," Adonis continued. "The three children of Ora and Gausica."

"Ora and Gausica," I breathed, the names of the god of stars and the goddess of earth rolling off my tongue. Ceralis was a *god*. No, not just a god... *Three gods* stuffed into the body of one overzealous, energetic Hollow – *Hollowed* – who liked bones and couldn't say a single sentence without getting distracted.

It... Made a lot of sense, really.

"He's also able to shapeshift," Adonis said. "Though it's not very easy to do now that there's three of them in there."

"Didn't... Didn't Medea slay all the gods?" I whispered.

The shadows shifted again. "No. She slew most of the Old Gods. The ones who live here, in Heladés, were spared. Archyr and Styxia went to sleep. Ceralis Ker Berethrou was untouched... It was only the gods who threatened Medea that were slayed."

Thin vines wrapped around my fingers; I didn't bother shooing them away. The familiar bite of thorns against my knuckles was oddly comforting.

"Does it hurt him?" I asked. "The collar, I mean. Does it hurt having the souls of his siblings squished inside with him?"

"He has never admitted to it." Adonis sat lower in his chair. "I think it gets loud in his head sometimes, but he isn't in any pain. He can take the collar off whenever he wants, too. Ceralis is my closest friend; I wouldn't force him to wear chains against his will."

He continued before I could dwell on the idea of poor Ceralis stuck listening to the voices of his siblings. "Nothing I have him do is against his will. He likes to find bones. He likes to guard the gates. He likes to go to Archyr and Styxia and make sure only the Hollowed are entering and only I am exiting. He was here before I was. Heladés is his realm more than it is mine, but he doesn't care about ruling over the Hollowed."

"Was... Was he upset when Medea killed his parents?" I asked.

The shadows moved, and it took me a second to realize Adonis was shaking his head. "Ora used his blood to impregnate Gausica. He left right after, or so I've been told. Gausica abandoned Ceralis Ker Berethrou right after giving birth. Her husband, Orinos, was not happy, but at least it wasn't another Eo situation."

I shivered. It never ceased to unnerve me how the Old Gods reproduced.

"So, Ceralis is…"

"He's two thousand years old. Give or take a handful of centuries."

I blanched. There was no way. No way! Ceralis barely looked older than me and acted half my age, yet he was *two thousand years old?!*

"How—" I started.

"I stopped counting the years," Adonis said, as if reading my thoughts. "I'm around his age. A bit younger. The Hollowed don't age, you know. Without flesh bodies, we are just souls."

I sat up, suddenly remembering what I'd overheard Ceralis say. *After all, maybe she can finally track down the other half of your soul.*

"You're not *technically* Hollowed, are you?" I asked.

The shadows flickered. I caught a glimpse of moonlight skin.

"I am not," he said.

"You're a god, aren't you?"

I could *hear* the grin in his voice. "I am."

Then…

The pieces slid together. Medea's tomb. The curse. The missing part of his soul. The secrecy, the knowledge of magic and myth, the role of king…

I asked, "You're Medea's twin, aren't you?"

And Adonis Nyx, grinning beneath the curse of his shadows, said, "Clever girl, Little Star. That I am."

CHAPTER FORTY-EIGHT

Shasi

I didn't sleep. Exhaustion wracked my body, deepening the bruises beneath my eyes and filling my bones with lethargic lead, but I didn't sleep. I couldn't. Not when I didn't know what the morning would bring. Not when I knew I couldn't defeat the monster at the temple yet was expected to slay whatever unknown beast awaited us on Olympus. Mirza, somehow, managed to bring me a hot cup of green tea with cardamom, which, while delicious, did little to calm my nerves. If anything, it made them worse, the familiar taste only bringing a bout of homesickness that coiled tightly around my stomach.

Mirza lay next to me on the floor. Auri snored in the corner, and Dio slept on the bed. We had agreed she needed it, since she needed to be well rested to open a portal to Olympus, then another to wherever we went after. She'd protested, but I could see the relief in her golden eyes as she curled up, wings closed against her back.

At midnight, when I realized I wasn't going to get any sleep, I went to the room next door to fetch Mirza, only to find him waiting in the hallway with a cup of tea. I drank the tea quickly and invited him in.

"What if the monster is even bigger than the one from the temple?" I whispered, stroking his dark brown curls away from his eyes. He had noble eyes, a dark blue that looked like sapphires against his warm skin. I'd always been so jealous of his thick lashes, even though he hated them enough he once threatened to pluck them all out.

"Shas, I think you're overthinking things," he whispered back. "You're one of the fiercest warriors I know. Just... Just think of it as a sparring ring."

I bit back the argument forming on my tongue that Mirza had been the one to tell me *not* to fight the temple beast. I sighed and dropped my hand, laying my head on his chest instead. His heartbeat was slow and steady.

Mirza continued, "this time tomorrow, it will be done, and we can go on with our lives."

I closed my eyes. "Isn't that what I said before your surgery?"

"It was good advice, Shas." He flicked the side of my head. "And it's advice that can be recycled now."

He was right. If everything went to plan – despite the plan being hastily scraped together and bound by nothing more than blind faith and superficial trust – this time tomorrow, we would have one more relic in our possession.

Mirza ran his fingers over my braid. "Hey, it could be worse, you know. You could be back in Svadaeva having more meetings with potential suitors. Oh, excuse me. You'd be getting drunk off maireya to avoid speaking with some sons of lords or whatever."

I grabbed his ear and yanked on it.

"I wish I could just be like Amma," I admitted. "Surrounded by suitors but with no real responsibilities. Don't get me wrong, I love Svadaeva, and I wouldn't abandon my crown, but..."

"But you don't want to marry some man whom you don't care about and give birth to his children?" he sighed. "I know. Trust me, I know."

"Welinas and Lysaen are going to go to war," I whispered. "Wallaekva and Caira will probably get involved, and if they do, Svadaeva is going to get involved. I... I need to be home for that. I can't blindly send my people to war without even being there."

Mirza's hand grabbed mine and squeezed it. "We'll be home before that. And I will make sure your mother and father don't send either of us to the frontlines. It'll be okay, Shas. I promise. Just close your eyes and try to get some rest, please."

Dio opened the portal after we breakfasted on lumpy porridge with nuts and syrup. I'd barely eaten anything, my stomach too queasy to hold anything down. I gripped my sword tightly as I stepped through the opening, going from the inn to a landscape full of trees. It wasn't as dense as the Foloi Forest, the trees here taller and thinner and spaced further apart, but it held the same aura. The aura of magic.

I clutched my sword to my chest.

Auri craned her head back, shielding her eyes with her hand. "So, this mountain is huge," she stated.

Suddenly, I found myself understanding why she always joked at the most inappropriate times. I laughed nervously.

"Did you figure out what an Avernus is?" Auri continued. She dropped her hand and began walking, stepping over a fallen log that wept gold sap. Flies were stuck inside, some long-dead, others still writhing in a futile attempt to be freed. I shivered.

"A lake," Dio said. "Apparently, Avernus is the only lake on Olympus. Some stories say it was formed by water nymphs. I'm willing to bet there's a perfectly reasonable explanation as to why it formed where no water source would've allowed it, but... Hey, I'm no scientist. I kill people for a living." She lifted her shoulders in a nonchalant shrug.

"And you couldn't open a portal directly leading us to the lake, because...?" Mirza asked. My tongue felt like lead in my throat.

"Couldn't find any pictures of it. Just a few paragraphs in a couple books here and there. I wouldn't have thought to look for it if Auri hadn't mentioned it," Dio explained.

I tripped over an upturned root. Mirza barely caught me before I ate dirt.

I sucked in a breath through my teeth. All I had to do was pretend this was the sparring ring. All I had to do was pretend whatever beast waited for me at Avernus was just some dummy the guards set up for me to spar against.

I just had to pretend my life wasn't at stake, and the lives of everyone I cared about wouldn't be destroyed if I didn't succeed.

No pressure.

We were walking in circles. There was no other explanation as to why it seemed like we'd passed the same log with the same flies trapped in the same golden sap a million times.

"You know," Auri said, not once looking up from the map in her hands. I'd learned, after she tripped over the log and sent the map sprawling, that it was a portrait of Medea with a map scribbled on the back in the same lyrical scrawl as the diary. I had no doubts she stole it from the temple, but I didn't accuse her of that. Not now. Not when my nerves held me by the throat, making it impossible for me to breathe, let alone speak.

She looked up from the map and said, "There's one part of this weird poem that keeps throwing me off. *A sword of silver to cut through all, through moonlit mirrors thine gaze shall fall.* What is a *moonlit mirror?*"

"Ri, I swear to everything holy, we have been walking in *circles*," hissed Dio. "Aren't you supposed to be able to feel the pull of the Relic, or something?"

At least I wasn't the only one irritated by the fact that we'd been following a loop for hours now.

"I *can* feel it," Auri said defensively. She shoved the map into her bag and pressed a fist against her sternum. "It's yanking on me, but it seems... All over the place. It feels like it should be that way, but that way looks like a steep cliff. I'm *trying* to find a way down. This is, like, my first time being anywhere away from the city, you know. So so*rry* I don't know where I'm going."

Dio stepped towards the drop Auri had pointed at. "There looks like a deer trail of sorts leading down. I think if we cut through the woods there we can get down."

"Or..." Cas pulled his lightning whip free. It crackled, sending all the hair on my body to stand on end. The back of my neck prickled as he unfurled it, then swung.

The whip wrapped around the spindly base of a tree, taut when he tugged on it.

"I'll carry you down one at a time," he announced. "Dio, you go first. Then Auri, then Mirza, then Shasi."

I knew he was making me go last to keep me safe, since we had no idea what awaited us at the bottom of the cliff, but deep inside, I wondered if it was because I weighed more than everyone else. I had muscle, sure – training daily with a sword carved out my thighs and biceps and back – but they were hidden under softness, under curves that wouldn't melt away unless I cut back on wine and pastries and the other delicious things the kitchen staff showered me with.

Dio didn't bother hiding the grimace on her delicate features as she wrapped her arms around Cas. He grinned, though it was more smug than anything else, and snaked his arm around her waist. Then, bicep flexing, he swung off the edge of the cliff. The lightning cracked and sparked, light veining through the darkness brought on by the trees. They were out of sight before the thunderous boom from the lightning faded.

It took two minutes before he returned. He repeated his steps with Auri, who looked ecstatic, then with Mirza, who cast me a gentle smile before vanishing.

I watched the flies struggling in the sap while I counted the seconds until Cas returned.

"You ready, Princess?" his voice came from behind me. I inhaled deeply.

"No. But what choice do I have?" I turned around to face him.

"You're the royalty here. You're the one who makes the decisions." His shoulders lifted in a shrug. "I won't force you to do anything, but I guarantee you won't want to be alone on this mountain for very long."

I nodded stiffly and approached him. His arm circled my waist, holding me with surprising ease. Mirza could lift me up, but I could always see the strain ingrained in his features. I never let him pick me up because of that, but –

Cas hopped off the edge of the cliff before I could finish my thoughts. I screamed, unable to help it. He just *laughed*.

We narrowly avoided trees, their branches reaching out to scratch my cheeks and legs as we went faster faster *faster*. The forest blurred, becoming a kaleidoscope of browns and greys and greens until a clearing came into sight, an oblong indent in the ground, caked mud and rocks scattered about.

The lightning bolt unraveled from the tree five feet above the ground. I screamed, clutching Cas with all my strength.

He landed on his feet; his head tossed back as he cackled.

I punched him in the shoulder. "You asshole! Give me a warning next time!"

Furious, I pulled myself away and turned to face the clearing. Auri held her hands over her chest, flat nose scrunched up in disdain.

"It's here," she said once Cas's laughter died down. "It's *right here*. The tugging says it's here. But there's no lake. There's no sword. *What the fuck does that mean?!*"

I nudged one of the mud-caked rocks with the toe of my boot. Scattered throughout the Svadaevan Desert were several oases. Svadaeva itself was the biggest one, built on the banks of a river, though there were dozens of others. Sometimes, when the summer months were especially brutal and dry, the scalding sun showing no mercy on the land, the smaller oases would dry up, leaving cracked mud and the brittle carcasses of palm trees behind.

"How long ago did Medea hide these Relics?" Mirza asked, turned towards Auri to direct the question to her.

"I'm not a historian," she said flatly.

"You were raised in a temple," he said pointedly.

"Yeah, and I ran away after deciding I'm atheist." She picked up a rock and threw it as far as she could. It landed with a wet *schlap* in the mud. "I didn't know about the Relics then. I don't think anyone really did."

She paused, throwing another rock before saying, "the stories, though, say she killed the gods a couple thousand years ago. The timeline doesn't make a lot of sense, though. She killed them a few thousand years ago, had a kid, somehow went into a stasis, the Hollows came seventeen years ago, two years after..." she trailed off, muttering to herself something incomprehensible.

"So, it's perfectly plausible that in two thousand years, give or take, Avernus dried up and the sword was misplaced," Mirza said.

Auri spun so fast my own neck ached with second-hand whiplash. She glared at Mirza with eyes so cold and so callous I worried for my friend.

"It is right here," she growled. "You can't feel it like I do. It's here. Undoubtedly. I just don't know *where.*"

Mirza held his hands up in defense. "Okay, okay, it's here. Sorry for doubting you. Jeez..."

"This lake didn't dry up two thousand years ago, though," Cas said. He pressed his boot into the mud, frowning when the muck stuck to the leather. "It dried recently. *Really* recently. Unless there was some massive rainstorm that got only *this area* soaked, this lake dried up only *hours* ago."

"How did an entire lake just *vanish?*" Dio grumbled. She sat on a rock, reaching into her bag to free the Chalice. She tossed it from one hand to the other

"I mean, we *are* dealing with gods and monsters and ancient, holy Relics," Mirza said. "An entire lake vanishing is the most realistic thing we've dealt with so far."

A vanishing lake was also the easiest thing we've had to deal with, but I kept my mouth shut.

"I'm going to go look for the Relic," Auri announced. She dropped her bag, opting to just carry with her a silver dagger, and began wading through the schloping mud.

Auri didn't return for hours. By the time she made it back to where the rest of us were, the sky had grown dark, a few stars peeking out from the thick overcast. She dramatically threw herself to the ground, falling onto a patch of grass. Mud was caked up to her knees. She looked more swamp creature than human girl.

"I couldn't find it," she said. "I just found bones and sicks and rocks and a whole lot of *nothing*. There has to be something we're missing. I can *feel* it. It's here."

"Did you try digging?" Cas joked.

"*Yes!*" Auri was exasperated. She groaned heavily and rolled onto her side, not seeming to care that her white hair got tangled with sticks and blades of grass.

For a moment, I wondered what it would have been like if our lives had been switched. If I'd grown up without the expectation of marrying well and having a horde of heirs. If I didn't have to worry about what my clothes said politically or how if I used the wrong fork, I might spark a war. I wondered what it would be like to be fearless.

The clouds above parted, revealing a sliver of milky moonlight.

I wondered, too, what life would have been like if Mirza and I had been born in different roles. If he was the prince and I, his bodyguard. Things wouldn't be as different since he and I had been inseparable since we met. We'd attended lessons together and went to parties together and had the same upbringing, but maybe... Maybe it would've been easier without the royal expectations placed on me at birth.

Maybe I just didn't want to be a princess anymore.

Maybe I just wanted to be a nobody.

Water lapped at my feet.

Maybe –

Wait.

I looked down. Where there was once mud was now *water*.

I stood quickly, my sword drawn. Above, the clouds had fully parted, revealing the full moon.

Lake Avernus was beginning to *fill*.

The lake didn't disappear for good. It was here the whole time.

I drew my sword, scanning the area for any signs of the monster I'd have to slay. The water kept rising, chasing after me no matter how far I backed up. There weren't any fish or reptiles in the mud, but if an entire lake could just magically appear, I didn't doubt crocodiles or –

A low, guttural growl sounded, rattling my bones, and churning my stomach. My palms grew slick, sweat loosening my grip on my sword.

A flash of light. Cas's lightning whip.

A glint of iron. Mirza's scimitars.

A gleam of silver. The daggers Auri and Dio held.

A glow of red, bright, and violent and bloodthirsty. Two eyes – four. No, six – staring through the dark night, piercing straight through my soul.

The beast *slithered,* like it was a snake, only it towered over us, taller than the spindly trees around the bank of the lake. From its thick, reptilian body, perched atop three slender necks, were three heads, as if this beast was some sort of eldritch copy of the Hound constellation.

I had been born to well-off parents. To a mother and father who doted on me and loved me, even though most royals couldn't care less for their children. I had Mother's harem, led by Amma, who were an extension of my blood family. I'd grown up inside a palace, drinking expensive wine and feasting on exotic fruits to my heart's content. When Mirza came to me to say he wanted reconstructive surgery, not only did I pay for it, but I also made sure he went to the best doctor in all Svadaeva. I was privileged. Not many people had the life of luxury I had.

But I didn't stay inside the walls of my palace all day, growing fat and ignoring the suffering outside. I trained with a sword, strengthening my body and mind in case my people were ever unsafe. I gave coins and hot food to the begging orphaned children, I offered jobs at the palace to the young women and tired men who needed a change when a position opened. I could wrangle crocodiles and throw the massive river snakes back into the watery depths where they belonged.

I was headstrong like Amma.

Fierce like Mother.

Tender-hearted like Baba.

Loyal like Mirza.

Determined like Dio.

Brave like Cas.

Free like Auri.

I was not going to let some *serpent* get the best of me.

I shifted my weight, rolling onto the balls of my feet. When the beast let out another rumbling growl, I charged, skipping through the squelchy mud, and leaping through the water to dig my sword into one of the serpent's necks.

Slice!

The blade cut clean through, meeting little resistance against the thick muscle and spine. The head fell into the lake with a *plop,* and I fell with it.

Blood so dark it looked black spurted, spraying down on me like a geyser.

The creature shot one of its four heads at me – wait. Four? Had I counted wrong?

I narrowly dodged the bite, catching a glimpse of razor-sharp teeth that would put the crocodiles back in Svadaeva to shame. Glistening saliva fell in globs, splashing into the water.

I *hadn't* counted wrong; it had four heads. Two had grown from the stump of the first one I'd cut off.

"Shasi, behind you!" Mirza screeched from the shore. One of the four heads had craned around behind me, using my moment of hesitation as a chance to strike. I dove underwater seconds before it could strike.

Maybe it was a fluke. Maybe it was hiding those two extra heads. Come on, Shasi. Think. Think!

I breached the water, gasping for air. My hair was heavy, weighed down and in the way. I raised my sword, grabbed a handful of hair, and *sliced.* The excess weight fell into the lake.

The monster struck, one of its heads heading straight for me. I swung my blade hard. As the decapitated head fell into the water, two more sprouted from the fresh, bloody wound.

Not a fluke.

I sucked in a breath through my teeth. The monster showed no signs of slowing down, but it had yet to land a hit on me.

When it struck again, I dug my blade into its throat, using it as leverage to hoist myself out of the water and throw myself onto its back. The monster shrieked, roaring in pain and anger, bucking itself as it tried to throw me off.

Come on, come on, come on! I grit my teeth together, trying desperately to free my sword. It was fucking *stuck,* the blade lodged deep between layers of muscle and sinew and bone tissue. The harder I tried, the more pissed the monster got. It threw its heads, teeth gnashing and snapping at me. Fangs tore through my arm, biting deep enough that yellowy fat cells and a glimpse of bone could be seen through the shredded flesh and fabric of my coat.

I couldn't even feel the pain. Not at first. All I could feel was *rage.* The white hot pain, searing and unbearable set in half a second later.

The monster bucked again. My fingers slipped, then fell from the hilt of my sword. My throat ached, raw like I'd swallowed sand, and it wasn't until my back hit the water that I realized I'd been screaming.

The moon winked at me in the sky above as I sank deep into the lake.

And then...

A flash of silver, deep in the murky muck. I blinked, eyes stinging, but it was still there. The monster hadn't come looking for me – yet – so I took my chances and swam towards it.

When I grabbed it, my heart skipped a fluttery beat.

A sword, made of perfectly polished silver with a jewel-encrusted hilt that fit *perfectly* in my hand.

With newfound strength, I kicked my legs, swimming for the surface. The lake seemed so much deeper now that it wasn't just a puddle of mud. I broke the surface, choking and sputtering as I coughed up murky lake water. The gash on my arm stung, but the hurt was an afterthought.

I zeroed in on the monster. It spun around, letting out a screech that nearly made me drop the Sword in favor of covering my ears. Hot, sticky liquid spilled down my jaw. Fuck. *Fuck.* I couldn't *hear anything*.

My legs turned to jelly beneath me; my chin slipped under the surface, my mouth filling with water. The beast drew nearer and nearer, my sword still buried to the hilt in one of its necks.

My gaze shifted further, focusing on the five people standing on shore.

Five?

I blinked; there were only four. Four people who were standing terrified. Four people who were watching with fear, with anticipation, with hope that I could somehow slay this beast and gain ownership of the Relic.

Medea, Mother and Executioner, I began to silently pray. The beast lunged. I grabbed the hilt of my sword. My arm screamed in agony – tendons peeled themselves away from bones as I heaved myself up.

Hear my prayer. Please. Lend me but a sliver of your strength so I might slay this beast. I shoved the Sword into its throat, then, with both swords, I pulled, knocking the pommels together as they scissored through flesh and bone. The monster might've roared. I couldn't hear a damn thing.

I don't care if I don't survive this fight. I just want to keep my friends safe. So, please, Medea. Please. I swung the Sword, knocking down another head. Silver light lit up around me. My vision blurred at the edges. All I could taste was blood blood blood.

Help me! With a final swing, with every last drop of energy and strength in my body, the Sword cut right through the remaining heads. Blood and viscera rained down on me, followed by chunks of flesh and meaty muscle and shards of bone.

The body of the beast, no longer regrowing heads, collapsed. And I, too exhausted to fight back, fell with it.

CHAPTER FORTY-NINE

KORE

Adonis left me alone so I could get some rest, but despite the post-fever aches and pains my body had succumbed to, I couldn't just idly lay in bed – in *his* bed – knowing there were four gods – and one asleep goddess – within the palace.

So, I rolled out of bed and shuffled to the adjacent washroom, pleased – albeit surprised – to find a massive tub inside. It was more of a pool, built in-ground and accessible by marble steps leading into the steaming blue water. Adonis had told me to rest. He *hadn't* told me I couldn't use the tempting pool-tub.

I glanced over my shoulder to make sure I was completely alone before stripping out of my clothes. I'd been in nothing but my chemise, my drawers, and my socks. Someone must've taken my heavier garments off when I was burning up with fever. I only noticed now. My cheeks heated, no doubt turning the same color as my hair. I tossed my rumpled clothes aside and quickly stepped into the pool, letting the water cover my body.

I couldn't help but groan as I sank deeper into the warm water, the heat easing all the tension from my muscles.

If only my mind would melt like the rest of my body. My thoughts raced at a million miles an hour as I waded through the water to the golden tray full of fancy crystal bottles. I picked out one that held a shimmering purple liquid that smelled like pear blossoms and dumped some out onto my palm. I rubbed my hands together, then began scrubbing at my scalp.

Adonis Nyx was a god. Not just any god; Medea's twin. And he was cursed to be shrouded in shadows since he was missing half his soul.

I picked up a crystal decanter, dipped it into the pool, then dumped it over my head to clean the suds from my hair.

Medea was alive. She was asleep in a tomb beneath Adonis's palace. How many people were aware of that?

I sniffed the various soaps, settling on a deep blue conditioner that smelled fainty of coffee and strongly of jasmine. I threaded my fingers through my hair, lathering each curl with a generous amount of Adonis's strangely floral soap.

He didn't smell floral. In the times my body had been pressed against his, he smelled of cloves and spice, of petrichor and graveyard dirt.

I pulled myself onto the ledge of the pool, using a brick of lilac soap to clean my body. Mother bought all her soaps at the market, never letting me pick out which scents I liked, leaving me with lumpy bars of oatmeal and goat milk soaps. They were better than the cheap olive oil soap most grocers carried but didn't come close to comparing to the silky smoothness of Adonis's soap.

I slid back into the pool to rinse off, already feeling much better. My body didn't ache as much and the sticky sweat residual from the fever was gone.

Eventually, I dragged myself out of the bath and dried off with one of Adonis's overly fluffy black towels. I put my chemise and drawers back on, wadding my socks into a ball to carry, and slung the towel around my shoulders to keep my hair from soaking into my chemise.

When I stepped out of the steamy bathroom, I spotted someone on the bed.

She was Hollowed, no doubt, with skin so pale only death could leech it of color, though it might've been a deep brown at one point. Her hair was styled into perfect inky ringlets, tied away from her soulless doe eyes. The only color about her was her deep green dress and her blood red lips.

"A human." She cocked a single, perfect brow. Her dark eyes shifted to my ears. "Ah. No. A mutt. How strange that he would let a mutt like you tarnish his belongings."

I gripped the end of the towel tightly and took a step back.

"Oh, how rude of me." The woman stood gracefully and brushed the nonexistent wrinkles from her emerald gown. "I am Madame Minniva Hedy, Adonis's fiancé and future queen of Heladés. You may call me Madame Hedy. Are you a servant? Why are you dressed so indecently?"

So, *this* was Minniva Hedy.

I wanted to punch her in her smug bitch face.

I dug my nails deep into my palms instead. Bitch or not, this woman was still Hollowed, so I had to be careful. I averted my eyes, gazing just past her instead. If she wanted to be petty, so be it.

Two could play at that game.

"A pleasure, Madame," I said, curtsying as low as possible. "My name is Etoile Astra. *Princess* Etoile Astra if we are being stringent with titles. Please, call me *Your Highness.*"

The corner of Minniva's eye twitched, but she kept that smug smile plastered on her face. Through her teeth, she said, "I didn't know there was a royal family set on muddling their pedigree with a half-blooded mutt."

"I could say the same about your future children," I snapped. Vines curled around my fingers, thorns biting into my skin. Around my feet grew carnivorous flowers, their little green jaws snapping at the air.

"Cute," she said flatly. "I was just coming in here to wait for Adonis. Imagine *my* surprise when I find a little tramp waltzing out of his bathroom practically nude. Does Adonis know you're here, *Your Highness?*"

Even if I wanted to leave, I couldn't. Not since I consumed those pomegranate seeds. I *knew* Adonis was going to marry Minniva. Hearing Ceralis encourage him to only solidified that, but...still. It *hurt*.

I had no claim over Adonis, but the way he held my throat, the way he pressed his body against mine until I was drowning in the scent of cloves and spice, the way my magic seemed to climax whenever he touched me...

Mother had always warned me not to humor the boys who gave me a wink of attention, because I'd just end up knocked up and kicked out and alone.

I had to wonder if that's what happened to her.

But Adonis hadn't just given me a wink of attention. He had saved me. He promised to teach me magic. He *had* taught me how to control it better. He took care of me when I was struck with fever, he told me the truth about his shadows. He snuck out every night to see me.

I, too, can make things that do not die. He'd written me a note, given me a flower – one I still had, tucked safely into one of the pockets of my dresses.

"If you're his fiancé, then where's your ring?" I crossed my arms over my chest to hide the droplets of blood my vines had drawn. I dug my nails deep into my palms.

Minniva glanced at her hand, the tips of her ears darkening with embarrassment.

"And if you're his fiancé," I continued, "how come Adonis carried me into his bed and let me sleep in it?"

In a blackened blur, Minniva Hedy charged, attacking me with the sharp fury of an enraged cat. Her nails tore at my face as she tackled me to the ground, sitting on my hips to pin me there. She grabbed a fistful of my hair and *yanked*.

I screamed, vines rushing out from thin air to wrap around Minniva's wrists, pulling as she ripped. Strands of curly red hair knotted around her fingers, looking almost like the red string of fate.

"Damnit bitch, let *go!*" She shrieked, trying to pull her hands from my hair and away from the thorny vines. The thorns bit deeper, refusing to let go, even as she struggled.

She changed tactics in a heartbeat, grabbing the front of my chemise and yanking my shoulders from the ground. Then, she slammed me down. The back of my head exploded in jagged shards of pain that crept into my vision. Blood filled my mouth from where I bit down on my tongue. Minniva grabbed my chemise again and slammed me down. This time my skull hit the ground with a wet *smack.*

She was trying to kill me.

The third time she pulled me up, my vines worked overtime to create a spongy net to protect my head.

With no way to return to the land of the living, to Lavoisin, to…my mother, I was already as good as dead. It shouldn't matter if Minniva Hedy killed me here, smashing my skull and brains to bits on the floor of Adonis's bedroom.

In the end, it really wouldn't matter. But the pain… Oh, gods, the *pain.* The violent, searing, furious pain that exploded from the back of my head to my sinuses, to my shoulders, to my toes, to my core, was too much to handle. Nausea roiled in my stomach, bile threatening to rise up my gullet. I wanted to scream, but my tongue was swollen and thick and too damn heavy.

When she slammed my head down again, I *erupted.*

Vines and brambles sprung from nowhere, enveloping Minniva in a thorny swarm. Spines and barbs shredded her flesh like paper, spilling ink-dark blood in rivulets. She opened her mouth to scream, but belladonna had clotted her throat, forcing her to cough out leaves and lethal berries instead. Ferns curled out from her ears, licorice dripping from her nose. The plants were inverting her, folding her inside out as they took root in her warm, wet insides.

Minniva Hedy, who had been Hollowed once, became Hollowed again as flora tore her apart. She screamed as her flesh ripped, her bones snapped, her organs squished. When the viscera settled on the ground, my vines dripping with gore, a plant lay where her body might have been. Roots still intact, the stalk thick and healthy, the leaves a vibrant green...

A mint plant.

Ceralis found me curled up in the corner of Adonis's room, as far from the bloody mint plant as possible, an hour later. I'd curled in on myself, shaking as I kept swallowing back vomit. I'd killed someone on Adonis's floor; I couldn't *puke* on it as well.

He didn't say anything as he sat down, then lay down, curled around me.

For a while, we stayed like that, with him curled around me, breathing into my damp hair, and me trembling as I choked back wave after wave of nausea.

When he finally spoke, his voice was soft – so soft, so uncharacteristically soft – and muffled as he kept his lips pressed against my hair. "Will you tell me what happened?"

I didn't want to. Even thinking about the mint plant in the puddle of viscera made my stomach cramp and my heart palpitate. I'd killed someone. No, that was putting it nicely. I'd *mutilated* and *ripped apart* someone until they were nothing but a *plant.* I'd murdered someone brutally out of jealousy.

She'd tried to kill me, but I hadn't been kind about what I'd done. There was no self-defense in turning someone into a fucking plant.

I took a shaky breath. My voice croaked, coming out scratchy and hoarse from all the bile I'd puked up. "She... She attacked me. She hit my head on the ground over and over and the plants just... They were inside of her, and they tore through her and... And then she turned into mint."

Ceralis brushed his fingers against the base of my skull, pulling them away quickly when I flinched. I didn't have to look to know that his fingertips were slick with blood.

He stood and picked me up as if I weighed nothing. He walked out of the room, away from the brutal crime scene, and to my own chambers. I buried my face in his shirt, breathing in his earthy, woodsy smell. Pine and earth. Sandalwood. Plants. Comfort. I nuzzled my cheek against his chest.

When we entered my room, Ceralis went to the bathroom. He set me down on the wooden bench under the frosted glass window. Without speaking, he rolled up his sleeves and began filling the tub with water. The smell of lavender and chamomile filled the air when he poured a bubbling elixir into the water. Knowing what he was doing, I peeled off my drawers, them my chemise. Ceralis was a god. He had probably seen more naked bodies in his life than I could imagine.

As he scooped me up again, he didn't even glance down at my chest or my legs. He just brought me to the tub and set me inside. Then, like a puppy, he sat on the floor and used a decanter full of water to begin cleaning my hair.

It stung. It stung worse than anything I'd ever felt before. Worse than the time I'd gotten trapped in blackberry brambles and Mother had to use alcohol to disinfect the wounds. Worse than when I was a child and fell off the table, biting through my lip when I hit the ground. I hissed and moved away instinctively; Ceralis set the decanter down.

"Do you want Donny?" he asked gently. "Or Enodia? The wound needs to be cleaned. If you'd prefer one of them to do it – or someone to just be here and distract you while I do it – please tell me. It might need stitches."

I didn't *want* stitches. I wanted to go home. I wanted my bed and my dresses and my cozy room. I wanted my kitchen and my garden and I... I wanted Mother. I wanted to curl up in her arms and tell her I forgave her and admit that she was right. I wanted her to show me her fae form and tell me about life in the palace. I wanted her to hug me and kiss my brow and tell me everything was going to be okay.

I hiccupped, unable to stop the tears as they steadily flowed down my cheeks, splashing against the bubbly water. Once I started weeping, I couldn't stop.

Behind me, Ceralis sighed. He shifted. Leather rubbed against metal eyelets, then clattered against the marble floor. Light flashed from behind me, then a soft hand took mine while another started rubbing my shoulder.

I opened my teary eyes to see a man kneeling next to the tub. He had the same big, black eyes as Ceralis, though his black hair was longer, brushing against his hips. His pale skin was nude, covered in nothing but a smattering of faint freckles. I craned my head back to see another dark eyed, pale skinned man rubbing my shoulders. His hair was shorter than Ceralis's, with the underside shaved close to his skull, showing off his elongated ears.

"Ker," the one holding my hand said in a voice deeper than Ceralis's, but with the same accent.

"Berethrou," the man rubbing my shoulders said, his voice slightly higher than Ceralis's.

"Ceralis," Ceralis said, in a voice that was just his, though emptier, and more tired.

He'd split himself into thirds just to give me a bit of comfort.

I squeezed Ker's hand tightly, though he didn't seem to mind. Not even as I cried harder, my body shaking with each sob. Ceralis poured more water over my head. He said something in a language I didn't understand, but he must have instructed Berethrou to fetch something, because he stopped rubbing my shoulders and hurried out of the bathroom.

Gentle footsteps padded across the floor, signaling Berethrou's return.

"Close your eyes, Miss E—Kore," said Ceralis. Warmth filled the base of my skull, the heat so intense it felt cold. I squeezed Ker's hand tighter, my knuckles turning white. Thornless vines, slim and green, sprouted in the cracks between our fingers. I pulled away once I felt them slithering over my palm. Ker was a god, but I still didn't want to witness what I'd done to Minniva again, especially not to one of Ceralis's siblings.

The intensity of the heat slowly trickled away, and when Ceralis – or Berethrou – wrapped a linen bandage around my head, I knew they'd given me stitches.

Ceralis said something in that strange other language again. I caught Ker's name. Ker looked at me, his dark eyes clouded with worry, but he nodded and slunk out of the bathroom.

"Miss Hedy tried to kill you, didn't she?" Berethrou asked. "She was always a jealous bitch. Adonis broke things off with her ages ago. She must've found out about you being here and came back. Adonis caught her cheating years ago."

I sniffled, rubbing my face with my forearm. Minniva had tried to kill me, but did that really justify what I'd done to her?

Ceralis picked up his discarded collar. Berethrou must've known what it meant because he said, "I'll see you again, okay? If anyone can break Adonis's curse, it's you."

Ceralis snapped the collar on, and in a flash of light, Berethrou vanished. The bathroom door opened moments later, and Enodia stepped inside.

"I figured you'd want a lady to help you clean up," Ceralis explained as he stood. "I'm going..." he trailed off. "I'll see you later."

He left, leaving me alone with Enodia. She didn't say anything. Didn't ask any questions – Ker must've explained the situation to her. She went to the cabinet and picked out a fresh brick of soap, using her stiletto nails to shear off the paper wrapper. She plucked a cloth and joined me by the tub.

"Lilac," she said, as if it explained everything. She dipped the soap and the cloth into water and began scrubbing at the flakes of blood and gore that freckled my skin. "You smelled like it already."

She cleaned my shoulders and chest, my neck, my face, the tips of my pointed ears, removing every last trace of Minniva from my flesh.

"Nearly two decades ago," she said when the silence became too suffocating, "I stepped foot on your continent for the last time. The birds up there are my friends, you know. Not all of them. Just the macabre ones; the crows, the ravens, the vultures. The scavengers and corvids and ones reserved for funerals and decay. I would visit them because they are the most observant creatures. They know the most about everything. They have the best gossip because nobody pays the ghastly and morbid any attention.

"When I visited for the last time, thirteen birds swarmed me. I'm used to my birds coming to me. When I crossed Archyr and Styxia, they would bombard me, telling me all the latest gossip and begging for treats and shiny treasures and shards of bones I found. But, as I said, my birds were the corvids and vultures. The thirteen birds that swarmed me were owls. Owls are Medea's bird. They are wise but ruthless, majestic but vicious. They flocked around me, scratching my skin with their talons, and littering my hair with feathers, only leaving when my grotesque birds came to me.

"'*Enodia,*' my birds said. '*Something terrible has happened. Something terrible has come.*'"

She paused, whether for dramatics or to rinse the soapy lather from my body with a decanter of warm water. I turned my head to look at her, silently asking her to continue.

"There are two natural exits on your continent for us to cross over Archyr and Styxia into. One is deep in the desert of Svadaeva – a place where an oasis once was, and an outpost now sits. That exit is closed now, after it was corrupted. The other is in a forest that spans across both the kingdom of Wallaekva and the queendom of Lysaen. The Lavoisin Forest. That was the exit I stepped out through. My birds led me into Lysaen, where I was met with a bloodbath. The Seelie and Unseelie fae had decided the other was responsible for that little Hollow butchery a few years earlier and figured the only rational way to deal with it was to commit genocide.

"My birds led me to Caira. Your mother's homeland." If she wasn't already aware of me knowing about Mother's bloodline, she didn't show it. "I found a boy there. A toddler. He was curled around the bodies of two desecrated fae, their wings removed and torn to shreds. He wasn't crying. He didn't even look scared when I approached. He just stared at me with green eyes. Thirteen owls surrounded the boy, whiter than snow with their feathers stained red with blood."

I turned around fully to face Enodia. "What's the point of this story?" I asked, my lips tugged into a frown.

Enodia just smiled. "One for death," she recited. "Two for mirth. Three for the daughter, four for the son's birth. Five for happiness, six for wealth. Seven for a secret, eight for health. Nine for passion, ten for bliss, eleven for uncertainty, twelve to be missed –"

I finished for her, "And thirteen to beware of Chaos's rift. I know that poem, Enodia. Every child learns it when they're learning how to count."

"Ah, but do you know what it *means?*" Her smile grew. "It means, when I looked into the dregs of my tea this morning, I saw one bird in the leaves. It means, Minniva was always going to die today. It means, Kore –" *how did she even learn my name?* "– that the boy had enticed a massacre when he was barely out of napkins."

My frown deepened. Maybe Ceralis was right – Enodia was a bit... out of it.

She leaned close, the tip of her pointed nose brushing against mine. "It means that Kaos is returning, Kore, and *you* have to kill the boy."

I swallowed the lump in my throat. If the boy had been a toddler during the civil war, he couldn't be older than eighteen or nineteen now. He was still a *child.* I couldn't kill him, even if he had somehow caused a mass genocide.

Enodia's grin grew so wide I half worried her cheeks would split and her jaw would unhinge like a snake's. She said, "the Hollowed are already dead, Kore. They're dead, dead, dead. You can't kill something that's already died and decomposed. Minniva was Hollowed, but *you killed the unkillable.* How do you kill a god? You must give it a body, a corporeal form. *You have to kill that boy before he becomes Kaos's vessel.*"

PART FOUR

INTERLUDE

KAOS AND THE VESSEL

Before the sky was blue, the grass green, and the ocean full of salt, there was Kaos and there was Eo. Eo and Kaos. And then there was Eo and Medea, Kaos and Adonis. And then there was Kaos and there was his vessel. Perhaps choosing a mortal as his vessel was a poor choice because mortal minds were feeble and weak and could hardly handle the possession. Because his mortal vessel spent most of his time throwing up blood and writhing in pain as his body morphed to fit the soul of a god. He had been born with eyes the color of grass – there had been someone with plant magic deep in his family tree, but he hadn't been gifted with the rare ability – but the more of Kaos inside of him, the bluer one eye became. Medea had two-toned eyes because of her father, and the vessel had two-toned eyes because his soul was being consumed and evicted to make room for the once-dead god.

The vessel, like Kaos's once-dead son, had a split soul. Many people had split souls. Where Adonis had his taken from him when he was sliced to bits and devoured, mortals were born with half their soul in a different body. They made up stories about how Fate and Time and Destiny, all ancient deities slain by Medea herself, tied the two halves together with a simple red thread. The vessel had been born with half a soul in his body, his other half in the body of a Wallaekvan boy who had three parents and a desire for vengeance. Maybe the half-soul made the vessel weak. Maybe it made his body unfit for housing a full soul. Maybe it was why he had snapped, unleashing a magic so devastatingly lethal it corrupted the minds of thousands, turning a once-peaceful land into a war-torn slaughterhouse.

Despite how pathetically weak the vessel was, Kaos still nurtured it, priming it to perfection for him to inhabit once his tomb was unlocked.

It was almost child's play hunting down the child of his daughter. She was of his blood, his flesh, and corrupting her the way he corrupted his vessel was simple. Filling her head with voices of his creation was so easy, he could do it without leaving his vessel's side. She had wards around her, but she was his flesh, his blood, and he'd sunk his teeth into her once. Sending the vessel to follow her was effortless. She was the only descendant of his bloodline who walked the earth, the world of the living, and thus, she was the only one who could unlock Kaos's tomb, freeing him to possess the body of his vessel.

He almost sank his teeth into her when she crossed through the collapsed exit, the doorway that once led to Heladés and now led to somewhere darker – an outpost once inhabited by many and now abandoned after their souls had been siphoned and their bodies left Hollow. He welcomed her into his realm, but she was forced out before he could truly distort and manipulate her.

"Follow the girl," said Kaos. *"And I will spare your soul-half."*

And the vessel, unwilling to let the mate to his soul perish the way he was perishing, had no choice but to agree.

Kaos had grown confident, cocky, arrogant. He had blinded himself to the fact that his weak, feeble, mortal vessel could commit genocide as a toddler. He had blinded himself to the fact that his vessel was just as cunning as a god was.

Once, it was Eo and Kaos, then Eo and Medea and Kaos and Adonis.

Now, it was Kaos and the vessel, the vessel and his soul-half, the vessel, and the daughter of a goddess.

Kaos and Eurydice, Eurydice and Auri.

CHAPTER FIFTY

SHASI

Drowning felt strangely peaceful.

There was a river that sliced through Svadaeva, but I'd learned to swim there. I wasn't afraid of the currents. I wasn't afraid of drowning because I didn't consider it a possibility.

Drowning should have scared me. I should have panicked the second my lungs filled with ice-cold water. I should have panicked when my sinuses nearly burst from the pressure and blood filled my mouth. I should have panicked. I should have trodden water, forcing myself above the surface because I *couldn't die.* There was no other heir to the Svadaevan throne. There was nobody else who could wield the sword I'd grabbed – the sword I wasn't even sure if I still held. I'd promised Mirza, hooking my pinky around his and pressing our thumbs together, that I'd marry him if we never found another partner.

I didn't want to marry anyone but him, and I realized that far too late. I had only realized I loved Mirza Issawi as my lungs filled to their capacity with the waters of lake Avernus.

I closed my eyes, willing the rest of my descent to the realm of the dead to be as peaceful as the fall was.

And then a hand grabbed mine.

And I was pulled from the depths of the lake.

And I was on solid ground.

And hands pressed against my chest, cracking my sternum and ribs as water was forced out and oxygen forced in.

And warm lips found mine as breaths filled my mouth.

And my eyes flew open, landing on the deep blue irises of the man I only just realized I *loved*.

Mirza was crying. He hated crying, because he thought men couldn't cry, and if he did, people would stop thinking of him as such and would go back to thinking he was a girl. My heart broke, and not because shards of my ribs punctured it.

I reached up, brushing shaky, hypothermic fingers against his cheek.

Twice now I had almost died trying to get Medea's Relics.

I opened my mouth to speak, only for nausea to hit me hard and fast. I rolled onto my side, emptying my stomach onto the muddy ground. As I coughed out more water, I finally noticed the wound on my arm.

I threw up again.

Dio was at my side in an instant, pulling the stopper from a small vial. I moved away from her, not caring that I practically sat in my own vomit puddle.

"Stop it," she hissed, thrusting the bottle at Mirza. "It's laudanum. It's not poison, I swear. Have him read the label to you. It'll help with the pain. You need stitches. Cas offered to give them."

"She's telling the truth," said Mirza. When I didn't reply, he sighed and read the paper label on the bottle. "Laudanum. Dose, ten to twenty-five drops, as an anodyne, sedative, hypnotic. Prepared by Smythe Ferguson, Lysaen. Poison, in excessive quantity. See? It's fine. It's medicine, Shas. You used to take it all the time when you couldn't sleep as a kid."

Even though I was hung-up on the word *poison,* Mirza was right. When insomnia kept me up until the sun rose in the mornings, Amma would slip a few drops of laudanum into my chai at night.

I opened my mouth and Mirza used the dropper to put ten drops onto my tongue. I swallowed, my throat rough and sore.

Mirza sat down and pulled my head onto his lap. He gently massaged my temples. "Your hair is such a mess, Shas. Amma would skin you alive if she saw it."

He was distracting me, forcing me to pay attention to him so I wouldn't notice as Cas pulled out a rather large needle and a spool of thick, stiff thread. I had no idea where he got it, but the sight made my stomach clench.

Mirza tipped my chin up, so I was looking at him, at those blue eyes framed by impossibly thick lashes.

"I'll trim it for you in the morning. Short hair suits you, but it would suit you even more if it was even," he continued.

Cold water was poured over my arm. I arched my back, screaming as the pain became too much. Auri, who wasn't assisting Cas, scooted over, and put her hands on my shoulders. Mirza whispered a thanks.

He continued, talking over my screams as fucking *Cassiel* slid the needle through my pinched flesh; "Remember when I cut my hair short for the first time? Gods, you wouldn't stop tormenting me about it. Amma looked ab-solutely mortified when she saw me. I think she was about to tell your mother to kick me out because I looked like a rat."

Though the tears rushing down my cheeks, I managed a broken laugh. "I-I remember. Half of it was so short it barely touched your ear, and half of it was still longer than your shoulders. A-Amma was s-so mad."

Mirza smiled. He brushed his fingers through my hair. "It's funny because I wear my hair longer than most men now. I still think she's mad at me because of that. Oh, well. She still lets me call her *Amma,* so she can't be *that* mad, right?"

"S-she's going to be so mad when we go home. S-she always hounded me to make sure I followed a strict s-skincare routine, since she s-said I'd have a harder time finding a husband with z-zits." Without access to my tinctures and creams Amma gifted me, my skin had become angry with me. My cheeks and forehead were pocked with acne that wouldn't go away no matter how many times I washed it with the soap from the inn.

"So?" Mirza asked. "All of us are breaking out. It's what happens when you go on an adventure to save the world. It doesn't make you any less beautiful. Frankly, I think it makes you look even more beautiful."

I choked on another sob.

"You're beautiful, Shas. I promise you that. And you're okay." He leaned down and pressed a kiss to my forehead.

"Done," Cas finally said. He'd wrapped my arm in a bandage, hiding the nasty gash from sight. The laudanum must've kicked in; I hardly felt the pain at all anymore. My eyelids had grown heavy. I could barely keep them open.

"Sleep," someone said.

I closed my eyes, letting the drug-infused sleep take me.

I woke to the gentle pitter-patter of rain against aluminum shingles and the concerned cooing of mourning doves. I blinked a few times and sat up.

I was in an attic. Racks of dusty, moth-eaten clothes were stuffed into one corner, a pile of hat boxes and bins overflowing with accessories and props in another. In the eaves above, the family of mourning doves had made a nest and sat huddled together to keep warm. A sea of blankets and mismatched pillows littered the ground. Auri and Dio were curled against each other, Cas was as far from them as possible, sleeping in a sitting position with his back against the wall, and Mirza...

Mirza was nowhere to be found.

I rubbed my eyes, catching sight of the bandage wrapped tightly around my arm. Blood had seeped through it, staining it a brownish red.

Nobody else seemed to be awake, so I made sure to be as silent as possible as I threw back my blankets and rose to my feet. My head throbbed, leaving me dizzy. I stumbled over my own feet, crashing into one of the support beams. The mourning doves cooed angrily, ruffling their feathers as if they could scare me off.

I found a steep staircase and, against my better judgment, descended it. I only tripped once before resolving to sit on my ass and slide down step by step.

When I reached the bottom and was greeted with warm light from gas lamps and sconces, I realized we were in an old theater. I ran my finger over the wall, frowning at the thick layer of dust I picked up. An abandoned theater, more like.

Mirza was sitting at a lopsided table, holding a tin mug in both hands. A folded newspaper stuffed with pastries sat abandoned on the table.

He looked up. "You're awake," he said. His blue eyes were limned with red.

"I am," I whispered. I slid into the three-legged chair across from him.

He pushed the newspaper towards me. "For you. We're in Orinos in case you were wondering." I was. "A smaller town just outside Welinas's capital. You already know that. Try that thing. It has chocolate inside."

I plucked the flaky pastry Mirza had pointed to and bit into it. Beneath the crispy, buttery layers was melty, gooey chocolate. I devoured the whole thing in just a few more bites. I'd forgotten how hungry laudanum made me once it left my system.

Mirza set his mug down, though his hands didn't leave it. He said, "How's your arm?"

I didn't want to think about it. It hurt. But it hurt more knowing I was the only one who had been injured on this adventure. I'd had a concussion, and now this. It *ached* to realize I wasn't strong and capable. I was just... someone born with a silver spoon in her mouth. Mirza would've been able to slay the beast without getting his arm torn open.

I was the weakest link. I didn't deserve to be here. I wanted to go home.

"Remember what you told me in the weeks leading up to my surgery when I was panicked and scared and kept asking if I was doing the right thing?" He brought his cup to his mouth and drank deeply. "The people of Welinas can*not* make coffee, by the way."

I looked up. "I said *shut up, Mirza.*"

He would sneak into my room at night and shake me awake. *"Do you think I'm making the right choice?"* he'd ask. *"What if I regret it in a few years? What if this is just a phase? What if I miss being your lady in waiting? What if –"*

"Shut up, Mirza," I'd said, and then I'd thrown a pillow at him.

He abandoned his drink in favor of unfolding the newspaper, smoothing out the wrinkles and wiping away the crumbs and smears of grease.

"Anxiety is a monster," he said, thumbs pressing over a seam in the paper. "A wicked, vile beast. Something that the monsters we've faced don't even compare to. It likes to convince you that you're weak because that's how it gets strong. I wish I could tell you to just ignore it, but I know that doesn't work. I wish I could make you some chai, but I know no amount of tea can drown it. Sometimes you just need to tell it to shut up. I know that face you're making. I know you're overthinking things. So, shut up Shasi."

I blinked.

"Nobody thinks you're weak. Yeah, rushing after that bull monster with no plan was stupid. But you're Shasi Dārayavahush. You're a damn princess, so you can do stupid things if you want." Mirza grabbed the last pastry and ripped it in half. He slid the larger half towards me. "Watching you fight that serpent monster was fucking *badass*. I've never seen anyone fight like that. Cassiel had to restrain me to keep me from going after you, you know."

I picked at the crumbly edge of the pastry. Bits of fruit and nuts were stuffed inside the dough. Delicious as it looked, my mouth was too dry, and I couldn't bring myself to eat.

"Those without battle scars have no proof that they actually fought," I said, quoting Amma.

"And now you have proof that you fought one of *Medea's beasts.*" Mirza ate his pastry in two bites. "Your sword was tucked in with you while you slept. It was glowing all night, so Auri hid it under some blankets, but it was with you."

It had been. I'd felt its warm blade when I got up.

I took a bite out of the pastry. Warm sugar melted on my tongue, followed by the tang of berries and the crunch of nuts.

"We have one Relic left," I said between bites. My stomach was finally catching up, letting me know – loudly – just how hungry it was. "Is it here in Orinos?"

Mirza shook his head. "Auri insisted we come here. Apparently, this is where she lives. She said we can't stay here long, but she wanted you to get some rest. And something about finding an ivy wall? I don't know."

"Where is the Relic?" I licked sugar crystals off my fingers.

"Apparently," he said, "It's somewhere on the border, around the Lavoisin Forest."

CHAPTER FIFTY-ONE

DIORA

I had been to Lavoisin exactly once. I'd been paid to get information from some local, since rumors said they knew about the Hollows, and I left them for dead after delivering a lethal dose of poison. It was such a small town that I had no real desire to ever return. If my mark's spouse recognized me, it would be over. It wasn't a secret that I killed people, but I didn't want anyone to know *how* I killed them.

I also didn't want an angry mob of humans coming after me.

But since I'd been to Lavoisin, I would be able to open a portal once I got some rest. In a desperate panic after Shasi lost consciousness last night, Auri told me to take us to Orinos. After I'd opened a portal, she dragged us to an abandoned theater to sleep.

Shasi's cries of pain kept me up most of the night. I'd given her more laudanum while she tossed and turned, and while it helped her for a few hours, I had to readminister the dosage multiple times.

The sun didn't rise, as thick clouds clogged the sky. Orinos was practically in a constant state of rain; the only telltale sign that it was morning was the humming of the trolleys and the clopping of hooves on the pavement outside.

The blankets next to me were still warm.

After breakfasting on warm pastries and hot coffee, I had finally gathered the strength – mentally and physically – to open the gate.

Lavoisin was the picture-perfect representation of the late-fall season, with the trees of the bordering forest a mix of evergreen and a rainbow of reds and oranges. Pumpkins grew in garden patches behind stone cottages, and the air had a perpetual smell of petrichor and cinnamon and warm spice.

And... There was a... Tree in the middle of the street...

Auri, determined as ever, began walking through the streets. Lavoisin was such a small town that trolleys hadn't been introduced yet, and the streets were far too narrow to accommodate for anything larger than a wagon. I almost wondered if *phonographs* had made it this far yet, considering how rural the sleepy town was. I hadn't seen one in the home of my mark all those years ago.

He was cheating scum, Dio. He deserved to die regardless. You saved his spouse a lifetime of heartache, I silently reminded myself.

Eyes focused on Auri, I didn't notice there was a person in my path until it was too late, and I ran right into them.

"Oh, excuse me," I mumbled, stepping back. The person, a woman with auburn hair and a pointed nose, looked at me with cold green eyes.

There was something off about those eyes.

"No, no," she said, offering a sad smile. "I wasn't paying attention. You're not from here, are you?"

I stiffened. Did... Did she recognize me? She wasn't the wife of my mark, was she? Her eyes looked off, but it wasn't because of *that*, right?

I shook my head, slowly.

Her shoulders slumped ever so slightly. "My daughter is missing. Have you seen her? She's about…" she glanced around, then pointed at Auri. "About her height. Red curls, green eyes, freckles."

My gaze narrowed. What was it about this woman?

"No, sorry." Cas grabbed my arm, pulling me away from the grieving mother. "We'll let you know if we spot her."

Mirza ushered Shasi after us, reminding her to keep her head down so nobody recognized her as the princess.

As I stumbled after Cas, I shot one last look at the woman. There was a shimmering gleam to the air around her. I had the exact same aura around me since I had mustered up the strength to glamour my ears away.

The woman was a fae. A powerful one.

A…familiar one. If I just stared at her for a second longer, I might be able to break the glamour…

Cas pulled on my arm, sending me splashing through a puddle. I cursed loudly. A little girl with ginger braids standing behind a makeshift table covered in roses eyed me like I'd just eaten horse shit.

"We're here to find the last Relic," Cas hissed. "Not stare at crazy ladies. She's probably just senile. We have a *different* crazy lady we need to follow."

Ahead, Auri was busy stepping over puddles, muttering to herself and absently rubbing her cursed arm.

"You're mean to her," I said flatly, wrenching my arm out of his grip. Cas narrowed his steely eyes, his heavy brow creasing in the center of his forehead.

"Look me in the eyes and tell me Auri isn't a bit crazy," he shot back.

I stopped walking, grabbed the front of his jacket, and yanked him close. "You forget, Cassiel, that I have the highest body count out of all of us. I kill pretty men for a living. Stop being mean to Auri. She's the youngest one here. She's scared. She's cursed. She… Remember the library?"

Cas yanked himself free, but his gaze never once left mine.

He was scared, too, and he was manifesting that fear by being mean.

"It's hard to light a candle, Dio," he said in a low voice, his tone deep enough to rattle my bones. "It's easier to curse the dark instead.""The fuck does that mean?"

"It means..." he stopped himself, then shook his head. "I don't know. Co—someone I knew once used to say that all the time. I trust Auri. I do. But she's been spiraling lately. Acting stranger. She talks to herself and seems to have conversations with someone who isn't there. I want to blame her curse – it's easy to – but there's something else – something more – going on with her."

Auri hopped over another puddle, though she missed, and splashed right into it, soaking the poor passersby who happened to be next to her.

Something *was* wrong with her. She'd been lucid and mature when we first met in the desert. She could hold a conversation. She stole things, sure, but she wasn't off speaking to herself. It was as if she was possessed.

Still... My heart ached for her.

Sighing, I pushed past Cas and caught up with Auri. I gave her a smile, her whole face flushed red.

I wanted to reach out and tuck one of her snowy curls behind her ear. I dug my nails into my palms instead.

"And at the end a tomb will lie, and he who enters is bound to die," I recited. "So, this last Relic is a tomb? How is that supposed to help us kill the Hollows? How did *Medea* use a *tomb* to defeat the Old Gods?"

Auri looked up. One of her eyes had a strange brownish tint to it. A strange trick of the light, since it went away just as suddenly as it appeared.

"I don't know," she said. "Maybe she put the dead gods there? Maybe *she's* in there. I bet a goddess would know how to defeat the Hollows."

I nudged her arm with my shoulder. "I thought you were an atheist."

She smiled. It didn't reach her eyes. "What would you do if you found out one of your parents was a powerful deity and the other didn't care enough to look after you once you were born?"

I frowned. Was she saying her parent was a god? That was impossible. Gods didn't mingle with humans. Medea slayed the Old Gods and has been asleep for centuries. Unless Auri was somehow hundreds of years old, it just didn't make sense.

She laughed awkwardly to dismiss the thought, saying, "Not like it's true. It would make no sense, wouldn't it? What's the timeline? How would it have worked? I'm atheist. Or maybe just agnostic. The gods existed, sure, but I don't like giving them – what?"

Auri turned her head, as if listening to someone else speak.

Cas was right; there was definitely something wrong with her.

"The forest," Auri breathed, brushing her knuckles over her sternum. "It's in the Lavoisin Forest. We need to hurry—"

I grabbed Auri's wrist. People underestimated my strength because I didn't built muscle the way men did. I killed for a living. Poisons were my weapon of choice, but I could strange a full-grown man with my bare hands seventeen different ways without breaking a sweat.

"Let go," she said.

I said, "No."

Auri tried tugging her arm free, her face scrunched up in concentration.

"What the fuck is wrong with you, Dio?" she hissed.

"I could ask you the same thing." I pulled her in close. To anyone watching, we looked like a couple sharing an intimate lovers' embrace. The truth was far from that. I continued, "You've been acting really weird, Ri. I know we've only known each other for, like, a week, but we've been through hell together, so I'm pretty sure you can trust us. You can trust *me*. What's going on?"

She stared at me like I'd grown a third eye.

"Stop pretending like you care," she finally snapped, yanking herself free with a sudden burst of force. "Go flirt with Cas or something. I'm sure he'd like that."

I stared at her in disbelief. Was this really the same girl who had been crying at the library because she was scared and overwhelmed? The same girl who shrieked when she saw scorpions and ate my street food when I couldn't digest it? The same girl who curled up next to me last night, because she was scared the bobbies would find her, because she was scared of being alone?

"Wait, are you acting like this because you think I like *Cassiel?*" I asked.

She didn't answer, but that was answer enough for me.

I balked. Cas. *Cas?!* She thought I had some schoolgirl crush on *Cassiel* and decided to act *psychotic?*

"Auri, I have no idea what you think is going on between me and Cas, but I guarantee there's nothing there," I said as delicately as I could.

She shrugged and resumed walking, her back to me.

"Auri!" I hurried after her, though she was determined to ignore me. "Ri, I... Cas is my friend. That's it. Though if *you're* interested in him, I think he has a lover already."

I'd noticed Cas brushing his hand against his pocket lately. It didn't take a genius to put two and two together; Cas had some secret lover and they'd given him a gift which he kept close.

"That's not it," Auri grumbled.

Then...

"I like women!" I blurted. A few people stopped what they were doing to stare. Auri spun around. Her cheeks were flushed, making the white of her eyelashes look paler, the pigment-less blue of her eyes glassier.

The black stain peeked out from under her collar. It hadn't been there last night.

Her gaze slid past me, landing on something behind me. Her eyes went wide before she turned quickly, covering her face with her arm.

"Don't look!" she yelled.

Curiosity got the best of me. I turned to see what she'd looked at.

A figure cloaked in darkness stood in the town square. Beneath its hood was a set of glowing red eyes, though the rest of its face was obscured in darkness. It seemed to float, as if it didn't have any feet.

A Hollow.

Mothers clutched their children to their chests, covering their eyes before their souls could be devoured. Mirza tugged his scarf up his chin and over his eyes. Shasi snatched a cloth from a nearby vendor to cover her eyes with. Cas, with his sclera lenses skewing his gaze, reached for his whip, slowly.

"Curioussssssser and curioussssssssser," hissed the Hollow, its voice distorted and chromatic, coming out in a dissonant tritone. *"Hissssssss sssssssscent isssss ssssssstill here. He hasssssssss not been gone long."*

Blood erupted from my nose. The hold I had on my glamour burst, as if I'd been holding it for days instead of hours. My wings were tucked safely into my corset, but my pointed ears sprung through my braids. I staggered, grabbing Auri's arm for stability.

Hollows consumed souls two ways: they stole names, which were the tethers to our souls, or they looked into our eyes and dragged it out that way. Everybody knew that. Everybody was warned to give nicknames and to avert gazes when meeting someone new, because once you lost your soul, you lost your life.

The little girl who had been selling roses was too young to have been alive when the Hollows came seventeen years ago. She didn't seem to have any parents. She didn't have anyone to teach her about the horrors of the Hollows, no first-hand encounters of the monsters.

She didn't stop to wonder why everyone was suddenly looking away, why a sudden stillness blanketed Lavoisin as everyone held their breaths and prayed the Hollow would leave or someone would kill it.

Cas pulled his whip free, but the little girl was too close to the Hollow now. If he struck, it would hit her, too. He reached his other hand into his jacket and slid the revolver pistol out.

"Would you like a rose?" the little girl asked. The Hollow turned its head. Red eyes met blue.

Cas fired the pistol with a *bang* that made my ears ache.

The Hollow had already unhinged its jaw. The girl's soul, a shimmery white thing that looked like pure, malleable light, had made it into the Hollow's mouth before the bullet hit its skull.

Both the empty corpse of the girl and the corporeal corpse of the Hollow fell to the pavement.

Lightning fast, Cas shot the whip out, hooking it around the Hollow's neck and yanking until its head and body parted. Beheading a Hollow was the only sure way to make sure they died and stayed dead.

I took a step back.

That girl could've been Tristan.

That girl could've been my baby bother and nobody would be there to protect him.

I swallowed back bile once, twice, then gave up and spilled my stomach on the ground.

I'd killed people before. I felt a euphoric rush when their lives left their eyes, when they realized I wasn't some lady of the night, but an assassin who poisoned my lips and killed them with my kiss. Before Cas, humans held no importance in my opinion.

But a girl – a little girl not even ten years old – had just been killed by a Hollow.

And *nobody* had tried to save her.

Everybody had just covered their eyes and hoped the Hollow – the creature they thought was fae in origin – would just go away.

I hadn't been any better.

Cas cursed under his breath. "Shit," he said. "We have to go. I wasn't planning on drawing any attention." He hid his lightning whip as best as he could under the folds of his jacket.

We left the poor girl's hollowed corpse on the pavement as we hurried down the street, following Auri as she went straight towards the forest.

We passed a house with an overflowing garden, cutting straight through the yard to enter the woods.

In the trees above us, thirteen birds ruffled their feathers, staring down with yellow eyes.

Owls were solitary creatures who hunted alone. They didn't like the company – the competition – of others, yet there thirteen sat, separated only by a few measly branches, watching with a gaze that was more foreboding than predatory. They were Medea's bird, but that didn't stop me from bending down and picking up a rock. I threw it at the birds.

Six flew away, then five, leaving one lone owl in the branches. It blinked slowly, then let out a screech so loud I dropped the remaining rocks in my hand.

I ran my tongue over my upper lip, licking off the dried flakes of blood.

Hollows had the ability to shatter glamours. That was the only explanation I could think of to rationalize why my glamour had broken in a bloody explosion.

If someone – if *anyone* – saw a fae moments before a Hollow devoured the soul of a human child, it would only make the tension worse. It would only push King Wilhelm to start the war he was urging.

I pulled my hood over my head.

Tristan would be forced to go to the front lines if war started. He'd have no choice, given how good he was at getting information. My brother was not a fighter. He could siphon secrets out of an impenetrable vault, but he couldn't handle a weapon. He'd die. He'd *die,* and I'd rather my soul be devoured than watch my brother, my only family, perish at the hands of the enemy.

Except...

Except humans *weren't* the enemy.

It was a civil war that killed so many faeries nearly two decades ago. It was the Hollows who sucked the lives from thousands. Tristan would be forced to fight in a war against people who were just as scared and innocent as he was.

He would die if he was sent to war, and I...

I hadn't even said goodbye before I left.

I balled my hands into fists. That person – my *mark* – had done this. He knew who I was, he knew I was coming, and he...

I was going to find that bastard, and I was going to kill him.

Inside my bag, as if reacting to my anger, the Chalice warmed, humming a silent song only I could hear.

Nothing is stopping you. You are a killer, Diora Hyoscyamus. Your strength comes from watching the life flee the eyes of those who have wronged you.

Find him. Kill him. Save your brother before it's too late.

CHAPTER FIFTY-TWO

SHASI

My arm burned. No, *burn* was an understatement. I'd taken the last of Dio's laudanum, even though I'd protested that we should save it in case someone else needed it more. It was my own fault for being weak, for being incompetent, and laudanum was expensive. It was Dio herself who grabbed my jaw and forced the dropper into my mouth. *("Stop being so goddess-damned stubborn for once in your royal life,"* she'd snapped, *"and take the damn medicine. You'll be more useful to us if you can actually hold your Sword.")*

The laudanum had helped for a few hours, but the severity of my wound was more than the drug could handle, and as we traipsed through the Lavoisin Forest, I gnashed my teeth together and tried to think of anything *but* the throbbing, searing pain pulsating from my forearm.

An hour went by, then two before Cas announced, "We aren't getting any-where. Let's take a break."

I exchanged a look with Mirza. Cas's words were code for *Auri is leading us in circles again and we need to subdue her before she leads us off another cliff.*

I sat down on a nurse log. Damp moss seeped into the seat of my trousers, but it was the least of my concerns.

Auri tore open her pack and dug through it to procure some nuts and fruit and stale bread. As she, reluctantly, handed everything out, I caught a glimpse of a leather book.

The journal Amma had me find.

"I have to piss," Auri suddenly announced. Dio scrambled to her feet, hurrying after her as Auri determinedly walked deeper into the woods. She'd left her bag unattended.

I leaned over and grabbed the diary before she could return.

The book felt familiar in my hands. It, along with my sword, were the only things I had left of home. This book was the last physical tie I had to Amma.

I opened the book, looking through it for any hint on the last Relic.

Instead, I found a mention of my Sword.

Of my Relics, only three of them should be virtually impossible to find. Unless, my dear, you are the one searching for them. Only you have my undiluted blood; only you can feel the tether. I hid the Lightning in the sky. I do not know who will end up being of worthy blood, but you will know, my dear. You will recognize their strength and determination and declare them worthy. I hid the Sword, my beloved Titanomachy, in Lake Avernus, a lake that is only visible beneath the light of the moon. Its guardian was entrusted to never let anyone near. And the last Rel

The rest of the page had been torn away, hiding the location of the final Relic for good.

Titanomachy. My Sword had a name. I brushed my fingers over the pommel.

The stories said Medea had sliced the final god, her father, to bits with her silver Sword. Titanomachy. The Sword that slew the Old Gods was fastened to my hip. Warmth spread in my chest.

I looked back at the journal. There were only a few pages left, so I flipped to the end.

The pride radiating from my chest dissipated in an instant.

Centuries upon centuries ago, I killed the gods because of something my father had done. The gods sided with him, the monster who exiled my mother and devoured my brother. It has been thousands of years, yet the hurt is still there. I wish more than anything that I could be there for you to protect you the way my mother, Eo, had.

I met your father on Ia two years ago. He did not know I was a goddess when we first met, but after I became pregnant with you, I told him. He was shocked and asked for space. It took him a week before he finally returned to me. He said he loved me, not the goddess I was. I never told him my true name, rather the nickname my mother called me. She was the goddess of storms, you see, so she called me her little zephyr. Auri.

Your father asked if you were a boy or a girl. I told him with a hundred percent certainty that you were a girl. He was the one who decided you should bear the name Auri.

You sucked away my magic while you were in my womb. Keeping a human form was virtually impossible as the months went on. I became weak. Your father left Ia to find medicine for me because I was dying. Perhaps it was my penance for killing the gods. I fled to the mainland to give birth. You were a stubborn child who came into the world screaming and bloody. I lost quite a bit of blood, and I was too weak to carry you, but I still cleaned the ichor from your skin (gods bleed gold, you see, and if anyone saw my viscera on you, they would know what you were), and I brought you to a temple, hoping your father would find you. I'm writing this with shaking hands. You are only a few hours old, hopefully inside the temple with milk in your belly. My brother prepared a place for me to sleep, because I need to go into a stasis to recover. I have entrusted my brother's closest friends, the gods Ceralis Ker Berethrou to bring this journal to a place you will find it when

The pieces clicked together like those from a puzzle. It made undeniable sense why Auri could *sense* the Relics now. She wasn't just an orphan; she was Medea's *daughter*. In all those paintings depicting the Mother and Executioner with her swollen, pregnant belly, it was *Auri Auri Auri*.

Auri, who was named after the goddess's nickname.

Auri, who had nearly killed Medea.

Auri, who sent Medea into a stasis hours after she was born.

Auri, who had inadvertently taken our goddess from us.

I slammed the journal shut and shoved it back into Auri's pack just as she and Dio came around the bend.

The daughter of the goddess said, "We found it."

Medea had declared this final Relic to be one of the three most difficult to acquire. The last one had nearly killed me.

My legs had turned leaden, refusing to let me stand. My heart sped up, pounding in my throat.

I can't I can't I can't I can't Ican'tIcan'tIcan'tIcan't...

I wanted to throw Titanomachy as far into the woods as I could, and demand Dio open a portal back to my home in Svadaeva. I didn't want to find the Relics anymore. I didn't want to deal with sleeping gods and their insane children.

I wanted to go home and curl up in bed and cry until the pain and fear went away.

I didn't realize I was yanking on my hair until Mirza took my wrists and pulled my fingers away from the mess of curls.

"Shas," he said. "You're okay. I promise you, you're okay."

I wanted to *scream.*

I thrashed, trying to pull my wrists free, but Mirza – Mirza, who had once been smaller and frailer than me, who had been so meek and shy and ashamed of his being – held tight. He was stronger than me now. He wasn't my lady-in-waiting. He was my personal guard, the *captain* of my guard.

He said, in a voice so gentle and soft that it shouldn't be the only thing I heard in the forest, but it was, "I will do whatever it takes to protect you, Shasi. I will salt this earth and burn it all to the ground if it means keeping you safe. Nobody – human or fae, Hollow or fucking *god* – will stop me from protecting you, because I love you – because I have *always* loved you – Shasi Dārayavahush."

People liked to whisper behind my back that I never knew when to shut up. That I was obsessed with my own voice and would talk for hours. They were right, in a sense. It was my Baba who taught me that my voice was my most powerful weapon, and silence would only make me miserable. Baba, who suffered from anxiety so terrible he had to drink lavender tinctures to relax his mind, taught me to make conversation with anyone and everyone, because women throughout the rest of the continent were silenced by men who thought they could trample them. There were women who didn't grow up in queendoms who never had the chance to develop a voice.

For the first time in my life, I was rendered completely speechless.

And, for the first time, I answered with my actions instead of words.

I grabbed the front of Mirza's shirt and yanked him close with strength I didn't realize I had and crushed my mouth against his.

His eyes went wide; he made a surprised noise that was muffled against my mouth, but he didn't pull away. Thank the sleeping *goddess* he didn't pull away.

Then, with the same fervor I'd given him, he kissed back. His tongue, warm and wet, swiped against my bottom lip, and I melted. I parted my lips, granting him access. His fingers fisted my curls, holding my head in place as he pressed his tongue against mine, drinking me in until my stomach twisted into a mushy mess of silken knots. His heart pounded against his chest; I could feel it against my knuckles as I tightened my grip on his shirt. He kissed me like the breath in my lungs was the only thing keeping him from asphyxiating, like my mouth was his lifeline, like he would crumble to ash as soon as he pulled away.

When I finally turned my head away, desperate for a breath, his blue blue blue eyes met mine, and he gazed at me like I was the moon.

"I've waited my entire life to do that," he whispered.

I took his hands and stood. My knees shook, but it was no longer from the anxiety.

"You're an idiot for not doing it sooner," I whispered back.

He gave me a crooked smile. It took everything in me to not grab him and kiss him again.

"Let's go get this last Relic," he said.

My lips too numb and swollen to speak, I gave him a silent nod and slipped my hand into his.

CHAPTER FIFTY-THREE

KORE

Every time I closed my eyes, I saw bloodied mint leaves and chunks of flesh and bone.

I didn't want to put on clothes, but Enodia convinced me that a shirt and bloomers would be clothes enough. I didn't ask if the loose black cotton shirt she'd given me was Adonis's – the spicy smell of it was answer enough. I pulled it on, struggling to get the neckline to sit just right without slipping over my shoulder before finally giving up. Wearing bloomers was useless, since the shirt practically covered them completely, but I kept them on over my drawers.

Ceralis brought me lavender tea laden with cream and honey. It sat cooling on my nightstand. I couldn't muster up the strength to sit up to drink it.

He also brought me a blanket, which he'd draped over me.

And a wooden box full of treasures, which he explained the meaning of to me one by one. A blurry photograph of the rock garden. A ceramic thimble with a tiny blue flower painted on it. A piece of green sea glass. A smooth stick with all the bark peeled off. The sharp needle from a gramophone. A handful of mismatched marbles.

And then, when I still didn't get out of bed, he brought Adonis.

The bed dipped, and I finally lifted my head. His shadows greeted me.

"Plant magic is extremely rare," he said as preamble. "But never in my life have I encountered someone with magic capable of turning something *into* a plant."

Great. So, he wanted to talk about me killing – re-killing – Minniva. I lay my head back down and pulled Ceralis's blanket over myself.

"I'm not mad, little star," he said gently. "If anything, I am in awe. I knew your magic was strong, but I don't think anyone could've guessed *how* strong. I have been trying to get rid of Minniva for years now."

I curled up tightly.

"She said you proposed," I mumbled. "She called you her fiancé."

"She's a damned liar," he seethed.

"Ceralis said she could help you find the other half of your soul," I whispered.

"He wasn't talking about her." His shadows hooked themselves on my blanket, pulling it back. "Little Star, he was talking about *you.*"

You.

You.

You.

The word echoed in my head.

"You're not mad?" I asked as I sat up. Adonis's shirt slid off my shoulder, but I didn't bother fixing it. I couldn't see if his gaze fell on the bare expanse of my throat, but something told me it didn't.

"I swear it on the life of my sister," he said truthfully.

I reached out, pushing my fingers through his shadows until I felt flesh. His hand was cold, lifeless, but I gripped it, nonetheless.

Flowers and vines erupted around us, creating a nest of flora. The white flowers that followed me everywhere surrounded Adonis, giving him the same affection they always did. Thorny vines encased us in a protective ring. Flowers sprouted in my hair, giving me a crown fit for a fae princess.

And the shadows.

They flickered. Beneath the haze, I could see Adonis's hand. His skin was pale, so damn pale, and his nails were long, almost like claws painted black. He had a beauty mark on his wrist, just barely hidden by the ruffled sleeve of his shirt.

The shadows around his face shifted. I caught a glimpse of deep blue eyes and dark lashes, bruises underneath. I saw the beginning of a straight nose, more beauty marks, black hair that fell across his forehead in long tendrils.

The whispers I saw of Adonis before the shadows smothered him again were beautiful.

"I believe," he said, his voice deep and rumbling and absolutely perfect for his dark beauty, "that your magic is tied to your emotions."

His shadows – no, his hand – reached out to touch the bandage across my forehead.

"She tried to kill me," I said.

And he said, "I know."

"It was self-defense."

"And you defended yourself beautifully."

"I'm a monster."

He cradled my cheek. My magic surged. His shadows faded ever so slightly.

"You are anything but."

I swallowed hard, trying to keep the tears from falling. I saw pointed ears. Hair that tumbled over shoulders. Sharpened canines.

"Then what am I, Adonis? Only a monster would kill someone and turn them into a plant."

His full lips curled into a smile I could just barely make out.

He said, "You are Kore, my Little Star. I know who you *are,* and I know what I hope for you to be."

I leaned into his touch. His hands were so deathly cold but his hold on my cheek was warm.

"What's that?" I whispered.

"My wife," he said. "The Queen of Heladés. If you'll have me."

I spoke before I could even think; "I will, Adonis. I will."

I drank Ceralis's tea. It was cold and a bit too sweet, but it calmed me enough that I closed my eyes, and when I didn't see Minniva's death replaying against my eyelids over and over again, I fell asleep.

I dreamed of white flowers and dark hair and blue eyes deeper than the night sky.

I would have slept for an eternity, just like Medea. My magic had drained my energy completely. I would've stayed in my flowery dreams if not for the loud *crash* outside my bedroom door.

I jolted upright, knocking aside Ceralis's box of trinkets. They clattered to the floor.

"I don't know!" came the unfamiliar voice of a man just down the hall. Forgetting I wore nothing but Adonis's shirt and my bloomers, I hurried to the door, throwing it open the peek outside. A man with hair the color of moonlight hurried after Adonis's shadowy form.

"The last time this many Hollowed appeared was during that faerie civil war," the silver-haired male continued. "I don't *know* why there's so many of them all of a sudden. Where's the Guardian?"

"I sent them to the Gates," Adonis said.

"These are just the Hollowed they're *letting in?!*" the other man exclaimed.

"I know, Thanatos," Adonis said. "I know. This... This is bad. Something is happening up there."

Mother.

I stumbled out of my room.

"What's going on?" I blurted. Both Adonis and the silver-haired man, Thanatos, turned to face me. Thanatos had the dark eyes and pale skin of a Hollowed, but I'd never seen a Hollowed with the same hair as his. I had to force myself to keep from staring.

Thanatos opened his mouth, but Adonis cut him off. "There's an influx of Hollowed arriving in Heladés. Mostly men, but women and children, too. Human and fae."

My eyes went wide. "Is—"

"I told Ceralis to keep an eye out for Ceres Astra, but they haven't seen her," Adonis said, as if he'd read my mind. I let out a breath of relief.

"Can I help?" I asked. "I... I can talk to some of the recently Hollowed. I'm still alive. I know what it's like to suddenly be stuck here. Please?"

Thanatos glared. Adonis ignored him.

"If you think that would help, then I'll allow it." The shadows gestured for me to come over. I hurried to Adonis's side.

He removed his jacket, holding it out. I blushed furiously but threw it on over my frame.

"Please be careful, little star," he urged. "They're scared, and that makes them dangerous."

"You shouldn't be letting a child handle this," Thanatos grumbled.

I followed Adonis down the halls. The sound of wailing grew louder and louder until we were in the foyer.

Hundreds of people were cramped inside.

There were men, their uniforms torn and bloodied. Women wearing blood-stained aprons over blue dresses, their hair messy and their faces tear stained. Children huddled by their parents with dirt smudged on their sunken cheeks.

I had been a child when the civil war between Lysaen and Caira broke out, but I recognized the uniforms of the Welinas army, the Wallaekvan army. I recognized the nurse uniforms of both armies. I recognized the pointed ears and fair features belonging to the fae.

Swallowing my nausea, I tip-toed down the stairs. As I tried to figure out who to talk to first, I felt someone tug on the hem of my borrowed jacket. I looked down to see a child no older than six or seven. A fae child, judging by his perfect features.

"Are the people with the explosion things gonna get us here?" he asked in a voice thick with the accent of Caira. It reminded me so much of my mother's accent that I nearly broke down right then and there.

I crouched down so I was at this height. "No," I said, even though I had no idea what he was talking about. "You're safe here. Can you tell me your name? I'm Kore."

The child blinked. He didn't know he was Hollowed yet. He didn't know that it was okay to share his name.

Then, reluctantly, he said, "Philip."

I held out my hand. A perfect orange gerbera daisy grew from my palm. I handed it to the boy.

"Can you tell me what happened, Philip?"

He took the flower, gripping its stem tightly. "Bad people came with these...these things that made a loud noise. They smelled like smoke. Like...like fireworks. It hurt, but now it doesn't hurt."

I brushed Philip's dark curls off his forehead. "I'm glad it doesn't hurt, Philip. You're okay now. You're safe, I promise. Can you do me a favor?" When he nodded, I said, "I need you to find all the other children without parents and bring them to the stairs. Tell them I will give them all flowers. You are a very brave boy."

The fear was overshadowed, albeit barely, by determination. Philip nodded, clutched his flower tightly, and wove through the throng of people to find the other orphans.

I stood and went to find the next person.

I spoke with humans and fae alike. Women and children, nurses, and soldiers. Every single one of them told me the same thing.

People attacked with explosion devices. With swords, with knives, with spears.

Ships had swarmed the ports in the east and west. Cities were razed to the ground, homes pillaged.

War had broken out on the continent.

And Heladés, the Underworld, was overflowing with the dead.

CHAPTER FIFTY-FOUR

AURI

*C*ome *sssssset me free,* said the voice. It had never used the singular pronoun until now, and it left a heavy weight of unease deep in my belly.

Come sssssset me free, and I will ssssssspare you.

"No," I muttered under my breath. My feet betrayed me, leading me deeper into the forest.

Dio followed me like a shadow. I could feel her presence without having to look over my shoulder. The tether in my chest pulled and pulled and pulled. I had no choice but to follow it, lest it rip my heart from my chest.

My entire arm was numb wherever the black stain touched it, tingling with the pins-and-needles sensation I got whenever my leg fell asleep.

The vesssssssssssel issssssss on itsssssss way, the voice said.

"Shut up," I snapped.

The voice did not shut up. It laughed, a wicked cackle that thrummed against my skull. I wanted to sink to my knees and cradle my head, but the tether pulled and pulled and pulled.

You are a curioussssss thing. Reveal yoursssssself. Give into the urge. Open the door.

I smacked the side of my head, like that would silence the incessant nagging. It didn't. If anything, it only made the laughter worse.

The tether pulled. The shimmering veil I had stumbled upon when I went off with Dio earlier came into sight. She was the one who said it was a glamour. I was the one who stepped through it, revealing a whole section of forest previously hidden.

The trees were older here, more gnarled and twisted, with their leaves completely fallen. Autumn had already made way for winter here, and the chill in the air only added to that. Nestled amongst the branchy foliage was a stone building, covered in moss and ivy, with crumbling columns holding the sloped roof up. Words in some ancient, symbolic language were carved into the space just below the roof. The door was sealed shut, as if whatever was inside wasn't meant to come out.

It wasn't a building. It was a tomb.

A Mausoleum.

The tether yanked.

Open it, demanded the voice.

"This... This is the last Relic?" Cas asked from behind me. I didn't turn. I couldn't. My eyes were glued to the Mausoleum.

"How did..." Shasi paused. "She killed the gods and put them here, didn't she? Unless... Unless *she's* in here."

There issssssss no goddesssssssss here, said the voice, louder now.

Ivy covered the door, just like the wall I'd touched in Orinos. I stepped closer.

"Auri, wait," Dio said. She reached out to grab me, but I took another step closer to the door, to the ivy, to the place where the voice was coming from.

Yesssssssss, the voice slithered around my brain.

I stepped up one of the stairs, then another. My hand *burned,* aching to touch the ivy as if that would quell the *hurt.*

"Auri, wait!" Dio screeched.

I stood before the door. Everything around me had become muddled, like I'd stuck my head underwater. All I could hear was the urging of the voice.

I reached out.

There was a thud behind me, like someone falling onto the dirt.

Dio's voice saying, "Wait, *Tristan?*"

I touched the ivy.

Light flared.

The world went black.

And then it wasn't black, but it was that wrong place with the wrong sky and the wrong constellations. It had been midday, but now the sky was dark with those wrong stars watching me like eyes. The Mausoleum was gone. In its place was a set of stairs leading *up*.

At the base of the stairs was the singing woman. She stared at the sky. When she noticed me, she startled, taking a step back.

"What have you done?" she whispered, fear in her stormy grey eyes. I knew those eyes.

"I... I don't know," I confessed. I looked at my hands.

At my hair. The ends had turned black.

The woman picked up her skirts like she was going to flee.

"Wait!" I called out. She hesitated long enough for me to ask, "Who are you?"

She looked at the sky, then at me. She smiled sadly. "Amelia," she said. "My name is Amelia."

She left, and darkness enveloped me.

CHAPTER FIFTY-FIVE

CASSIEL

Tristan Edelweiss was excellent at appearing out of nowhere, but the look of pure horror plastered on his face told me he had not planned on being here. His wings were out, their multicolored membranes twitching slightly.

Dio took a stumbling step closer. "Tristan?" she asked impossibly softly. His two-toned gaze slid to her.

"Dio," he whispered. "I *really* didn't want you here. I didn't want you to see this. Please... Please open a portal. Go home. *Please.*"

She took another step closer, but he took a step back. I grabbed her arm. I felt the sting before I realized she'd slapped me.

"I'm not going home, Tristan," she said. She tried so damn hard to keep her voice steady, to keep it from wavering. "Not without you. Please... Please don't leave me. You're all I have left."

And then I realized what had her so worked up.

In Tristan's hand was a revolver pistol.

"Dio, I've been with you this entire time," he confessed. "I've been following you ever since you jumped through that portal to Svadaeva. No, that's a lie. I haven't been following you. Or you, Cas. I've been following the daughter of the goddess. He promised he wouldn't hurt you if I found her for him. I killed a Hollow for you to find. So you could see that they aren't human or fae. I tried to leave hints for you. I tried to help you."

"Auri," whispered Shasi. "You were following Auri. *You* were the one who shot the Hollow in Svadaeva."

Tristan tightened his grip on the pistol. "You're so strong, Dio. Strong and brave. I wish I could've been a fraction of the person you were." His voice warbled. Panic and fear and desperation filled his tone.

He continued, "I love you Diora. I do. Don't ever forget it. I never deserved your kindness. Not after killing your parents."

"There is this *darkness* in me." His voice *shattered* like glass, and my heart – my soul – screamed for him. But when I stepped closer, Dio shot me a dangerous glare, and Tristan...

Tristan raised the pistol, pressing the barrel right against the side of his head.

Tears spilled down his cheeks. He was *terrified*. Dio noticed the pistol, too, so she froze.

"Tristan, please," she begged. "Please. I don't know what you're talking about. Just... Just please come home. I need you. I'm supposed to protect you."

"You did a good job of protecting me," he whispered. "But I'm a liar. I kept so much from you. I'm a fucking *monster*. I slaughtered our people. It was my fault the war broke out, and it's my fault it's happening again. He won't leave me alone. He killed Eurydice Edelweiss over a decade ago, and now he's going to kill me. I love you so much, Dio. You were the greatest family I could've asked for."

And when he shifted to look at me, I lost it. I didn't cry when August had his stomach torn open. I didn't cry when Cora had her soul sucked from her body. But tears stung my eyes now as I watched my soul-half make amends with death.

"The god of the underworld likes music," he said. His finger hovered over the curved trigger. "Find him and bargain for my soul with your Hollow song. Find *me*, Cassiel Orpheus Jäger."

Auri touched the door. A flash of bright light flooded the woods.

"Tristan!" I shouted. I lunged. Black shadows escaped from the Mausoleum. Thirteen corvids flew from the trees around us.

Bang!

Tristan crumpled to the ground before I could reach him.

The god of the underworld likes music.

I ran to Tristan's side, falling to my knees and scooping his still-warm body into my arms. I tried not to look at the mess his head had become.

Dio was *sobbing*, screaming at me to let him go. I didn't. My soul ached like I'd been the one who had my brains blown out.

Tears ran down my cheeks as I clutched Tristan's body to my chest. As I moved him, something slid out of his pocket. A tiny notebook, opened to the first page.

Property of Tristan E. Edelweiss.
How to kill a God.
Step one: give it a body.
I will not be his body.

Slowly, I set Tristan's body down. His heart wasn't beating. Gods, he was gone.

I pocketed the notebook and stood. I wiped my eyes with the back of my hand.

Find me, *Cassiel Orpheus Jäger.*

I pulled the matchbox from my pocket and slipped the string out. Without breaking eye contact, I tied the string around my ring finger. A silent promise. A wordless vow.

Auri's bag lay opened on the ground. I'd never been talented with music, but I knew my mother's song. The Lyre was tucked inside. Shasi and Mirza were busy dragging Auri away from the mouth of the Mausoleum. Dio was shrieking, cradling Tristan, and pressing glowing gold hands over his chest as if she could bring it back. Nobody noticed as I slipped the Lyre out and stuffed it into the folds of my jacket.

Find me, Tristan had said.

I stared at the mouth of the Mausoleum. There was a humming coming from inside. I recognized the tune instantly. The Song of the Hollow; my mother's song.

I stepped into the darkness.

I'm coming, Tristan. Wait for me.

EPILOGUE

THE TRAIN, THE VESSEL, AND THE GODDESS

The seats were upholstered with red velvet that matched the deep wine of the curtains. The curtains were closed. They could not be opened, despite how they fluttered in the nonexistent breeze. There were six people aboard the train, spread out throughout the single carriage. An elderly man sat hunched in one seat, both hands holding the curved pommel of his wooden cane. A woman in a flimsy hospital gown held her face in her hands as she sobbed silently. A child with the sunken eyes of someone stricken with consumption lay across a bench, staring at the ceiling. A uniformed soldier held a perfect posture even in this place, their spine straight and rigid. The Vessel, who was no longer a vessel now that his brains lay scattered across the mulchy forest floor, sat near one of the windows. There was nobody in the seat across from him, and the window above the opposite seat was also sealed shut, but that didn't stop the Vessel from looking. He'd ridden on a train only a handful of times, but he knew the etiquette and minded his manners. He kept his wings tucked up against his back and took up as little space as possible. He didn't have a ticket, which made his hands clammy, but it didn't seem like anyone had a ticket.

And there was the woman sitting next to the Vessel.

The train was mostly empty, with a plethora of seats to choose from, yet when the woman boarded, she scanned the train and took a seat directly next to the Vessel.

She was pretty, in a Hollowed way, but the Vessel didn't stare. Well, he tried not to. It was hard when she was sitting so close to him. Her hair was long and dark, pin straight save for two tufts at the top of her head that resembled horns. Her ears were long and pointed, her skin deathly pale, and her eyes as dark as ink. She wore a deep purple dress with a high collar and a cinched waist and a bustle that kept encroaching into the Vessel's space.

She had a strange smell to her. Woodsy and citrusy and sweet at the same time, almost like a bruised fruit. It wasn't bad per se, but it was strong. Nobody else on the train had doused themselves in perfume. The Vessel suddenly felt very self-conscious of his own smell.

The Vessel could not look out the windows to see if the train was moving, but the droning *clickety-clack* made it seem like it was. It must be moving.

The train stopped after an eternity that spanned only a few minutes. The elderly man and the sickly child got off. The Vessel caught a peek of sunlight – or, maybe moonlight – through the train door before it closed, and the *clickety-clack* started up again.

It did this a few more times. It stopped again, and the weeping woman left. Then again, and the soldier departed. Then, it was just the Vessel and the woman.

Clickety-clack, clickety-clack, clickety-clack.

"The gods made you, Vessel," the woman finally said. There was something familiar about her voice, but the Vessel couldn't place it.

"Don't call me that," he said.

She continued as if she hadn't heard him. "You were given a power. I don't want to see it wasted. How did you start a war when you were a toddler?"

The Vessel looked at his hands. "There was this...this fire inside me. It hurt. Nobody would listen to me when I told them about it. My mother and father ignored me. When I started crying because of the pain, Mother put me in a cold bath and Father gave me cold milk to drink. Nothing helped. It kept building and building and building until it exploded, and all the darkness – all the fire – came rushing out. It infected the minds of everyone, convincing them to turn to slaughter."

"He had plucked you out from the very beginning. He wanted that power for himself. He wanted to use your body so he could harness the power," the woman said.

"Where are we?" asked the Vessel. He did not want to think about the massacre he'd caused. It left a sour taste in his mouth.

"We are on a train," she said. The Vessel was not impressed with her antics, but he kept his opinion to himself.

In the distance, a muffled song sounded.

Two coins for your fare

For the boat at the dock.

We dance this revelry

On the shores of the loch.

The woman said, "I don't like how they always assume it's a boat. It's a ferry sometimes, but it's a train most of the time. Do you have two coins? Any coins will do."

The Vessel reached into his pocket. It was empty. He kept his notebook in there. Frowning, he dug through his other pocket. He wasn't sure why he needed to pay two coins, but he didn't want to be kicked off the train for not paying the toll. Finally, he pulled out two coins. He handed them to the woman. She pocketed them.

"Who's singing?" he asked when the woman didn't say anything else.

She frowned. "A Hollow. She always sings that song. It drives me crazy. I guess you can hear it here because she unlocked the gate."

"She?"

"Medea's daughter. Auri. The cursed one."

The Vessel hoped she was okay. He didn't like the idea of the Shadow killing her.

There were sconces on the walls. The Vessel looked down, expecting to see the two shadows he was used to. He saw none. The woman didn't have one, either, but the benches did.

"Hollow," the Vessel said suddenly. "You mean there's a Hollow here?"

The woman's dark lips curled into a smile. She said, "The Hollows were not allowed here. They were supposed to be confined in their land. In Enochis. *This* is where the Hollowed live. The Hollows were ripped from their bodies prematurely. They are not Hollowed like you are."

It made little sense, but nothing about the Vessel's life made any sense. Still, if the woman next to him wasn't Hollow, but rather Hollow*ed,* it wouldn't hurt to ask for her name.

"Who are you?" the Vessel asked, not offering up his own identity because it seemed the woman already knew who he was.

"I am the goddess of doors and gates and crossroads. The goddess of the Waiting Space between life and death – the Nowhere."

She turned towards Eurydice and gave him a fanged smile.

"My name is Enodia."

To be continued...

Acknowledgements

I remember walking in from lunch/recess for circle time in third grade (yes, we still sat on a rug for stories and called it circle time in third grade). So far, we'd had pretty fun "story units" throughout the year. We learned about the Oregon Trail and Balto and the Iditarod. But that day we came to class and sat down, and my teacher opened up the *Odyssey* and my entire life changed. I went home that day and reserved every single book on Greek mythology imaginable from the public library, and when that wasn't enough, I checked out every book from my school library. At that time, the game Poptropica released its "Greek Mythology Island", and you'd best believe I played through it no less than a dozen times. It's funny how one tiny little thing such as reading a book can change someone's life. This book would not exist if my third-grade teacher Mrs. Giles did not teach us about Odysseus and his adventures. So, for that, thank you.

Another teacher I'd *love* to thank is my twelfth-grade anatomy teacher, Mrs. Mrosla, who, after learning I was taking the class so I could be a writer, cornered me at lunch when I was with all my friends and told me to give up on my dream of being a writer because they never make it. I hope you're aware you are the least favorite teacher at the entire high school :)

I have always been a pretty solitary person, but there were some people who supported me throughout this journey. Dani, my love, my soulmate, my besto friendo. Thank you for listening to my nonsensical ramblings about my book, about hot anime characters, about literally everything I had to say. I love you so much. Raven, my biggest fan. Thank you for (kinda sorta) inspiring the cover. For hyping up my characters and story. For being an all-over amazing friend. I am beyond lucky to be friends with someone like you. Chris, my absolute love and twin flame (soul-half!!!). You only came into my life during the middle of this story, but you will be there until the very end. To Lysandra, my cat, who didn't really do much and pushed my laptop out of the way to sit on me more than once, thank you for being the most important part of this story.

Thank you to my siblings, not for helping but for being weirdos and making me laugh. Benny, Lucas, Penny, Fiona, Finn, thank you. A big thank you to Penny for being my best friend, for drawing me lots of One Piece fanart, for generally just being a goober.

Thank you, Dad. Thank you for always supporting me even though you haven't read a book in ages. Thank you for staying up with little me to read me stories and play I Spy and for listening when I rambled about Greek Mythology way back in 2008.

Thank you, Mum. You got the very first ever copy of this book. Every time I'd write a bit of foreshadowing or a plot twist, I'd think of you and try to figure out if you could guess it. You probably can. Thank you for sparking my love of books and writing when I was just a tiny child.

Thank you to the Gods and Muses who helped me write this. I appreciate your guidance every day. So mote it be.

Thank you to the members of Avatar: Johannes Eckerström, Jonas Jarlsby, John Alfredsson, Henrik Sandelin, Tim Öhrström, Simon Anderson. This book was inspired by your song *So Sang The Hollow*. Thank you for writing the music that had me throw my phone across the room so I could race to open a document and begin writing.

And most importantly, thank you, the reader. Thank you for picking up my silly little book about silly Greek myths. Thank you for giving it a chance. Thank you for making it all the way to the end (unless you're weird and you read the acknowledgements first).

Till next time <3

POSTSCRIPT

THE CAT

Somewhere deep in the continent, nestled between shelves of books, a grey cat opened her yellow eyes. She stretched and yawned and stood on two legs.

It was time for the New Gods to return.

ABOUT THE AUTHOR

Emma T. Shannon has been writing since before knowing how to actually write. On the rare occasions where they are not writing, Emma can be found hunched over a drawing, circling the same shelf at the local bookstore, obsessing over 2D men, and singing loud enough to annoy the neighbors.

Emma lives in the dreary PNW with their tiny house tiger Lysandra, their tiny house dragon Andarna, two cursed dolls, and more tarot cards than they know what to do with.